An Unlikely Suitor

Books by
Nancy Moser

Mozart's Sister

Just Jane

Washington's Lady

How Do I Love Thee?

Masquerade

An Unlikely Suitor

AN
UNLIKELY SUITOR

Nancy Moser

BETHANY HOUSE PUBLISHERS

Minneapolis, Minnesota

Published by Bethany House Publishers
11400 Hampshire Avenue South
Bloomington, Minnesota 55438

Bethany House Publishers is a division of
Baker Publishing Group, Grand Rapids, Michigan.

Library of Congress Cataloging-in-Publication Data

Moser, Nancy
    An unlikely suitor / Nancy Moser.
      p. cm.
    ISBN 978-0-7642-0752-5 (pbk.) 1. Dressmakers—Fiction. 2. Socialites—Fiction.
3. Female friendship—Fiction. 4. Courtship—Fiction. 5. Social classes—Fiction.
6. Immigrants—New York (State)—New York—Fiction. 7. Italians—New York (State)—New York—Fiction. 8. New York (N.Y.)—History—19th century—Fiction. 9. Newport (R.I.)—History—19th century—Fiction. I. Title.
    PS3563.O88417U55   2011
    813'.54—dc22

                                                2011002921

To my mother, Marguerite Young.
By teaching me to sew
you taught me to face all challenges
with confidence and creativity.
Thank you, Mom.

CHAPTER ONE

*L*ucy's eyes shot open.

Something was wrong.

The darkness of the windowless bedroom did nothing to ease her nerves.

What had awakened her?

Lucy heard the soft breathing of her sister, Sofia, in the hammock slung above her cot, and listened for the snores of her uncle. Or the sounds of her aunt moaning as she tried to get comfortable upon their shared mattress on the floor.

But the room was silent. Had the unaccustomed silence slid into her dreams, warning her that something was amiss?

Lucy pushed herself up on her elbows and noticed the bedroom door was ajar. The faintest of lights announced someone was up.

She left the cot as quietly as possible so as not to wake the others, and peeked into the main room of their apartment. Lucy's uncle and aunt sat around the table with her mother, their voices low, their upper bodies leaning toward each other, forming a triad of dark hair and olive skin. A single sheet of paper was displayed on the table between them, with the occasional finger jabbing at its presence. The paper was the cause of their midnight meeting, some evil declaration that made sleep impossible.

Her curiosity and concern propelled her to enter the main room, but she closed the door so Sofia could sleep. At the sound, the three at the table looked up, their foreheads creased in worry.

"What's wrong?" Lucy asked.

Mamma looked at the others, then to Lucy. "I heard footsteps in the hall, then heard the sound of a paper being pushed under the door." She lifted its corner and handed it to Lucy as if it were the filthiest of rags.

Lucy took it closer to the gas lamp in order to see. One word stood out among the rest. "Evicted? We're evicted?"

"We have a week," Uncle said. "One week or they'll tear the tenement down around us."

The tenement on Mulberry Street where they'd lived for most of Lucy's twenty-four years needed tearing down. It had been old when they'd moved in after immigrating to New York City from Italy. Yet in spite of its flaws, it was home—all the home they could afford. Especially since her father had died four years previous.

Lucy still missed Papa. She'd been his *dolce ragazza,* his sweet girl. Even when Sofia had come along after they'd arrived in America, she hadn't usurped the bond between Lucy and her father. Perhaps because he'd never had a son, Lucy had become that son, that heir, that confidante he primed to lead the family when he was gone.

But who could have known he would be gone years before his time, in his prime? There was still so much to learn from him, so much to say to him. All she had now were the remembered snippets of wisdom he'd peppered throughout his talk, priceless gems she now held dear, as precious as actual jewels. The one she repeated most often was *Morto un papa, se ne fa un altro*: Life goes on.

Dante Scarpelli had lost his life in an accident on the docks where he had worked. Uncle Aldo and her cousin Vittorio had been there, and had seen how the careless methods of the shipping company had been to blame. But there'd been no investigation. No compensation. The death of another I-tie meant nothing to the businesses that hired them. Not when there were a thousand others waiting for a job.

They'd nearly had to move right then. The loss of her father's income had been a mighty financial blow. Lucy and Sofia worked twelve- to fourteen-hour days at a sweatshop in the garment district, Mamma worked at home with Aunt Francesca making paper flowers for women's hats, and her uncle and cousin continued their work on the docks. But without Papa's contribution, their combined income was barely enough to get by. It didn't help that the rent was continually raised even as the conditions of the rickety building deteriorated. Sometimes Lucy wondered if she could cause the walls to crumble just by staring at them. If she had such power, she would walk down the street and stare at building after building, causing their destruction. It was hard to imagine what their neighborhood of Five Points would look like if it were razed to the ground, if everything could be started fresh.

Actually . . . that's exactly what was going to happen.

Lucy looked at the paper again. A park named after Christopher Columbus was going to be built on this spot. A park with actual trees and grass would be an obvious improvement—but at what cost?

They would pay the price. The five Scarpellis who'd been left behind.

Cousin Vittorio had abandoned them the year after her father's death, lured by the wilds of Oklahoma, seeking adventure and free land. Lucy couldn't blame him for going. If she could get away from this place . . .

Angelo Romano.

Lucy's heart still hurt at the thought of this man she'd loved. Brown eyes and fascinating dimples had been instrumental in getting her to accept his proposal of marriage. But when Papa died, Lucy realized she couldn't abandon her mother and Sofia at the height of their sorrow, and couldn't withdraw the income she provided for her family's survival.

And so she'd invited Angelo to come live with them after the wedding.

He'd laughed at her.

A knife in the heart would have hurt less.

Lucy was forced to choose between gaining a husband and maintaining her family. She never let herself ponder whether she'd chosen rightly. Yet added to her grief over her father's death was the grief over the death of her future as a wife. But what choice did she have? *La famiglia sempre.* Family forever.

Papa would have been sad she'd never married—whether it be to Angelo or any of the other men who'd paid her attention. He'd always commended her on her character and strength. *La buona moglie fa il buon marito.* "A good wife makes a good husband, Lucia."

But now there would be no husband for Lucy. No marriage. *Niente.*

Angelo became a sweet memory, and one year added to another, and another, and another, and now at age twenty-four, Lucy knew she was too old to marry. It was not an option.

Would it ever be an option? What did Americans call her? An old maid?

Her aunt's words interrupted her thoughts. "Tomorrow, Aldo. Tomorrow you go and find us a new place to live."

Uncle's head shook back and forth, his focus on the floor.

"What you mean no?" Aunt said.

He raised his head to look at them, his dark eyes sad. "I mean no. I refuse to find another hellhole in this city. We are going west, Francesca—to Oklahoma to be with Vittorio."

"West?"

"Sì." Uncle's head nodded once with emphasis.

Lucy couldn't believe what she was hearing. "You can't leave us," she said. "We took you in when you came from Naples. For nine years we've opened our arms to you, our home to you."

There were two types of people in the world: givers and takers. Relatives or not, her aunt and uncle were takers. It made her resentful to see Aunt Francesca feign a headache, making Mamma do twice the work. It incensed her when Uncle Aldo insisted on buying himself special pickles from the Jews up on Delancey Street, even though he was the only one who liked them—and who knew kosher from not, anyway?

The thought of her aunt and uncle moving out had crossed Lucy's mind on a daily basis over all nine years. But now, the idea that they were going west to start an exciting new life, leaving Lucy, Mamma, and Sofia behind to fend without a by-your-leave or even a thank-you . . .

Resentment was *her* problem. Mamma was always gracious, always kind, always giving. To a fault she was giving. Her aunt and uncle didn't deserve half the kindness Mamma extend—

Aunt looked imploringly at her husband. "Aldo, please. I don't want to leave Lea alone with her girls."

His face softened, but Lucy could tell he'd made up his mind. "Vittorio has been pleading with us for months. I haven't wanted to leave for the very reason you state. But now"—he pointed at the paper—"the decision has been taken from us. Besides, it will be much easier finding lodging for three rather than five."

"But where do we find such a place? How do we find such a place?"

It was the first time Lucy's mother had spoken. Her questions hung in the air between them, unanswerable.

Then her gaze fell upon Lucy. In recent years her mother's eyes had lost their vibrancy, and now, even more than before, they looked weary and defeated.

Lucy leaned down and wrapped her arms around her mother. "I'll find us something. I promise."

She felt her mother relax, but instead of finding satisfaction in her relief, Lucy felt the weight of the world fall upon her shoulders.

If only she hadn't promised.

❧❧

"I'll find us something, I promise."

At her sister's words, and upon hearing the scrape of chairs against the floor, Sofia rushed from her eavesdropping perch back to her hammock. As the bedroom door opened, she put a hand to the wall, stopping the hammock's swing.

She closed her eyes, feigning sleep, as the light from the main room cut a swath through the room.

"Look, the girl sleeps while the rest of us worry," Aunt Francesca whispered.

"Oh, to be young and ignorant," said her uncle.

Lucy shushed them, but Sofia knew the action wasn't in her defense. Sofia was well aware of what her sister thought of her, what everyone thought of her. She was the spoiled youngest child, the selfish one.

Unfortunately, this assessment was accurate, and though Sofia regretted the truth behind this description, she wasn't eager to change. Being the least of her family had its advantages. No one expected her to excel at anything, and since what they *did* expect was the worst, it was easy to give it to them. She counted herself lucky that her family issued few penalties for her behavior, merely accepting it as the norm.

The main consequence of Sofia's disposition—the one that *did* bother her more than she would ever admit—was that her family ignored her views, or worse, didn't believe she had any. When she'd first sensed Lucy getting up this night, when she'd heard the door click shut, she'd immediately climbed out of her hammock to stand at the door, listening. Separate, on the fringe, unconsulted.

Not that she would have added anything to the discussion about eviction but more fear and worry, perhaps even more than the rest of them had shown. For, unlike the rest of them, living on Mulberry Street was the only life Sofia had ever known. When her family—when all her neighbors—told stories of the old country, she was excluded from the shared memories. Actually, she had *no* memories to call her own. From morning to night she was with her family. As a child she'd appreciated their company and protection from the dangers of the street, but now, at fifteen, she longed for time alone, for the chance to experience a life separate from theirs.

But with the night's discussion of big changes coming their way . . . Sofia wasn't sure how she felt about that.

Unable to feign sleep any longer, she leaned over the side of the hammock and whispered to her sister, "We're moving?"

"Hush now," Lucy said. "Don't worry. I'll handle everything."

Sofia lay back. She knew Lucy's words to be true. And yet . . .

To move, to live in a different place, on a different street, with different sights, smells, and sounds . . .

Could Sofia be different too?

It was a frightening, exciting thought.

Lucy barely slept. Once the four adults of the family finished discussing the eviction, they'd all tried to get back to sleep—Mamma on the thin mattress she'd shared with Papa in the main room, Uncle Aldo and Aunt Francesca on a similar mattress on the floor of the only bedroom, with Lucy on her cot nearby. Uncle never did snore that night.

Only Sofia slept on, oblivious to the crisis spinning around her. As usual. Oh, to be a child again, to live with the assurance that someone older and wiser would handle whatever needed to be handled.

It was Sofia who roused the adults from their beds.

"Up, everyone!" Sofia jumped down from her sling, sending it swinging wildly. "We'll be late for church."

Amid moans and much stretching, the family rose and got dressed. The lines at the outhouses—five stories below in the alley—were long, as usual, for everyone worked six days a week and went to church on Sunday. Lucy had heard about modern buildings that had such necessary rooms inside. What she wouldn't give for such luxury.

"Why are you so quiet?" Sofia asked as they walked to the service at St. Patrick's Old Cathedral.

"It's nothing for you to worry about," Lucy answered.

Yet as soon as Lucy gave the answer, her thoughts turned in its direction. There was plenty of reason to worry, because a place for them to stay wasn't going to fall from the sky—no matter how hard they wished for it or even prayed for it. Someone had to make an effort to find an apartment. They only had a week.

Looking at her uncle walking with her aunt and mother a few steps ahead, she knew he wouldn't be the one to accomplish such a thing. In the nine years since his family had come to New York, he'd never once offered to find his wife and son a place of their own. Lucy knew this had been a point of contention with her mother and father, and had heard the two of them speak of it in hushed tones on many occasions. When the Scarpellis had invited the three newcomers to stay with them back in 1886, they'd always assumed it was a temporary situation. Her father had even been instrumental in getting Aldo and Vittorio jobs on the docks where he worked, and Mother had let Francesca be a part of her at-home work of making flowers for hats.

But as one year flowed into the next, as temporary became permanent, her parents' private complaints stopped. Family was sacred.

And perhaps it *had* been for the best. For when Papa was killed, the presence of Aldo and his family was a blessing—both for their company and for their income. And a year later, though they could have used Vittorio's income too, Lucy wasn't bitter about her cousin leaving to find a better life out west. Family was family, but . . . she also knew there *could* be a proper time to be a bit selfish. There was nothing evil about having your own dreams.

What if I leave? Just go away like Vittorio and start over?

She shook her head against the thought. If she were a man, she might consider it. But as a woman, with few ways to make a living, she needed to choose a safer route.

Which was . . . ?

Fulfilling her promise to find them a new home. Lucy caught up with her mother just as they turned toward the entrance of the church and tugged on her sleeve. "Mamma, I'm not going in with you. I have—"

"Of course you're going in. Come—"

"No." Lucy lowered her voice. "I have to find us a new apartment."

"That can wait."

"No, it can't. I can't risk time off from my job to look for one. We need a place to live. Now."

Mamma motioned for Francesca and Aldo to go on in, and to take Sofia with them. "And how are you going to do that?" she asked. "On the Sabbath? Today is a day of rest."

There was no time to rest. Surely the Almighty would forgive her for helping her family on this one and only free day. "I have to try. You

14

pray and I'll do what *I* can do." Besides, God listened to Mamma's prayers much more than Lucy's.

Mamma's eyes skirted past the people to the endless streets beyond. "A girl alone? It's not safe."

"A woman alone. I have no choice, Mamma. *We* have no choice."

Mamma cupped Lucy's cheek with her hand. *"Dio sia con voi."*

Lucy was glad to have God's company. If He would do His part, she would do hers. If He was busy elsewhere? That was all right too.

Lucy's line of vision alternated between the left side of the street and the right, searching for elusive *FOR RENT* signs.

She'd knocked on a few doors but hadn't found many people home. Those who had answered were asking too much, or blatantly told her they didn't rent to her kind.

Regarding that . . . she'd purposely avoided their old neighborhood around Five Points. Most of the buildings were in as horrible condition as their own. Would they also be torn down to make way for some park or factory? Lucy couldn't risk being moved twice.

And so she'd walked north, past the Jewish neighborhood running along Bayard, past Grand and Stanton . . .

The buildings were better there, more solid, and often made of brick. She turned onto a street that was full of shops—real shops. She was used to the pushcarts of Mulberry Street that dappled the street like pebbles interrupting the flow of a stream. The pushcarts sold common goods like pans and baskets, and fruit, bread, and flowers. But these shops had their goods displayed in the windows: cheese, sausages, crocks, books . . . and dresses. One window showed a mannequin wearing a gorgeous blue gown of satin brocade with pink bows at the bottom of the sleeves and at the neckline. Lucy was used to the rather bland work of sewing sleeves and linings into coats whose colors did nothing to brighten her weary days. Once in a while, they were given women's blouses to work on, but even then the colors were depressingly neutral.

Remembering the task at hand, she forced herself to move on, yet her eyes rebelled at the thought of looking anywhere but at the prettiness of the—

With a start, she ran into a man exiting a door.

"Scusi," she said.

"Pardon me," the man said as he tipped his hat and took a step back. "I'm afraid my mind was elsewhere."

He had a ring of keys in his hand. He fumbled for one in particular and tried the key in the lock. Lucy saw that the door was not to a store, but was nestled between two storefronts.

"This blasted lock."

"May I?" Lucy was used to finicky locks. The one on their apartment only worked if she tilted the key in a downward angle. She tried the same method and it worked. The door locked.

"There you are," she said, trying the door as evidence.

He looked surprised by her success. "With all the rentals I own, you'd think I'd get used to the idiosyncrasies of the locks."

"Rentals?"

"I have a small apartment above the store here. I have rentals all over Manhattan."

"An apartment, you say?" Her heartbeat strengthened. This was a good street with nice shops.

"Are you looking for one?"

"I am. My mother, my sister, and I are being evicted."

His long face lengthened even more. "For nonpayment—?"

"No, no, sir. We've lived in the building for twenty years. But now they're tearing it down—tearing down an entire row of buildings to make a park."

The man studied her as if assessing her character. She was glad she was wearing her best navy dress for church but felt the need to persuade him further. "Does the apartment have good light? My mother makes flowers for hats and works at home."

"Hats?"

She nodded. "And my sister and I work in the garment business."

His eyebrows lifted. "You're a seamstress?"

Of a sort. "For twelve years now. My sister is only fifteen, but she's worked four years in the trade." In the sweatshops. The horrible, disgusting sweatshops.

He put a hand to his mouth and shook his head. But beneath the hand he was smiling. "Come with me, Miss . . . ?" He waited for her name.

"Scarpelli. Lucy Scarpelli."

"Come with me, Miss Scarpelli. Today may be your lucky day."

She hesitated. Although he looked to be a man of fine bearing, she didn't know him.

He laughed at her uncertainty. "Five steps, Miss Scarpelli. Ten at the most."

He walked up the sidewalk and motioned toward the doorway of the shop that contained the beautiful dress.

She'd get to see it in person? Lucy walked after him and noticed the sign painted on the window: *Madame Moreau's Fashion Emporium.*

"Is this a dress shop?"

He laughed. "Don't let Mrs. Flynn hear you call it that."

"Who is Mrs. Flynn?"

"The woman I hired to run the place. Irish through and through, but she'd like people to believe she's Madame Moreau."

"Where is Madame Moreau?"

He cupped his mouth with a hand. "She doesn't exist. I thought a French name would be a lure to our society customers." He fiddled with the ring of keys, finding the correct one for the door. "Come inside."

The warning of Lucy's mother intruded. *A girl alone? It's not safe.*

The man sighed. He was running out of patience. "My name is Thomas Standish and I'm happily married with three children—who are waiting for me to get home for Sunday dinner. If you need more references than that to trust me, I—"

"No. I mean, yes, I'll come inside."

He swept an arm toward the interior.

The main room had numerous dress ensembles displayed on mannequins, making her forget the initial blue one. Scattered about were lush velvet chairs, a sea green settee, and two full-length gilded mirrors on stands.

"It's beautiful."

"Yes, well, the upper set expects sumptuous surroundings, so that's what we give them. There are two private fitting rooms over there, but when the dresses are near completion, the women do love to come out here to see themselves."

Lucy glanced at the window. "And be seen?"

"Is that not the point?"

Lucy fingered the lace on a sleeve with huge leg-o'-mutton sleeves. She wasn't keen on the trend—it made women look ridiculous to have puffed sleeves twice the size of their head—but the sleeves were popular because their volume made the wearer's waist look tiny in comparison. And like it or not, the style wasn't the fault of this shop. Fashion was declared elsewhere and women followed. She turned the cuff over and saw that the stitching was straight, and the presence of interlining gave the cuff body. It was obvious the sewing standards were high. She turned to Mr. Standish. "All the work is done here?"

"Indeed it is. In the back." He walked through a curtain and lit a gas lamp inside the next room. Then he held the curtain aside for her to enter. "Come in, Miss Scarpelli."

The workroom was set up with many work stations. There were two treadle sewing machines, a large cutting table, and a wall of spindles, filled with spools of thread. It was a far cry from the dingy sweatshop where she and Sofia sat shoulder to shoulder with dozens of other women, under minimal lighting and the weight of boredom, as they sewed the same type of piece over and over and over.

"So all the dresses are custom-made?"

"Every one. With stores like Bloomingdale's, Macy's, and Tremaine's luring women to buy off the rack, we live on our reputation for extraordinary custom-made clothing for society's elite."

The notion of creating something beautiful and using good-quality fabrics and trim was enticing. Lucy longed to be creative, and often, during her tedious work, daydreamed of how she would design a dress or a blouse or skirt. "So the outfits are custom designed too?"

He put down the scissors he'd been playing with. "Are you a designer?"

She almost said yes, but decided truth the better choice. "I've never had the chance. But I would like to try. I would like to learn."

His gaze moved from her face to her toes and back again. "You didn't design the dress you're wearing, did you?"

Lucy knew her outfit was marginal. Her dress was at least six years old. It had the distinction of being her "best" because it was the least worn looking, yet it was very old-fashioned, with narrow sleeves and an out-of-style bustle.

Mr. Standish was waiting for an answer. "I didn't design my clothes, and I certainly know their shortcomings in both design and quality. But when a family needs food and the rent is due, the desire for something new and fashionable is set aside."

"To pay the rent."

"On time."

He made an odd sound, as if he didn't believe her, a notion that was dispelled when he said, "Then that makes you a better tenant than my last two—the last of which moved out without notice and left the place a mess."

"I know of such people, but I assure you, Mr. Standish, my family shares none of those vices."

"I believe you." He strolled around the cutting table that sat in the middle of the room. "And perhaps . . ." He stopped. "Perhaps your lucky day is also mine."

Lucy held her breath. Was he talking about an apartment, a job, or both? She forced herself to act calm. "How so, sir?"

"I've wanted to expand our offerings to hats."

"My mother could handle that expansion with ease."

"And with the sewing of gowns for the upcoming season in Newport in full swing . . . we are heartily busy."

"Three additional sets of hands, savvy with needle and thread, would be an advantage."

"But the apartment . . ." He resumed his stroll. "It's small."

"How much is the rent?"

"Sixteen."

Lucy tried to control her excitement. They paid seventeen dollars a month now, and this building was far better than their tenement. But they also had two fewer people to help with the rent. "I'll give you fourteen."

He considered this a moment. "You'll make up the difference keeping the shop clean?"

"Of course."

He extended a hand. "It appears we have a deal, Miss Scarpelli."

She coughed once, then again, expelling the tension that had accumulated in the minutes that had transpired between bumping into Mr. Standish and gaining both lodging and jobs for her family. She shook his hand. "We have a deal."

"I surmise you don't have the rent money on you?"

"You surmise correctly." She thought of the coins in the money jar at home. Was there enough for the rent? "I'll pay you all I can, and the rest you can deduct from our paychecks until we are square. Would that be satisfactory?"

"I believe something can be arranged. When would you like to move in?"

Her thoughts sped through the logistics of moving. They could borrow a cart from someone . . . she might even hunt down Angelo, since he and his father used a cart for their business. And since Uncle Aldo was still around, he could help with the heavy lifting, not that they had that much to—

"A day, Miss Scarpelli. What day would you like to move in?"

"The day after tomorrow? And we could start work the day after that."

He laughed. "I admire your spunk and work ethic." He took out his key ring and removed a key, pressing it into her hands. "Here you go. I'll stop by later to collect the first portion of the rent."

"Thank you." Lucy palmed the key and pressed it to her heart. Just like that, their problems were solved. She thought of Mamma in church this morning, praying . . .

They exited the store and Mr. Standish said his good-byes. Lucy was left with the key—and the door to their apartment. Only then did she realize she'd not even looked at the space.

What if it's awful? What if it's so small the three of us can't even live there?
There was only one way to find out.

She unlocked the door and was greeted with a set of dark, narrow stairs. She took a match from a container on the wall and lit the wall lamp. The light—though dim—helped ease her wariness. She went up the stairs to a landing. And one door. This was it.

The same key that opened the bottom door opened this one. Lucy opened it slowly, expecting the worst. She saw . . .

Light. A bounty of glorious sunlight.

To her left, the entire front of the main room was lined with windows. In a small alcove near the windows was a stove, a sink, and shelves in a kitchen area. Off the main room were two doors. The one straight across from the entry was open, showing a bedroom at least the size of the one on Mulberry Street. And the other smaller door led to something Lucy had never dared hope for: a bathroom! There was a toilet, a small sink, and . . .

A bathtub.

Lucy stepped into it, clothes and all, and sat down. Such luxury was beyond her ken. Only then did she notice the tub needed a good scrubbing. And the sink had an ominous orangey coating in its bowl, and the toilet . . .

Lucy climbed out of the tub and brushed off her clothes. With her eyes freshly attuned to details instead of space, she saw that the apartment needed a lot of cleaning. It was obvious Mr. Standish's previous tenants had left quickly, with little regard for what they'd left behind—or the condition of the apartment itself. There was a smattering of discarded furniture that may or may not be usable. A man's shoe was in the corner, trash was scattered throughout the room, and the kitchen shelves were marked with a myriad of ancient spills.

Upon closer inspection, Lucy smelled something sickly sweet and found the kitchen sink filled with the remnants of more than one peeled apple and fruit flies dancing above their feast.

She turned toward the main room and put her hands upon her hips, measuring the challenge. She'd have to give it a good dose of elbow grease—before her mother and sister saw it.

Speaking of . . . they were probably sitting at home, worried for her life and limb amongst the fearful streets of New York.

Such a surprise she'd have for them.

ॐ

"Where have you been?"

Lucy closed the door behind her. She was greeted by all four members of her family, waiting for an answer.

She'd be happy to give them one.

Lucy had pondered this moment all the way home. She didn't want to burst in the door, shouting the news. She wanted to mark the moment with a little drama.

And so, she removed the key from her pocket and dangled it in front of them.

"What's that?" Uncle Aldo asked.

"A key."

"We can see that," Aunt said. "But what—?"

Sofia ran to her, nabbing the key away. "It's the key to our new apartment!"

Lucy nodded, seeking her mother's smile.

Mamma did more than smile; she wrapped Lucy in her arms, leaning this way and that, cradling her head against her own face. *"Ah, cara ragazza! Grazie, grazie!"*

Lucy had expected her mother to be happy, but her exuberance was surprising, and revealed a worry beyond what she'd previously expressed.

Once Mamma let her go, they all began talking at once.

"Where is it?"

"How many rooms?"

"How much?"

She reveled in the knowledge that she had one more surprise for them. But first she gave the details.

"A bathroom?" Mamma said.

"With a real bathtub," Lucy said, "and an indoor necessary and running water in the kitchen."

Aunt tugged on her husband's arm. "Perhaps we should stay."

Lucy nearly panicked. Although they could all fit in the new apartment, her hopes for the future involved just the three of them living there.

"No," Uncle said. "We promised Vittorio. I'm getting the train tickets tomorrow."

Aunt nodded and the crisis was averted.

"When can we move in?" Mamma asked.

Lucy had thought it through. "Tuesday. Tomorrow I'll go make it ready for you and—"

"What you mean, 'make it ready for us'?"

Lucy didn't want to let them know how dirty it was, only how clean it would be once she was through with it. "I just want to make sure it's perfect."

"The fact we have a place to go . . . that makes it *perfetto*." Mamma looked heavenward. *"Grazie a Dio."*

It was time for the other surprise. Lucy extended her hands to her mother and sister. She needed physical contact for her next announcement. "I have something else to tell you that will make things even more perfect."

Sofia tried to guess. "You found a thousand dollars in a trunk in the apartment."

Lucy ignored her. "I found jobs—for all three of us."

"We have jobs."

Lucy shook her head. "Not like these jobs. Not in a fancy dress shop catering to society ladies."

Mamma blinked, her mouth open. "Where? How?"

"Madame Moreau's Fashion Emporium just so happens to be the shop directly beneath our apartment. The owner's been wanting to expand their offerings to hats, and Sofia and I will be seamstresses. Real seamstresses in a nice workroom with our own work space and good lighting and—" She thought of something else that would impress them. "Out front there's an elegant room where the ladies come to see dresses and look at fabric choices. The chairs are covered in velvet and—"

"What's velvet?" Sofia asked.

"Velluto," Mamma said. "Like Mrs. Romano's shawl, the one she wears to show off."

Sofia nodded.

"But this velvet isn't black; it's pale green. Very sophisticated." Lucy could say more, but she knew they already had an image of the place.

"I get to make hats?"

"With all the trims, feathers, and flowers you want."

"Probably flowers we made right here in this room," Aunt Francesca said.

"Perhaps," Lucy said.

Aunt bit her lower lip and Lucy could almost see her thoughts churning. "Would they have a job for me?" She glanced at her husband. "I want to see our son, but Oklahoma is so far away, and—"

"Enough, wife. We're going."

Aunt sat back down, still uncertain.

"Come now." Mamma motioned all of them close. "Let us fall to our knees and thank God for answering our prayers."

The five of them knelt, bowed their heads, and prayed silently. Lucy prayed too, thanking God, but . . .

But also thanking herself.

She'd done very well. Like Mr. Standish had said, today was her lucky day.

CHAPTER TWO

*F*or the first time in her memory, Sofia awakened on a Monday and didn't go to work. Lucy had told her there was no reason for both of them to go to the sweatshop to quit and collect their pay.

So Sofia was blessed with something incredibly rare: free time.

But didn't she deserve it? Though she'd only been working at the sweatshop for four years, before that she'd worked at home, making paper flowers with her mother and aunt, since she was five.

What little free time she had, she spent reading dime novels, which she either bought in their entirety as soft-covered books or collected from magazines over many issues. Mamma called them an extravagance, but Papa had told Mamma to let her be, that if Sofia could escape in a good story, so be it. Though Papa had been gone for years now, Mamma hadn't defied his wishes and prohibited the treat. Sofia earned ten cents a sleeve, sometimes seventy cents a day. Surely she deserved to buy a book every week. Up until today, Sunday afternoon was her only time to indulge herself, to escape to the Wild West, or into one of Laura Jean Libbey's romances.

She loved how Mrs. Libbey's stories usually revolved around a poor young girl who fell in love with a man far above her station. And they always—always—married in the end, and knowing that never ruined the stories one whit.

This morning, Sofia saw an opening for some reading time. So before Mamma ordered her to help pack for the move, she grabbed her latest title, *Little Rosebud's Lovers*, and ran down the five flights of stairs to the stoop outside their tenement. There, she sat upon the top step, just to the right of the door, leaned her back against the building, and found the place she'd left off. . . . A handsome stranger, Percy Fielding, was discussing the county fair, where he planned to see Maud, the woman of his affection. Yet the local man he spoke with talked of a stepsister, Rosebud. . . .

"Who gave her the name of Rosebud?" said Percy.
"Oh, she's been called that ever since she was born, and she has the sweetest face, with red cheeks and pretty dimples, that you ever saw; but she is no young lady. Little Rosebud is only a romping, merry-hearted child of sixteen, with a face like an apple-blossom, framed in long, fair, curling flaxen hair, soft and clinging as a baby's, and great blue roguish eyes, and the sweetest little scarlet mouth you ever saw."

Sofia looked up when an argument between Mrs. Roselli and a customer over a loaf of bread got heated. Noise. Mulberry Street was always noisy, whether it be from the pushcart owners calling out their wares, horses' hooves on the cobblestones, or homeless children trying to sell a stray piece of wood, some matches, or a discarded newspaper.

She pushed the distractions away and returned to the book's description of Rosebud. Blond, blue-eyed, and merry. Nothing like Sofia herself, yet she also knew that before the story ended Rosebud would face great peril before finding love and redemption. There was satisfaction in seeing the rich humbled and the poor raised up. Not that Sofia believed such things actually happened. Although the

An Unlikely Suitor

neighborhood was filled with families that had come to America to make a better life, the streets were not paved with gold. They were but worn and dirty cobblestones made slick with the droppings of man and animal alike.

Within a page Sofia nodded with satisfaction as poor Rosebud began her descent into hell. . . . *And pretty Little Rosebud Arden would know the bitterest woe that ever came to a bright, sunny girl's life, as she drained to the dregs the bitter draught which would be held to her lips by the hand she loved. . . .*

Sofia could hardly wait.

❧

Just a peek . . .

Lucy was tempted to peer into the window of Madame Moreau's, but refrained. Today—dressed in her worst work clothes for the task of cleaning their new apartment—was not the day to make her presence known. Only two days more and she could enter with confidence.

She set down the basket of cleaning supplies in order to negotiate the key in the door to their apartment, angling it downward as she'd had to do when first meeting Mr. Standish. Her easy success made her smile. She was an expert already. It was meant to be.

The door at the top of the stairs also succumbed to her key and she entered—and immediately saw a vase of white and yellow flowers on a table.

There was a small note stuck within its blooms. *Miss Scarpelli, I feel bad for the horrible condition of this flat. Hopefully, these flowers will bid you fair welcome. Mr. Standish.*

Lucy allowed herself a moment to enjoy the fragrance. She appreciated Mr. Standish's gesture, but would have preferred the more practical one of having the place cleaned.

"Chi fa da sé, fa per tre," she said with a sigh. If she wanted something done, she would have to do it herself.

And so she did.

As usual.

❧

Lucy pushed hair away from her face with the back of a hand. She got up from her knees, arching her back to counter the ache.

Was she finished?

She scanned the main room. The windows were washed, the floors swept and scrubbed, the facilities in the kitchen and bath as spotless as she could make them.

Her hands begged for attention. They were red-raw from the hot water and soap, yet she didn't really mind. At least there *was* hot water in their apartment. Back home they'd had to go into the hallway to gather water from a shared spigot, and then heat it on the stove. Baths had been taken in the main room, in a hip bath, and the more intimate needs were attended to in communal outhouses.

Now to arrange the furniture. What was left behind was rickety— Lucy had thrown away one precarious chair—but the rest was usable.

She remembered that the mattress to the bed was sticking out the back window to air. She hauled it back in and placed it on the frame, choosing the best side up. The room held a small table she placed beside the bed, and a three-drawer dresser—one drawer for each of them. And there was even an armoire for hanging clothes. Lucy shivered at the memory of cleaning out the mouse nest she'd found inside.

The living room contained a small table for eating at and two chairs. In addition, there was an upholstered chair. Even through the seat cushion, Lucy could feel the springs, but if you sat just right, it was the softest chair she'd ever sat in. Mamma would like it.

Mamma and Sofia would like all of it.

"I did well," she said aloud, breaking the silence.

The silence. What was silence?

Lucy sat in the chair and rested her arms upon *its* arms. It was odd to consider the lack of silence in her life. In a tenement full of families there was always noise. Even in the middle of the night they could hear people moving about. The walls were thin, and privacy didn't exist. Not to mention Uncle Aldo's snoring.

She closed her eyes and held her breath to allow the silence to fully wrap around her—and didn't like it.

Lucy breathed heavier to break through the nothingness, and after f that effort, opened her eyes and stood. Silence and solitude were foreign conditions that would take getting used to.

A familiar sound broke into the moment, drawing her to the window. Horses pulled a lovely carriage to a stop in front of the dress shop. The driver got down from his perch and opened the carriage door. A fine lady emerged wearing a navy suit adorned with red piping. She said something to the driver and went inside.

This was the sort of woman Lucy would be sewing for. She faced the room, raised her chin, and placed her hands primly, one upon the other. "How may I help you this morning, ma'am? I just happen to have the most exquisite ensemble, designed especially for you." She cocked her head, hearing the woman's response. Then Lucy said, "My name? Lucy Scarpelli." A pause. "You've not heard of me? Let me assure you, you will."

With a laugh, Lucy dropped her hands and did a pirouette in the middle of the room.

Why not dream?

Her life was just beginning.

Sofia's free time didn't last long before her mother and aunt found her and demanded she come help with the packing. A lifetime of accumulation and not enough crates made the chore difficult. And added to the chaos were Uncle Aldo and Aunt Francesca packing for their trip west.

Lucy came home late in the day. Sofia tossed her a roll of twine. "It's about time. Tie up that stack of bedding."

Lucy stood inside the door, scanning the room. She looked as though she could cry.

"What's wrong?" Sofia asked.

"When I left this morning I didn't realize it would be the last time I'd see the place as it's always been."

Mamma took the twine from her. "Consider it a blessing, Lucia. Sometimes it's best not to have time to wallow in the 'last' of things."

"But it's not home anymore."

Sofia hadn't taken time to think of it that way, yet what Lucy said was right. In the length of a single day, the apartment had been stripped of the items that made it home. Now it was simply two rooms with peeling wallpaper, a single cracked window that overlooked a narrow alley, and a stove that barely provided heat and made cooking a challenge. Would the kitchen in their new place be better? Would they see sunshine? Would the bedroom have natural light and air?

"Do you want this pan?" Mamma asked Aunt Francesca.

Uncle Aldo shook his head. "She does not. There isn't room and I'm certain our son has plenty of pans."

Sofia was less certain. She couldn't imagine Cousin Vittorio caring about pans or pots or anything domestic. She hoped he lived in a respectable place in Oklahoma, but she also knew he had a penchant for exaggeration. She did not trust his letters, bragging about his new life. What would her aunt and uncle find when they met their son?

Suddenly Mamma pressed a shirt to her face. Was she crying?

Sofia put an arm around her shoulders. Without a word Mamma offered her the shirt. Sofia inhaled the scent of her father.

"We came here together. We made this home together."

Sofia felt her throat tighten but refused to give in to tears.

Lucy smelled the shirt too, then handed it back to Mamma. "It would sadden Papa to be here and see our building demolished, to see the old neighborhood change so drastically."

Mamma's eyes lost a bit of their sorrow. "Would he like our new place?"

Lucy nodded. "He would."

"Then I will like it too."

Mamma amazed her. She never let anything bother her. What life handed her she embraced—or at least set aside without complaining. Sofia wasn't keen on change, any change. Even though their life was hard, would this new life Lucy concocted be any better?

It had better be.

CHAPTER THREE

*L*ucy braced herself to see him again.

Angelo Romano, her ex-fiancé, was helping them move. He possessed two key essentials: a two-wheeled cart and a strong back.

Lucy hated having to call on him, but all their other requests for help had been answered with good excuses. People couldn't risk their jobs to take off work and help the Scarpellis move. Because Angelo worked for his father, he had some leeway in such things. But would he associate her need for his services with her need for *him*? Four years had passed. Surely he wouldn't still want to marry her.

There was a knock on their door and Lucy felt her stomach flutter. She opened it. "*Ciao*, Angelo."

With cap in hand he leaned forward to kiss her cheek. "*Ciao*, my dear Lucy."

My dear Lucy?

He looked past her. "Signora Scarpelli. You're looking well."

Lea smiled at him and handed him a crate of dishes. "You are very kind to help us, Angelo."

With a wink to Lucy he said, "Didn't your husband always say, '*Mal comune, mezzo gaudio*'? Trouble shared is trouble halved. I'm glad to do it."

Lucy immediately gathered a load of belongings. Perhaps if she kept him busy Angelo wouldn't have time to court her or ask questions she couldn't answer.

For she didn't love him anymore. He was far too frivolous and flighty, and in hindsight she realized their marriage would have caused more anguish than joy. If she ever found a man—if—she wanted someone with a practical nature who could ease her burdens, not add to them.

Sofia came out of the bedroom. "Angelo!" She ran to him, hugging him awkwardly around the crate.

He set it down and gave her a proper embrace. "Ah, my *piccolina*, it is nice to see you again."

Sofia stepped away, taking offense. "I'm not your *piccolina* anymore, Angelo. See? I am a grown woman." She drew herself to her full height with her hands on her hips.

"Sofia!" her mother said.

"Well, I am."

It wasn't proper for Sofia to draw attention to her figure. Lucy interceded. "Come now. Let's carry a load to the cart."

Angelo returned to the crate of dishes, then held the door open for Lucy with his shoulder. "Ladies first," he said.

She'd made a horrible mistake asking him to help.

Angelo and Aldo pulled the cart, heavy-laden with the belongings of the Scarpelli women. Such a sight was not uncommon in their old neighborhood, as people often moved from here to there in hope of better accommodations—or to escape paying overdue rent. But as the group made their way to the north, to the newer sections of the city, Lucy felt conspicuous. The ethnic boundaries became blurred and she saw judgment in the eyes of many who did not appreciate the influx of

Italians into their neighborhood. Some people walking on the sidewalks looked aghast at the haphazard mountain of crates, mattresses, and chairs, and hurried on their way as if they feared being tainted by the sight of it. Lucy wanted to boldly step in their path and demand they tell her just how else a person was supposed to move to a new home.

With this image still in mind, Lucy had the men stop the cart on the street *before* they reached the windows of the Fashion Emporium. She hated to care so much what the ladies inside thought of her, but also knew her instinct regarding their reaction was correct.

With their destination reached, everyone looked to Lucy for direction. "So," Uncle Aldo said, arching his back, "where is this wonderful new apartment?"

"Up there." Lucy pointed to the row of windows above the shop. "Behind those windows is the main room."

Her mother's eyes grew wide. "So much light."

Lucy nodded with satisfaction. "And air. There's a window in the bedroom too, so this awful heat will be conquered."

"I get the bedroom!" Sofia said.

"Mamma gets the bedroom." Lucy looked to Mamma to see if she smiled—but Mamma was busy untying the rope that held everything to the cart. The idea that suddenly everyone would beset the apartment en masse reminded Lucy of her plan to show her mother and sister the place in private.

"If you all could just wait here a moment while I take Mamma and Sofia upstairs alone . . ."

"So what are we?" Aunt Francesca said. "Aren't we relatives too?"

Uncle Aldo nipped her arm with his hand. "Leave them alone, wife." He winked at Lucy. "This is Lucia's special moment."

Lucy winked back at him. He was a good man and she might actually miss him.

She retrieved the key, opened the street door, and struck a match to light the lamp. "See here? Our own private stairway."

Mamma looked upward. "Only one flight?"

"Only one."

Sofia raced up the stairs to the landing. "There's just the one door. This is ours?"

Lucy followed after her. "This is ours." She waited to open the door until Mamma had also reached the landing. Then she used the key and swung the door wide. "*This* is ours. Our new home."

Just as the light from the windows had first drawn Lucy into the room, so it did for her mother and sister. "Look at the view!" Sofia exclaimed. "We don't have to look into someone else's window across the alley! We can see the street and watch people come and go." She opened the sash, leaned out, and called to the family below. "Look here!"

Angelo called up to her. *"Ciao, piccolina!"*

Mamma bypassed the windows when she spotted the kitchen. She ran a hand along the edge of the sink as if it were made of solid gold. Lucy turned on the water. "Look, Mamma. Not just running water, but hot water." She backed up to show more. "And a real stove and oven. We can bake our own bread now."

Mamma's eyes were rimmed with tears as she took Lucy's face in her hands and kissed her. *"Cara ragazza mia. Bella.* It is beautiful."

Lucy wasn't certain *beautiful* was the right word for the apartment, but—

Sofia interrupted. "Look, Mamma! A bathroom!" Mamma and Lucy found Sofia climbing into the bathtub, just as Lucy had done at her first sight of it. "I'm going to take a bath every day, two times a day, and sit and soak and read and fall asleep. You'll have to serve me my meals in here."

"You'll be making your share of the meals, sister. With all three of us working at the shop . . ."

"You spoil everything, Lucy. I doubt you even know how to pretend to be a grand lady."

Mamma ignored both of them and went into the bedroom. She turned to Lucy. "A real bed?"

"It's for you, Mamma. This whole room is yours. No more sleeping on the floor in the living room."

Mamma sat on the bed but shook her head no. "I can't take this room. You and Sofia—"

"No," Lucy said. "You deserve this room, and it's yours."

Sofia looked around. "So where are you and I going to sleep?"

"On the mattress we brought from the other place, right here, in the main room."

Sofia put on her pouty face, but before she could give the mood full reign, Lucy tugged on her arm. "There will be none of that; there will be no complaining in this house. Not for one second."

Sofia yanked her arm loose. "You don't get if you don't ask."

Sofia did enough of that. Her sister's selfishness was like a pebble in Lucy's shoe. She couldn't understand how Mamma was always so forgiving. If she were Sofia's mother she'd . . . she'd . . .

God help her if she ever had a child like Sofia. Which she wouldn't, because she was never going to marry. What did she need with children, anyway? Her experience with Sofia had stifled all maternal longings.

There was a knock on the door. It was Aunt Francesca. "Are you ever going to let us in?"

Lucy helped Mamma to standing. "Enter," she said. "Welcome to our new home."

⚮

Mamma and Aunt Francesca stood in full embrace, sobbing. "When will I ever see you again?" Aunt said.

Mamma murmured something in her ear. Yet the truth was, this might be a final good-bye. America was a vast place, not easily traversed.

Lucy had already said her good-byes to her uncle and aunt. Feeling the strength of her uncle's arms reminded her of her father's embrace. Although Uncle Aldo had never taken her father's place, his very presence had eased her father's passing.

And now Uncle would be gone too. They would be three women, alone. The idea frightened her, yet offered an odd exhilaration at the challenge.

Angelo cleared his throat to get her attention. He stood at the door, hat in hand. Although Lucy had done her best to avoid any private

35

contact, such evasion could not be continued. He'd taken much time and effort to help them. He deserved her thanks.

As she walked toward him, he surprised her by drawing her out of the apartment to the landing at the top of the stairs. "Well, then," he said. "You're settled."

"Thanks to you, and to your father's cart. Please thank him for me."

He nodded, then looked past her to the apartment. "It's a large place, much better than the last."

Lucy suddenly worried that his compliment was a prequel to the suggestion they get back together, marry, and he move in. Her thoughts rushed to this conclusion, and she offered an awkward answer that was wanting in subtlety. "If you're wanting to move in here with us, Angelo, I apologize for giving you the wrong impression. I—"

He leaned his head back in full laughter. "You think I helped you because I still want to marry you?"

Lucy was horrified. "No, of course not, but . . ."

"Four years have passed, Lucy. Although I admit you hurt me, I've moved along with my life." He nodded toward the apartment. "You have done the same. I am happy to see you happy."

She hated the thought that he'd gotten over her. "Are you happy?" she asked him.

"I am happy. And married," he said. "With a son and a daughter."

Lucy's legs faltered enough to make the stairway a danger.

Angelo righted her with a hand. "I thought you knew."

She was suddenly angry and slapped his hand away. "How would I know? I haven't heard from you in all this time."

"And I've heard from you?" he asked. "Not until you needed my father's cart and another set of strong arms. Not that I mind, but . . ."

She felt the fool. Not for being ignorant of Angelo's marriage and children, but for thinking he would still be interested in her after all these years.

Lucy tried to regain her dignity. She set her chin and extended her hand to him. "Thank you very much for your services today, Angelo. My family appreciates your special effort."

"It's not your family I care about," he said softly. "I did it for you, Lucy. And if you ever need me again, please ask."

With that said, he kissed her cheek before rushing down the stairs and onto the street. Once more Angelo became a sweet memory and Lucy chided herself for opening her heart and mind to romance for even a moment.

Uncle Aldo and Aunt Francesca came to the door to leave. Each gave her one last embrace and kiss good-bye before they too descended the stairs.

Lucy heard Mamma's soft cries and entered the apartment. The click of the door behind gained special meaning.

"We're all alone!" Mamma cried.

Lucy and Sofia did their best to comfort her.

And comfort themselves.

❀

Sofia turned on her side, pulling the sheet with her.

"Stop it," Lucy whispered. "That sheet is for both of us."

Sofia flopped over again, facing her sister. "I don't like sleeping out here. I'd rather have my old hammock than sleep on this hard floor."

"We have a mattress. Be thankful for—"

The bedroom door opened and Mamma came out. "I can't sleep in there."

"Why not?"

"It's too soft."

Sofia scrambled to her feet. "This is your mattress, Mamma. Try this one."

"Sofia!" Lucy was appalled at her sister's insensitivity.

"No, no, Lucia. Your sister is right. I would much rather sleep on the mattress I'm used to. You girls take the bed."

Lucy grabbed a hunk of Sofia's nightgown, holding her back. "But I want you to have it, Mamma. I want you to have the bedroom all to yourself."

Sofia pulled out of Lucy's grip. "Don't argue with her, Lucy. If she wants the mattress in the main room, let her have it."

Lucy heard the creak of bedsprings as Sofia made herself comfortable. She tried to read her mother's face in the moonlight.

"Mamma," she said softly, "you don't have to do this."

Mamma put a hand to Lucy's cheek. "I want to do this. Go on now. Go claim a spot before your sister takes the entire bed for herself."

Reluctantly, Lucy did as she was told.

※❋※

Why do I do that?

Sofia turned toward the bedroom window, but she didn't close her eyes. For to do so would allow her mind to replay her latest act of selfishness. Why hadn't she let Mamma have the bedroom?

Honor your mother and father.

She cringed at the Commandment. What she should do is get out of bed, go into the main room, kneel by Mamma's side, and put a hand on her shoulder to wake her. *"Come into the bedroom, Mamma. I was wrong. I'll sleep here."*

But as one minute passed to another, the generous thought faded.

And sleep allowed her to be selfish one more time.

CHAPTER FOUR

*H*ow do I look?"

Sofia glanced at her mother and at Lucy, dressed in their Sunday best. "You look very nice."

Mamma shook her head. "I do want to make a good impression."

As did Sofia. She knew how much was riding on their jobs at Madame Moreau's Fashion Emporium. Working as one of a hundred in a dingy sweatshop was one thing, but working in a fancy store was by far another. Sofia knew the basics of sewing, but what if they expected her to know more? She'd be glad to learn, but what if they wanted her to know more *now*?

Lucy stepped toward her and tucked a stray piece of hair behind Sofia's ear. "Work doubly hard these first few days, all right?"

Even though Sofia had just suffered the same thoughts, it was annoying to hear Lucy say them aloud. She batted her hand away. "You act like I don't work hard. I know how to work hard."

"I know you *know* how, but I need you to do it. You don't want to move again, do you? Before you've even had a chance to soak in that bathtub?"

That last reference hit its mark. "I'll do fine. Stop worrying."

But there was a crease between Lucy's brows. "I just want Mrs. Flynn to like us."

"Why shouldn't she like us?" Mamma asked.

Lucy hesitated before answering. "She may not appreciate Mr. Standish hiring three extra sets of hands, sight unseen."

"Does she know we're coming?" Sofia asked.

"I hope she does, but I can't be sure."

Nothing like walking into a lion's den.

⚜

A bell on the door announced their arrival. With their first breath in their new employ, Lucy noticed Madame Moreau's smelled like women, a smell she had overlooked during her first visit with Mr. Standish. Now, knowing she belonged here, her senses were awake and eager to claim the space as part of her life.

Perfume. That's what it was. The lingering scent of perfume. How many wealthy ladies had lounged in this reception area, awaiting the moment they'd see the luxurious fashion being made just for them.

Mamma ran her hand along the top of a velvet chair. She whispered for their ears alone. "It is better than Mrs. Romano's shawl."

Lucy stifled a laugh when a woman entered from the workroom. Her welcoming smile immediately changed when she saw they were not one of her customers. "May I help you?"

Lucy stepped forward, extending her hand. "I'm Lucy Scarpelli, and this is my mother, Lea, and my sister, Sofia."

The woman nodded but did not offer her hand. "What can I do for you?"

Her tone held a distinct *Why are you here?* challenge. It was clear Mr. Standish had not informed the woman of their arrival. Or their hiring.

Mamma spoke low to Lucy in Italian. Lucy put a finger to her lips and smiled at the woman. "We are here to work. Mr. Standish hired us on Sunday and told us to come to work today."

The woman shook her head. "Sunday? He's not here on Sunday."

"But he was," Lucy said. "He was here checking on the apartment upstairs. We happened to meet, and in doing so, met each other's needs. We moved into the apartment yesterday and were to report to work today."

The woman made a face as if the entire situation held a sour taste. "I don't need three more workers. I have no idea what he was thinking."

Lucy couldn't believe Mr. Standish hadn't informed her of their coming. "I assure you, we have years of experience and will be an asset—"

The bell on the door announced another arrival. Lucy was ever so glad to see Mr. Standish walk in.

He removed his derby hat and nodded to the ladies. "Well, well. I see you've all met each other without me."

"So it's true?" the woman said. "You hired these three?"

He ignored her question. "Mrs. Flynn, I assume you have met Miss Lucy Scarpelli? And you must be her lovely mother." He nodded toward Mamma.

"And I'm the sister. Sofia."

He smiled. "Very nice to meet you, sister Sofia." He looked to Lucy. "You're all moved in abovestairs?"

"We are."

"It is a very lovely apartment, Mr. Standish," Mamma said.

His brow furrowed and Lucy explained. "I spent all of Monday cleaning so it showed its best face to my family when we moved in yesterday."

"Yes, yes, good for you." He turned to Mrs. Flynn. "See there? Hard workers, one and all."

Mrs. Flynn crossed her arms. "But I don't need any more workers."

"Actually, you do. Remember how I wanted to expand our offerings to include bonnets and hats?"

"Yes, but—"

"Mrs. Scarpelli has considerable expertise in making the very same."

Mamma shot Lucy a glance. "Considerable expertise" was an exaggeration to be sure.

Mr. Standish continued. "And Miss Scarpelli has more than ten years' experience in the garment trade, and Miss Sofia will help where needed." He gave her a wink. Sofia's smile told Lucy she was charmed by him.

Mrs. Flynn was less so. "This is all very well and good, but I wish you would have warned me—informed me—of their coming."

"Yes, well. I meant to come earlier this week, but my other business kept me away." He cleared his throat. "Mrs. Flynn, you've been complaining about how busy you are with the sewing for the Newport summer season. Plus, you often mention the pressure of keeping the shop organized and clean. So now I have addressed both of your problems—for Miss Scarpelli has agreed to the latter as well as the former."

She shrugged. "Well. I guess that's that then."

"Indeed it is." He put his hat back on and tapped the top of it. "With that accomplished, I will leave you ladies to the work at hand. Good day."

He left them staring awkwardly at each other. Lucy spotted Mamma taking Sofia's hand. It was up to Lucy to break the tension. "What would you like us to do first, Mrs. Flynn?"

With a *harrumph*, the pudgy woman turned and said, "Follow me." *That* they could do.

There were six women sewing in the workroom. Sofia forgot most of their names as soon as they were mentioned, but for two. Tessie was a young redhead with an Irish lilt to her voice, and Dorothy was their mother's age. These two had actually smiled when they'd been introduced. The other four barely looked up from their work. Sofia couldn't tell whether it was because they resented this influx of new-comers or simply didn't care. Had there been other new workers that had come—and gone? Was that the issue? Did the women hold off from being friendly because they doubted the three of them would last under Mrs. Flynn's rule?

Mrs. Flynn's opinion of their presence was abundantly clear and evident by her brusque tour of the workroom. "The cutout area is here, the bolts of fabrics are in the back, and fabric scraps go in this barrel and the trim in this smaller one."

The scrap barrel enticed like a treasure chest of jewels. Sofia would like nothing better than to dig through it with Mamma right beside her. Just walking by she saw lush satins that made her long to dip her hand in, just to *feel* . . .

Mrs. Flynn continued the tour. "The pressing is done over there, the threads are kept on the spindles, and the trims and other supplies are stored in the back room. Just so you're wise about it, I know the number of every hook and eye, every button."

Sofia resented the implication but said, "Yes, Mrs. Flynn."

The woman spun toward them. "To the customers I am Madame Moreau, so it's best you get used to calling me *Madame* now, so they'll be no slipups. I'll be—"

The bell on the front door chimed and she left them. A thick French accent was adopted as she greeted the customer. *"Ah, Madame Stewart, entrez! Venez, s'il vous plaît."*

Tessie giggled and put down the blouse she'd been trimming with lace. "I shouldn't laugh. She's actually quite good at what she does. No one has called her on her ruse yet." She shrugged. "If it keeps me working, she could speak Russian, for all I care." Tessie stood. "Will you be sewing or cutting?"

This was easily answered. Sofia had never cut fabric in her life. "Sewing." She glanced at the sewing machines. "But I want to learn to cut, and to use that machine. I'll do that."

Her comment elicited a tittering among all the workers. Dorothy explained. "I admire your pluck, girl, but putting scissors to fine fabrics that cost many dollars a yard and working with Madame's prized machines are a chore you work up to, not jump into."

Sofia's embarrassment was heightened when Mamma pulled her close like a child who needed to be drawn to her mother's hip.

"I am supposed to make hats," Mamma said.

This time the women looked impressed, and a girl sitting at a far table nodded. "Maybe now Madame will stop forcing us to try. We're no good at it, that's for certain."

"And if it'll keep the dollars from flowing to Wilson's Millinery, Mr. Standish will be happy," Tessie said.

Lucy looked around the room for a place to settle. "Where should we sit?"

Dorothy perused the room. "The table nearest the lobby is empty. When it's winter and the cold seeps through the curtain you'll see why, but here in the summer the breeze might be inviting. It should be a good place for the new hat department. And you too, Lucy."

Lucy gathered a chair for Mamma and for herself.

"And you, Lucy? What is your specialty?" Dorothy asked.

It was Lucy's turn to laugh. "I've sewn lining into wool coats for ten years, so I'd appreciate doing anything else."

A girl on the machine looked up. "You worked at Kennard's?"

"Yes."

Sofia stepped forward. "I worked there too."

"I was there three years," the girl said.

"On the sixth floor?"

"Under the Beast."

Sofia moved closer. She didn't recognize the girl—had she been introduced as Ruth or Rachel . . . some name with an *R*—but Sofia's lack of memory wasn't surprising. The sweatshop employed a couple hundred girls and each sat in her own spot. Mingling was frowned upon.

"He's not there anymore," Lucy said.

"His sins finally catch up to him?"

"His ambition. He moved to a better position."

"Hopefully not around young women."

"Ah," Tessie said. "Groping hands and large demands?"

"That's the sort."

Sofia had heard Lucy's stories of "the Beast," but luckily he'd been gone before she'd started to work there.

A young girl hemming a skirt spoke up. "Actually, we have our own Beast."

Tessie moved beside her and placed a hand upon her back. "Yes, well . . . you've learned to stay clear of Bonwitter now, haven't you, Dolly?"

The girl nodded.

"Who's Bonwitter?" Sofia asked.

"The bookkeeper. He comes in three times a week to order supplies and pay the bills—including our wages."

"What's wrong with him?"

The girls exchanged glances. "He's grabby."

"More than that, I just don't trust him."

Sofia's mind flitted to something else. "By the way, what are the wages?"

"Sofia!" Mamma said.

"What? Don't we have a right to know? Lucy said Mr. Standish never told her straight out."

The women exchanged glances. "That's not for us to tell you," Dorothy said. "Let's just say they're not enough but better than nothing."

It would have to do. For without this job that's exactly what they'd have.

Nothing.

They all heard the rise and fall of Madame's voice in the other room, along with the higher pitch of the customer.

"Who does the designing?" Lucy asked.

"Madame's fairly good at it," Tessie said, but her shrug indicated a lesser talent.

"Good at copying other designs mostly," Dorothy added. "But she leaves it to us to figure out how to do it. Mavis there makes the patterns and Ruth does the cutting."

"Does no one else help the customer with the designs?"

"Who has time? Besides, we never get a chance to talk with them except when we're doing a fitting."

"And then we don't talk; we're just hands, doing the work," Dolly said.

"While Madame talks. And talks," Mavis said.

More soft laughter.

"It's her best talent."

45

Suddenly, the curtain dividing the workroom from the lobby was pulled to the side. "Leona, join us, *s'il vous plaît.*"

Leona, who was at the sewing machine, gathered a pincushion and exited through the curtain.

Tessie found a basket of buttons and placed them in front of Sofia, patting a chair near Dolly. "Sort these and string like ones together."

It was demeaning work, child's work. "But I can sew too," Sofia said.

"I'm sure you can, but do this for now."

Tessie handed Lucy a blouse. "These cuffs need hemming."

It was rather funny actually. For Lucy to be handed a sleeve. Once again, a sleeve.

Dorothy led Mamma to the scrap bin. "See if there's anything salvageable in here for bonnets or hats."

Sofia saw Mamma's eyes light up and was happy for her.

Everyone returned to work and Sofia settled into her button sorting. Their jobs weren't as glamorous as Lucy had implied, but they were certainly better than their last ones. This would work.

It had to.

❦

Lucy hadn't tried to overhear, but with her position next to the curtain that divided the workroom from the lobby and fitting rooms, she couldn't help it.

"I wish I had a hat to complete the costume," the customer said. "Something in this green with some flowers or feathers."

"*Oui*, Madame Stewart," Mrs. Flynn said. "As soon as Leona gets finished marking the hem, I will have you meet our newest addition, Madame Scarpelli, a milliner of the highest degree."

Lucy set her sewing aside and rushed to Mamma, who'd divided the scrap barrel by colors. "Mamma! Your big chance has come." She told her about the woman's words.

"I must see the dress first," Mamma said.

Dorothy was listening. "You could bring Leona some more pins."

"Does she need—?"

46

Dorothy handed her a pincushion. "Don't say anything. And just a quick peek. Will that be enough?"

"It will have to be," Mamma said.

Armed with the pincushion, Mamma smoothed her hair and went through the curtain.

"Where's she going?" Sofia asked.

"She's making herself indispensable," Lucy said.

In just a few moments, Mamma returned. "It's a sage green dress with pink accents. I wish I had my flowers."

"Make some," Lucy said.

"I'll do it," Sofia said.

Mamma plucked some green fabric from the scrap pile. "This is left over from the dress!" She looked around. "I need some stiffener. Interfacing?"

"I'll get some," Dolly said.

Sofia found some pink ribbon. "Ribbon roses, but how big?"

"One large flower, two inches," Mamma started, "and a half dozen smaller."

"I need pink thread," Sofia said.

"Here." Ruth brought her some from the spindle wall, along with a needle and some small scissors.

Soon everyone was involved as Mamma expertly covered the many layers of starched material with the green fabric, adding interest by making small pleats across the crown. She added a poof of ivory lace, along with two pale blue feathers, and finally, Sofia's ribbon roses.

Dolly peeked through the curtain. "Hurry! She's getting ready to leave."

Mamma finished her final stitch, cutting the thread with her teeth. "Here."

Dorothy shook her head. "No, Lea. You are the creator. You show it."

"But I can't—"

"I'll go with you," Dorothy said.

Mamma looked petrified but, with Dorothy's hand upon her elbow, exited the workroom.

All sewing stopped as the women gathered by the curtain to eavesdrop.

"What is this?" Mrs. Flynn said.

Dorothy did the talking. "Mrs. Scarpelli overheard your need for a hat and has created one for you."

Mrs. Stewart answered. "In this short time?"

Mamma found her voice. "All the ladies helped."

"I wish I could see," Lucy whispered.

They didn't have to see, for they all heard Mrs. Stewart's exclamation of *oohs* and *ahs*. "It's absolutely perfect," she said. "I didn't know you had a milliner here."

"She's a new addition," Mrs. Flynn said. "I brought her in especially for you."

"What?" Lucy asked.

"Witness another of Madame's ways," Tessie said. "Everything is her idea, and all talent stems from her alone."

Mrs. Stewart was speaking again. "The ball gown you are working on . . . I would like a spray of flowers for my hair, perhaps with some beadwork. Can you do beadwork?"

"Of course," Mamma said.

"She is an expert at beading," Mrs. Flynn added. "Go on, then, Mrs. Scarpelli. Back to work."

The women parted so Dorothy and Mamma could enter the workroom. Sofia flung her arms around her mother. "I'm so proud of you!"

Mamma shook her head. "I am so proud of all of you. For you to help me, when you don't even know me . . ." There were tears in her eyes. *"Grazie."*

Dorothy put her arm around Mamma, but her words were for the lot of them. "We are a family here, Lea. And now our family has been increased by three."

Lucy felt her own tears threaten. All her fears of being accepted evaporated. To witness such kind cooperation. To see Mamma glow with the satisfaction of creating something beautiful . . .

They were the luckiest women in the world.

☙❧

Lucy handed Sofia a broom.

A broom? "It's after closing. What am I supposed to do with this?"

"It's part of the arrangement I made with Mr. Standish. Reduced rent if we clean the shop after hours."

"But I'm tired."

Mamma slapped the side of her arm. "And we're not? It's the end of our first day. We need to make a good impression. *Chi ben comincia è a metà dell'opera*: A good start is half the battle."

Yes, yes.

Lucy used a feather duster on the worktables and Mamma tidied the trim and scrap bin and the pile of bolts, which left sweeping the floor to Sofia.

"Why do I always get the worst job?" she asked.

Mamma looked up. "You want my job?"

"Actually . . ." Sofia handed Mamma the broom. At least she'd get a chance to touch the pretty fabrics.

She was folding over a stray edge of a bolt to set it on the pile with the others when the bolt slipped from her hands and fell to the floor.

"Careful with that!" Mamma said. "That fabric is expensive."

As Sofia collected the bolt, the fabric slipped off and into her arms. It was a royal blue nubby silk. She'd never felt anything so exquisite.

The temptation was too much.

Sofia wrapped it around her torso. "Look at me. I'm a lady." She tucked in the end, making it secure.

Mamma looked to scold her, but after a moment's hesitation retrieved a feathered hat she'd been making. "You need a bonnet, *mademoiselle*."

Lucy stopped her dusting. "You shouldn't play with those things. They aren't ours."

She could be so stuffy sometimes.

Sofia drew a length of gold braid from the basket and tied it around her middle, cinching the silk into her waist. "Now, where is my wrap? It's chilly tonight."

Mamma yanked the remains of a pink satin from its bolt and waved it in the air. "Here you are!" She draped it around Sofia's shoulders.

Sofia laughed—and found the sound foreign. She spotted a long string of buttons she'd strung together that very day. She pointed and instructed Lucy. "My jewels, please!"

Reluctantly, Lucy brought the strand and placed it around Sofia's neck. "This is silly."

"Yes, it is." Sofia raised her chin and took several long strides across the room, flaunting her fashion.

Mamma got into the fun by putting on a half-sewn chemise with only one puffed sleeve. "It's the newest fashion," she said, pulling at the one puff.

Lucy stood by, shaking her head. "We really should stop."

Sofia tossed her a length of lace fabric. "Sometimes you're like pasta without any sauce, sister."

Unenthusiastically, as if it were painful, Lucy draped the lace around her shoulders. Sofia took a red ostrich plume and stuck it in her sister's hair. "See? You look just like a lady in one of my novels."

"Lady of the evening, more like."

Sofia was glad when Lucy left the feather alone, and was surprised when she even tied some ribbon in a bow and pinned it to her shawl.

"Better?" Lucy asked.

"Bella, bellissima!" Sofia said, kissing her fingers.

As they played, even as they eventually put their props away and got back to cleaning, Sofia reveled in the laughter and frivolity. Life was serious business, yet she remembered laughing quite a lot when Papa was alive. Had the laughter died with him?

Perhaps. Until this evening, playing among the silks.

How odd that this simple act gave her hope.

Their new life just might work out after all.

Chapter Five

"*S*it up straight, dear."

Rowena Langdon abandoned her comfortable slouch and straightened her spine. Her corset pinched, claiming victory. The fashion of tiny waists was fine for those to whom God had granted such a trait, but to women of slightly wider build, it was torture.

The family carriage jostled left, forcing Rowena to stay herself with a hand against the leather wall.

"Must we suffer every bump?" Mother asked.

Rowena was glad an answer wasn't required. She was tired of talking, or rather, listening. In the past two weeks her mother and father had made it more than clear that she was to marry Edward DeWitt. On and on they went, as if it were the only topic in the world.

Not that there was anything wrong with Edward. He was a handsome man, quite a catch. But there was something disturbing about being *told* to marry someone—for business reasons. It lumped a girl into the category of a highly bred brood mare or piece of prized Manhattan property.

Rowena's and Edward's fathers were recently partnered in a business that sold and installed the elevators that had become a necessity in the tall buildings taking over the skyline. Earlier that year the American Surety Building had scraped the sky at twenty-one stories. Rowena couldn't imagine being up so high. The four stories of Macy's department store was quite enough for her.

Why the two sets of parents were insisting their children be partnered was not exactly clear, but Rowena was in no position to argue. Girls with physical infirmities were not on the top of any gentleman's marriage list.

At the thought of her bad leg, Rowena adjusted her skirt over it. Today was not going to be pleasurable, for she and her mother were on the way to Madame Moreau's Fashion Emporium for another fitting. They were leaving for the summer season in Newport soon, and had ordered two complete wardrobes. Over thirty ensembles each.

Rowena knew she should be thankful her father was willing to expend such money on fashion, but when that fashion only accentuated her lopsided stance . . .

The fact was, no matter how much satin and lace Rowena put on, she would never be a swan.

❧

Lucy was in seamstress heaven. The tedium of her sweatshop days was over, making each new challenge as invigorating as a breath of morning air. After hemming the cuffs—her first assignment—she'd been asked to hand stitch lace to a bodice, and was now carefully tacking the facing of a voile blouse. Having never experienced variety, she now embraced it. Even Sofia was being allowed to do some real seamstress tasks. And her declaration that she would learn how to work the sewing machine? Leona had been kind enough to begin the task of teaching her. To have a machine make a run of stitches in just a few seconds was mind-boggling.

The women in the shop continued to be kind. Dolly was the least talkative, though Lucy had often seen her and Sofia with their heads together. The fabric cutters, Mavis and Ruth, acted like best friends and didn't seem eager to expand their close circle. Dorothy and Mamma had formed a bond, most likely based on their common age. And Lucy enjoyed Tessie's talkative nature.

Dorothy came through the curtain, her head shaking in disgust. "These socialites who expect us to create dozens of new outfits are one thing, but wanting changes at the last minute is quite another." She motioned to Lucy. "Come with me and bring a notepad and pencil. I can't keep all of Mrs. Langdon's requests in my head."

Once again, the distraction of a new task was welcome. Up until now, Lucy had not been invited into the presence of the customers.

There were two of them. The older woman held herself with stately aplomb. Her blond hair revealed streaks of gray, and her face displayed lines around her eyes and forehead. Yet there was beauty there. It was not hard to imagine her as a young woman, turning heads and breaking hearts.

The other customer appeared to be her daughter, due to the shared shade of blondness and the turn of her narrow nose. She was not as beautiful as her mother was—or even had been—but Lucy wasn't sure if that conclusion was accurate or due to the awkward way she held her body and the shy manner in which she avoided all eye contact as she gave her attention to the floor.

"Stand up straight, Rowena," her mother commanded.

Rowena did her best, but it was with her best attempt that Lucy noticed a flaw in the girl's stance. Despite her best efforts, Rowena's posture was far from straight. Lucy didn't want to stare, but it appeared one shoulder was lower than the other and the issue continued with her hips, causing the entire ensemble to lose its symmetry and the center line of buttons to curve awkwardly rather than stand tall.

"Lucy . . ."

Dorothy was behind Rowena, tugging at this and pulling on that, trying to make the dress hang straight. "Write this down," Mrs. Flynn said. "Make a tuck in the back yoke on the right side. Add another row of lace to hide the seam. Adjust the—"

Lucy wrote on the pad, but her eyes were glued to the dress. What Madame was saying and what Dorothy was doing wouldn't help the line of the dress. If anything, it would accentuate the difference in the girl's shoulders.

Lucy's mind buzzed with ideas of her own. Her ears heard what Madame was saying, her hand wrote the words down, but her thoughts flew of their own accord, finally landing on, *Yes, I think that would work.*

Before she lost the idea, she spoke aloud. "What if we put an extra pad on her hip and even one on her shoulder so the dress would hang—"

Mrs. Flynn strode toward her, grabbing the pad and pencil away. "Silence, missy," she hissed. "Go back to the workroom, where you belong."

Lucy looked to Dorothy, who shook her head the slightest bit. Lucy had spoken at the wrong time and would receive no help from her. *Could* receive no help.

Yet as Lucy turned to leave, she caught a glance from Rowena, a wistful smile, as if she was appreciative but had resigned herself to the limitations of her fashion. The passive resignation wrenched Lucy's heart.

As soon as Lucy entered the workroom, she blurted out, "I can help her. I know I can."

The others wanted to know what had happened, and Lucy told them. "If only they'd let me play with the design a bit, I'm sure I could come up with something that would minimize the girl's—"

Mrs. Flynn interrupted by flinging the curtain aside as she entered the room. She strode directly to Lucy. "Who do you think you are?"

Dorothy slipped in behind her, carrying Rowena's dress among others. She offered Lucy a glance, but no more.

Lucy knew she should feel guilty for speaking up in front of a customer, but was surprised that wasn't the emotion she was feeling at all. Anger filled the spaces that frustration had left behind. She was about to say something to Mrs. Flynn when she spotted Mamma, shaking her head, warning her to keep her mouth shut.

Fine.

"Well?" Mrs. Flynn said, after her rant.

The woman was expecting an apology. That was the last thing Lucy wanted to give, yet it was the one thing she *must* give. "I'm sorry," she said.

"It won't happen again." Mrs. Flynn offered a statement, not a question.

Lucy wasn't sure she could promise *that*. But Mrs. Flynn was waiting—as were the rest of the women.

"I will do my best."

Mrs. Flynn's eyebrows rose.

"I promise," Lucy added, hoping that would appease her. Or confuse her.

A skirt slipped from Dorothy's arms, ending the exchange.

"Back to work," Mrs. Flynn said.

While Madame Moreau was out of the room, Rowena turned to her mother in a whisper. "I want to hear what that girl has to say."

"She is an underling, dear. She is not a designer. Besides, she was rude to speak out of turn."

Out of turn or not, Rowena wanted to hear the girl's ideas. For the first time since her accident, a dressmaker was truly seeing her problem and, more than that, was offering solutions. That the girl was in the back room being chastised was untenable.

"Mother, please go after her. Don't you want me to look my best for Edward?"

Her mother blinked once, and then again, as if acknowledging and then conceding the point. But before she could act, Madame returned from behind the curtain with Dorothy. The outspoken girl did not join them.

"I do apologize for the rude behavior of the seamstress," Madame said. "She is new here and hasn't yet learned her place."

"But—"

"We understand," her mother said. "And we appreciate your expertise."

And so, that was that.

It wasn't fair.

But what was?

Sofia had suffered enough drama for the day with Mrs. Flynn arguing with Lucy.

And Lucy had been worried about Sofia's work?

During the break for lunch, Sofia took her sandwich and slipped into the storeroom to read. Little Rosebud had just become homeless and Sofia was eager to see how she got out of her latest crisis.

She spotted a space behind a grouping of three barrels and tipped them in order to squeeze into the spot. It was a perfect place for hiding away. She turned to the right page and was just beginning—

When a chubby, balding man slapped his hands on the top of a barrel.

"What are you doing out here, girlie?"

Sofia put a hand to her chest, calming the beat of her heart. "You scared me!"

His smile was crooked and revealed a row of bad teeth. "What do you have there?"

Bonwitter. She'd seen him before, but not one-on-one. She put the book on the floor, near her back. "Just a novel."

"Let me see it."

"Why?"

"Because I'm your boss, that's why."

Considering Mr. Standish was her boss and Bonwitter was just the bookkeeper, she wanted to argue with him, but sensed it wouldn't be the wise thing to do.

His face grew stern. "Hand it over."

She had no choice. As expected, he read the title and laughed. "*Little Rosebud's Lovers*? Isn't that a bit racy for a young girl like you?"

Sofia awkwardly got to her feet and smoothed her skirt. "I'm not so young."

She immediately regretted her words, for he made no secret of eyeing her figure. "I can see that."

Sofia felt her cheeks redden. Even though his features more closely resembled those of a neighborhood baker or butcher than someone to be feared, there was something about Bonwitter that made her stomach tighten and her nerves tingle. If only she could get out of her hiding place. Yet there was no way to leave with the three barrels and Bonwitter barring her escape. So she held out her hand, palm up. "My novel, if you please?"

"I do not please." To her horror, he held the pages before her and ripped them in two.

"Don't!"

He tossed the pages onto a barrel. "Trash to trash. You're here to work."

"But that was mine! You had no right."

He leaned over the barrels, placing his face inches from hers. His breath was foul and the skin around his nose blotchy. "I have a right to do whatever I please, girlie." He traced a finger up her arm.

Sofia pulled away, shoved a barrel toward him, climbed out, and ran back to the workroom.

She'd never encountered anyone like Bonwitter. Weren't evil men supposed to look evil, with dark hair and eyes, and a sweeping mustache? That's the way they were always described in her novels. The fact that he looked more pudgy than wicked strangely added to his menace.

Lucy saw her come in. "What's wrong?"

"Bonwitter ripped my book apart."

All the ladies looked up from their lunch, but instead of being outraged, they seemed resigned.

Lucy noticed their attitude too. "He can't do that," she said. "Can he do that?"

Tessie shrugged. "Who and what's to stop him?"

Certainly not Mrs. Flynn, for she clapped her hands and said, "Lunch is over. Back to work."

But as Sofia returned to one of the sewing machines, Lucy slid past and whispered, "Don't worry. I'll handle it."

Lucia Scarpelli, defender of the weak.

Sofia Scarpelli.

The weak.

Lucy's nerves were aflutter as she marched into the back room to confront Bonwitter. Yet how could she let his affront to her sister go unanswered? *Chi pecora si fa, il lupo se la mangia.* Those who make themselves sheep will be eaten by the wolf. Bonwitter was definitely a wolf of the nastiest kind.

She found him holding a clipboard, checking things off a list.

He raised an eyebrow. "May I help you?"

"You can buy my sister a new novel to replace the one you ruined."

"And why would I do that?"

"Because you shouldn't destroy other people's property."

He crossed his arms and nodded, a smug smile on his face. "And who are you to tell me anything?"

Suddenly, Lucy was at a loss. She had no rights here. No power. "Just leave her alone, all right?"

But when she turned to leave, Bonwitter grabbed her arm and yanked her close. He dropped the clipboard and used his other hand to grope places he shouldn't.

With difficulty, she removed herself from his grasp. "Get away from me!"

He was not put off so easily and moved closer, his hands ready. . . . The memory of his greedy touch propelled Lucy to action.

She spotted a yardstick leaning against a stack of fabric bolts. In one motion she grabbed it and slapped it hard upon his hands.

He shrieked.

Unfortunately, his pain was replaced by anger and he lunged toward her. "You stinking dago. You can't get away from—"

The door to the storeroom opened. Mrs. Flynn showed her surprise at seeing them, and looked to Lucy, to Bonwitter, then to Lucy again. Finally, "Don't you have some work to do, missy?"

Lucy nodded and rushed past her into the workroom. She was unable to hear the exchange that passed between them, but knew Mrs. Flynn was well aware of Bonwitter's penchant for cornering the seamstresses in the back room.

Luckily, Bonwitter only came into the store a few times a week.

Lucy had already noticed that the work atmosphere on the days he was away was like a sunny day compared to a day overcast with clouds.

She returned to her table. The other women stopped their work. "So?" Sofia asked.

She decided not to mention the groping. "I slapped his hands with a yardstick."

A few of them laughed. "Did it break?" Tessie asked.

"Unfortunately, no."

Dorothy held a needle to the light and squinted as she threaded it. "Next time, try smashing it over his head. That's what I'd—"

"Shh."

The door to the storeroom opened and Mrs. Flynn returned. Would she make mention of Lucy's encounter? Lucy was in enough trouble for talking with a customer.

Mrs. Flynn walked behind Lucy's chair, causing a shiver to course through her.

"Next time a no will suffice, don't you think?" she said.

Lucy knew she should respond with a simple "Yes, Madame," but the memory of Bonwitter's hands propelled other words from her mouth. "Actually no, Madame. I will do whatever it takes to defend myself and my sister from the likes of him."

Mrs. Flynn yanked at Lucy's shoulder, forcing her to turn and face her. "The likes of him disperses your wages, missy. I've calmed him down this time, but next time you'd better find another way—if you want to keep your job."

A fire stirred in Lucy's belly. "But what about his job? If he's the one acting out of turn, we shouldn't have to suffer for it."

Lucy could hear the others take a breath. She'd gone too far. Again. She caught a glance from across the room where her mother sat making bonnets. Even Sofia gave her a warning look.

Mrs. Flynn's finger came within an inch of her nose. "You are not queen of the hill, missy, and you'd better—"

A bell chimed from the next room, indicating they had a customer.

"Watch yourself," Mrs. Flynn said. She left the room to attend to the patron.

"That was close," Dorothy said. "Madame has fired many a girl for less back talk than that."

Lucy didn't doubt it. From talking with Tessie and Dorothy, she knew in the past six months the shop had gained and lost at least a half dozen workers for a variety of offenses, real and imagined.

"Lucia, come here, please."

Her mother beckoned Lucy to a corner where they could have some privacy. She knew what Mamma would say. She always knew. But that didn't mean Lucy could avoid hearing it. Her mother was . . . her mother.

Once Lucy reached the corner, Mamma turned her back to the other workers and lowered her voice. "You are far too outspoken, and twice in one day?" she said. "This is a good job. We must keep it."

"So I'm to let that cad put his hands on me?"

Mamma shook her head no, but seemed unable to give her answer verbally. "We must tolerate such things in order to survive."

Lucy despised this truth.

When Bonwitter came into the room, Lucy wanted to look away. But she couldn't. The way to beat a bully was to confront him—or at least look at him eye to eye.

Upon seeing her stare, he hesitated just a moment before approaching her. But before he reached her, Mavis interceded. "Sir? We need some more muslin. I thought there were ten bolts in the storeroom, but we're already down to four, and—"

"Then you must have been mistaken," he barked. "But I've already ordered ten more. They'll be delivered tomorrow."

With that, he left them.

Tessie put her hands on her hips and mimicked him, easing the moment.

Mavis went back to work, cutting out a muslin pattern for a jacket. "I know there were ten bolts back there just a week ago. I don't use *that* much, even if this is our busiest time."

"That's because Bonwitter's taking them home," Ruth said. "Probably has them stacked up like a throne."

"Or he's selling them for profit." Lucy hadn't meant to say it aloud, but the silence in the room told her others had thought of it too.

"He wouldn't dare," Dorothy said.

"He dares plenty," Dolly said, implying more than muslin.

"Exactly." Lucy hatched a plan. "If Mrs. Flynn won't fire him for abusing us, then maybe she'll fire him for stealing. We just need to catch him in the act."

"How do we do that?" Dorothy asked.

Lucy added that question to the other questions swirling in her head about Rowena's alterations. . . .

She wasn't bored here. Not one bit.

The one thing Rowena hated above all else was mingling. Mindless chitchat where neither party learned a whit more about the other, or at least nothing of consequence.

Yet society demanded this very thing. Whether it be at a gathering for dinner, the opera, the races, a ball, or a reception for a funeral or wedding, all women of bearing were expected to smile, talk about nothing, and listen as if whatever was being said *to* them was essential to life as they knew it.

And perhaps it was. For wasn't that the definition of high society? A mingling of like-minded people with a common goal? Rich, like-minded people.

Among the elite Four Hundred of New York City, the goal was fourfold: to celebrate and encourage each other's egos, make more money than anyone else, show off that money as ostentatiously as possible, and intermarry and propagate so no one else gained a chance to infiltrate the hallowed halls of their divine community. It was all quite civil, in a maniacal sort of way.

The butler announced Edward's entrance into the Langdon drawing room. Edward came in holding his top hat in the crook of his arm. He offered Rowena a smile, clicked his heels together, and gave her a quick nod. "Miss Langdon. How are you this evening?"

Horrible. I don't want to go out to dinner with these people. Do you?

She set aside her feelings and answered with her own slight dip and nod. "Quite well, Mr. DeWitt. And you?"

"Actually, I'm quite hungry."

His honesty was pure refreshment and gave Rowena a bright inkling that perhaps, just maybe, there *could* be a true connection between them. What a joy it would be to find personal pleasure in the match *and* please her parents. And Edward's.

She suffered a small laugh at herself. All this speculation from Edward stating he was hungry?

"Are you ready to go out, then?" he asked.

"I am always ready for Lobster à la Newburg."

Edward laughed. "I do like a woman with an appetite."

She added another point to Edward's scorecard.

✑✐✑

Wah-wah, nah-nah, blah-blah.

The conversation around their table at Delmonico's was as inane as she'd feared. Edward, having recently moved to New York City from Boston with his family, seemed immune to her source of annoyance. Even though he was a newcomer, he was quite able to banter with the rest of them. In fact, they appeared far more interested in him than in Rowena. Which wasn't *that* much of a surprise. Ever since she'd come out—four years ago—society had accepted her presence with a nervous concession, as they would do with an eccentric aunt or a slightly senile uncle. Although no one ever—ever—spoke of her handicap, it was always in the room, a stigma preventing her from full entry into their sacred circle.

She glanced at the clock on the mantel. Eleven-thirty. They'd been done with dinner for two hours, yet had kept the poor waiters busy with various requests for additional food, even though no one had eaten their meal in its entirety.

Harriet Adams cupped her hands to her cheeks and exclaimed, "I just don't know what I'll do if I don't attend every ball in Newport. If you gentlemen don't keep me dancing, I'll be forced to dance with my uncle Elijah, and he has two left feet."

"Maybe *I'll* dance with your uncle Elijah," said Reggie Cosgrove. "Since I have two right feet, together we'll make a pair."

"Or go round and round in circles," said another.

"Poor man," Harriet said.

Harriet. Uncle. Poor. Rowena suddenly remembered something her father had told her that morning. "Have you read Harriet Beecher Stowe's latest book, *The Poor Life?*" she asked the group.

The room fell into complete and utter silence. Then Reggie said, "Harriet who?" He paused a short second, then burst into laughter. "Are you sure your uncle's name isn't Tom?"

"And why would I want to read about anyone who's poor?" Harriet said.

More laughter. Rowena had reached her fill and stood. To his credit, Edward stood also. "I need to go home, please. If you don't mind?"

"Of course," he said, and pulled out her chair.

Harriet spoke first. "Don't leave us, Rowena." To Reggie she said, "Apologize to her, you oaf."

Reggie stumbled to his feet, plainly drunk. "Ah, come on, Rowena, I didn't mean to run you off."

Rowena paused at the door and faced them. "Believe me, you do not possess the power."

She took Edward's arm and exited the room accompanied by a bevy of *oohs* and laughter.

Good riddance.

Once in the carriage she had second thoughts. "I apologize, Mr. DeWitt. I usually am not so short with them, but—"

"No, no, you did me a favor. Somehow they manage to be boorish *and* boring."

Edward was a gem.

CHAPTER SIX

hat are you doing?"

"Shh," Lucy said, getting out of bed.

"It's not morning, is it?" Sofia asked.

"No, not morning."

It was the middle of the night. Lucy couldn't sleep. Her thoughts twisted with her anger at Bonwitter and her frustration regarding Rowena Langdon's clothes. Finally admitting she couldn't change Bonwitter, her mind had free rein to think about helping Rowena.

But Mrs. Flynn will be mad.

Her ideas swelled, making the threat of Mrs. Flynn's ire lose its bite. The ideas demanded full release, so she got up, dressed, and slipped downstairs and into the shop.

She purposely left the lamps off in the front lobby and felt her way through the dark until she reached the curtain to the workroom. Only when it was fully closed behind her did she light the lamps.

It was eerie being there alone. The silence was almost frightening.

Almost.

To dispel it, Lucy made some noise as she found Rowena's outfits hanging in the wardrobe closet. There were two dozen ensembles so far. There was no way she would have time to fix them all. But if her ideas worked and even one gown addressed Rowena's unique body issues, then hopefully Lucy could work on the rest of them with the customer's—and Mrs. Flynn's—blessing.

She found the day dress Rowena had been wearing when Lucy had offered her opinion. The skirt was a pale beige, settling somewhere between cream and tan. The bodice was a light yellow, accordion-pleated *mousseline de soie,* bisected with pearl buttons. The sleeves were of the current leg-o'-mutton fashion—voluminous from shoulder to elbow, padded with eiderdown, yet tight to the wrist. Just as the bustles of the eighties had grown ridiculous, these sleeves and the overt attention to the upper torso often went too far with layers of lace, festoons, and flounces threatening to choke. . . . Would fashion ever leave women alone and let them be comfortable in their clothes instead of making them look like some overwrought gewgaw? Did fashion designers ever ask women what they'd prefer? Who made these decisions?

Men, most likely.

Men or no men, comfort or no comfort, it was not in Lucy's power to make such changes in the status quo. Nor did she have the time.

Which was ticking by . . .

She held the dress before her, seeing how the buttons lined up perfectly. It was made for someone with a conventional figure, not someone with physical issues.

Lucy looked at the pinning Mrs. Flynn had ordered in her attempt to solve the problem. It would only pull the fabric off grain. Lucy's solution was the best solution.

And so, she set to work.

The clock in the workroom read four. In the morning. The early morning.

Lucy had finished Rowena's dress and was pleased with the results.

The true test would come when Rowena tried it on. Somehow, Lucy had to arrange to be in the room when that happened. She had to *see*.

And take credit. Although she knew a truly humble person would let Mrs. Flynn accept the glory, Lucy also knew if she ever wanted to rise in her profession, she had to prove she could do more than hem other people's work.

Lucy set the workroom to rights again, and was about to extinguish the lamps when she decided to use the shop's facilities. It would be better not to risk waking up Mamma and Sofia.

Before she lit a lamp in the tiny room, she noticed something odd. Light was coming in through the wall. Lucy kept the light off and moved toward it. There was a small hole in the wall the size of a coin. She peered through it and saw the storeroom, where she'd left a lamp burning.

She stood upright, her thoughts rushing to uncomfortable places. Was Bonwitter spying on them while they were using the necessary? She shuddered. And looked through the hole again. Directly in view was their stock of muslin.

Then she got an idea.

Perhaps a great idea.

❦

"Shh. Let your sister sleep."

Lucy was vaguely aware of her mother and sister moving about the apartment, but sleep was a demanding master.

She dozed until she felt her mother put a hand upon her shoulder. "You must get up, Lucia. Sofia told me you worked through the night, but Mrs. Flynn will not accept tardiness, for any reason."

Memories of her nocturnal busyness won out over sleep. She had to get to work to be there when Rowena and her mother came back for more fittings.

And then there was her plan regarding Bonwitter . . .

Lucy sped through her morning ritual and bested her mother and Sofia to the stairs.

"Maybe you should get less sleep more often," Mamma said. "I do wish you'd tell us what you were doing."

"You'll see soon enough."

When they entered the shop, the workroom was already abuzz. The beige dress was displayed on the cutting table, and Mrs. Flynn and Dorothy were examining it. "If you didn't do this, who did?" Mrs. Flynn asked Dorothy.

"I did." Lucy stepped forward.

Her boss looked skeptical. "When?"

"Last night."

"All night," Mamma added.

"How did you get in?" Dorothy asked.

Lucy produced the key. "We have a key so we can clean."

Mrs. Flynn held the dress by the shoulders. "It doesn't hang straight at all. Look at this, the bodice is off center."

Lucy shook her head. "So is Miss Langdon. The dress will hang straight on her."

Mrs. Flynn lowered the dress and eyed Lucy. "You ignored my wishes; you ignored the alterations we were set to make. You have no right to risk our customer's patronage, not to mention the expense of the fabric and other materials."

"It will work," Lucy said.

Mrs. Flynn flashed her a look. "You're willing to risk your job on this?"

Lucy felt a sharp pull in her stomach. Would it really come to that? If this one dress failed, would she lose her job? She'd made the alterations without being able to try the dress on Miss Langdon in the process.

Mrs. Flynn was waiting for an answer.

Lucy hedged. "The girl needs help. The normal methods of dress-making won't work with her, and—"

"You think I don't know that?"

The other women in the room looked away and made themselves busy. Doubt slid front and center. Had Lucy made a horrible mistake?

The doubt let humility and regret have their way with her and

Lucy found herself sincerely saying, "I'm sorry, Madame. My intentions were good, but I should have consulted you first."

By the lift of her left eyebrow, it was apparent Lucy's apology took Mrs. Flynn by surprise. "Well, then. You're new. You didn't know, but now you do. All designs must go through me."

"Yes, Madame."

"Now, back to work, all of—"

The bell on the front door announced a customer. Mrs. Flynn left them.

"Lucky Lucy. That's what we should call you," Tessie said. "None of us have ever spoken to Madame like that."

"And lived," Mavis added.

Sofia rolled a length of ribbon into a circle. "You should have gotten me up. I could have helped."

"Hush," Mamma said. "You stick with the rules, young lady."

Sofia tossed the ribbon onto a table, where it unwound and fell still. "But why does Lucy get to—?"

A stern look from their mother silenced her.

Lucy took up the hem she'd been working on the day before. As she sewed she thought about the dress she'd altered for Miss Langdon. She'd adjusted the hem after inserting a pocket full of padding on the skirt's hipline. Another pad had been carefully hidden beneath the three ruffles of the mousseline at each shoulder. It was further disguised with a lapel of black guipure lace that matched a godet detail around the waist. If you didn't know . . .

This *had* to work.

❦

Timbrook entered the drawing room and announced, "Mr. DeWitt is here, Miss Langdon."

Rowena immediately set her embroidery aside. "Show him in."

She wasn't expecting him. Or had she missed something on her calendar? Actually, since being so rude to the group last night at Delmonico's, she'd feared he wouldn't want to see her again at all.

Rowena put a hand to her hair and wished she were wearing

her pink day dress instead of this plainer green one. She bit her lips, pinched her cheeks, and—

Edward entered the room.

He paused and nodded, and she did the same. "I hope I'm not disturbing you," he said.

"Not at all. You are always welcome here, Mr. DeWitt. Please sit down." She indicated a chair near her settee.

As he took his place she noticed a book in his hands. She couldn't see the title because he placed it on his lap and covered it with his hands. She purposely kept her eyes away, to let him take the initiative.

He got right to the point. "I've come with a gift." He handed her the book.

It was a copy of *Uncle Tom's Cabin.*

Rowena was taken aback, not certain if he was being kind or making fun of her by hearkening back to her comment about its author at Delmonico's.

He must have noticed her reticence, for he quickly added, "It's a favorite of mine, and since you're obviously knowledgeable about the book and its author, I wanted to give it to you as a gift. I'm only sorry I couldn't find *The Poor Life*, which you mentioned."

She released the breath she'd been saving. "That's very kind of you, Mr. DeWitt."

"Please call me Edward. And may I call you Rowena?"

She felt a glow ignite from within. This was a very good sign. "Of course."

Since an opening had presented itself, she brought forward an issue that had been bothering her. "I did want to apologize for my rudeness last night. For me to purposely provoke the group like that . . . it's not like me at all."

"Then why did you do it?"

She'd never expected him to ask. "I . . . I get weary of the nothingness of chitchat."

He laughed. "Then I'd better fine-tune the subjects of my conversations. Would you like to talk about current events? I hear there's a new country in the world: Formosa. Or would you rather talk about music? What's your favorite opera? Apparently *Romeo and Juliet* will be at the Metropolitan this next season."

Rowena felt herself redden, this time from embarrassment. "You're making fun of me."

His face turned serious and he reached to touch her hand. "Not at all. Forgive me if I've offended you. I agree with your view about shallow conversation. I would honestly enjoy speaking with you in depth about any subject of your choosing."

Rowena felt like a fool. For she knew nothing about Formosa, and for him to specifically mention the tragic love story *Romeo and Juliet* . . . But then, a far different subject sprang from her lips. "How do you feel about our obligation to marry? Don't you find it awkward?"

Edward's raised eyebrows revealed surprise. But once again, he put her at ease. "It's awkward and rather embarrassing, and yet . . . you are a charming woman, Miss—Rowena. If I am obliged to follow my parents' instruction, I'm pleased you are its subject."

Rowena felt tears threaten. "You are the kindest man."

He shook his head. "But I'm not. All credit to kindness comes about because of you."

She was unused to such compliments, to any compliments, and it made her fear they were offered out of pity. "I know I'm not like other women." She realized she was looking down at her leg, and quickly looked up at him.

He took her hand fully in his and offered a reassuring squeeze. "No, indeed you are not. Thank God."

Indeed.

That's exactly what she'd do: Thank God.

Suddenly the curtain parted, and Mrs. Flynn came into the work-room. She strode to Lucy's side and spoke softly. "Please come with me, Lucy. Miss Langdon is wearing your gown."

"Does it fit?"

"Just come." She walked toward the curtain.

The moment of truth had arrived. Lucy's nerves sprang to

attention. She smoothed her hair. She vaguely heard soft words of encouragement from the other women. *Please let the dress work.*

As soon as Lucy entered the room she knew her prayer had been answered. Rowena Langdon walked toward her, her hands outstretched, her face beaming. "You? You're the one who created this miracle for me?"

Lucy glanced at Mrs. Flynn. Had she actually given Lucy the credit?

Mrs. Flynn avoided her gaze. Lucy turned her attention to Miss Langdon, allowing her hands to be taken up. "So you like the dress?" Lucy asked.

There were tears in the girl's eyes. "I have never felt so pretty— never felt pretty at all." She smiled. "Until now."

Rowena's mother put a hand on her daughter's arm as if a bit uncomfortable with the contact she'd made with Lucy. "We are indeed grateful, Miss . . . ?"

"Scarpelli," Lucy said. "Lucy Scarpelli."

In spite of her mother's preference, Rowena held on to Lucy's hands a bit longer. "Can you rally the same magic for all my new outfits?"

Mrs. Flynn interrupted. "It's not magic, I assure you. There are many hours involved and much tedious handwork, *mademoiselle.*"

It was obvious the woman was working toward an extra charge of some kind. Lucy would've done the work for nothing. Just to know she'd helped Rowena feel pretty was payment enough.

The bell on the front door announced a new arrival. All heads turned to see Mr. Standish.

"Good morning, ladies. Mrs. Langdon, Miss Langdon. How nice to see you both."

His greeting was reciprocated.

He studied Rowena's dress. "My, my," he said. "How lovely you look."

Rowena beamed. "It's Lucy's doing. You are aware of my . . . dilemma, Mr. Standish, but now . . ."

He made a turnaround motion with his finger, his gaze glued to the garment. "To that I say, *what* dilemma?" Her revolution complete, he took her hands and kissed them. "You are lovely, my dear, and this dress only accentuates your beauty."

Miss Langdon blushed. And though it seemed Mr. Standish's flattery was a bit overboard, upon a second look, Lucy saw he was right. She'd considered Rowena a pretty girl, and the dress removed any awareness of her infirmities, but it seemed with that removal was an addition—a glowing countenance that indicated the woman standing before them was confident and worthy of admiration.

Lucy felt a wave of pride rush over her. And awe. She'd undertaken the task of fixing Rowena's dress as a challenge, to prove herself *to* herself—and others. But to know she'd achieved something far beyond the sewing . . . had touched the wearer, had changed her . . .

Mr. Standish turned to the mother. "Are you pleased?" he asked.

"Very. It seems Miss Scarpelli has accomplished what no other seamstress has been able to achieve."

An eyebrow rose. Mr. Standish looked upon Lucy. "You are responsible for this dress?"

A long explanation swept through Lucy's mind, yet she simply replied, "Yes."

"Bravo, Miss Scarpelli. You never told me you were so skilled at fitting."

I didn't know I was. She shrugged. "I enjoyed working with Miss Langdon."

Rowena perked up. "And I with you, Miss Scarpelli."

Mrs. Flynn interrupted. "Actually, we have many skilled seamstresses who can work—"

"No," Rowena said. "I want Miss Scarpelli to sew all my things." She turned toward her mother. "Don't you agree?"

Mrs. Langdon sighed. "Yes. I do believe that's the way things should proceed."

Mrs. Flynn shook her head. "But Miss Scarpelli is new here and should go through more training. Plus, she has other work assigned—"

Mrs. Langdon's eyebrow rose. "Work more important than a wardrobe for my daughter?"

They all looked to Mrs. Flynn. Lucy almost—but not quite—felt sorry for her. There was no way she could deny Mrs. Langdon's request.

Mr. Standish stepped in. "Your wish is our command, Mrs. Langdon. Miss Scarpelli will be in charge of your daughter's wardrobe." He looked at Mrs. Flynn. "Correct, Madame?"

"*Oui*. I'm certain something can be arranged," Mrs. Flynn said.

"Will be arranged," Mr. Standish said.

Mrs. Flynn hesitated, then gave in. "Will be arranged."

He nodded. "I'll come in tomorrow to check on the progress."

Mrs. Langdon plucked a thread from her daughter's sleeve. "Now let's have Rowena try on her other outfits so Miss Scarpelli can make more of her alterations."

Lucy tried not to smile.

But failed.

༄

The unfortunate aspect to being Rowena Langdon's personal seamstress was the amount of work it entailed. Nearly thirty outfits ranging from walking ensembles to ball gowns. The ball gowns would be the most challenging to alter because the bare arms and décolletage made extra padding harder to hide. At least the fashion tended toward having a short puffed or ruffled sleeve for evening wear. The sleeveless styles of a few years previous would have been far more difficult to adapt.

The fortunate aspect to being Rowena Langdon's personal seamstress was her company. The girl was surprisingly candid—especially when her mother commandeered Mrs. Flynn and Dorothy to fit her own costumes and Lucy and Rowena were left alone in one of the private fitting rooms.

"I am to marry, you know," Rowena said as Lucy worked to adjust a blue day dress.

"Congratulations."

"No congratulations are due—as yet. I misspoke. I am not yet betrothed, but my parents have agreed with his parents—in theory—that the two of us would make a good match."

Rowena did not sound enthused. Lucy would have liked to ask if she loved the man, but knew that would be too presumptuous.

Rowena continued. "A proposal is the goal of this year's season in Newport. Edward and I are to fall in love and, as Father says, seal the deal."

Lucy hated the air of resignation in Rowena's voice, yet knew the wealthy had a fondness for arranged marriages. There were some advantages to being poor.

Though not many.

Rowena gazed in a mirror while Lucy worked on the train of her dress. "This is the first time I've been excited about getting new clothes. That's your doing, Miss Scarpelli."

Lucy spoke through a mouthful of pins. "I'm glad I could help."

"It's extremely important for me to be beautiful so Edward likes me and . . ." She looked over her shoulder, seeking Lucy's eyes. She lowered her voice. "He needs to desire me."

Lucy nodded. Attraction, desire, love. Attraction always came first, but as far as the other two? Which came first? It was not something a woman could control. Actually, there wasn't much about the whole courting experience that anyone could control—which was yet another reason Lucy was glad to abandon the notion. Why would anyone choose to be a part of such a confusing, haphazard association?

Rowena turned forward again. "I have absolutely no idea how to be desirable in that way. It isn't in my nature."

"Nor in mine," Lucy said.

"Really?"

"I'm far too practical to be flirtatious."

Rowena laughed. "And I'm far too impatient." She sighed deeply. "I'm so glad we met, Miss Scarpelli. I see God's hand in our friendship."

God's hand? Friendship? Although Lucy enjoyed Rowena's company, she hadn't allowed herself to think they were friends. As far as God bringing them together . . . ?

Rowena was waiting for her response. "I'm glad we met too, Miss Langdon. And I—"

"Call me Rowena," she whispered. "At least when we're alone."

"Rowena," Lucy repeated.

Calling a wealthy patron by her first name. Perhaps God *was* involved.

⚜

Sofia pricked her finger and put it in her mouth. How appropriate. For once again, Lucy was the subject of praise and Sofia was merely her little sister, or even worse than that, completely ignored.

Why didn't you think of a way to help a customer? Why didn't you stay up all night to work on it?

Sofia shook the questions away, for she had no good answers. The truth was, she wasn't creative like Lucy, nor as hardworking. To willingly forfeit sleep was absurd.

Then you'll never receive praise. You'll never get anything special if you don't push yourself. Sacrifice a little.

The voices in her head needed to be silenced, so Sofia set her sewing aside, slipped one of her novels into the fold of her skirt, and escaped to the back room.

"Lucy, Lucy, Lucy," she said under her breath. "She gets everything. No one even thinks about me."

"Except me."

Sofia whirled around and saw Bonwitter watching her from the shadows. How appropriate. She knew from her stories that evil always lurked in the dark. If she'd known he was there today, she never would have risked the storeroom.

Without another word, she headed back to join the others.

He lurched forward and stopped her with a hand on her arm.

"Let go!"

He pulled her close. "I prefer you to your big sister any day." He ran a hand over her bottom. And squeezed.

With all the energy she possessed, she shoved him away.

The memory of his hand upon her body followed her as she ran into the workroom.

⚜

"Lucia. Stop working. You must eat."

Lucy looked up from her sewing, and with that one small act moved from one world to another. Ever since Rowena and her mother left after their fittings, Lucy had been consumed with executing the changes. She'd not looked up or even held a thought beyond the work. The work. The work.

Tessie tugged at her sleeve. "Come on now. It's lunchtime. You working through will make us all look bad."

With the mention of food, Lucy realized she was hungry. And as she looked across the room she found her eyes had trouble focusing. She rubbed them as Mamma set a lidded tin of vegetable soup before her and broke a hunk of bread from a fresh loaf.

Mamma looked around. "Where is your sis—?"

Suddenly Sofia burst in from the storeroom. Her face was a mask of panic. She ran into her mother's arms.

"What happened?" Mamma asked as she stroked her hair.

"He . . . he . . ."

Lucy knew exactly who *he* was. She looked toward the storeroom and spotted a shadow pass the open door.

Bonwitter.

Lucy marched into the storeroom. *Where is that man? Just let me at him.*

"Looking for someone?" Bonwitter asked.

He leaned a shoulder against the wall, his hands in his pockets. Calm. Unconcerned. Haughty.

Lucy strode toward him, moving close enough that he felt the need to stand erect and step away. "What did you do to my sister?"

There was a flicker of panic, quickly shrouded in arrogance. "I don't know what you're talking about."

He did. He knew very well.

But Lucy also knew he'd never admit any wrongdoing. Types like him never did but seemed to feel a sense of entitlement, as if all the laws of the land, and the moral commandments under God, only applied to everyone else.

He resumed his leaning. "Don't you have something to do, Miss Scar-pel-li?"

His words made her offer a soft laugh. Oh yes. She *did* have something to do. Something very important to do.

Lucy turned on her heel and left without offering him the satisfaction of another spent word.

She'd have the last word. Of that, she was certain.

❧

Where Lucy's thoughts had previously been consumed with her work for Rowena, after lunch, they were consumed with Bonwitter. She suspected he was stealing stock, but proving it . . .

Midafternoon, she got her chance.

Dorothy came in from the storeroom and announced, "That muslin you wanted is being delivered, Mavis."

Mavis was busy cutting out a pattern for a tennis dress. "Good," she said. "I'm on my last bolt."

Lucy remembered the conversation when Mavis had mentioned they were down to four bolts and Bonwitter had said he'd just ordered ten more. Ten, plus the one bolt that was currently left . . .

"It's being delivered now?" Lucy asked.

"As we speak." Dorothy took up her needle.

Lucy set her sewing aside and went to the necessary. She kept the lamp off, closed the door, and was drawn to the spy hole in the wall.

Directly in her line of sight were Bonwitter and a deliveryman. The man was setting ten bolts of muslin on the stack, making eleven all told. But then, as soon as the man left, as if on cue, Bonwitter took six of the bolts and put them somewhere out of Lucy's sight. Was he creating a stash he could pick up later?

Lucy rushed to the storeroom, hoping to see where he was putting the goods.

When she entered, she saw him arranging a tarp over a row of barrels. He started, then continued his work. "What do you want, girlie?"

Lucy went to a shelf and chose a spool of thread from stock. She held it up for his inspection, then left. Her mind whirled. Back at her worktable she set the unneeded red thread aside. Then took it back.

Perhaps it could be useful. . . .

❧

Lucy's nerves remained on edge the rest of the workday. As soon as Bonwitter left, she hurried back to the storeroom, to the tarp over the barrels.

And there they were. Six bolts of muslin, slipped behind the barrels. Obviously, he planned to come back some other time and spirit them away through the alley door.

Was he cocky enough to do it during the day? Or would he wait for darkness? Lucy guessed the latter, when all good thieves did their best work.

Lucy returned the tarp to its place. She thought about telling the others, or at least Mrs. Flynn, but feared Bonwitter would come up with an explanation as to why some of the bolts were separate from the rest.

She had to catch him in the act, and more than that, follow him to see where he took the goods. Only then . . .

But if Bonwitter had done this before, if he had a large stash of supplies, how could Lucy prove that he had stolen *these* particular bolts?

So evolved her plan.

She was going to mark them. Yet for that act she needed a witness—and not Mamma or Sofia, for their testimony would be tainted by their familial ties. She thought of the other women. Who had the most clout *and* was the most trustworthy?

Lucy went back to the workroom and gathered the red thread and a needle. "Dorothy, could you help me with something in the storeroom, please?"

Dorothy looked curious, but followed. Once in the back, she asked, "So? What do you need me for?"

"I need you as a witness." Lucy showed Dorothy the six bolts.

"But why are they here, and not on the—?" She put a hand to her mouth. "Bonwitter?"

Lucy nodded. "He hid them here to pick up later." She held up the needle and thread. "I'm going to mark them with a red X."

"What good will that do?"

"When we find the goods elsewhere, it'll prove they're from our shop."

"We?"

"Me. Unless you want to come along . . ."

"I want to see Bonwitter get his comeuppance as much as anyone, but I have children at home. I can't risk losing this job and . . ." She shrugged. "Are you sure you want to do this, Lucy?"

Not really. "I have to do this. I have to rid this place of him, for all our sakes."

Lucy began sewing a small X along the fold of the fabric. "You see me doing this, yes?"

"I see you."

"So you *will* vouch for me if he's caught?"

Dorothy hesitated. "If it gets that far, I'll vouch for you."

Lucy bit off the thread from the first X and moved to the second. "Do you think he's going to pick them up tonight?"

"If he's smart, he will. Every minute these bolts are hidden is a risk."

Dorothy shook her head. "You're assuming Bonwitter is smart."

"He is smart. But I'm smarter."

Dorothy crossed herself. "May God protect you."

❦

"You shouldn't have to do the cleaning tonight, Lucy," Mamma said. "Not when you barely got any sleep last night, working on Miss Langdon's dress." She nodded toward Sofia. "Sofia can sweep up."

Sofia draped herself over Mamma's upholstered chair, one leg dangling across its arm. "If Lucy wants to do it, let her."

Mamma pinged her leg with a finger. "You reap what you sow, child."

"Sew, mother. *S-E-W.* I sew all day. And I'm tired."

"And we aren't?"

Sofia got up with a sigh. "Fine, I'll go."

"No," Lucy said. "I really want to do the cleaning tonight." *I need to do it.*

Mamma studied her face, and Lucy had to look away from her discerning eyes. Then Mamma put a finger beneath Lucy's chin and lifted it. "What are you up to, Lucia?"

"I'm making things better for us, Mamma. I promise." She kissed her mother's cheek. "Don't worry. I know what I'm doing."

Papa always said, "*Volere è potere:* Where there's a will there's a way." Hopefully, she possessed both.

⁂

Lucy entered the shop in darkness—and kept it that way. She felt her way through the lobby, then the workroom, and into the storeroom. Pale moonlight from an alley window offered a shadowy scene.

Lucy had pondered long and hard about where she could hide. She didn't want to be hemmed in because she wanted to be able to slip out the back and follow Bonwitter with his goods.

She chose another row of barrels a short distance from the ones in question. With difficulty she rocked one forward, away from the wall, and squeezed into the created space. By looking through the gap between her barrel and its neighbor, she had a good view.

Lucy tried to get comfortable. A mouse squealed as she did so and skittered to some new hiding place.

There. She was settled.

All she could do was wait.

CHAPTER SEVEN

ucy opened her eyes.

It was dark. Her back hurt, her legs were cramped—

Then she remembered where she was, hidden away behind some barrels, waiting for—

Boots sounded upon the wood floor. She heard the expulsion of air as effort was expended.

Lucy peered through the space between the two barrels that formed her hiding place. Bonwitter was removing the bolts of muslin from *their* hiding place and stacking them one upon the other.

Once they were manageable, he carried them to the back door, which he'd left ajar. He pushed it open with a shoulder, then closed it behind him.

Lucy scrambled between the barrels and ran to the alley window. She spotted Bonwitter climbing into a small cart. As soon as the horse began to move, she slipped out the door and hurried after it, dodging behind boxes and barrels in the alley, keeping him in her sight.

She thanked God the streets of New York would not allow Bonwitter to travel quickly. She only hoped *she* could be quick enough.

⧉

Eighty-nine Bowery. Eighty-nine Bowery.

Lucy repeated the address as she hurried back home. This was the place Bonwitter had stopped and removed the bolts of muslin from the cart. He'd gone inside, and she'd waited until she saw a light go out. He must live there too. She hoped he lived there. If it was just a warehouse he might find a way to weasel out of her accusations. *"I don't own that warehouse. The goods inside aren't mine."*

It would be hard to prove. But if he also lived there . . .

Eighty-nine Bowery. Eighty-nine Bowery . . .

⧉

Lucy was the last to get up. Again.

Sofia stood in the doorway of the bedroom. "I don't see why Lucy gets to sleep in, day after day."

Her sister sat up in bed and hung her legs over the side as if they were leaden. What was her problem?

Sofia smelled coffee brewing. Mamma sidestepped her chores in the kitchen to stand beside her in the doorway. "Two nights in a row, Lucia?"

"I . . . I cleaned the shop, remember?"

Mamma lowered her chin, pinning her with stern eyes. "Did you?"

"I said I did, didn't I?"

Something was up. It wasn't like Lucy to snap at their mother. And the fact that Mamma didn't chastise her for it . . . Once again, Sofia felt left out. She'd noticed Lucy getting into bed late, but had no idea what time it had been.

But Mamma did have something to say. She entered the bedroom and faced Lucy. "*I* cleaned the shop, Lucia. When you didn't come back, I went downstairs and found the shop dark—and dirty. I swept the floors and took out the trash. Would you care to explain yourself?"

Lucy looked toward the window, then down to the blanket. Sofia was glad to see her discomfort. Her saintly older sister was in trouble? It was a momentous occasion.

Mamma tipped her head toward the kitchen. "Go get us some coffee, Sofia."

"No," she said. "I deserve to hear too."

With a sigh, Mamma obviously decided not to fight both daughters. She sat beside Lucy on the bed. "What's going on, daughter? It can't be good, otherwise there would be no need for secrecy and deception."

Lucy glanced at Sofia, but Sofia didn't move. No way would she miss this.

"I suspected Bonwitter of stealing and last night I caught him, and—"

Mamma gasped. "You confronted him?"

"No, no. Even I wouldn't dare that. But I saw him do it, and followed him to a building. I saw him take six bolts of muslin inside."

Sofia sat on the end of the bed. "No wonder Mavis keeps having to ask him to order more."

Lucy nodded. "When Mr. Standish comes in today, I'm going to tell him in front of all the ladies."

Mamma studied Lucy a long moment. "Do you really think he'll react well? Most men wouldn't like having their business ability shown up by a young woman. After all, he hired Bonwitter. He gave him the power he's misused."

"But why wouldn't he want to know Bonwitter is a thief? Mr. Standish is in business to make money. If Bonwitter is taking that money . . ."

Sofia offered another opinion. "He's more than a thief. He tore my book in half, he grabbed me, and he's grabbed some of the others too. He's evil."

"That's a strong word, Sofia."

She risked saying more. "But, Mamma, what good has he ever done any of us?"

Mamma hesitated, then said, "He pays our wages. If we confront him . . ."

Lucy spoke up. "Actually, Mr. Standish pays our wages—and his. When I tell him, all the other ladies will attest—"

Mamma looked pensive. "You need to tell Mr. Standish in private."

Sofia didn't like that idea. "But I want to be there. I'm the one who's suffered under him."

Mamma shook her head, the decision final. "Lucy needs to talk to Mr. Standish alone."

Which meant once again, Lucy would get the glory all to herself.

❧

Lucy's stomach danced uncomfortably when she heard Mr. Standish's voice in the lobby. She stole a glance at Mamma, who offered a level look. *Patience.*

Unfortunately, patience was a virtue Lucy sorely lacked. When she heard her boss talk on and on with a customer and Mrs. Flynn, she felt she would burst from the waiting. *Stop your talking. Come in here. Don't you realize I have something important to tell—*

Lucy pricked her finger, forcing her back to reality. She put it in her mouth to stop the bleeding. Poised in such a fashion, she saw Mr. Standish enter the workroom.

"Good morning, ladies," he said in his usual jovial manner.

He began his rounds, strolling between the worktables, chatting with all the women. Lucy restrained herself from rising and going to him. She had to wait her turn. Soon enough he would come to her table and—

When he stopped at Mamma's place, Lucy could wait no longer. She rose and joined them.

"Well, hello, Lucy. How are you?" His face changed from cheery to concerned. "Is something wrong?"

Lucy ignored Mamma's disappointed look. "May I speak with you, sir? In private?"

He looked taken aback but swept an arm toward the storeroom. *What a perfect location for our talk.*

Lucy moved to the stack of muslin before turning toward Mr. Standish to begin. "I'm afraid I have some awkward, unfortunate news for you, sir."

"Is something wrong with your apartment?"

She shook her head vehemently. "Not a thing. We're very grateful for it and are very happy there."

"So your news involves . . . ?"

Lucy got right to it. "Mr. Bonwitter."

It was clear by his expression that her answer was unexpected. "Go on."

She decided to start with the most profane, to ignite her boss's high morals. "He's been very inappropriate with many, if not all, of the women working here." She hesitated but a moment before adding, "Including my young sister."

Mr. Standish looked appropriately appalled. "In what way? I mean . . ." He shook his head. "Never mind. Any forwardness, any impropriety is unacceptable."

Lucy pointed to the spy hole. "In addition to the unwanted physical contact, I believe he's been spying on us."

At first Mr. Standish didn't see the hole in the wall, but then he stooped and peered through it. "I don't see anything."

"That's because the lamp in the necessary isn't turned on."

He drew in a breath, and a hand went to his mouth. "That's unconscionable. Deplorable." He looked at Lucy. "It's unacceptable."

She nodded sadly, then moved back to the stack of muslin. The joy she was experiencing was surely sinful, yet she couldn't wait to tell him more. "Unfortunately, there is another item to discuss."

He ran a hand across his face. "And to think I trusted that man."

It was the perfect opening. "He has fully betrayed that trust, sir. For he is a thief."

"A—?"

She pointed to the muslin and told the entire story, from her first suspicions to the actual theft. "I followed him. I saw him bring the bolts into this building." She pulled out the slip of paper that contained the address.

"He lives here."

It was a statement. "I suspected as much when he didn't come out again."

"I simply can't believe a man who has charge of all the accounts would betray my trust in such a manner."

Lucy felt a wave of panic. Didn't he believe her? "If you'd like to ask Mavis, she can attest to the discrepancy in the muslin stock."

"No, I don't need—"

Lucy didn't want there to be any question, so she entered the workroom and asked Mavis to come out back.

"But why?" Mavis asked.

"Just come."

Lucy presented Mavis to Mr. Standish. "Tell him about the odd things occurring with the muslin stock." Mavis looked uneasy, as if she thought she would get blamed, so Lucy added, "I've told him about Mr. Bonwitter stealing."

Mavis relaxed and told what she knew.

Mr. Standish kept shaking his head. "And did he . . . was he inappropriate with you?"

Mavis was totally at ease now. "Of course. He gets grabby with all the girls whenever he gets a chance."

"Thank you, Mavis. I appreciate your candor. That will be all."

"You going to sack him?" she asked.

"At the least."

Mavis gave Lucy a wink and a smile, and returned to the workroom. Lucy could easily imagine the chattering that would follow.

Mr. Standish took in a deep breath and let it out slowly. He nodded once to Lucy, as if coming to a conclusion. "I owe you a great debt, Miss Scarpelli. It was very courageous of you to go to such an extent to prove the deception, and to come to me with your knowledge. Let me assure you, Mr. Bonwitter will feel the fullest extent of my ire—and the law's."

"You're welcome, sir. I only want what's best for the shop—and the girls."

"As do I, Miss Scarpelli. As do I."

Together they strode into the workroom. The ladies had gathered around the cutting table, and Lucy joined them. Mr. Standish paused.

"I wish to apologize to all of you fine women for the dreadful, unsuitable behavior of Mr. Bonwitter. I had no idea . . ." He hung his head a moment and Lucy felt sorry for him. Then he regained his strength and she saw a firm resolve in his countenance. "I promise you will never see his face in this shop again."

Dorothy began the applause. Mr. Standish blushed, then left them. He would have a difficult day ahead.

Once he was gone, the ladies gathered around Lucy, hugging her, kissing her cheeks, lauding her brave actions. Even Mrs. Flynn gave her a special nod and said, "Well done."

Then suddenly, Lucy remembered something. "I never told Mr. Standish about the red X's!" she said. "Bonwitter will deny everything. You know he will."

"What red X's?" Tessie asked.

Lucy let Dorothy explain.

"That was good thinking," Leona said.

Lucy was mad at herself. "If Mr. Standish doesn't know about them, then Bonwitter will come up with some other explanation. Without proof he won't go to jail."

"But Mr. Standish won't let him back in here," Dorothy said. "That's our main concern, yes?"

Yes. And no. With Bonwitter on the streets—with an angry, vengeful Bonwitter on the streets . . .

Lucy shivered. This wasn't over yet.

Lucy tried to concentrate on her sewing, tried to revel in her victory. And yet . . . without the information about the red X's, Bonwitter could get off.

Mr. Standish was probably at the police station or at Bonwitter's right now. And so Lucy hired a boy off the street for a nickel, ordering him to run a note to the nearest police station. Whether he would deliver the message or merely pocket the money was questionable.

Mamma strolled by her table and put a hand on her arm. "Don't worry. It's out of your hands now."

Which was the problem.

꧁꧂

It was nearly quitting time before Mr. Standish came back to the shop. "Gather round," he said to the ladies.

Lucy didn't like the look on his face. She approached him, "Did you get my message? My note?"

"What message?"

Oh no. "I forgot to tell you that I sewed red X's into the six stolen bolts of muslin, as a marker to prove they were ours."

Mr. Standish stood mute.

"Is Bonwitter in jail?" Tessie asked.

He shook his head. "He was not arrested."

"What?"

"I accompanied the police to his house this morning and we discovered the muslin in question, as well as other sewing goods. I accused him of theft, but he offered a lengthy explanation about how he was readying to start his own dressmaking supply store, and the goods were legally his, bought and paid for from a supplier."

"But they're not his," Leona said.

"He was very convincing, and the police had no grounds to arrest him." He looked at Lucy, his face drawn. "I wish I would have known about your X's."

Dorothy raised her hand. "I can vouch for them, sir. I saw her do it. I was her witness."

Mrs. Flynn spoke. "Can't you tell the police about them now?"

"I fear it's too late."

"It's never too late for justice," Dorothy said.

Mr. Standish put on his hat and tapped the bowl of it. "I suppose I must try." He headed for the door, then paused. "But do take comfort in knowing he's been fired. He will not return to Madame Moreau's. I guarantee I will be dutiful about finding a replacement with true character."

"That's something," Sofia said.

"But not enough." Lucy paced between the tables. "If only I'd told Mr. Standish about the X's."

Mamma put an arm around her shoulders. "You've told him now. He'll take care of it."

"If it's not too late," Dolly said.

She was shushed by the others, but her statement held true.

Rowena sat at her mother's desk, composing a letter to her best friend, Morrie. They'd known each other since they were children, and he alone knew the real Rowena, good and bad. He'd also proven himself to be a wise counselor. Barely a day went by when they didn't talk.

Until recently. For Morrie had already gone to Newport. Since he'd left New York, Rowena felt as though she were missing an important appendage to her person. Yes, her leg was one appendage that was crippled, but her peace of mind felt the lack of Morrie's strengthening presence.

She could hardly wait until she was also in Newport. She and Morrie would have much catching up to do. Until then, letters would have to suffice.

> My dear Morrie,
> I hope you are well in Newport. The house here is abuzz with preparations for our departure. As usual, Mother has ordered both of us a new wardrobe, but this time I am actually excited about it. I have met a talented girl, a seamstress, Lucy Scarpelli. She has done wonders with my outfits, and has magically made my infirmity fade from view. If I didn't know better, I would propose that I could run and play as we did as children. Remember how we used to climb in the stables and walk along the rafters?

She stopped the motion of her pen, letting the pleasant Morrie-memories settle. She could go on and on about the past, but he would see through her reminiscences and know she was revisiting those times as a way to deal with changes in her present. Morrie, above anyone else, knew how poorly Rowena dealt with change. And being told to fall in love with Edward was the biggest change of her life.

If she was falling in love with him. Having never been in love, she had no model to measure against. She cared what happened to Edward. She thought about him often, kept account of his attributes, and anticipated their next meeting. But was that love or merely infatua—?

"Hello, sister. Here I am, ready to assume the role of chaperone *extraordinaire.*"

Rowena glanced at the clock on the mantel. Between the letter and her daydreaming, she'd lost track of time. Edward would be there any minute to take her on a carriage ride through Central Park.

"Just a moment. I want to finish this letter to Morrie."

Hugh took a place behind her, trying to read it. "Tell him hello for me. And tell him I'll be ready for a race with that new mare Father bought."

Rowena nodded, added the message from Hugh, and put the page in the envelope she'd already addressed.

And none too soon, for Timbrook announced Edward's arrival.

He looked dashing in his gray morning coat and blue Windsor tie. Rowena loved how he was always fashionable yet didn't dress like a dandy who lived for fashion. Edward, the man, always shone above whatever clothes he wore.

It was a lovely day, and the open carriage allowed them to fully appreciate the Central Park Reservoir, the trees, and the blue sky. Rowena adjusted the angle of her parasol to keep the sun off her face.

Hugh arranged the seating so Rowena could sit next to Edward while Hugh faced backward in the carriage, across from them. Being a weekday, the park was far from crowded, and with Hugh to entertain them with witty banter, Rowena was fully content.

Until . . .

"So, Edward. With our money and with you at the helm of our fathers' business, the Langdon and DeWitt families will surely give the Astors and Vanderbilts a good run for their money."

Rowena heard Edward pull in a breath. She couldn't believe her brother's audacity. To mention who was bringing what to the table was the epitome of uncouth. "Hugh, this isn't the time," she said.

"Then when is, my dear Wena?" He stretched his arms across the back of his seat. "Although our fathers may barely talk about it—at least in our presence—I assure you, between them, they have been quite candid." He looked directly at Edward. "Or perhaps they've been candid with you? I know I don't deserve to hear the gory details, but you, as heir to the business, have surely earned their trust." He raised an eyebrow in a challenging way.

Finally Edward spoke. "With your talent for getting to the point, I can definitely see a place for you by my side. There's no reason we can't both take over when the time comes."

Hugh shook his head. "Unfortunately, my father has deemed me a man of few talents and much mischief." He shrugged. "I dare not argue with the first, and must admit to the latter."

Rowena was horribly uncomfortable with the entire conversation. "Hugh . . . you know Father has a place for you in the business. He's said as much."

"But not the helm." He stretched his arms above his head and plucked a leaf from a passing branch. "I may be an heir, but alas I am not the chosen heir."

Rowena leaned toward him to touch his knee. He moved it to the side, avoiding her touch. Then he pointed to a food vendor and turned to the driver. "Stop! We need refreshment." He hopped out of the carriage, leaving Rowena and Edward alone.

"I'm sorry for his outspoken ways, Edward. I assure you it's not directed at you per se, but stems from his frustration."

"I appreciate his candor," Edward said. "And honestly, I'm not thrilled at being thrust into the business as the successor. Although I appreciate what our fathers have done, the elevator business is not my first love."

She hadn't known this. "Then what is?"

He smiled and looked past her to a place unseen to all eyes but

his. Then he turned to her and said, "My first love is you, Rowena."
He leaned forward and kissed her gently on the cheek.

So this is what it felt like to fall in love.

⁊❧

The workday ended with no more news about Bonwitter—which
was fine with Sofia. If she never heard his name again . . .

The three Scarpelli women went upstairs to their apartment. Sofia
helped Mamma with dinner and watched Lucy mope.

Who cared about some stupid X's, anyway? Or whether or not
Lucy told Mr. Standish about them? Her sister could get obsessed with
details. She'd already played the heroine. What else did she want?
Someone to write a dime novel about *her*?

"Come, Lucia. Eat," Mamma said as she placed two plates at
the table.

"I don't want anything."

"Nonsense."

Lucy shook her head.

She was acting like a baby being coaxed into eating its gruel. "If
she doesn't want to eat, Mamma, let her not—"

"Shh!" In one quick motion Lucy stood and froze.

Sofia had heard it too. Feet on the stairs. No one came up to their
apartment. No one had a key to the door on the street level.

Bonwitter?

There was a knock on the door. Mamma whispered, "Girls, go in
the bedroom. Shut the door."

"No, I'll—"

"Go," Mamma said.

"See what you've done," Sofia told Lucy. She gladly went into the
bedroom, but Lucy stayed in the main room with Mamma.

Sofia looked around the bedroom for something to use as a weapon.
If only she'd thought to get a knife from the kitchen. But now, her
only choice was a hairbrush. She held it to her chest and closed the
door most of the way, standing to the side so Bonwitter wouldn't be
able to see her.

Lucy, doing what Sofia had not, grabbed a knife and held it behind her back. She nodded to Mamma, who asked, "Who is it?"

"It's Mr. Standish. I need to talk—"

Mamma opened the front door and Sofia opened hers. Realizing she was holding the hairbrush, she ran it through her hair. They'd been silly, getting worked up over nothing. If Bonwitter wanted to get them, he wouldn't knock on the door, he'd break it down.

"I'm sorry to come so late, ladies, but—"

"No, no. Come in, come in," Mamma said.

He saw the sisters and nodded. "Girls." His gaze moved to the knife in Lucy's hand. "You were expecting someone else?"

Lucy got to the point, "What did the police do with the information about the X's?"

"Girls," Mamma said. "Where are your manners? Mr. Standish, please sit down."

He took Mamma's chair, and Sofia and Mamma pulled other chairs close. Lucy stood.

Unfortunately, the look on Mr. Standish's face did not reveal a victory.

"The police were very interested in the information about the X's, Lucy. They commented on the wisdom of such a move. So for that, we all commend you."

"I don't want commendation, I want—"

"He's gone."

"Gone?" Mamma beat Sofia to the question.

"The police went to Bonwitter's house to check for the X's and found him gone. Moved out."

The implications were horrendous. "Not only will he not be arrested, he's on the loose?"

"I'm afraid so."

Sofia remembered Bonwitter's eyes, the smell of his breath, the pain of his grip. "He'll come after us, won't he?"

"Will he?" Mamma asked.

Lucy crossed her arms, making a protective wall over her chest. "He'll at least come after me. I cost him his job and set the police on him."

Mamma crossed herself, and Sofia heard her utter a prayer.

"I'm afraid there is that chance," Mr. Standish said. "For not only has he lost his job, he's lost his source for stolen goods. I'm so sorry, Lucy. You did all the right things, but—"

"But one. I didn't tell you about the X's in time."

He raised a hand. "We each have many should-have-dones to suffer. But know that I do not take Bonwitter's freedom lightly. I have informed the neighborhood policemen to keep an eye out."

Neighborhood police wouldn't have much incentive protecting three working-class women. "That's not enough," Sofia said. "We need to move to a place where he can't find us."

"I didn't mean to bring this kind of danger upon us," Lucy said.

"No, indeed you did not." Mr. Standish stood. "But let me assure you, I will do my best to keep you and your family safe. I promise."

He refused Mamma's offer of dinner and left them. Sofia looked out the window and saw him walk across the street to talk to a policeman. "He's there. He's really going to stand there and guard us."

Mamma pulled the curtain closed. "Come, girls. Let us eat, thank God for Mr. Standish, and pray for God's protection. *Che sarà sarà*— what is to be, will be."

This was all Lucy's fault.

Rowena opened the window of her bedroom and stood before it. There was absolutely no breeze. Summers in New York could be unbearable. At least in Newport there was relief from the breeze off the ocean.

Speaking of which . . . Mother had instructed all of them to make a list of what to pack for Newport.

Rowena stood to the side of the lace curtains and spread open her dressing gown. For the briefest moment she felt some relief. But when there was a knock at her door she pulled it shut again. "Yes?"

"It's me, Wena. Let me in."

What did Hugh want at this time of night?

She let him in. He too was ready for bed, wearing his pajamas and a robe.

"What?" she asked. "You're not going out tonight? What will your friends do without you?"

He put his hands in the robe pockets. "Don't be cruel, Wena. Not you."

She *was* being cruel and chastised herself for it. "I'm sorry. Have a seat. I'm trying to put together my list for Newport, but am finding it difficult to function in this stifling heat."

He went to the window and was able to open it a few inches more. He leaned against the sill, looking out over the darkened street below. "No air out here either."

She feared for his safety. "Hugh, come in. You'll lose your balance."

He came inside and sat upon the edge of her bed, hooking his slippered feet on the side rail. "I saw Edward kiss you today."

Rowena felt herself blush, and returned to the chair and her list on the table close by. "It was just a small kiss."

"Don't get defensive. It's not like you haven't kissed—" He paused and studied her face. "You haven't been kissed before, have you?"

She dipped her head to her list, trying to hide her blush. "None of your business."

She expected another snide remark but was surprised when he simply said, "Edward is a good man."

It was not like Hugh to concede an attribute in another. "You're a good man too, brother."

With his hands perched on the bed near either hip, he straightened his arms and shrugged. "I wish you were right."

She'd never seen him so pitiful. "I am right. You are a good man. You just have to show it more often."

With a soft laugh he hopped off the bed and strolled around the room. "It's far easier to be otherwise, far easier to be the wag and the life of the party."

"Can't you work hard *and* play hard?"

He stopped fingering a bird statue on the mantel and looked at her. "Why should I try? The business won't be mine to run, it will be Edward's."

Rowena felt bad for him, and yet . . . . "Must you be in charge? Can you find fulfillment in another role?"

"Accept being a prince when being king was in my grasp?"

She stood to go to him. "But was it in your grasp, Hugh? Was Father considering you for that role before he and Mr. DeWitt set their sights on Edward?"

His face struggled to maintain composure, and Rowena saw flashes of the little brother who still lived within this grown frame. He offered a laugh that was only partly successful. "Cruel twice in one conversation, Wena? Perhaps being kissed has changed you for the worse."

His words wounded her and she embraced him. "I'm sorry. I didn't mean to hurt you." She could feel his heart beating wildly.

He didn't return her embrace but gently pushed himself free. "I accept your apology, for how can I do otherwise when the truth is being spoken?"

"But, Hugh . . . if only you'd try to do something to improve your reputation. Perhaps then, Father and Mother would—"

There was another knock on the door and their mother entered. Her face revealed her shock at seeing Hugh present. "Son, daughter . . . I've come to check on your list, Rowena."

She lifted it from the table as evidence. "I'm working on it."

"And you, Hugh? Have you made your packing list?"

He shrugged. "Lists are overrated."

She was taken aback. "Nonsense. You don't want to arrive in Newport without the necessities, do you?"

Hugh patted down his chest and the pockets of his robe and said, "It appears I have those." He strode to her, kissed her on the cheek, and said, "Good night, Mother." With a backward glance, he added, "Wena."

Mother shook her head. "I don't know what I'm going to do with that boy."

"He's trying," Rowena said.

"Trying to do what? Cause us heartache and embarrassment? Cause us worry and frustration?"

Rowena had no words in his defense. To change the subject she offered her mother the list for her approval.

And, of course, received it.

CHAPTER EIGHT

ofia!"

Sofia awakened from her bad dreams of Bonwitter to find Lucy already gone from their bed.

The outcry was repeated. "Sofia! Mamma!"

Her dreams rushed to meet reality. Was Lucy hurt? Had Bonwitter hurt—?

Sofia found her sister at the living room window, pointing to the street below. Sofia took a look. "What? I don't see anything."

"Exactly," Lucy said. "Where's Mr. Standish? Where's the policeman?"

Sofia shared her first awful thought. "Bonwitter killed them."

"Enough, *piccolina*," Mamma said as she expertly twisted her long hair into a bun. "They've been watching over us for a week now. Night and day. We will be safe at work—*if* Bonwitter's even a true threat to us."

"Oh, he's a threat," Lucy said.

"How do you know?" Sofia asked.

97

"How do you *not* know?"

Lucy had a point, and Mamma was also right. They were safest in the workroom filled with many women.

The sooner they got there the better.

❧

The bell on the door jangled and Mrs. Flynn motioned to Lucy. "Come. It has to be the Langdons."

It was. Mrs. Langdon led the way, carrying a basket lined with cloth. Were they bringing a special gift? Greetings were exchanged and then the basket was handed over.

"Merci," Mrs. Flynn said.

"Oh, don't thank us. We found it outside, on the stoop."

With another glance, Lucy noticed that the fabric covering the contents of the basket was muslin. Her nerves stood on end. "Let me take that," she said, heading to the workroom. "I'll be right back."

Mrs. Flynn gave her a quizzical look, but let her go.

Lucy brought the basket to the main worktable. Ruth objected. "Move that thing. I'm trying to cut—"

"It was by the front door. I think it's from Bonwitter."

The women tentatively moved forward to see.

"How do you know?" Tessie whispered.

"It's just a feeling."

"Open it," Dorothy said.

"Carefully," Sofia said.

Ruth handed her a pair of scissors. "Use these to move the fabric aside."

Their caution added to her own, and Lucy slid the scissors under one of the edges of fabric and flopped it back.

A red X appeared.

The women gasped.

"It *is* from him!" Tessie said.

Sofia cowered behind her mother. "Don't open it!"

Lucy had to. She had to see. She used the scissors to open another flap of the muslin, and saw another red X. The impact of seeing them had faded, but the implication had not. He'd found her out. There would be no convicting him now.

With the opening of the third flap, Lucy could see what was inside. She quickly covered the contents and carried the basket toward the back.

"What's in it?" Tessie asked. "I didn't see."

"You don't need to see," Lucy said. "It's a dead rat."

"But why?"

"Because I ratted him out. Now, if you'll excuse me, I'm taking this out to the alley."

She left the women discussing it without her. Although she'd appeared strong for their sake, the sight of the red X's and the rat shook her mightily. Yes, she'd done a good thing getting Bonwitter out of the shop, and had attempted another good deed in getting him convicted for theft. But since he'd been able to talk himself out of the charge and had moved to who knows where . . . she'd put herself and everyone at the shop in danger.

After dumping the entire basket in the garbage she leaned against the doorjamb and closed her eyes. *I'm sorry for putting everyone in danger, but I'm not sorry for turning him in.* She opened her eyes a moment. Should she be sorry for *that*? Had she overstepped her position?

Mamma appeared at the door. "Come inside. Madame says the Langdons are waiting."

Lucy had forgotten all about the customers. She rushed through the workroom and paused but a moment at the curtain to try to capture some calm, some confidence. Then she applied a smile and entered the lobby.

"Oh, there you are," Rowena said. "Is everything all right?"

Rowena was already wearing a pale yellow evening dress Lucy had altered. "That's my question for you. Do you like the dress?"

Rowena turned toward the mirror. "Very much. Once again, you've done just the right thing."

At least in this.

⁂

Rowena stood very still while Lucy arranged a lace flourish on her blouse and attached a blue ribbon choker with flat bows that marked the back of her neck.

"The blue of the ocean sky," Lucy said. "If this ensemble doesn't bring to mind the essence of summer, I'll never sew another stitch."

"You'll do no such thing!" Rowena studied her image. The pink satin in the oversized puffed sleeves was tucked into elbow ruffles of scalloped lace. A flat lace collar dipped low in a V, and the bodice was covered with a sheer lace overlay that flounced over a blue satin waistband. The skirt wasn't gathered at the waist but folded in deep pleats, and the fabric was a floral sateen of blue and pink flowers.

Lucy pulled the pouf of the sleeves to even better advantage. "You're as fresh as a summer garden. Your fiancé will swoon at the mere sight of you."

Although Rowena loved the outfit, and indeed found it perfect for Newport, *it* was perfect. *It* was lovely. Looking past the dress to the girl wearing it . . . making Edward swoon? "I fear I don't possess the capacity to make men swoon, no matter what the fashion."

Lucy gave her a chiding look. "You mustn't say such a thing. You have a fuller beauty than anyone I've ever known."

Rowena put a hand on Lucy's arm and looked into her deep brown eyes. "You are a true friend. Not truer than many, truer than *any*."

Lucy placed her own hand on top of Rowena's. "As you are to me."

As if on cue, they both glanced toward Rowena's mother. For she would not approve . . . in no way would approve. How sad that friendship was constrained by rules and class rather than emotion and need.

Lucy stepped away to look at the skirt and blouse. "That's the last one. You are fully prepared to take Newport by storm."

Rowena smiled. Briefly. For now their time together was over. She would be going to Newport for six weeks. Lucy would be left behind, working. Rowena had learned more about Lucy than she knew about any of the society friends she'd known for a lifetime, and she'd shared more about herself. They'd chatted like two sisters, talking about fashion, men, and families. They'd talked about being frustrated with various aspects of their lives, longing to be happy, and wanting to feel they had worth.

Soon Rowena would be off to Newport for the rest of the summer.

Hopefully, in the autumn she'd return to the shop, needing a new set of clothing for the New York social season, but until then . . .

Rowena leaned forward and whispered for Lucy's ears alone. "I wish you could come with me."

Lucy suffered a laugh and immediately covered it with a hand. "If wishes were horses . . ."

"Then beggars would ride."

When Lucy went back to the workroom to get Madame to wrap things up, Rowena approached her mother. "Could I ask a friend to go to Newport with me? You've said so in the past, but I've never brought anyone."

Mother adjusted her gloves. " 'Tis rather late notice, dear. And who were you thinking of?"

Rowena hesitated, and in that hesitation her mother looked past her, to the workroom, and back into her eyes. "No. Absolutely not."

"But we've grown so fond of each other, Mother. I've shared things with Lucy that I've never shared with another—"

Mother stood. "Which was an error on your part. We've always taught you to be polite to everyone, respectful of your elders, and considerate to those of lesser rank, but you cannot socialize with them, Rowena. You can't be friends with a seamstress, especially not an Italian seamstress."

"But we are friends."

"You're mistaking her professional attention with friendship. I assure you she does not expect to be invited anywhere within your circle. In fact, I suffer to say she would be mortified to find herself in such a situation. Do you wish to cause Lucy discomfort?"

"No, of course—"

Mother waved a hand, dispelling the issue into the air between them. "Then I'll hear no more of it. Lucy has provided a service to us; she has achieved what no seamstress has previously accomplished. Yes, you should feel gratitude for her insight, but she is being paid for her services. And honestly, I know she'd rather have the money. They all would."

Rowena looked away, gazing at the curtain that hung between

Lucy and herself. But with her mother's words the curtain gained substance and became solid. It was an unyielding rampart, fortified to keep them apart.

The delight in the new wardrobe faded with the loss of a friend.

Lucy moved a piece of pasta around her plate. And around.

"You're not eating."

"I'll eat your portion if you don't want it," Sofia said.

Mamma intervened. "You will do no such thing." She turned back to Lucy. "Are you worried about Bonwitter?"

Always. But instead of admitting it, Lucy shrugged. "I'm sad."

"About?"

"Not seeing Rowena again."

Mamma blinked as though the subject had never come to mind. "You can't be friends with her, Lucia. It's like asking a queen to be friends with a washerwoman."

Lucy took offense. "I'm far from being a washerwoman, and Rowena is far from being a queen."

"She's rich."

"That is neither her doing nor her fault."

Mamma sighed and looked toward the window as if gaining supporters there. "The world does not work the way we wish it to, daughter. It never has and never will."

Lucy set her fork down, her appetite fully gone. "The ways of the world could change," she said. "Rowena and I spoke as friends, shared things that only friends share."

"What kind of things?" Sofia asked.

"Private things."

"Like what?"

"Sofia." The tone of Mamma's voice made her hush. "Even if Rowena wanted to be your friend, Mrs. Langdon would move against—"

"But what if she likes me?"

"She would move just as I would move against the very same

102

friendship. For the sake of my daughter, to protect her—to protect you—from pain."

Lucy knew it was no use arguing. She also knew what Mamma said was true.

But that didn't mean she had to like it.

Lucy bolted upright, yanked out of sleep.

She held her breath and listened.

"Lie down," Sofia said, adjusting the lone sheet they used in the summer heat.

Lucy got out of bed. She moved into the main room as if the slightest noise would—

"Lucy?" Mamma whispered.

In the moonlight, Lucy saw she was also awake and was sitting upright on her mattress.

Lucy tiptoed to her side. "Did you hear it too?"

Mamma nodded and looked toward the door.

Lucy hadn't had a chance to settle on the source of what had awakened her. But to know that someone was outside their door . . . Last time it had been Mr. Standish, but even he would not come calling in the middle of the night.

Mamma attempted to stand, and Lucy helped her. It was then she saw the glint of a knife blade in Mamma's bed. She pointed at it.

"Get it," Mamma whispered.

Lucy got the knife and put it in her hand as if to defend. It was an odd feeling to grip it so. Together they moved to the door. Lucy put her ear to it, held her breath, and heard . . .

Nothing.

She stood aright. "Whoever was here, I think they're gone."

Mamma wiped her hands upon her nightdress, crossed herself, then let one hand move to the knob and the other to the key sticking out of the lock. Her breathing was labored and Lucy wished she could have both roles in what was about to happen—to throw the door open, and to charge at whoever dared intrude upon their home.

Mamma looked at her and mouthed, *"Uno, due . . . tre!"*

She turned the key and yanked the door open.

The darkness revealed nothing.

Knife poised, Lucy held her breath. She was afraid to peek around the corner to see down the stairway. The dark stairway.

There was no sound, which meant the intruder was either gone or waiting in the shadows. They needed light, but the stairwell light was at the foot of the stairs. She whispered to Mamma, "Bring a lamp over."

Mamma went to the kitchen table and Lucy heard the striking of a match. Then Mamma came close with a kerosene lamp.

With one hand still on the knife, Lucy held the lamp high and risked a look down the stairway.

It was empty.

She allowed herself to breathe and stepped onto the landing and—

Slipped!

The knife flew out of her hand and down the stairs, Mamma rescued the lamp, and Lucy landed hard, sprawled upon the landing and the first step.

Which was wet.

She lifted her foot and spotted something greasy upon it. Her hand was covered in the same goo, a grease . . .

"Animal grease?" Only then did her senses allow her to confirm the substance. "Mamma, move the light over here."

As Lucy attempted to stand without sliding farther down the stairs, Mamma held the lamp over the dim space. "All the steps are covered with grease. Every one."

"You could have been killed," Mamma said.

"I think that was his intent."

Sofia appeared at the door. "What's that stuff all over?"

"Grease, à la Bonwitter."

She stepped back. "He was here?"

"We both heard him." Lucy motioned for them to go inside.

Mamma inspected Lucy's nightdress. "It's ruined."

"Better the dress than a leg or a back."

"Take it off."

Lucy shook her head. "I might as well leave it on. If we're ever going to get out of here, the stairs need to be cleaned."

"But shouldn't the police be shown?" Mamma said.

She rubbed her hip, which surely would be bruised. "I'll offer my nightgown as evidence—and my bruises if they wish for more. Now help me get a bucket of hot water, some soap, and a brush."

Lucy made good work of it. The smell of the animal grease was horrible, and the slimy feel on her hands made her long for a very hot bath.

And a very long sleep.

Once again, she was working alone. If it wasn't staying up all night working on Rowena's clothes to help her look beautiful, it was catching Bonwitter in the act. Or venturing off into strange parts of town to find her family lodging, making the deal for an apartment *and* jobs, then coming over to clean the place. Once again, alone.

She stopped scrubbing and arched her back, feeling very much the martyr. Why did she have to do everything? Why did she have to take charge of all the problems of the world? Why did she . . . ?

Lucy let the words be spoken. "Why do I always have to be the hero?"

Overwhelmed in body and mind, she sat on a step, grease and all.

Was this need to *do* a good trait or a fault? A strength or a weakness?

She used to live for the times when Papa would take her face in his hands and tilt it upward. He'd look into her eyes and say, "Well done, Lucia. You are a gift from God." And then he'd kiss her forehead. Oh, how she missed him.

Her hand moved toward that forehead now, but Lucy stopped its movement before it plastered grease on the one portion of her body that the awful stuff hadn't tainted.

Grease. If she didn't clean it up, no one would.

She got back to work.

CHAPTER NINE

*R*owena sat in a wicker rocker on the veranda facing the sea. A vast expanse of lawn divided her from the actual ocean, but she could see miles of water beyond the green— water stretching out to meet the sky.

They'd been in Newport for two days now, and Rowena had already attended one dinner party, one afternoon tea, one tennis match, and a visit to the Astors' home, Beechwood, to pay homage to Caroline Astor and acknowledge her peerage over Newport—and New York—society.

Rowena was bored to death. She missed Edward. As was oftentimes the case with the men of the families, they arrived from the city on the weekend, taking short and numerous breaks from the work that made all this luxury possible. Morrie was around, but the two times she'd tried to see him, he'd been busy.

And so she sat alone, looking out to sea, wishing for the absent company of Edward.

And Lucy.

Her mother's words returned to her: *"You can't be friends with a seamstress, especially not an Italian seamstress."*

How silly was that? Her own grandparents had been immigrants from England. Her grandfather had opened a clock store, which had been the impetus for her father to garner an interest in how things worked. That her family had succeeded beyond any expectation, that they'd built this grand house in Newport, should make them sympathetic to people like Lucy who were just starting out, people who were using their God-given gifts to an amazing degree.

Mother came out on the veranda, her calendar book in hand. "Oh, there you are, dear. We need to go over the invitations we've received so there are no mistakes."

A mistake would be to accept the wrong invitation in lieu of the right one, to a better house, invited by a better family.

Rowena stopped her rocking. "Actually, I'm quite content doing nothing."

Mother sat in the settee close by. "Nonsense. We are not here for you to relax."

Rowena let a laugh escape.

"I amuse you?"

"No, no. Never that."

She felt her mother's eyes, but was allowed her indiscretion, for they both knew Mother was never amusing, rarely witty, and possessed the sense of humor of a hawk peering out for its prey.

Mother opened her date book. "You will be blessedly busy this season, dear."

Busy. Busywork. That's what these parties were. Rowena got nothing out of them and offered nothing to them. Perhaps when Edward arrived there would be some relief, but . . .

If only Lucy were there. How Rowena would love to show her the sights. To see Newport through Lucy's eyes would bring her much delight.

Her mother was going over the dates and times, but Rowena had stopped listening. It was appalling that Lucy wasn't welcome there as a friend, yet odd that she would have been embraced if she were their servant. How—

Suddenly, Rowena got an idea.

"Rowena?"

She must have gasped or made a sound, for her mother looked at her with a modicum of alarm. Rowena smiled sweetly. "What were you saying about Wednesday afternoon?"

Rowena pretended to listen, but her mind whirled with other possibilities.

༺❀༻

Rowena yanked at the lace around the neckline.

The stitches gave way.

As did Rowena's heart, for it was pounding wildly.

She moved to the next dress and tore the sleeve from the bodice.

And then another. And another.

After more than a dozen outfits were damaged, Rowena stepped to the center of her dressing room, her breath heaving in short fits.

She sat on the large ottoman to collect herself.

It was not an easy task, for as she looked across the rows of gowns edging her dressing room, the full implication of her actions took hold. She *did* need Lucy's help now, for who better to repair these awful injuries to her clothing?

She imagined her mother's voice: *"But how did this happen, daughter? And why didn't you notice it earlier? And why were only your clothes—?"*

The last question spurred her to action. If she was going to present the scenario that their clothing was damaged in transit from New York, it would make no sense that only Rowena's garments were affected.

I have to get in Mother's closet.

She cracked open the door leading from the dressing room to the hall and peered out. She looked to the left. Sadie was entering her brother's room next door, her arms full of fresh linens. She looked to the right.

The coast was clear.

108

Rowena entered the hallway and strode quickly toward her mother's bedroom. Hopefully Mother was still downstairs working on their social schedule. She knocked on the door and, receiving no reply, went inside.

Mother's adjoining dressing room was even larger than Rowena's, with dress racks encompassing three walls. She rummaged through the racks searching for dresses from Madame Moreau's. The tug of a bodice seam on one, the tear of a cuff on another, the—

"Rowena?"

Her heart plummeted to her toes and her face grew hot. She turned toward her mother and put a hand to her chest. "You frightened me."

Mother looked askance. "What are you doing in my dressing room?"

Rowena's thoughts rushed toward a logical answer. She pulled out the last dress she'd damaged. "Look at this."

Mother stepped forward and examined the tear. "How did this happen?"

"I don't know," Rowena said. "But I was going to wear one of my dresses from Madame Moreau's this morning and found similar damage. Quite a few of my outfits are torn in some way. It got me wondering whether yours had suffered a similar fate."

Her mother looked through the rack to Rowena's left and pulled out the dress that had already met Rowena's yank and tug.

"How could this happen?"

Rowena shrugged. "I remember Lucy telling me about an employee at the dress shop who got fired because of Lucy's courage in catching him in the act of stealing. Remember the basket left on the stoop? It had a rat in it."

Mother shuddered. "You think he damaged our clothes as a way to get revenge on Lucy?"

"I know of no other explanation." *That I can share.*

Mother continued looking through her clothes, but Rowena stopped her. "Don't bother yourself with this. I'll go through the racks. So far I've found nearly twenty outfits with damage."

Mother turned toward the door. "I'll call Margaret and get her started on the repairs."

Rowena stepped toward her mother, stopping her with a hand. "I don't think Margaret's skills are of a level to do more than sew on a button. Remember how she blundered the hem of your blue lawn?"

Mother's eyes darted, as if she was mentally going through the staff who might have the talent—

Rowena intervened before she came up with a name. "I have a solution," she said.

"Then say it."

"Let's bring Miss Scarpelli here. Since she was instrumental in the creation of the dresses, she'll be able to repair them with an expertise beyond any other servant who pretends to know how to wield a needle and thread. Besides . . ." Rowena peered at the floor, trying to look pitiful. "With the custom alterations she made to my outfits, I would not feel comfortable handing them over to someone who isn't aware of why some extra padding is here, or a tuck is put there."

Mother was eyeing Rowena in a way that made her feel wholly uncomfortable. Did she suspect the truth?

Finally, she spoke. "Of course the fact that Lucy is your friend, that you wanted her here in the first place . . ."

Rowena took her mother's hands in hers. "I won't deny the solution pleases me on more than one level, Mother. And I know you were right in refusing my request to have Lucy come here as a guest. But now, she would be here as a worker, as a seamstress."

"A seamstress only."

"Of course." The fluttering in Rowena's chest was far different from the experience a mere half hour before. The joy she would experience if her mother would let Lucy come . . .

Rowena met her mother's pale gray eyes and added, "Please, Mother?"

Her mother's eyes flashed with a hint of hardness before she nodded. "Write up a note and I'll have a telegram sent. I will not have her come by steamer, though. It is far too luxurious."

"I'm sure the train to Wickford Junction will be fine, and then the short boat ride—"

"Tell Hugh to arrange it."

Rowena kissed her mother on the cheek. "Thank you, thank you, Mother. You've made me very happy."

"And solved the problem of the torn dresses."

Rowena couldn't hide her smile. "Of course. That too."

❦

"First class, Wena? For a seamstress?"

"Please, Hugh?" Rowena said. "Just do it. I'll pay the difference from my allowance. Lucy is more than just a seamstress, she's a good friend. I'd really like her to be pampered a bit for her inconvenience."

He buttoned a vest over his striped shirt. "So Mother doesn't know about this?"

"She knows Lucy is coming. She gave her approval for that. But no . . . she doesn't know about first class." She appealed to her brother's rebellious side. "It will be our secret. I've kept enough of yours."

Hugh threaded a bow tie around his collar. "I suppose I could—"

She grabbed his face, kissed him on the lips with a loud *whack*, and walked to the door. "I love you, brother!"

He called after her, "This Lucy must be someone pretty special to deserve all this trouble."

❦

"Any threats from Bonwitter today?" Tessie asked Lucy.

Lucy sighed dramatically. "What have I asked all of you?"

Tessie shrugged. "Not to ask about it anymore."

"Because?"

"Because you're sick of wasting another moment of your life worried about such a disgusting, despicable, disgraceful, desperate, dumb, disgusting—"

"You said *disgusting* twice," Lucy said. "And I believe you added a few more nasty traits to my previous list."

"I could add more," Tessie said. "That was only the D's."

Lucy tied a knot in her thread. "The point is, I'm done with him."

"Until he does something else."

"Tessie!"

"All right, all right."

Dorothy looked up from her sewing. "Work, Tessie?"

The girl reluctantly returned to her table. Lucy felt the same reluctance, not because she wanted to talk about Bonwitter—because she truly was trying not to think about him—but because she was having trouble concentrating on the dresses she was making. They were pretty enough, and the fabric was luscious enough, but she had no personal stake in them. Once again, she was merely a seamstress. What difference did it make whether she was stitching on a collar, a cuff, or some trim upon a train? She'd been spoiled working on Rowena's wardrobe. Each item had offered Lucy a challenge, and each solution had rewarded her with a dose of satisfaction. Why, she hadn't even met the woman who would wear the dress she was working on today. An anonymous wearer would take her work and waltz away into the city.

Waltz. During one of Lucy's conversations with Rowena, Rowena had talked about how much she wished she could waltz properly. She'd said the one-two-three, one-two-three sashay and swirl made dancers look as if they were flying. But Rowena was unable to dance well in her condition. Lucy had never heard of such a dance, and Rowena had said, *"I would love to teach you, and watch you sweep around the ballroom in the arms of some dashing partner."*

Talking about such things was a lark, yet Rowena had a way of making it seem possible.

But Lucy was not one to daydream. Why waste thoughts on scenarios that were unattainable? She might as well dream about being the Queen of Sheba.

And yet, when Lucy closed her eyes, with a little effort she *could* imagine herself in one of the gowns she'd made, with long gloves up to her elbows and jewels at her neck and ears. She would gaze into the eyes of her dance partner, and he would smile back at her, his blue eyes sparkling at the sheer joy of it.

Blue eyes? Where did that come from? Italians had brown eyes. Blue-eyed men were as inaccessible as . . . as . . .

Waltzes, gowns, gloves, jewels, and dance partners.

⚜

Mrs. Flynn was headed toward the foyer to see who'd come in the front door when a young man peeked his head through the curtain.

Mrs. Flynn was sent on her heels, a hand to her chest. "Young man! You frightened my heart into my toes."

He came fully into the room and removed his cap. "Sorry, ma'am. Telegram?"

Mrs. Flynn took it, but the boy didn't leave. He seemed to enjoy the bevy of females, and grinned at the lot of them. Sofia grinned right back. He was tall and lanky, and very cute.

Mrs. Flynn physically turned him around. "Go on now. You did your duty. Shoo."

He tipped his hat, winked at Sofia, and left. Mrs. Flynn waited to hear the door's bell tinkle before she addressed the issue of the telegram.

"I can't remember the last time we got a telegram," Dorothy said.

Sofia didn't want to sound stupid but had to ask. "What's a telegram?"

Dorothy thought about it a moment. "I don't rightly know but for the fact one person can send a message to another without going through the mail."

Dolly raised a hand. "My family got one once to tell us Uncle Harry died. All the way from Virginia."

Leona shushed them. "What's it say, Madame?"

But Mrs. Flynn wasn't opening it. She was staring at the envelope. "Madame?"

The woman collected herself, then walked over to Lucy. "It's for you."

A series of gasps stirred the room.

"Me?"

"Who died?" Dolly asked.

Sofia mentally listed faraway family members and glanced at Mamma—who looked worried. Had something happened to her aunt and uncle or her cousin Vittorio?

113

Lucy dispelled her worry with logic. "If it was a death in the family, it would be addressed to Mamma, not me."

"Then it must be good news," Tessie said.

Sofia's relief was replaced with envy. Of course it was good news. It was addressed to Lucy, wasn't it?

Mrs. Flynn slapped the telegram onto Lucy's table. "Here it is. Good or bad."

Lucy removed a folded note as Mamma and Sofia moved close to see.

"What's it say?" Dolly asked.

The three of them read it silently and Mamma quickly put a hand on Lucy's arm. Sofia could only shake her head in disbelief.

"What?" Dorothy asked. "You must share."

Lucy read the note aloud: " 'Wardrobe ruined. Come to Newport immediately. Ticket at train station. Leave tomorrow 10 A.M. I need you. Rowena Langdon.' "

Mrs. Flynn took the telegram away to see for herself. "What does she mean her wardrobe is ruined?"

"I don't know," Lucy said. "That's all it says."

Sofia felt as though the rest of the room had pulled away and she were standing alone, witnessing the moment from afar. Lucy was going to Newport? She'd been invited there by Rowena, a wealthy patron? How could this be? Why did Lucy constantly get the breaks?

Tessie ran to Lucy and took her hands. "That's not all she said. She wants you to go to Newport on the train. Immediately! Newport!"

"I've never been to Newport," Ruth said.

"You've never been out of New York," Leona said.

"Neither have you."

Neither have I.

"Have you been on a train before, Lucy?" Dorothy asked.

"Never."

"It will be an adventure—though I have no idea how long the trip will be." She looked around the room. "How far is Newport from here?"

No one knew.

"I'm sure it's hundreds and hundreds of miles away," Tessie said. "So that means hours and hours on a train."

"I've heard they're very loud and bumpy," Dolly said.

Sofia hoped so.

"I've heard they go up to thirty-five miles an hour," Ruth said. "I would be afraid of going so fast."

Sofia wouldn't be afraid. It would be exhilarating.

"Do they have food on a train?" Mamma asked.

"And they must have . . . you know." Tessie nodded toward the necessary.

Lucy laughed. "I don't care about the answers to any of your questions. I'm going to Newport. I'd go by donkey cart if need be."

"You can't go."

Mrs. Flynn's pronouncement halted the room.

"Why not?" Lucy asked.

The bell on the door caused Mrs. Flynn to lower her voice as she turned toward the lobby. "You have work to do here, Lucy. The Langdons' wardrobes are complete. It is not our responsibility to repair them after the fact. We've done our—"

Mr. Standish came through the curtains. "What's not our responsibility?"

Lucy hurried toward him, and Sofia hated that her sister had every right to do so. She was a special friend of Mr. Standish, *and* Rowena Langdon.

Sofia was special friends with no one.

Mrs. Flynn began her explanation. "We were just talking—"

Lucy held the telegram toward him. "Pardon me, but I just received this urgent telegram from Rowena Langdon."

Mrs. Flynn flashed Lucy a look, but Lucy was oblivious, giving all her attention to Mr. Standish. He read the note, then looked up. "Her wardrobe is ruined?"

Mrs. Flynn stepped between them. "I assure you, the clothing we delivered to the Langdons was in perfect condition. We would never give a customer something that was in need of repair."

"I'm not accusing you," Mr. Standish said. "But apparently, in the process of moving the garments from here to Newport some damage was done."

"A lot of damage," Lucy said, pointing to the note. "She says *ruined*."

"I am not disparaging Miss Langdon's assessment, but I would imagine they are not ruined as much as damaged in some way. Otherwise, she would be ordering a complete new wardrobe."

"Ruined or merely damaged, Lucy cannot be spared," Mrs. Flynn said.

"Are you indicating someone else should go in her place?" Mr. Standish asked.

Mrs. Flynn faltered.

He continued. "The telegram *was* addressed directly to Miss Scarpelli, and didn't the Langdons previously request that Lucy be in charge of Miss Langdon's fashion?"

"Yes, but—"

"But?"

"Lucy is new here. Her experience is limited and—"

"In the short time Lucy has been with us, she's managed to impress the Langdons so much that they specifically asked for her, plus she took it upon herself to catch a thief and a cad, thus saving me money and saving the rest of you ladies from . . ." He blushed. "From further humiliation."

Mrs. Flynn would not be deterred. "But Bonwitter hasn't been caught. He's—"

"Which is another reason for Lucy to leave town for a while." He looked at Lucy. "There haven't been any more threats or incidents since the greased stairs, have there?"

"No."

"Then hopefully he has either left the city or gotten himself arrested for some other crime. But if not—until we can be sure the man is accounted for and brought to justice—I think it only prudent Lucy goes to Newport. It will serve a dual purpose: helping a client and keeping her safe."

"But I want to go too," Sofia said.

Mamma shushed her.

Mr. Standish smiled. "I think we'd all like to go. Newport is a magical place during the season."

"You've been there?" Lucy asked.

"Once. I was never privy to the society fêtes, but I always enjoyed standing on Bellevue Avenue to watch the daily parade of carriages."

"Parade?"

He leaned toward them, as if sharing a secret. "Surely you ladies have guessed by now that the rich live to be seen."

Lucy held her hands to her chest as if pleading for mercy. "So, Mr. Standish? May I go?"

He nodded once. "You may."

"But what about the work here?" Mrs. Flynn asked.

Mr. Standish surveyed the room. "I'm sure all the ladies are quite willing to work extra hard so Lucy can gain this opportunity."

Sofia was appalled to see everyone nod. She wanted to raise a hand and say she was *not* willing to work extra hard so Lucy could get *any* special privilege. And wasn't Bonwitter a threat to Sofia and Mamma too? He wouldn't know she was out of town. There was no reason to think he wouldn't continue his mischief.

Mr. Standish handed the telegram back to Lucy. "Then it's settled. You make hard work of it today, young lady, to ease Mrs. Flynn's worries. And before you leave tonight, gather together a valise of threads and materials you may need. If more is required, have the Langdons send another cable."

"Yes, sir. Thank you, sir."

"Mrs. Flynn . . . if you will. I have some other business to discuss."

The two of them went into the lobby, enabling the women to crush Lucy with their exuberant attention.

It was sickening.

⁂

Seam tape!

Lucy stopped her sewing to add seam tape to her list.

So the day had gone. As she worked diligently on her assigned work, she made a list of what to take along to repair Rowena's clothing.

The two words *wardrobe ruined* haunted her. If the clothes were truly ruined, she would need to make replacement pieces, and would need yards of fabric. Lucy took solace in Mr. Standish's suggestion that if she needed additional supplies, she could send for them.

As for her personal packing . . . there was little need for her to make a list. She only owned one dress, and two skirts and blouses—and one of those was far past its prime. It was not as though she needed gowns. She was going to Newport as . . . as . . .

As what?

An employee? A servant? A friend?

This last would have been her preference, but Lucy knew it was wishful thinking. Although she and Rowena had gotten along famously, her practical nature had to acknowledge that amiable chitchat did not a friendship make. Rowena had been beholden to Lucy and, therefore, had gone out of her way to be polite and attentive. That was all.

But she said "I need you."

"To repair her clothes. That's it."

"What did you say?" Dorothy asked.

"Nothing." Lucy took a moment to rub the tiredness from her eyes.

"You don't have to push yourself," Dorothy said. "Madame told you we'd pick up the slack."

Lucy looked around the room for Mrs. Flynn, then remembered she was in the fitting rooms with a customer. "Actually, Mr. Standish *told* Madame you would pick up the slack."

"Either way, you can't work yourself sick. Your Rowena needs you fully well and capable."

"She's not 'my Rowena.' "

Tessie chimed in, putting her clasped hands to her chest and sighing dramatically, " 'I need you.' "

"To fix her clothes," Lucy said.

She saw Leona slip something into Mamma's hand. There'd been something secretive going on all afternoon. Whispers forehead to forehead, and a concentrated bustle that nearly silenced the usually chatty group.

Lucy didn't mind, because she didn't have the capacity for chitchat today and was relieved for the lack of Dolly's discourse about some new beau she thought she was in love with, or Sofia's complaining, or Tessie's gossip about the rich set, or even the not-so-rich set. Lucy had no idea where Tessie got her information, or whether she made it up, but there was usually enough of it to fill the air for at least half of every day.

Lucy glanced at Mamma again and received a smile in return. She was at work adding ribbon to a smart straw boater.

Ribbon!

Lucy added it to her list.

All day long there'd been a buzz in the workroom that grated on Sofia's nerves. Everyone was excited for Lucy.

To make it worse, there was a secret afoot. Mr. Standish had suggested—instructed—Mrs. Flynn to have a new outfit made for Lucy's trip. So beyond their usual work, they'd spent the day cutting and sewing a present for her sister.

Sofia had been assigned to sew the skirt on the sewing machine. Each stitch was like a prick to her nerves. Each laugh and secret whisper was a nail. Making things worse was hearing Lucy ask Tessie and Dorothy to watch over *her* while Lucy was gone. She didn't need anyone looking after her. Lucy was acting like she was some great protector whose presence would be missed. Sofia could take care of herself—and Mamma.

Mamma must have seen her mood, for when they were finishing up, she appeared by Sofia's side. "*Breve orazione penetra,* Sofia."

Sofia looked up from her sewing. "What?"

Mamma nodded once. "You heard me. God listens to short prayers. I suggest you say a few."

Mamma left her, and Sofia was faced with her horrible attitude. A part of her wanted to embrace the anger and resentment, but another part . . .

Why couldn't she be happy for Lucy? Why was she always jealous? Why couldn't she let the envy go?

Sofia stroked the brown poplin of the skirt. Lucy would look pretty in this color. And shouldn't she look pretty? Wasn't she representing all of the Scarpelli family—all the ladies at Madame Moreau's—in Newport?

Sofia glanced toward Mamma and found her mother watching her.

A prayer. She needed to pray like Mamma instructed.

But what should she say? The truth of it was she *liked* being angry. It gave her a feeling of power.

Power? That was silly. Her anger didn't gain her any power. If anything, it made her weak. Needy. Susceptible to all sorts of bad thoughts.

But how could she change? It was embarrassing to think that God knew of her bad behavior and thoughts. And because of that, He wouldn't want to hear from *her*.

And yet, because Mamma was waiting, Sofia bowed her head, clasped her hands to her chin and prayed.

Help!

It was a rather pitiful prayer considering her sins, yet hadn't Mamma said that God listened to short prayers?

If so, He'd be ever so pleased with Sofia's.

⁂

I can sleep on the train tomorrow. I hope.

Lucy held on to this thought as the workday drew to an end. She was always tired after the twelve-hour days, but today she felt as though the last bit of energy was slowly seeping out of her pores and any moment she would collapse into a puddle on the floor to be mopped up and put in a slosh bucket.

Anything else? Concentrate, Lucy. You must think of every possible need. . . .

She stood in the storeroom, a satchel in hand, filling it with extra laces and trims from Rowena's dresses, pins, hooks and eyes, scissors, thread, needles, padding, a few yards of muslin . . .

Suddenly, she was not alone. All the ladies burst into the room as a pack, laughing and smiling.

"What's—?" She looked to Mamma to see what was going on, but Mamma's face revealed only a smile.

Dorothy stepped front and center. "The lot of us want to wish you well on your journey tomorrow."

Lucy was truly touched. It had crossed her mind that there could have been some jealousy or bitterness among the ladies. After all, she'd only altered Rowena's outfits. These other women had made them from scratch. "That's so very nice of you," she began.

But before she could say more, Tessie stepped forward and pulled a caramel brown skirt from behind her back. And then Leona displayed an ivory blouse with bulbous sleeves, while Dolly stepped forward with a blue fabric belt. "These are for you."

Lucy was speechless.

They brought the clothing close for her inspection and Tessie explained. "We got the key to your apartment from your mother and brought down one of your blouses and skirts for size. We all know the extent of your wardrobe . . ."

There were knowing snickers.

"And we thought it just wouldn't be proper to descend on Newport without a smart-looking outfit. Topped off with . . ." She nodded to Mamma.

From behind her back, Mamma produced the straw hat she'd been working on all day. Three different ribbons formed stripes, and white silk flowers made it natty.

Dorothy offered a bit of wisdom. "I've heard it said that a working professional woman will be satisfied with six dresses in her wardrobe, but a fashionable lady will feel destitute with less than sixty."

Lucy laughed. "I am one step closer to the professional require-ment, thanks to all of you."

"Try them on!" Mavis said.

Lucy undressed right there and put them on. The brown light-weight wool draped beautifully from her hips in the popular seven-gore style, with the interest being in the back, a contrast to the flat front. The face of the blouse was highlighted with tiny pleats, with deli-cate lace edging the high collar and cuffs. The blue satin belt hooked in back. Lucy touched the upright collar with awe. "Thank you," she whispered. For the clothing and the friendship it revealed were unexpected blessings.

The ladies applauded and Lucy turned full circle, her arms outstretched. "You look beautiful" was oft repeated.

She felt beautiful. "I've heard it said clothes make a man, but—"

"Or woman," Ruth said.

"Or woman, but I truly have never worn anything that proved that statement. Until now." The threat of tears was alarming. She was not a weepy woman.

Mamma pulled her into an embrace. "Ah, *bella*. Shh."

Mamma's arms gave her a moment to renew her strength, and when she hugged each lady in turn, the threat of tears had passed.

But then she saw Mrs. Flynn, standing on the edge of the group. What did she think about the women spending time—and materials—on this gift?

"You can take the cost of all this out of my check, Madame."

The woman pursed her lips, then shook her head. "You don't pay for gifts, missy. Besides, you are representing Madame Moreau's Fashion Emporium." She looked to the floor, then back. "Actually, all this was Mr. Standish's idea."

That man.

༺ఞ༻

Up in the apartment, Lucy opened the suitcase Mrs. Flynn had let her borrow. "She's been ever so nice about all this."

"You know her bark is worse than her bite," Mamma said.

Sofia played with the clasps on the suitcase. "And Mr. Standish makes her be nice."

"Where would we be without him?" Lucy asked. She moved to the bed, where her new clothes were laid out. "I can't believe they did this. Or that I didn't notice during the day."

"You had other things on your mind," Mamma said. "Here. Let me fold those. If you roll them up they won't get creased. See?" She carefully folded the skirt on the seams, then rolled from the waist down.

Sofia sat upon the bed, closely missing sitting upon the sleeve of a blouse. "I suppose if you need more clothes you can borrow them from Rowena. After all, she is your bosom friend."

"She is no such thing," Lucy said, surprised at her own vehemence. "She simply needs my help."

Sofia fingered the cuff of the blouse until Mamma took it away. "I wish I could go. I've never been on a train."

"And I have?" Although Lucy was used to Sofia's complaining, tonight she was in no mood. "Can't you be happy for me?"

Sofia shrugged.

Mamma pinged her knee with a finger. "We are a family, we three. What brings joy to one, brings joy to all. Joy *and* sorrow."

Her mention of sorrow made Lucy think about something else. She stopped Mamma's busyness with a hand. "You must be extra careful while I'm gone to protect yourself from Bonwitter."

"He hasn't bothered us in a week."

"I don't trust that he's gone completely. Just be aware. Please?" She looked at Sofia too. "Promise me."

"I promise," Mamma said.

Lucy's sister remained silent. "Sofia? Promise me you'll be careful." A shrug and a nod would have to suffice.

"I hope I can sleep tonight," Lucy said as they were getting into bed. "I have to rise extra early to get to Grand Central Station to catch my train by ten. I'm so glad Mr. Standish offered to go there with me. I have no idea where I should pick up the ticket the Langdons purchased. Plus, I suspect the bustle of such a place will be overwhelming."

Good, Sofia thought, and immediately felt bad for it. So much for God answering her prayer for help. She still felt jealous. She still hated that Lucy was going to Newport and she was staying home.

Once she and Lucy were settled, with the sheet pulled up and smoothed to Sofia's liking, Mamma came in the room.

"What, Mamma?" Lucy asked.

Mamma moved to the bedside and knelt beside it. She looked at both girls. "*Corre lontano chi non torna mai.* He runs far who never turns,

123

girls. You must stay the course. Don't be distracted from being all you can be."

Lucy nodded, but Sofia had no idea what *all* she could be. Did Mamma know? Did God?

Mamma bowed her head, placed it in her clasped hands, and began to pray in Italian. Sofia clasped her own hands beneath her chin and closed her eyes, letting her mother's prayers take care of Lucy's safe journey. But since the door to heaven was open, Sofia added a few prayers of her own, a few longer prayers.

Help me not be jealous. Help me be a better person. Change me. . . .

The last prayer made her open her eyes. Could God change her? And more than that . . . did she really want Him to?

CHAPTER TEN

r. Standish helped Lucy out of the carriage. "Watch your step."

She was immensely glad he'd offered to take her to the station to make sure she found the right train. She'd heard stories hailing the busyness of Grand Central Depot. Three distinct railroads shared the same station, but each had their own waiting room, ticketing area, and baggage handling. To add to the confusion, they all held very similar names: the New York Central and Hudson River Railroad, the New York and Harlem Railroad, and the New York and New Haven Railroad.

Mr. Standish led Lucy across busy 42nd Street, and stood before the entrance of the massive four-story structure. "Now, then. Let me see the note from the Langdons one more time."

Lucy removed it from her reticule. Mr. Standish read it again. "I do wish she would have indicated which line it was. But I assume the New Haven will get you to Newport."

He assumed? He didn't know?

"Will you ask someone?" she said.

He offered her a reassuring smile. "Never fear, Miss Scarpelli. I *will* get you to the right train, on time." He picked up her two bags, putting one under his arm, and held the door for her to enter. He immediately sought a man wearing a uniform with a flat cap, and asked the needed questions. Lucy saw the man point. Mr. Standish thanked him and rejoined her. "Over there. He says the New Haven line *will* be the one to get you to Wickford Junction, where you will go to the landing and get a steamer to Newport."

"A boat?" The last boat Lucy had been on was the huge ship that had brought them from Italy to America.

"Newport is on an island, you know."

She was shocked. "I didn't know that."

He laughed. "I think there will be many things about Newport that will shock and surprise you. Now, come. First off, we need to pick up your ticket."

They moved through the station past hundreds, if not thousands, of people who all seemed to know where they were going.

Mr. Standish talked to a man sitting in a booth that had wrought-iron rails dividing his space from the public. He procured a ticket and was all smiles as he brought it to her. "My, my, are you going to have an adventure," he said. "The Langdons purchased you a first-class ticket. You will be traveling in high style."

First class? Lucy shook her head. "But I don't want to travel with society people. Can't I just travel with those of my own class?"

"I suppose you could, but . . ."

She was causing him distress. *And* she was being ungrateful. "I'm sorry. It's just unexpected. I'm not one of *them*. I don't know how to act. What if they question my being there and want to kick me out?"

"You simply show them your ticket. A conductor will ask to see it after you're on the train, and once he's approved your place, no one can argue. Your seat has been paid for. You deserve to be there." At her continued distress he added, "Enjoy it, Lucy. Enjoy all the advantages that come because of your association with the Langdons. I'm sure this train ride is but the first of many amazements."

His words frightened more than excited her. When she'd come to America she'd been too young to understand the immensity of the voyage, but now, she felt as if traveling to Newport, traveling among the rich and powerful, was as daunting and life-changing as traveling to a new country. For the wealthy *had* created a kingdom for themselves, one with its own rules, rulers, and boundaries. One that was wary of all outsiders, invited or not.

"Come, now," Mr. Standish said. "This way."

They passed through a vast waiting room lined with tall oak benches that extended a full foot above any seated person's head. Perched on each end were globed light fixtures that rose from the top of the benches the height of a man. The ceiling climbed to at least thirty feet, and the walls were decorated with half-columns and arched doorways. There was an echo in the room which accentuated the movement and conversations swirling about her.

Lucy and Mr. Standish didn't pause to sit down but continued through an archway to a vast exterior area of tracks and trains. It was open on the sides, but covered from the elements by a metal roof. The air was heavy with thick vapor from the steam engines, and the sound of trains coming and going was deafening: clacking and squeaking and the alarming sound of the trains' whistles announcing themselves. As if anyone could ignore them. It was all rather frightening and Lucy immediately understood why people waited inside until it was time to board.

Which it was.

"There it is," Mr. Standish said, taking her to a track nearby. "This is your train." He sounded confident, but she noticed that he asked a train employee, just to be sure.

Seeing the ticket, the man was suddenly attentive, and took the two bags from Mr. Standish. But when he saw Lucy, he looked confused. Obviously, she didn't fit the image of a first-class passenger. Lucy knew what such traveling attire should look like, and though she was dressed in her new skirt and blouse sewn by the ladies, she was far from fashionable. To be so she needed a matching suit, heavy with soutache trim, gloves, and a hat with an abundance of ribbons and feathers, and probably a veil.

Mr. Standish said a few words to the man, and he nodded.

The steward was waiting for her. It was time to say good-bye.

"Mr. Standish," she said with a sigh. "Once again you've saved me, once again I'm in your debt."

"You have saved yourself, Lucy. Your tenaciousness, creativity, and work ethic will serve you well in Newport." He took her hand and held it between his two. "Be confident and be yourself."

"I'll try."

He reached a hand into his pocket and pressed some coins into her hands. "For food and gratuities along the way."

Gratuities? She'd never thought about that.

Then he stepped back and tipped his hat. "Safe journey, Miss Scarpelli. Don't worry a moment about anything here. I'll watch over your mother and sister as if they were my own."

She felt her eyes grow misty, for she knew him to be a man of his word. Then she turned toward the steward and weighed her decision: she could act as if she belonged or cower in a corner. Making her choice, she walked toward the steward, trying to hold her chin erect, trying to look confident.

The steward offered her a hand to climb the steps to the train car. "Now to the right, miss."

She entered a car that had to be as sumptuous as a Vanderbilt mansion. There was a carpeted center aisle with benches on either side, just wide enough to seat two. Benches faced each other, enabling intimate conversation between two couples. The seating was upholstered in a patterned velvet of navy, red, and green, with the upper portion of the back tufted and buttoned in a rich green to match. There were spaces above the seats that pulled down for small storage, and these—and the ceiling of the car—were painted with intricate patterns and scenes edged in gilt filigree.

Her stomach clenched as she walked past other travelers, decked out in their finest traveling ensembles. At a glance she knew firsthand the quality and cost of their clothing.

As they knew hers.

She kept her head down and quickly found a seat facing the end wall. Hopefully no one would sit across from her. She hugged the armrest closest to the window. The steward stood in the aisle with her bags. "Are you comfortable here, miss?"

"Very," she said.

"Then I'll put your bags up here. Just ask for assistance if you need to get at them," he said.

She remembered the money in her hand and procured a coin for him. "Thank you."

He shook his head and said softly. "The gentleman took care of that, miss. And he asked that I take special care of you." Then he tipped his hat and offered her a wink. "Relax and enjoy the trip, miss. If you need anything, anything at all, my name is Ralph."

Once again, Mr. Standish had gone above and beyond. She looked outside for him, but he was gone. A tinge of fear fell upon her, but she quickly shoved it away. She was safely on the train. Ralph had been assigned to help her. There was nothing to worry—

A couple moved into the bench seat across from her. She panicked and wanted to move away, yet knew that would be rude. Maybe if she kept her gaze focused out the window . . . If only she'd brought along a book to read. That would have provided an excuse to avoid eye contact.

"Hello," the woman said.

Suddenly, the words of Mr. Standish returned to her: *"Be confident and be yourself."*

Lucy gathered a breath, smiled, and answered. "Hello." She purposely looked both the woman and then the man in the eye. "It's a lovely day to be traveling," she said. As if she traveled much. At all.

"What is your final destination?" the man asked.

"Newport."

"Really," he said.

Lucy's confidence faltered until the woman said, "How wonderful. We're traveling to Newport too." She settled her small beaded purse into the space between herself and her husband, then put her gloved hands in her lap. "Since we are traveling companions, we should introduce ourselves. I am Mrs. Garmin, and this is my husband."

With a hint of reluctance, he tipped his hat, then looked away.

"I'm Lucy Scarpelli. Very nice to meet you."

"Scarpelli," the woman repeated. "What a lovely name."

Her husband raised an eyebrow and Lucy wondered if he was thinking of something derogatory. I-tie. Ginzo. Dago. Guinea. Tony. She'd heard them all.

The conductor came through and asked to see their tickets. Although Lucy knew her ticket proved she belonged there, she was still nervous until he moved on.

The train whistle blew and Lucy felt the car jerk into motion. She gripped the armrest.

"Is this your first trip on the New Haven?" Mrs. Garmin asked.

"This is my first trip on any train, anywhere." With the words freshly spoken, Lucy wondered if she'd made a mistake being so honest.

Then Mr. Garmin startled her by calling out across the railcar, "Joseph! You old goat." He excused himself to talk to his friend.

Mrs. Garmin edged toward the center of her bench. Lucy hoped her disapproving husband would spend the trip seated elsewhere.

"There, that's better," she said. She was looking toward the far end of the car. Lucy turned around to see Mr. Garmin sitting with two other men. Mrs. Garmin went on to explain. "My husband comes out with me at the beginning of the season to see that the house is opened properly, but then he commutes back to New York during the week, and then to Newport for the weekend." She smiled confidentially. "We would take a steamer from Long Island for the shorter trip, but I have never liked being on the sea for any length of time. The rocking of the train is tolerable, the rocking of the ocean is not."

"It's nice he's traveling with you," Lucy said.

Mrs. Garmin leaned forward as if sharing a confidence. "But it's also very nice when he goes back to New York. You see, Newport is a very female environ. We let the men visit so we have proper dance and dinner partners, but for the most part, we are not particularly saddened by their absence." She hastened to add, "I speak only for myself, of course."

"Of course." But Lucy imagined Mrs. Garmin spoke for many wealthy women. What a life they had. As their husbands worked hard to pay for their lavish habits, all the women had to do was sit back and enjoy the benefits.

Mrs. Garmin pointed at Lucy's grip. "We are at full speed now, my dear. You can let go. We are perfectly safe."

Lucy relinquished her grip and found the feeling of speed was not as frightening as she'd imagined.

"Over thirty miles in an hour," Mrs. Garmin said. "We are indeed lucky to live in such a modern age. What would take days by carriage can be accomplished in six hours."

"We'll be in Newport in six hours?"

"Oh no, my dear. We'll be in Wickford Junction. There we catch the steamer to travel the bay to Newport. But by later this evening you should be safely ensconced in your . . . Do you have family in Newport?"

"No . . . I . . ." Lucy hesitated. Yet since Mrs. Garmin had shown a generosity of spirit in spite of Lucy's obvious lesser status . . .

The woman reached across the space between them and let her fingers touch Lucy's knee. "It's all right, dear. I'd love to hear your story. We all have a story, you know. Very few of us end up where we started."

Lucy was overcome by a swell of gratitude.

And so she began . . . "Have you ever heard of Madame Moreau's Fashion Emporium?"

<hr/>

"I can't believe the police haven't caught that cretin, Bonwitter," Mrs. Garmin said as she buttered her bread. "How fortuitous you're leaving town. To live in such fear must be excruciating."

Lucy nodded and wiped a crumb from her bodice. "Mr. Standish has promised to watch out for my mother and sister, but evil men have ways of getting what they want."

Mr. Garmin cut a piece of steak and held it in midair as he answered her. "If he were bothering my family, I would hire a private investigator to weed him out and bring him to justice. The law is far too lenient with such men. They must be caught and dealt with now, before their crimes escalate into something more serious. Unfortunately, the latter is usually the way of it."

His wife put a hand on his arm. "Don't say such things, my dear. You're frightening Miss Scarpelli. After all, she still has family in harm's way."

He chewed the meat, making his mustache dance. "Well, then. Yes. I'm sure your Mr. Standish is handling things just fine."

"I will pray for your family's safety," Mrs. Garmin said.

"Thank you. I'd appreciate it." She looked to Mr. Garmin. "As I appreciate this dinner, sir. It's very kind of you to include me."

He blushed, set his fork down, and indicated for a waiter to take his plate away. "I'm just glad my wife has found someone to talk with."

Mrs. Garmin put a hand to her mouth, though she made no effort to lower her voice so her husband couldn't hear. "It leaves him free to talk shop with the men."

He cleared his throat and rose. "If you ladies will excuse me, I shall continue doing just that."

"Of course, my dear."

"Again, thank you, sir. The meal was delicious."

"Yes, well . . ." He nodded and left them.

"He's very nice," Lucy said.

"He pretends to be gruff, but he's not. I'm very blessed to have found love with the man I married."

It was an odd way of putting it, but Lucy understood. Marriage came first, and then—if the couple was lucky—love followed. It was like Rowena had told her during one of her fittings. She was supposed to fall in love with a man her parents chose for her. It was as if love were a goal to be claimed rather than a sentiment that claimed its recipients.

Lucy did not agree. Love was not a noun, was not a *thing*: it was a verb, an action. A mode of being. It could not be forced, but rather it forced itself into people's hearts, sometimes unawares.

She thought of Angelo. . . . She *had* loved him, and the feeling had taken her by surprise. When she knew their future was impossible, her decision to stop loving him had only been accomplished with dogged determination, will, and pain.

The waiter removed their dinner plates. "Would you ladies like to see the dessert selections?"

Mrs. Garmin smiled and raised her eyebrows at Lucy. "Yes?"

"Oh yes. Please."

The waiter brought a tray that held four choices. "This is our German chocolate cake, this a lemon sponge cake with raspberry sauce, and these last two are cheesecake with strawberries and an apple strudel. Your choice, ladies?"

One of each? Lucy had never eaten any of them. She'd had chocolate but once, and the cake here had four layers of it. But she'd never had raspberries, and couldn't imagine a cake made out of sponges or cheese. The strudel was the least exotic, as she had eaten apples before.

"What if we choose two different items and share?" Mrs. Garmin said.

"That would be perfect."

"You make the first choice."

"I choose . . . the German chocolate cake."

"And I choose the cheesecake, please."

As the waiter was leaving, two ladies stopped him in the aisle. "Can you bring our desserts to this table?"

"Of course, ladies."

The women stood before them. Their eyes flitted over Lucy but landed on Mrs. Garmin. "How nice to see you again, Martha."

"Abigail."

The other woman made her greeting. "Do you usually come out this week?"

"I believe last year it was a week later." Mrs. Garmin waved a hand toward the chair her husband had vacated. "Please join us."

Abigail sat next to Mrs. Garmin, and the other woman sat on a chair beside Lucy. Lucy's nerves, which had been soothed in the Garmins' kind presence, were reignited.

"So," Abigail said. "Introductions, Martha. Who is your new . . . friend?"

"Abigail, Frances . . . I am pleased to introduce you to Miss Lucy Scarpelli. Lucy, this is Mrs. Samuel Wilson and Mrs. Oscar Berkeley."

The ladies nodded. Slightly.

Abigail spoke first. "Miss Scarpelli. You are traveling alone?"

"I am," Lucy said.

"With no chaperone?"

Mrs. Garmin spoke up. "Lloyd and I have taken her in. You see, she is on a very important mission—a mission of mercy, if you will."

"Indeed?"

Lucy was very willing to let Mrs. Garmin take the reins of the conversation. "Miss Scarpelli is a very talented dress designer. She made the entire wardrobe for Mrs. Langdon and her daughter, Rowena, and—"

"Oh my. Poor, poor Rowena. How is she doing?"

It was a question set for Lucy to answer. "She is quite well. But unfortunately her clothing was damaged in transit and she sent for me to come and make the repairs."

"Oh my," Mrs. Berkeley repeated. "It is just her luck. Nothing ever goes right for that girl."

"She *is* quite sweet," Abigail said. "It's so sad she has proven to be unmarriageable."

"Oh, she's not unmarriageable," Lucy said. "She hopes to become engaged this summer."

By the looks on the ladies' faces, Lucy realized she'd said too much.

"You know this for a fact?" Mrs. Berkeley said.

"You never mentioned this to me," Mrs. Garmin said.

"I . . . I . . ."

"I wonder if they've gotten the Fleming boy to propose. He's had his wild time, and I know his parents have been wanting him to settle down. Maribel Yearling refused last year, and—"

"Don't the Astors have a cousin who lives overseas? I would think new blood would be the most likely to agree to marry her."

"No one will agree easily," Mrs. Berkeley said. "With her . . . infirmity. There's no guarantee she can ever have children, you know."

Lucy was shocked. "Why wouldn't she be able to have children? It's just her leg and hip that are . . ." She let her words fade away. Again. Too much. "I'm sorry. I shouldn't speak about what I don't know."

Mrs. Garmin waved a hand. "Oh, why not, my dear? Do you think any of us know what we're talking about?"

Abigail looked peeved. "I know for a fact the Astors have a cousin."

"I'm not saying there isn't a grain of truth in all we say here. But I would bet a diamond to a dollar that Miss Scarpelli has had more conversations with Miss Langdon than any of us ever have." She gave each woman a look, expecting an answer.

"I know her mother but have never spoken directly to Rowena," Abigail conceded.

Mrs. Berkeley offered a shrug as her answer.

Mrs. Garmin nodded once. "So, then. We are pleased if Rowena has found a beau. Good for her. And good for Miss Scarpelli to be such a skilled seamstress that they trust her to make the ruined right."

"What is the name of your shop?" Mrs. Berkeley asked.

My shop? Lucy decided not to nitpick. "Madame Moreau's Fashion Emporium."

Abigail perked up. "I've been there! I had you make me a gown for the opera last season."

"Did you like it?" Lucy asked.

"Very much so. Perhaps you designed—?"

"No, no," Lucy said, knowing at least a portion of the truth must come out sooner rather than later. "I've only worked there a short while." She thought of correcting Mrs. Garmin's description of her as a designer, but decided the extra leverage in status might be to her advantage. "But I know the work the designers do, and it's of the highest quality."

"Which dress was it?" Mrs. Garmin asked Abigail. "The navy toile?"

"The burgundy velvet."

The ladies *ahh*ed in appreciation.

"How long are you staying with the Langdons?" Abigail asked.

"I'm not sure. I haven't seen the extent of the damage." Lucy wasn't even certain how long she wanted to stay. Would her visit be wonderful? Or disastrous?

"Might you be available if I have need of some alterations or repairs?"

"Of course. I'd be happy to be of service."

Their desserts arrived, a lovely frosting to their conversational cake.

⬥⬥⬥

"It's just through that door, to the right," Mrs. Garmin said.

Lucy had been embarrassed to ask where the necessary was, but after their large meal it had become essential. Sure enough, at the end of the next car was a door with the proper signage. She went inside and was surprised to see a commode and a sink in a setting as sumptuous as the rest of the train. There was even a roll of paper on a holder, something she'd never seen before. How odd that a train would be so modern.

She looked at herself in the mirror and was appalled to see a spot of food had fallen on her blouse. She wished the ladies had said something, yet she knew doing so was a delicate matter.

After cleaning the spot, she exited the necessary and returned to her original seat. Mrs. Garmin was nowhere to be seen, nor was her husband. It was just as well. Lucy could barely keep her eyes open. As the day was far from over, it would be advantageous if she could manage even the smallest of naps.

She removed her hat and placed it in her lap, then leaned her head against the back cushion. The movement of the train rocked her to sleep—and sweet dreams.

CHAPTER ELEVEN

The needle broke.

Sofia uttered an epithet, which caused some of the ladies to giggle and Mamma to flash her a look.

"Want to learn some Irish cuss words, Sofia?" Tessie asked.

Mamma answered for her. "She most certainly does not. She's just a child."

Mamma's words repeated themselves in her mind. *"She's just a child, a child, piccolina. . . ."*

Without consciously choosing to do so, Sofia pushed her chair back, sending it toppling backward. She faced the room. "I am not a child! I'm a grown woman. Stop treating me like a baby."

A moment of silence was interrupted by full laughter.

"Baby Sofia."

"Want some help, little girl?"

Heat rushed into her face, making her feel as if she would burn up if she didn't get some air. She stormed from the workroom, through the lobby, and onto the street—where she ran into a man pulling a cart.

He grabbed her arms, righting her. "Whoa there, lass. What's yer hurry?"

Surprised to hear the youth in his voice, she turned toward him, found him nice looking, and took his head in her hands, kissing him fully on the lips.

He pulled away but kept hold of her arms. "Well, now, lassie. What e'er sent you into my arms, I'm thanking God for it." He started to pull her close again when—

"Sofia!"

Mamma stood in the doorway of the shop, her eyes wide. She pointed at the spot in front of her. "Come here. Now!"

The man let her go, tipped his cap to Mamma, and shrugged. "Sorry, lass. But e'en I ain't brave enough to go against anyone's mamma."

Sofia heard laughter all around and realized she'd gained an audience. Why had she kissed him? She'd never kissed anyone. To have her first kiss be wasted on a stranger—a stranger who reeked of sweat and smoke?

She strode toward Mamma but didn't stop in the spot indicated. She needed to get off the street. Once inside she would deal with Mamma's wrath.

Mamma closed the door behind them. Sofia saw the briefest glimpse of heads through the curtain, then saw them disappear into the workroom. She whispered to her mother. "I'm sorry, Mamma. It was a stupid thing to do, but—"

Thankfully Mamma kept her voice low, her breath hot in Sofia's ear. "I'm sorry if I called you a child, but that's no reason to hurl yourself onto the street and kiss—"

Shame washed over her, and Sofia flung herself into the comfort of Mamma's arms.

Mamma shushed her and murmured soft words. "Tell me what's wrong."

Sofia removed herself from the embrace, shaking her head. She couldn't say it without sounding exactly like a child.

"Lucy?" Mamma asked.

Sofia looked into her mother's soft eyes and found safety there. "I'm nothing compared to her."

Mamma's eyebrow rose, indicating this wasn't what she'd expected to hear. She took Sofia's hands in hers, squeezing hard. "You are not Lucy and she is not you, and that's the way God meant it to be. Being the oldest forced your sister to find her way, to find her strengths. Perhaps being the youngest has prevented you from your own discovery. Or perhaps you've liked letting Lucy be in charge?"

"I don't like—"

Mamma's look stopped her interruption. For hadn't Sofia enjoyed being the youngest, the little girl to Lucy's mature woman? Hadn't she benefited from Lucy's dependable care?

She began again. "I don't want to be that little girl anymore."

"Then grow up." Mamma kissed her forehead and linked her arm in Sofia's. *"La pratica vale più della grammatica."*

Since Italian was her second language, Sofia wasn't sure what that meant.

Mamma translated. "Experience is the best teacher."

Sofia nodded but wasn't sure how to gain experience.

It all sounded rather frightening.

༺❀༻

Lucy lurched forward and awake.

"We're here," Mrs. Garmin said.

"We're at Wickford Junction," her husband corrected.

Lucy pressed her back against the seat and rubbed her sore neck. After a deep breath in, then out, she asked, "Can you give me instructions as to where I go next to catch the steamer ship?"

"We can do better than that," Mrs. Garmin said. "Mr. Garmin has insisted you accompany us to our shared destination."

Lucy noticed Mr. Garmin roll his eyes and knew it had been his wife who'd done the insisting. "Thank you, sir. That's very kind of you."

The next hour was spent transferring to the Newport and Wickford

Railroad, which took them to the Wickford harbor, where they boarded a steamer for the seventy-five-minute ride to Aquidneck Island and Newport.

Lucy spent the entire boat ride at the railing, looking over the water of Narragansett Bay. She vaguely remembered standing at the railing as a little girl, crossing the vast Atlantic. That trip had taken days, and this, but a little over an hour. And yet she was making the same sort of journey, leaving one land for another, one known way of life for something completely new.

She took a break from the view of the water and turned around, leaning her waist against the railing. Although Mr. and Mrs. Garmin had gone out of their way to guide her from the train to the steamer, once on board, they'd left her on her own. Perhaps with Newport so close, they'd felt the need to gently withdraw from their association. What could be tolerated amid the close confines of a train car would not be allowed within the circle of Newport society. And so walls had been erected in preparation for their going ashore.

So be it. Lucy had been the one to gain from their friendship—no matter how short-lived. And once in Newport she would gain her own society at the Langdons'.

Lucy saw Mrs. Wilson walking on the deck with her husband. She smiled. "Hello, Mrs. Wilson."

The woman nodded slightly, then looked away.

"You know that girl?" Lucy heard her husband ask.

"She's just a seamstress the Langdons have called in."

"Ah," he said, as if that explained her entire existence.

Just a seamstress. When the ladies had discussed her talent during dessert, they'd given her the impression she was admired, that she had a talent worthy of merit.

Lucy turned to face the sea, relieved it accepted her without judgment.

The wharf was crowded. Lucy searched the crowd for a friendly face. Surely the Langdons had sent someone to meet her. Surely they would be looking for her. If only Rowena had come . . . After her long day of travel, Lucy longed to see a friendly face.

People bustled around her, all seeming to know where they were going. She spotted the Garmins moving toward a carriage. She wished Mrs. Garmin would look her way. She would have felt ever so much better to have parted with a smile. But the woman entered the carriage, never looking back.

Lucy's attention was drawn to a young man wearing a short-collar shirt, a brown vest, and a cap. He carried a sign: *L. Scarpelli*. She resisted the urge to run to him. Instead, she raised a hand. "Sir? Sir?"

Their eyes met and he gave her an appraising look. "Lucy Scarpelli?" he asked.

"Yes."

He touched the brim of his cap. "Haverty. I've been sent to fetch you to the Langdons'." He took her satchels, led her toward a cart, and helped her into the seat beside him. Watching other ladies from the train get into fine carriages accentuated the gulf of their status.

So be it.

Haverty expertly made his way through the congested harbor and onto a residential street. The homes they passed were pleasing and Lucy said as much.

"You ain't seen nothing yet. These are but shacks compared to where we're heading."

"The Langdons have a large home?"

He laughed. "Larger than large. But the thing is, here in Newport they're called *cottages*. Millions of dollars, dozens of rooms, and gold dripping off the walls." He glanced at her. "You impressed yet?"

"Only if you're telling me the truth."

"You can be the judge of that." He pulled on the reins and yelled at another carriage that had cut him off. "Stupid tourists. Can't live with 'em, can't live without 'em."

"What's a *tourist*?"

"Someone who comes visiting and thinks they own the place. It's not just the rich who come to Newport in the summer. The town swells up like a boil on a horse's—" He glanced at Lucy. "You get the picture."

Lucy held on to the side of their bench seat for her very life. Although she was used to traffic in the city, there was a certain wildness to the traffic here, as if everyone was in a hurry to get their holiday started and didn't care whom they ran over in the process.

"Do you live here all year round, Mr. Haverty?"

"Just Haverty. Nope. I'm with the Langdons in New York the rest of the time. Come down here a few weeks before the family to get things ready, and'll go back a few weeks after."

Since Haverty seemed willing to talk, Lucy decided to ask him more. "Can you tell me about the family? Is Miss Langdon well? Is there anything I should know to help me get along while I'm here?"

"Snoopy little thing, aren't ya?"

"I prefer to say I'm inquisitive. I'm coming in blind and simply wish to know the lay of things."

"Knowledge is power; that's for certain," he said. "Let's see if I can get it in a nutshell. Miss Langdon's gentle as a fawn in the forest, kind to everybody, not demanding at all. She'd lay down her life for a friend, though I can't say as others would do the same for her."

"She doesn't have any good friends?"

"Can't say as I've been too impressed with any of the young ladies she's forced to hang around with. Just because she's different . . ."

Oh. That.

He changed the subject. "She has one brother, Hugh, who's as opposite from Rowena as a wolf to a sheep. Hugh thinks he's king of the world—a jolly king. He doesn't take much seriously." He gave her another look. "If I was you, being a pretty girl and all, I'd stay clear of him best you can."

Wonderful. Another Bonwitter. "Any other advice?"

"Work hard and stay invisible."

Lucy didn't understand. "As I'll be repairing Miss Langdon's clothing, I don't see how that's possible. Besides, she invited me here."

"You've never been a servant, have you?"

"I'm still not a servant."

He laughed. "Well, then, you're going to have a time of it, ain't you?"

"What do you mean by that?"

"You'll see."

⊗

Rowena's boredom was at an end. Today Lucy was arriving, and yesterday Edward had arrived. Although she was still required to attend numerous social occasions she would have preferred to skip, the attending would be made far easier knowing Edward would be present at most.

Rowena looked across the grass at the other two couples who'd accompanied her and Edward to watch the sailboat regatta. She and Edward had taken their place upon the grassy knoll overlooking Narragansett Bay first, and she expected the others to sit close by.

But they didn't do that. She watched as Winnie Rutherford pointed to the grass a good twenty feet away, instructing her companion to lay the blanket there. The other couple sat beside them, leaving an awkward patch of green as testament to their rudeness.

And Rowena's and Edward's ostracism.

She felt bad for Edward. Since his family was new in Newport, they were suspect. The bastions of society were high and wide, and there was no guarantee of acceptance no matter how much money one made—or displayed. Why, just the other night at Delmonico's, her friends had talked to Edward as if he were one of them. But today . . . Acceptance into society was fickle. Further proof could be seen in the case of Mrs. William K. Vanderbilt, who had been ostracized since her divorce the previous spring. Such a thing was simply not done, but Rowena had heard her mother say that though they wouldn't invite Alva to *their* house, they probably would go to a party Alva was having later this season. The presence of the Duke of Marlborough was the draw. Apparently, Alva was arranging for her daughter, Consuelo, to marry him.

There were others who kept tabs on who was in and who was out: Mrs. Stuyvesant Fish, Mrs. Cornelius Vanderbilt II, Mrs. Hermann Oelrichs, Mrs. William Backhouse Astor, Jr. . . . . These ladies were an unofficial but recognized panel of judges who gave—or withheld—their favor at will. And whim.

Of course, Rowena's position was not exactly solid. Her family was accepted because they'd been in Newport before the patriarch of all the Vanderbilt clan—the Commodore—had even thought about running a railroad, much less climbing any ladder other than the one in a train car's berth. But Rowena knew her infirmity, along with her brother's frivolous nature, tested their position.

If only she and Edward could have come here alone. But such private outings were not allowed at this point in their relationship, so she'd let her mother arrange the outing with the other couples. In truth, she disliked them as much as they tolerated her. But for them to be so blatant about it . . .

Rowena pretended to be preoccupied with her parasol, even though she knew it would open if she really tried. And oddly, as Edward stretched his legs out beside her, she noticed scuffs on his buff-colored shoes. But instead of thinking *He should polish them*, the shoes made her think of Morrie. Morrie's shoes were never polished and often displayed a disturbing amount of dirt and grass. Yet she wouldn't have it any other way. For by his shoes, Morrie always revealed a refreshing evidence of fully living. Being all staid and polished only revealed that a person was idle and had servants to help showcase that idleness. *Living* was a coveted trophy most of her set would never win. Caught in her memory, she moved the blanket aside so she could feel the grass.

"Would you like me to smooth the blanket?" Edward asked.

She smoothed it back herself. "I like the grass, the feel of it."

"I'm more a city boy." He took a deep breath but shook his head. "This fresh air . . . my lungs don't know what to do with it."

His comment was disappointing. Who could not like the soft musk of the grass, the rainbow of colors in Newport's gardens, the sea air, the waves, the endless sky?

Unable to delay any longer, Rowena finally let her parasol open and looked absently at the other couples. It gladdened her heart that Winnie's hair was frizzing in the humidity. So much for perfection. And there was a distinct amount of sweat on her companion's brow, sweat that he tried in vain to eradicate by fanning himself with his straw hat.

Rowena felt her own trickle of perspiration course down her spine between skin and corset. Yet its presence gave her no distress. She loved the outdoors, and if she could have rid herself of this ridiculous corset, dress, and petticoats, along with the veil, hat, and parasol, she would have played the child, skipping over the knoll in her bare feet like she used to do with Morrie before convention, age, and injury ruined their fun.

The other couples talked amongst themselves, often behind upraised hands. Again, the utter rudeness astounded but did not surprise her. Rowena was glad the breeze took their words out to sea.

Odd that the upper crust saw no need for subtlety. When they wished to discuss a person, they did so with little or no attempt at hiding the act. As now. When Rowena looked in their direction, she usually found them with their heads together, talking in low tones, their eyes fixed on Edward and herself. It was very disconcerting.

On one such occasion, Edward noticed it too. "Are we entertaining enough for you, ladies? Or would you like me to dance a jig?"

Not waiting for their reply, he stood and did a funny little dance.

He received laughter from the others and gratitude from Rowena. When he returned to his seat on the grass, he said, "There. At least now I've chosen their attention."

She was touched by his willingness to play the fool to gain her comfort. "Be assured they are not chattering to disparage you but to mock me, or rather what they consider the absurd idea of me *with* you. Or is it *you* with me?"

"Why are they so cruel? Haven't they known you your whole life? Being from Boston, being new to New York and Newport, I should think *I* would be the subject of their rudeness," he asserted. "I've heard my mother and father talk of the bolted doors of society and how difficult it is to pry them open."

"But you are a handsome, eligible man, and charming besides. Those traits are very advantageous when it comes to being accepted by the younger set here. See the way Mary Grant is smiling at you? With one smile in return she could be yours forever."

He turned toward Mary and waggled his hands beside his ears. Alarmed, she looked away.

"You're fearless."

"Foolish."

"Guileless."

He seemed to like that word.

The regatta played out before them, the tall ships and smaller sailing vessels cutting through the water of the bay with the ease of paint from an artist's brush. The sails captured the wind's magic, and Rowena was brought back to happy times aboard her family's yacht, and even happier times on their small sailboat, where she and Hugh would bob and dance with the waves and wind. She'd taught Hugh how to sail, but now . . . only he enjoyed the privilege.

Rowena lifted her veiled face to the wind and closed her eyes. "Oh, to sail again . . ."

"So you like to sail?" Edward asked.

She regretted showing her interest. "I used to."

"No more?"

"No more." *Please don't ask me. . . .*

"What happened?"

And there it was. The opportunity or the curse of explaining her infirmity.

Rowena glanced at the other couples, who were thoroughly enmeshed in their own gaiety. She *could* tell Edward. If they were ever to be married, she *should* tell Edward.

"You don't have to tell me," he said.

Which, of course, gave her the courage to do just that. "I loved to sail. Our family spent hours on our boat."

"But . . . ?"

"I hurt my leg and everything changed."

He nodded. "I'm sorry."

"Me too. Now, even if I felt inclined, I wouldn't be able to keep my footing and balance. That experience, the exhilaration of having the wind caress my face, the sound of the sails popping taut, and the smell of the ocean spray . . ." It made her sad to think of it. "So be it. Life goes on."

"I don't like the sea."

"What?" The fervor of her exclamation surprised her. "How can you not?"

His shrug was like a slap and his attitude far more hurtful than anything the other couples might have said behind closed hands. How could he shrug about the sea? What was there not to like? Suddenly, her pleasure at being able to share her love of sailing seemed tainted.

It was not aided by his next words.

"Perhaps your inability to sail will be a good thing, since I don't like to sail."

She found herself gawking at him. He looked at her, at first confused, then said, "That didn't come out as I meant it to."

Indeed. She turned her attention to the regatta, to those lucky people who were doing what she could never do again: ride the wind.

The Langdon home was set on the crest of a vast lawn and was reached by a drive through stone and wrought-iron gates. Lucy had never seen such an expanse of space belonging to one residence. In the city, buildings were close together and green space was sparse—except for Central Park, of course.

As it was dusk, the house seemed to glow with light. Its silhouette against the darkening sky revealed a myriad of turrets and rooftops.

Lucy must have made an audible sound, for Haverty chuckled. "Quite the cottage, eh?"

"Quite."

Haverty bypassed the front entrance and steered the horses around to the side, near the back. "Here we are."

Lucy was disappointed not to enter the house from the front. Surely this was a servants' entrance. She knew she wasn't society, but the Langdons had paid for a first-class ticket on the train and steamer. To be so blatantly put in her place upon arrival was distressing.

Haverty helped her to the ground and took her satchels down a few steps into the basement.

A girl in a maid's uniform looked up from her sweeping. "Watch your feet, Haverty. I don't need no dirt on my clean floor."

"Are you saying I'm dirty?"

"Don't I know it," she said. She looked at Lucy. "Who are you?"

"I'm Lucy Scarpelli. I'm a seamstress. I was sent for in order to mend Miss Langdon's wardrobe."

"Well la-di-da, aren't you the fancy one, being *sent for* and all that."

"Enough grousing, Fanny. You're just mad because it ain't you. Where's Mrs. Donnelly?"

"I saw her in the pantry, going over the order with Cook."

"Come on, then," Haverty said to Lucy.

Lucy knew she should have said something nice to Fanny like *"Nice to meet you,"* but she couldn't bring herself to do it. Hopefully Fanny's attitude wasn't universal throughout the house.

After a few twists and turns, they reached a huge kitchen that was as large as the Scarpelli apartment in New York—times ten. Two women were kneading bread. Both eyed Lucy suspiciously.

Haverty walked past them to a room replete with floor-to-ceiling shelves, stocked with all manner of food and baking supplies. A stout woman wearing a mobcap was counting boxes. A very slim woman wearing a striped blouse and plain skirt carried a clipboard and was marking off a list. Both stopped their work.

"Yes, Haverty?" the thin woman asked.

"This here's Lucy Scarpelli, fetched from the dock." He looked to Lucy. "This is Mrs. Donnelly, the housekeeper. She's in charge."

"Nice to—"

Mrs. Donnelly handed the clipboard to the cook and shooed Haverty and Lucy out of the narrow room. "Well, now. I trust your trip was satisfactory?"

"Very much so," Lucy said. "It was very nice to be treated—"

Mrs. Donnelly shook her head. "I heard through the grapevine they bought you first-class fares. Unprecedented, that's what it is. Apparently, you have Miss Langdon to thank for it."

"I will thank her, then," Lucy said. She'd already grown tired of defending her mode of travel. Could she help what class of ticket was purchased for her?

The housekeeper's right eyebrow rose. "I suppose you'll be wanting to settle in."

"That would be nice."

Mrs. Donnelly spoke to Haverty. "Up on three, the west corner."

"Addy's old room?"

The housekeeper flashed him a look. To Lucy she said, "You're off the hook tonight, but I'll inform the Langdons you've arrived. I'm sure they'll send for you first thing in the morning."

"Thank you."

"I suppose you're hungry too."

Starving. "I could eat something."

"I'll have Sadie bring you a tray. Now go. The rest of us have work to do."

Whispers followed Lucy and Haverty out of the kitchen, as the bread makers exchanged opinions about this newcomer.

So be it. Let them talk. She wasn't here for them. She was here for Rowena.

❦

Lucy put the last of her clothes in the dresser and shut the drawer. There was a knock on the door.

"Come in."

It was a maid, carrying a tray. "I'm Sadie. I hope you likes potato soup."

"It's a favorite," Lucy said.

Sadie put the tray on the narrow bed. Lucy noticed bread, jam, and some strawberries, along with a glass of milk.

"Thank you," Lucy said.

"Well, you're welcome, then," Sadie said. "But don't get used to it. This is the last time you'll be served round here."

"I don't expect to be served."

"Good. 'Cause you won't be. You're no better'n the rest of us, you know."

Lucy was surprised by her tone. "I know."

149

"Just 'cause Miss Langdon likes you don't mean you can put on airs."

"I have no intention of doing any such thing." She hated the chip on this maid's shoulder, because she was proof the attitude was shared. She didn't consider herself a servant, but she certainly didn't want to be considered an enemy by those who held that position.

Sadie eyed the hat Lucy had placed on the spindle of the chair-back. "I do likes yer hat."

"My mother made it for me."

"Would she make one for me sometime?"

"Perhaps."

Sadie moved to the door, then nodded back at the chair. "You'd best find a new place for the hat, though—at least at night."

"Why?"

"You'll be wanting to wedge the chair under the doorknob."

"Because . . . ?"

"Because the last girl who stayed here didn't. Servants don't get no locks on our doors, you know, and Master Hugh . . ." She moved into the hall. "If you want breakfast, be in the kitchen by half past six. 'Night."

"Good night."

Lucy sat upon the bed and practically inhaled the food as if it were her last meal. Once that was accomplished, she felt the fatigue of her trip take over. To think she'd started this day in her own apartment over the dress shop . . .

She began to undress, but as she undid the third button on her blouse, she stopped long enough to wedge the chair beneath the doorknob.

One of her father's proverbs came back to her: *Fidarsi è bene; non fidarsi è meglio.*

To trust is good; not to trust is better.

At least for now.

Rowena ran into Sadie, coming down from the third floor. "Is Miss Scarpelli here?"

Sadie nodded upstairs. "Just got her settled into Addy's room."

Rowena had never been up to the servants' quarters. "Which room is that?"

"The one on the west. If you needs her, I could go get her, miss."

Rowena lifted her skirts. "No thank you." She began the trek upward.

The third floor held a long hall and many doors, none of them marked. Rowena began knocking on the rooms that faced west. No answer. No answer.

Finally, she heard scuffling inside a room, and the door opened.

Rowena pulled Lucy into her arms. "You're here!"

Lucy seemed a bit uneasy about the display of affection, so Rowena let her go. "How was your trip?"

"It was lovely. I've never traveled first class."

Rowena doubted she'd ever traveled at all. Rowena entered the tiny room but, finding its only chair small and tenuous, remained standing. "I'll take credit for that. Mother wanted to send you third-class tickets, but I thought that since you were interrupting your life to come to our aid, and since time is of the essence, it would be to our advantage to have you arrive as rested as possible. She still doesn't know, because I had my brother Hugh arrange it." Rowena paused for the *pièce de résistance*. "I paid for it out of my own allowance."

"You didn't need to do that."

"But I wanted to." She looked at the contents of the room. There was a mirrored dresser, a washstand, and the small chair. Rowena moved to the window. "I do wish you faced the sea. You would have a magnificent view of the ocean and the sunrise."

"I don't think Mrs. Connelly was too concerned about my view."

"Mrs. Donnelly."

"Donnelly."

Rowena let the lace curtain fall into place. "I wish I weren't going out tonight so we could talk. Did you have something to eat?"

"I did."

Rowena was rather disturbed by how awkward it all seemed. Lucy was so quiet, almost standoffish. "Well, then," she said. "I expect you must be tired. Have a good night's sleep and I'll see you in the morning."

"Good night, Miss Langdon."

Rowena was going to correct her, but instead just offered a nod.

❦

Sofia lay on her bed, in the bedroom she usually shared with Lucy. In the bed that was empty *of* Lucy.

I always wanted to have a bed to myself.

And so, toward that end, she spread her arms and legs wide, claiming the mattress as hers and hers alone.

Within moments she pulled her limbs close. Venturing beyond her space was almost frightening.

"Sofia? Are you all right?" Mamma called from the next room.

Sofia hesitated. Was she all right? She'd always wanted to be free of Lucy's shadow. Now she wasn't the youngest daughter; she was the only daughter.

And as such . . . shouldn't she act more grown-up? What did that entail exactly?

Offer Mamma the bed. That's what Lucy would do.

An inner argument began. They each had their own bed; there was no need for them to change. Mamma preferred her mattress on the floor, and—

"Sofia? Answer me. Are you all right?"

Before she could deny it, Sofia heard herself say, "I miss Lucy."

Mamma left her mattress and joined Sofia in the bed. She held up her arm, drawing Sofia into its safety as she'd done a thousand times before.

"Shh, *piccolina*. It will be all right."

Sofia would be a grown-up tomorrow.

CHAPTER TWELVE

*L*ucy hesitated a moment before entering the Langdon kitchen for breakfast. She braced herself for disapproving looks and comments. She couldn't blame them. She was the intruder—an intruder who'd been invited by the family, who'd already received special privileges.

Lucy was startled when a maid came through the door and nearly collided with her.

"Oh!"

"Pardon me," Lucy said.

"You in or out?" the girl said.

"I'm coming in."

The girl nodded to a door across the room. "The help eats in there. You'd better hurry before the men eat all the bacon."

Lucy crossed through the kitchen and entered a dining room. Seated around the table were servants in uniform. All talk stopped. A silver-haired man at the head spoke. "Mrs. Donnelly, would you do the honors, please?"

"Certainly, Mr. Timbrook." She rose from her chair. "I would like to introduce all of you to Miss Lucy Scarpelli, who arrived last night."

"First class," a young man said under his breath.

"Claude . . ."

Mrs. Donnelly continued. "She's come to repair Miss Langdon's wardrobe."

"I have a button or two that needs sewing," another man said.

"She can sew my buttons anytime."

Mr. Timbrook slammed a hand upon the table. "Silence! Have you lost your manners? There will be no talk like that at my table."

"Sorry, sir."

"Sorry, Mr. Timbrook."

The head man pointed at a chair. "Here, Miss Scarpelli. Please take a seat and have some breakfast. The days are long and hard here, and proper sustenance is essential."

Lucy sat in her assigned seat and the dishes of eggs, bacon, and toast were passed.

Mrs. Donnelly renewed the conversation. "Have you been a lady's maid long, Miss Scarpelli?"

"Oh, I'm not a maid; I'm a seamstress at Madame Moreau's Fashion Emporium. I helped create a wardrobe for Rowena and her mother. I mean, Miss Langdon."

As soon as she finished talking, Lucy knew she'd said something wrong. The faces around the table—which had softened slightly after Mr. Timbrook's admonition—had hardened again. Even Haverty's face lost its friendly edge.

"Maybe you should go eat with them, then," the cook said. "If you're so important as all that."

Although she'd only spoken the truth, Lucy realized she'd set herself apart—on purpose, if she was honest with herself.

"It's because she's used to first-class treatment," a maid said. "She's slumming it, eating with us."

Mr. Timbrook chastised her. "Miss O'Reilly, that will be enough."

"She's the one who started it, sir, acting like she's better'n the rest of us."

Lucy tried again. "I didn't—"

A young boy ran into the room and handed a note to Mr. Timbrook. All talk ceased until he read it. He carefully folded the note and slipped it under his plate. "Miss Scarpelli, you are wanted in the morning room at once."

Sounds of derision accompanied her exit.

Let them make fun of her. She *didn't* belong with them.

She didn't belong with the Langdon family either.

So where *did* she belong?

Once out of the kitchen Lucy realized she didn't know where she was going. The boy who'd brought the note was running ahead of her. "Boy?"

He stopped and she caught up with him. "Will you show me the way to the morning room, please?"

He eyed her warily. "Don'tcha know?"

"I'm new here."

"Come on, then, but you better hurry. When the family wants you, they wants you now."

Good to know.

❦

Rowena stood at the window in the morning room and looked out upon the lawn. Servants were busy pruning, picking weeds, and manicuring the yard, yet she barely noticed their movement. In a few minutes, Lucy would come into the room and be formally introduced to Newport. In a few minutes their friendship would truly commence.

Rowena heard a knuckle against woodwork and turned to see Lucy in the doorway. She rushed forward, extending her hands in welcome. "Lucy! Your first day in Newport begins."

Lucy looked a bit overwhelmed but took Rowena's hands and let Rowena kiss both of her cheeks.

The awkwardness from the night before remained. Was it the lavish setting? Or being away from her family?

"Did you sleep well?" Rowena asked.

"I did."

Would Rowena ever get more than two words from her? She led Lucy to a settee. "As you can imagine, I've been extremely distressed because of the damage to my wardrobe. You are a lifesaver coming here to make things right."

"I'm very glad to be here."

Silence fell between them, and Rowena started to panic. This wasn't the way she'd dreamed it would be. Not at all. What could she do to make Lucy feel welcome? What could she—

Lucy smoothed her skirt upon the cushion. "I'm ready to get to work. Have you missed any engagements because of the damage to your clothes?"

"Just one dinner. But today I'm supposed to go on a picnic with some friends."

Lucy nodded. "The mauve seersucker?"

"A torn sleeve."

"Then let me get to work."

"Excellent."

It was all so formal, as if Lucy were a servant and Rowena her mistress. Rowena had brought her here to work, yet her unspoken job was to be Rowena's friend. But how could they transition from one to the other?

Rowena was at her wit's end. She let her hands fall into her lap. "This feels incredibly awkward, and I wanted it to feel comfortable, like two friends getting the chance to spend time together. Back in New York we talked like sisters."

Lucy looked around the drawing room with its satin wallpaper, thick patterned rugs, and filigreed woodwork. "This is not New York."

Ah. So that was it. "Actually," Rowena said, "this room was supposed to evoke France. Father nearly died when Mother insisted the oak paneling be painted white. It doesn't match the rest of the house at all."

"It's very . . . fancy," Lucy said.

Rowena offered a laugh. "That it is." And in hindsight, perhaps it wasn't the first place they should have met. Checking her motives, Rowena asked herself if she'd chosen this room *for* its opulence. Was she trying to show off to her friend?

Perhaps more than a little. It was no wonder Lucy was acting formal and distant. "I know," Rowena said, standing. "Let's go up to my room. It's much homier."

But before they could exit, her mother entered the room. "Look, Mother, Miss Scarpelli has arrived."

"None too soon."

"I came as quickly as I could, Mrs. Langdon. And I'm eager to get to work."

Rowena took Lucy's hand. "That's where we're going now, Mother. I'll show Lucy all that needs to be done."

"You can't cancel your picnic," Mrs. Langdon said. "Edward will be there. He's expecting you to come."

"I won't miss it, Mother," Rowena said. "Lucy has assured me the seersucker will be repaired in time."

Mrs. Langdon looked skeptical, but Lucy let Rowena pull her from the room and followed her up the stairs to the second floor. Rowena wished she was capable of running up the stairs but, as usual, moved slowly, lifting her skirt with one hand and holding the railing with the other. Each step gained the attention of both feet before she moved on to the next. It was incredibly tiresome.

But Lucy didn't seem to mind the slower pace. While her feet did the walking, her gaze moved from left to right, up and down. Her interest made Rowena look at their home with new eyes.

The staircase and the walls along the way were a dark walnut. The spindles were intricately carved and so close together as to nearly be one piece of continuous wood. These same spindles had caused Rowena and Hugh no end of frustration as children when they'd tried to drop grapes or olives down upon their parents' guests. Many a plump olive had found itself wedged in place.

The paneled walls extended two stories beyond the second, culminating in a stained-glass skylight featuring a woman floating among a puffing of clouds in a striking blue sky. Rowena and Hugh had named her. Hugh had suggested Gertrude—which was so *not* right—but Rowena had won out with Anastasia. Birds flew past Anastasia, carrying sprigs of flowers and leaves in their beaks.

Lucy paused at the railing on the second floor to look down, and then up. "It's like being in a tunnel leading to heaven."

"Father would be pleased to hear you say that. He named our home *Porte au Ciel*."

"Gate to Heaven?"

Rowena was pleased. "You know French?"

"In this case it's similar to Italian: *porta al cielo*."

"Mmm. How lovely. I wish I could speak another language. My tutor tried to teach me French, but I have no talent for it whatsoever. As for the house, my grandfather built the first version forty years ago, then after he died, Father made it larger and grander—though this house is like a poor cousin's barracks compared to the two Vanderbilt palaces that have sprung up in the past few years. Father has insisted he will do nothing to compete, that to do so would be gauche and so . . ." She realized she was talking too much. She opened a door off the wide hall that ran along three sides of the atrium. "Welcome to my abode."

Lucy walked inside and smiled. "After seeing the other parts of the house, it's not what I expected. It's very warm and inviting." She looked at Rowena. "It suits you. It matches your character. It's very . . . right."

Somehow the compliment bothered her. "I don't feel very right. I think all sorts of bad thoughts."

"I can't imagine you doing any such thing."

Rowena nodded, accepting full responsibility for this flaw. "Be assured I may do the right thing, but not always with a willing heart."

"At least your actions are right. Most people don't *do* much of anything."

"You're very kind."

Lucy shook her head. "But I'm not. I'm rarely kind at all. My biggest fault is that I say what I think."

"That's a good attribute."

"Not when I speak without thinking through how the other person may feel about it."

Rowena remembered a quotation. " 'Discretion is the better part of valor.' "

Lucy stopped her exploration of the bird figurines on Rowena's mantel. "I have no idea what that means."

Rowena bit her lip as she thought about it, then burst into laughter. "Neither do I. But someone famous said it once."

"Someone more famous and smarter than us."

Rowena wagged a finger at Lucy, though she was smiling. "Don't disparage my intelligence, Lucy. Without the full function of my body, it's what I must lean on the most."

Lucy offered the slightest glance at Rowena's leg, making Rowena regret bringing up the subject. She knew Lucy was curious, but that was a discussion for another time. First things first.

"Actually, Mother and Father have the large bedrooms. I purposely chose this smaller one because I enjoy the golden tones of the oak." She moved toward the fireplace and extended an arm toward the painting above the mantel. "Besides, how can I resist having a marriage scene from the Renaissance watching over me?"

Lucy peered at the painting, studying it.

Rowena offered commentary. "It looks like a formal Italian wedding with the men in long robes and the pages in tights."

"Not like any Italian wedding I've been to."

Of course not. It was a painting of aristocracy. Rowena chastised herself for bringing it attention.

But she'd kept the best for last. "Here's my true inspiration." She pulled the sheer curtains aside and thrust open the window to showcase her view. "See what you're missing by having your window look to the west?"

Lucy leaned against the sill and took it all in. The breeze made wisps of her hair dance as the curtains fluttered.

"It's the most lovely view I've ever seen."

"To which I take absolutely no credit." She remembered a verse she'd had to memorize for Sunday school. " 'By the word of the Lord were the heavens made; and all the host of them by the breath of his mouth. He gathereth the waters of the sea together as an heap: he layeth up the depth in storehouses. Let all the earth fear the Lord: let all the inhabitants of the world stand in awe of him. For he spake, and it was done; he commanded, and it stood fast.' "

"How beautiful."

"I can't take credit for that either."

Lucy took hold of the finial on the footboard of the bed. "This entire home is like walking into a make-believe world. My family has lived in two rooms all our lives—and for years there were seven of us."

"In two rooms?"

Lucy ran her fingers along the curved footboard. "Now there are just three of us in a three-room apartment. Now we have our own bathroom and running water and a bathtub. My sister makes good use of it too. She loves to read her books there."

Rowena was shocked. "*Now* you have a bathroom?"

Lucy sat upon a fringed bench at the foot of the bed. "Until our present apartment above the dress shop, we lived in a tenement on Mulberry Street with dozens of other families. We got our water from a spigot in the hall, and had to go down five flights to use the necessaries in the alley." She ran her hands along the sateen fabric, then looked up at Rowena. "Does that shock you?"

Rowena sat on a chair near the fireplace. "Probably as much as all this shocks you."

Lucy smiled. "This house is a lovely surprise and I'm very glad to be here, to see where you live. But I'm even more glad you never had to see where I lived."

A measure of silence fell between them, but now, it was void of discomfort. It was as though a settling had occurred during their exchange, a calm water after the height of a wave and the pull of the ebb tide.

"Now, then," Lucy said. "If you don't mind showing me the clothes? Since your mother doesn't want you to miss the picnic . . ."

"Because Edward will be there—along with a dozen others, of course."

"I remember now. Edward is your intended."

"As per our parents' plan."

"You wanted him to desire you."

Rowena felt herself blush. "I believe I've made some progress in that department."

Lucy grinned. "Do tell."

"He has said kind words."

Lucy's face fell. "A brother can say kind words."

True. "But he defended me when people were rude."

"Which makes him a gentleman. But what about *desire*?"

Rowena hesitated, but only for a moment. She *had* wanted a confidante. "He kissed me."

Lucy's interest was renewed. "More than once?"

Actually . . . "Just the once." She was quick to defend him. "But as you yourself said, he is a gentleman by nature. He would never take advantage."

"Is that a relief or a disappointment?"

Rowena laughed nervously. "A relief, to be sure."

"Oh."

With Lucy's reaction, Rowena rethought her answer. Perhaps it would be better if Edward did try to take advantage. If his desire for her grew, it would mean his need to marry her would increase also. But she couldn't fathom the idea of defending her virtue against a man who was letting lust rule. Which begged the questions: Was their relationship at its proper place? Should she be doing something differently?

"Are you all right?" Lucy asked.

She regretted the transparency of her face. "Enough about Edward. You are here for the clothes. Come with me."

Rowena opened a door on the fireplace wall that led to a large dressing room.

Lucy gasped.

Rowena tried to see it through her friend's eyes. At the head of the room was a large window, hidden with discreet sheers, but on either side of the room were high rods upon which were hung all manner of clothes, most recognizable as coming from the Emporium, but some others besides. To their sharp right was a shoe rack that stood eight feet from bottom to top, lined with her boots and slippers. And on the other side of the door was a similar shelf unit that contained her hats, many displayed on hatstands to protect their shape.

Lucy strode to the center of the room, turning full circle next to a massive Tiffany-blue velvet ottoman. "You were wrong about the atrium," she finally said.

"Wrong?"

"It's not the reason this house is called Gate to Heaven. *This* is the reason!"

"And you are the creator, for most of its contents are the work of your hands."

"You are too kind, Miss Langdon."

"Rowena. Please, Lucy. Remember I am Rowena—at least when we're alone."

Lucy spotted the mauve seersucker suit and removed it from the rack. The sleeve was pulled from the bodice.

"Is it fixable?"

"Of course. Let me fetch my satchel of sewing supplies and—"

"One moment." Rowena rang a bell.

Within a minute, her lady's maid appeared at the door. "Yes, Miss Langdon?"

"Margaret, I would like you to meet Lucy Scarpelli, the talented clothing designer who created my wardrobe this season. She has come to make repairs—"

"Pardon me, miss, but I could've repaired the damage."

"You have enough duties, Margaret. You don't need me adding to your burden." *Actually, I will be glad for your absence.*

Margaret only shrugged.

Rowena pointed to a suitcase near the window. "There. On your way out, would you please bring Miss Scarpelli her supplies?" She looked to Lucy. "I had them retrieved while you were at breakfast."

Margaret's gaze moved slowly from Rowena to Lucy, but she picked up the suitcase and set it at Lucy's feet. With a thud.

"That will be all, Margaret. Lucy will attend me from now on."

As Margaret left, Lucy asked, "Is she your lady's maid?"

"In theory," Rowena said. "But she much prefers helping my

162

mother, hence my point in calling her in here today. Now, with you here to help . . . she'll be relieved to be away from me."

"Why?"

"She treats me like I'm unclean, as though my infirmity is contagious."

"How silly," Lucy said. "Back home I often see people with handicaps: a missing limb or a finger, or a growth on the face or hand, all far more obvious than yours. Never once have I considered these people contagious."

"Ah, but society demands perfection."

Sadie came to the open doorway and bobbed a curtsy. "Begging your pardon, Miss Langdon, but your mother wishes to see you in the morning room. She says to tell you it won't take long."

Rowena sighed and turned to Lucy. "I will return. Make yourself at home."

❀

Lucy was glad for the time alone in the dressing room. Although she'd worked on these beautiful gowns, to be in their presence as one luxurious whole elicited feelings she'd never had before. She was practically giddy.

She strolled past the shoes, choosing a dainty pair of ivory silk pumps that were complemented by a curve of brocade and satin piping. She lifted her skirt and held one against her own foot. It looked as though it could fit. The fun she could have playing dress-up. . . . She thought of Sofia. Her sister would dive into the clothes with fervor.

The hats were next to gain her attention. Lucy placed a wide-brimmed mauve hat on her head, tying the wide ribbon under her chin. She moved to the full-length mirror close by. The ostrich feather bowed with her movement. A hat like this could make the plainest woman feel pretty.

Lucy realized time was passing. Although she knew Rowena wouldn't mind her innocent act of appreciation, she didn't want anyone else to walk in on her play, so she returned the hat to its stand and began to examine the familiar items hanging around her.

One by one she pulled them out for examination and found the damage. Some lace pulled off and unruffled at a cuff, a side seam opened, a flounce dislodged, some buttons missing, a length of trim hanging loose. When she'd received the telegram telling her the entire wardrobe was ruined and she was needed immediately to make the repairs, she'd imagined damage caused by a trunk that had burst open in transit, or perhaps items shredded by carriage wheels or water damage or—

"Am I found out?"

Lucy turned to face Rowena. And then she knew. Her disjointed thoughts rushed to a single conclusion—the only possible conclusion. "You caused the damage?"

Rowena raised a hand, palm forward. "I confess."

"But why?"

"You know why."

Lucy did know, or at least suspected. Yet she couldn't say it aloud in case she was wrong. It would be far too presumptuous.

Rowena said it for her. "I wanted you here, Lucy. With me. In Newport. During the fittings I became fond of you as a friend. And I guessed you felt the same about me. Was I wrong?"

Lucy slipped the dress back on the rack. "No, you weren't wrong. I felt a deep connection with you from the start, one I've never felt with anyone but family."

Rowena smiled and let out a deep sigh. "And so. As my dear friend, as the one person in the world who had the ability to make me feel pretty again, I didn't want to lose contact. Now if you were of the same . . . if you ran in the same circles as I, I could simply invite you to come here as my guest. But—"

Lucy said it for her. "But since I'm of the working class . . ."

"I had to be creative." Rowena strolled past a rack of clothes, her fingers skimming the sleeves. "I hated to cause damage to these lovely garments in which you'd invested so much work, but I could see no other way."

Lucy had another thought. "What of your mother? How did you explain the damage to her?"

"I detest that I had to lie, but lie I did. I told her it was obvious someone had broken into our trunks en route and had been rough with our clothes."

"*Our* clothes?"

"I'm afraid I damaged some of hers too."

Lucy was amazed by Rowena's act. She never would have guessed her capable of such a thing. But then, a gap in Rowena's story demanded attention. "Pardon me for bringing this up, but why would anyone damage your clothes? Why wouldn't they just steal them?"

Rowena stopped all movement, her mouth agape. "I don't know. That would have been the more logical thing to happen, wouldn't it?"

Lucy laughed. "It's clear you don't have the mind of a thief—which is a good thing."

"But Mother . . . did she see through my explanation as quickly as you did?"

"Obviously not."

Rowena sat on the ottoman, her head shaking. "Or if she did, she chose not to say anything." She looked directly at Lucy. "She knew I wanted you here. Could she have simply allowed my ruse?"

"I don't know her. Could she have been so kind?"

Rowena considered this a moment. "If that's so . . . why didn't she tell me she knew?"

All Lucy could do was shrug. "Whether she knew or not, I'm very grateful to her for allowing me to come."

Rowena shook her consideration away. "My mother is hard to understand. Sometimes she's my champion and other times she works against me."

Lucy thought of her own mother and could pinpoint moments when she'd felt the same way. "Perhaps that's what motherhood is: being loving *and* being tough."

Rowena looked at the watch pinned to her blouse. "She will be very tough with both of us if I'm not downstairs, dressed in the seersucker, in two hours."

Lucy weighed the quality of the light. "May I move a chair by the window?"

"You may do whatever you need to do." While Lucy moved the chair and got out the necessary supplies, Rowena retrieved the dress. Lucy got to work mending the sleeve.

Although the work was tedious, Lucy felt none of that emotion as joy took over. Not only was she in Newport with Rowena, not only had she been invited there, she had been summoned because Rowena cared for her as a friend. Lucy had never had a real friend.

She was the luckiest girl in the world.

⊙⊗⊙

Ninety minutes later, Lucy buttoned the back of Rowena's ivory voile top. Though bloused in front, it was cinched tight at the waist and neckline with embroidered bands. She remembered making twenty-two buttonholes for the tiny mother-of-pearl buttons that lined the back opening. She hated the task of buttonholes, especially in such delicate fabric, especially for a blouse that would remain hidden beneath a seersucker jacket. For no matter how warm the day, she knew Rowena would never remove it.

Speaking of . . . Lucy retrieved the jacket with its peplum waist and large embroidered collar. She held it while Rowena slipped it on, then adjusted the wedge that corrected the height difference of her shoulders and puffed out the enormous sleeves to best effect.

Next came the hat, which was small and flat but for rosettes and bows made from two shades of blue ribbon. Mamma had done a good job on this one, making it subtle but complementary to the rest of the suit.

Bone-colored kid boots rounded out the costume. "How do I look?" Rowena asked.

Lucy pointed to her own cheeks. "You're pale. A picnic in the sun will do you good."

Rowena pinched her cheeks and bit her lower lip. "But surely you know it's considered gauche for ladies of bearing to have a suntan. Although rosy cheeks *are* well considered."

"But why?" Lucy asked. "Surely showing evidence of being out in the sun and fresh air would be a good thing."

Rowena seemed a bit uncomfortable at the subject and merely shook her head. Then Lucy understood. "Is it because a darkened skin makes you look of lower class?"

Rowena offered a pained expression. "These are not my standards, Lucy, but they are standards nonetheless."

Lucy felt a gulf open between them, one that could never be altered any more than the color of their eyes or hair. They were what they were.

"Please don't be sad," Rowena said. "I meant no offense."

"I know you didn't." *You* didn't. But that still didn't remove the offense.

Rowena headed to the door. "To make amends, I do have a surprise for you."

"What is it?"

"I don't have time to tell you right now. But when I get back . . ." She smoothed her skirt and gathered her gloves. "Well, then, I'm off. Wish me well with Edward."

Lucy set aside her hurt and sincerely offered Rowena her best wishes.

Once she was alone, she turned back to the racks, chose another item, and returned to her mending.

The total silence of the room quickly enveloped her. Silence was still a rarity. At home and at work she was always in the presence of others, and the sounds of the street were but a few feet away.

Others . . . How were Mamma and Sofia doing? Was Bonwitter bothering them? Was Mr. Standish watching over them as he'd promised?

If only they could be here and see this house. When Lucy had first been invited she'd placed an image in her mind of what the house of a wealthy person would look like, yet her imagination paled in comparison to the reality of this . . . cottage.

Such a term was laughable. Why would they call these mansions cottages? Was it an inside joke? Or did it expose an essence of guilt for owning such places—such palaces—in the first place? Lucy would be embarrassed to have so much.

Of course it was easy for her to say such a thing, since she did *not* have and would *never* have . . .

She shook the thoughts away. Back to mending.

⁕

Edward helped Rowena to a bench on the lawn and sat beside her. Then he giggled, stifling it with a gloved hand.

She looked toward him. "What's so funny?"

He leaned back. "I dare not say."

"Then I dare you *to* say."

His eyes skimmed the eight others in their picnic party, all lined up neatly on a row of benches and chairs in the grass. "I've never attended a picnic where the participants sat in a neat line, nor one where servants set up tables with fine china and crystal."

Rowena looked down the row of top-hatted men with their spats and walking sticks, alternating with pastel-clad women—except for Mrs. Burnwald, who was still dressed in mourning. Rowena had never considered any of this odd. It was the way picnics were accomplished in Newport.

"You'd prefer to sit on the ground and let insects infest your luncheon?"

"Absolutely not," he said. "I'll fight any ant to the death if it dare attack my *foie gras*."

His tone was a concern. As an outsider it would behoove him to accept whatever mode of entertainment there be, in whatever form it was presented. "Do you mock us, Mr. DeWitt?"

He put a hand on her arm. "I tease you. If you'd rather I didn't . . . ?"

Teasing. He was teasing.

She put her hand on his, letting it linger. "You're good for me. You make me see things with a lighter view." She glanced back over the group, with their row of parasols at attention, even though the seating was situated in the shade. "When I was a child I used to go on less formal picnics, with hunks of bread and ham stolen from the pantry."

168

"Ah so. You are a thief?"

"Actually, my friend Morrie did the thievery. I merely told him where the food was kept." The memory took her away from the moment, and she smiled at the recollection of searching for lucky four-leaf clovers and feeding most of the bread to the birds.

"Should I be jealous of this Morrie?"

"Oh no, no. He's just a very good friend."

"A friend who has the ability to make you smile with fond memories."

She felt her face grow warm, for her picnics with Morrie were but one of many happy times together.

"You're blushing. Was the young Morrie bold on this picnic?"

Not on that one. But Morrie *had* delivered her first kiss. She'd been thirteen, and he two years older. He'd just helped her down from her horse where she was learning to ride sidesaddle when they'd suddenly noticed their close proximity and he'd leaned down to kiss her on the lips. She hadn't known what to do, so had popped the tip of his nose with her hand. Which had led to his doing the same for her, and . . .

"Hello? Rowena?"

She blinked the memory away just in time to accept a glass of lemonade from a footman.

Lucy rubbed her eyes. She'd been sewing for hours and the close handwork had taken its toll. She scanned the room for a clock, found none, but was certain many hours had passed. She set the dress aside and stood.

When would Rowena return? Should Lucy be here when she got back, or could she go up to her room? Was that considered against the rules?

She stretched her arms overhead and decided by the ache there and in her shoulders and neck that she would have to risk it. If someone stopped her, so be it. She could claim ignorance without lying.

Lucy was glad there was a door directly from the dressing room to the hallway. To go through Rowena's bedroom without her present would be uncomfortable.

Luckily, the hallway was empty. Lucy paused a moment to gain her bearings. Which way to the stairs?

She turned to the left and found the back stairs, but before she could begin her ascent to the next floor, a young man barreled up the stairway from the main floor and nearly collided with her. His trousers and shirt were covered with mud. She couldn't imagine what a stableboy or gardener was doing amid the private quarters of the house, but merely lowered her eyes to move past.

"Well well, look what we have here," the man said.

She was amazed at his cheeky manner. "I am not a *what*, I am a *who*. Now, if you don't—"

He laughed and put a hand on her arm, stopping her escape. "Point taken. And so then, *who* are you?"

The nerve of the man. She took a moment to blatantly take note of his messy clothes. "You're getting mud on the carpets."

"Then clean it up."

"Excuse me?"

He gave a little salute with two fingers to his forehead, then added, "I'll see you later, Lucy. I'll make sure of it." He walked off, down the hall from whence she'd come.

Lucy? He knew her name?

"How do you know—?"

He turned to a door, opened it, and smiled back at her. "I know everything that goes on around here. Everything. Ta-ta." He entered the room and closed the door behind himself.

Lucy was confused. He'd been messy like a servant, yet he'd entered one of the rooms as though he owned—

She gasped at her obvious mistake. He belonged here. He was part of the family—was he Rowena's wanton brother, Hugh? And to think she'd called him on his messy clothes.

Taking a break in her room was doubly needed.

Within the span of a few seconds, Lucy knew something was wrong. Her hat was gone from its perch on the dresser, the empty satchel that had held her clothing was missing from under the bed. She opened the drawers and found all her clothing gone too.

"They stole everything!" She repeated the words as a question. "They stole everything?" Who would do such a thing?

The need for answers dispelled her need for rest. Lucy headed belowstairs in search of Mrs. Donnelly or the butler, Mr. Timbrook. Spotting neither, she entered the kitchen.

"Pardon me . . ." She couldn't remember the cook's name.

"All right," the woman said, looking up from cutting up a chicken. "I'll excuse you. But what for?"

Two kitchen maids laughed softly.

Fine. She'd be the brunt of their jokes all they wanted, if only she could get her things back. "I went up to my room and found all my possessions gone."

"Yes, well . . ."

"I know I'm new, but I will not be treated in such a manner. If this is some sort of joke . . ."

The cook put down her meat cleaver and eyed Lucy with raised brows. "So being moved to the room of the lady's maid, right next to Miss Langdon, isn't good enough for you?"

"What?"

One of the maids spoke. "Care to tell us your secret? How do you rate coming here first class and getting moved next to the young mistress?"

"What are you talking about?" Were they talking about the dressing room?

Cook shrugged. "If you can't find the room, that's your problem. *I* have work to do."

No. It couldn't be. "I just came from there and none of my things—"

"You're still accusing us of stealing?" Cook asked.

"No, no, but . . ."

Cook flipped a hand at her in dismissal. "Go on, then. Go back to your domain and stay out of ours."

Lucy suffered sudden regrets at her accusation. She didn't want the servants to hate her. The consequences were troubling and unknown.

"Get on with you," Cook said. "Leave us peons to our work."

"I . . ." Lucy didn't know what to say, so said nothing and left. She hurried upstairs, hoping she didn't encounter anyone else who knew of her preferential treatment.

She hesitated at the door to Rowena's dressing room and knocked. When no one answered, she went inside. Her things were not inside. There had to be some other room nearby. Cook had said there was a room for the lady's maid here.

Lucy walked the perimeter of the room and saw no other door. Was she somehow supposed to sleep in here, amongst the clothes? Flummoxed, she put her hands upon her hips and sighed. It was then her gaze fell upon the opposite side of the room, where she spotted the top of a doorjamb above a rod heavy with dresses. She spread the clothes to either side and discovered a door. She opened it outward toward the next room, and entered. There, sitting on a bed, were her missing satchel and hat.

The room was no larger than her bedroom back home, but the furnishings were of nicer quality. The bed had an oak head- and footboard, and the dresser was crowned with an oval mirror. A tan upholstered chair sat in the corner, and a small window overlooked the back lawn. The floor was covered with a blue and maroon oriental rug, and there were hooks on the wall for her clothing.

The only odd thing about the room was that there was no door leading to the hallway. The only way in and out was through the door behind the dresses. And yet, as Lucy sat upon the bed, it made her feel rather safe. She was neatly tucked away in her own little space, far removed from the rest of the household.

"I can be happy here," she said aloud.

"I'm glad."

Lucy started as Rowena's voice came from the doorway. "You discovered my surprise. Are you pleased?"

"It's a lovely room."

"It's a quirky room, hidden away as it is. And I will admit I had you moved here for personal reasons. I like the idea of having you close. I hope you don't mind. I had your personal things moved while you were at breakfast. I should have told you before I left for the picnic. I didn't mean to worry you."

"I don't mind a bit." Lucy was glad she could be honest with her answer.

Rowena dangled a key before her. "This is the key to my dressing room. You can come and go through there."

Lucy pocketed the key. Then she remembered where Rowena had spent the afternoon. "How was the picnic?"

"Quite delightful. Come and help me out of this and I'll tell you all the details."

Lucy's stomach growled. And no wonder. She hadn't eaten anything since the few bites at breakfast. Lunch had been bypassed as she worked on Rowena's dresses, and now that it was dinnertime, she wasn't sure what to do.

After helping Rowena on with a dinner gown, she couldn't find the courage to go down to the kitchen to dine with the servants. She didn't feel up to enduring their disdain.

If only there was some way to venture into the pantry, where she could grab a loaf of bread or some cheese . . .

She suddenly remembered Rowena had ordered tea brought up late in the afternoon. Rowena had invited Lucy to join her, but Lucy had declined because it just hadn't seemed proper. But maybe . . . if Rowena hadn't consumed all of it . . .

Lucy ventured into the dressing room, then tentatively into Rowena's bedroom. There, on a table near the fireplace, was the tea tray. The tea water was tepid, but Lucy poured herself a cup. And the plate of scones held but one half left behind.

Lucy started to devour it, then realizing it might be all she'd have for dinner, ate it slowly, savoring every bite. She licked her finger and smashed it against every crumb on the plate.

So much for preferential treatment.

※※

"Ahhhh!"

Everyone in the workroom looked toward Mamma. But where was she?

There she was, under her worktable, half lying on the floor. Sofia knelt beside her. "What's wrong, Mamma? What are you doing under here? Give me your hand."

Mamma pushed her hand away. "I dropped a tin of beads and went to pick them up and twisted my back. I can't move."

Mamma ended up inching her way out from under the table, and with the help of the ladies, got to her chair. But when that position caused pain, and since it was the end of the day, Mrs. Flynn told her to go upstairs to the apartment so she could lie down.

Tessie helped Sofia get Mamma up the stairs and to bed. Every movement, no matter how slight, made her groan.

"Are you sure I can't get you anything?" Sofia asked.

Mamma closed her eyes. "I just need to rest. I need to let my muscles relax."

Sofia thought about the cleaning they did every night. "Don't worry about the cleaning. I'll do it."

Tessie piped up, "I'll stay behind and help if you'd like."

It was a tempting offer, but after kissing a stranger the other day, after behaving so childishly, handling the cleaning on her own was a must. "Thanks, but I'll be all right."

After getting Mamma a glass of water and setting some bread and butter close enough for her to reach, Sofia headed downstairs to clean.

"Be careful," Mamma said.

Her words took Sofia aback. Careful?

Oh. Bonwitter.

She'd be alone in the shop. Although they hadn't been bothered by Bonwitter for a while, he was still out there.

Why had Mamma reminded her?

Sofia locked Mamma inside the apartment and entered the empty shop, locking that door too. The silence rushed around her like a phantom taking her captive. She held her breath, not knowing what to do to break the awful spell.

The truth was, she was rarely alone. Yes, she liked to go off to read, but she was always near others. She couldn't remember a single time she'd been so utterly on her own.

Light a lamp!

She was rather ashamed to realize it had always been Mamma's job to step into the dark lobby and light the gas sconces. *I've been letting someone else take care of me even in that. . . .*

Once the lamps were lit, the fear abated, but only a bit. Sofia took care of the silence by making as much noise as possible. She began singing as she burst through the curtain to the workroom and lit those lamps. " 'East Side, West Side, all around the town. The tots sang 'ring-around-rosie,' 'London Bridge is falling down.' Boys and girls together, me and Mamie O'Rourke, tripped the light fantastic on the sidewalks of New York.' "

She gathered the scraps and deposited them in the bin. But she needed a broom and the dustpan.

They were in the back. In the storeroom.

Another dark place. Sofia hummed and opened the door tentatively. Where *was* the lamp in here? During the day, the alley window provided light, and at night . . . Mamma or Lucy always lit the lamp.

With only the light from the workroom cutting a swath into the blackness, Sofia tried to remember if the lamp was to the left or right of the door.

Right. Just a few steps to the—

"Hey there, sweet Sofia."

Her heart stopped, and a match was struck. Bonwitter lit the lamp and grinned at her.

"What are you doing here?"

"I've come to see you, girlie." He looked past her to the workroom. "Your Mamma's not with you tonight."

Sofia thought fast. "Yes she is. She's cleaning the lobby."

He strolled toward her, making her back up. "No she's not. I saw you and Tessie taking her upstairs. It's just you and me."

Sofia lunged for the broom and held the straw end toward him. "Stay away from me."

He was not deterred and continued his approach, his eyes intense. "Where's your sister? I haven't seen her around lately."

It gave Sofia some comfort to know Bonwitter had gaps in his knowledge. "She's probably halfway to the police by now."

For a quick moment he looked worried. "She wasn't here with you. I haven't seen her since—"

"Lucy came in after me, and as I said, I'm sure she's talking to the coppers right now. You'd better leave, unless you want to get caught." She was surprised her words sounded forceful, because inside she felt she would faint from the fear.

"You're a feisty thing, aren't you? How 'bout you and I act out a scene from one of your trashy novels?" He raised his eyebrows suggestively.

"Stop that!" She was appalled when her voice cracked. She cleared her throat and tried again. "Get out of here!"

He grabbed the end of the broom and they struggled for control. He yanked it away from her and flung it across the room. Sofia looked for something else to use as a weapon, but there was little to choose from. She grabbed a tube of cloth and swung it at him. She hit his shoulder.

"Whoa there, girlie. You've got quite an arm on you." But then he grabbed the end of the tube as he'd done with the broom.

There was no way she could win this battle. She needed to get away. She moved right, then quickly changed direction when he came after her and managed to get to the door leading to the alley. The lock slowed her down, and he grabbed her, but his hold lessened when she stomped hard on his foot.

The door opened and she ran through it, down the alley, with Bonwitter in fast pursuit.

The street. The main street . . . just a few more yards . . .

She burst out of the alley and immediately ran to a man walking with a woman on his arm. "Please, help me! A man is chasing—"

Bonwitter ran out from the alley and pulled up short.

"Say there," said her savior. "What do you mean running after this young lady?"

With his chest heaving, Bonwitter ran a hand through his greasy hair, tugged at his vest and coat, and pointed at Sofia. "This isn't over." Then he walked away.

The woman put her arm around Sofia. "Are you all right? Did he hurt you?"

"I'm fine."

"No, you're not fine. You're shaking." She turned to the man. "William, let's get this girl home."

That sounded wonderful, and Sofia could think of nothing better than to be upstairs with Mamma. But she remembered the back door to the shop was open. The gas lamps were flaming. She needed to lock up. "Can you bring me to the back door of the shop, please? I'll be fine once I'm inside."

The couple escorted her down the alley, and the man insisted on waiting until he heard the bolt on the door lock up tight.

Home, get home became Sofia's goal. She picked up the tube of fabric and rolled the material smooth, then looked around for the broom. It was on the far side of the storeroom, amid the shadows.

Suddenly, her ordeal returned to her with fresh teeth and she was newly afraid. There was no way she could turn out the lamps. No way she could venture onto the street and up the stairs to her apartment. Bonwitter might be waiting for her.

Sofia looked toward the alley window, half expecting to see him peering in at her. She moved into the workroom and was beginning to go into the lobby when she started to worry after *those* windows. If Bonwitter was outside he would be able to see her, stalk her.

She closed the curtain of the workroom tight, and did the same with the door to the storeroom. The workroom was safe—or safe-er.

Yet standing there exposed . . . Sofia crawled under Mamma's worktable and pulled the chair in behind her. She scooted into a corner and drew her knees to her chest to wait out the night.

Keep me safe. Keep me safe. . . .

Sofia started to wakefulness at the sound of a door opening. Within seconds she remembered where she was, and why. Had Bonwitter come back?

Her heart beat wildly, and she pulled her feet even closer to her body, making herself as small as possible. Maybe if she held her breath, he wouldn't know she was—

"Sofia?"

Mamma!

Sofia pushed the chair away so she could exit her hiding place. "Here, Mamma. In here!"

Mamma came through the curtain and, with one hand to her back, held the other one out to Sofia, helping her crawl from under the table and to standing. "What are you doing? You didn't come up and it's the middle of the night and—"

"Bonwitter was here. He was going to hurt me and—"

The details didn't matter. Mamma was there. She was safe.

For now.

CHAPTER THIRTEEN

amma knocked on the bathroom door. "Sofia, come. We'll be late."

Sofia stood behind the door, hugging herself. The memory of her encounter with Bonwitter enveloped her like a dense fog. "I'm not feeling well this morning, Mamma. Make my excuses to Mrs. Flynn."

Mamma's voice softened. "I know you had a hard night, *piccolina*, but you can't let that man keep you from making a living."

She edged away from Mamma's words and stepped into the bathtub, sinking down amid its high cast-iron walls. She pulled her knees to her chest as she'd done in her hiding place under the worktable. If only she had a blanket to drape over her head, she would truly feel—

"Please, Sofia . . ."

"I just can't Mamma. Not when he's still out there."

At first Mamma didn't reply; then she said, "I'll talk to Mrs. Flynn first thing and she'll get word to Mr. Standish. He will come and make everything right."

But would he? In spite of his efforts—and the efforts of the police—Bonwitter was running free.

Free to hurt me.

Sofia heard the front door closing and the muffled sound of Mamma's feet upon the stairs.

And then silence—an awful silence that made Sofia fear the sound of her own breathing, the beating of her own heart.

She scrambled out of the tub, and out of the apartment. Being with the ladies would ease her fears.

Perhaps.

⁂

"Oh dear. Pardon me," Lucy said.

Rowena looked askance as Lucy helped her with her morning dress. "If you don't mind my asking, am I hearing hunger pangs?"

Lucy covered her midsection with a hand. The pains had plagued her all night, receding for a time, only to grab on with new vengeance.

Rowena turned to face her. "When was the last time you ate?"

Lucy decided to ignore the half scone because it seemed so pitiful. "Yesterday morning."

"Why haven't you eaten the other meals?"

Lucy wasn't sure how much she should say. To bring the wrath of a family member down upon the servants would not help her situation. But the fact remained, she needed to eat. "I don't feel at ease eating with the others."

"Why not?"

"You've treated me in a manner far above most—"

"This is ridiculous. They should rejoice in your treatment, not condemn you for it." She walked toward the bell pull that would summon a servant.

Lucy rushed to stop her. "Please don't."

Rowena studied her a moment. "Is the situation that bad?"

Lucy shrugged. And yet, she *was* living in a no-man's-land between the servants and the family.

"This is ridiculous." Before Lucy could stop her, Rowena rang for help.

"You really don't need to intervene."

"It appears I do. You must have sustenance. I need you healthy."

Lucy conceded. "I *will* work better if my stomach is full."

"I need you healthy because you are my friend."

Lucy was touched.

There was a knock on the door and Sadie entered. "Yes, miss?"

"I'm giving you a special assignment, Sadie. Do you think you can manage it?"

Sadie nodded. "Of course, miss."

"I'm assigning you the job of bringing Miss Scarpelli her meals, up here to her room."

Sadie's face fell. "Up here?"

"Three meals a day, without fail. Do you understand?"

"Yes, miss."

"Starting with breakfast. As soon as possible."

Sadie bobbed a curtsy. "Yes, miss." She nodded at Lucy, but there was a tightening of resentment in her eyes.

Oh well. At least she would eat.

༺❀༻

Lucy cut the thread and held the dinner dress for a final inspection. One more down. Dozens to go.

As she tackled the repair of Rowena's wardrobe, Lucy wished Rowena had done a lesser job of creating a need for Lucy's services. Without the benefit of a sewing machine, the handwork was tedious and seemed never ending.

And yet, Lucy also didn't want the work to be done too soon. When else would she ever get a chance to be in such a house, in such a place?

She hung the dress upon the rack and detoured to the window. The grounds beckoned, and Lucy remembered Rowena's words said just this morning. *"You are not a prisoner in this house, Lucy. Do your work, but also feel free to go outside and take a stroll. There is a lovely Cliff Walk that edges all the properties and the sea. To the homeowners' chagrin, it's public. But by all*

*means, take advantage of it. You'll find the views of the water breathtaking—though
please be careful. The rocks can be treacherous."*

While she made up her mind, Lucy closed her eyes and took a
deep breath. The confident breeze that entered the opened window
was starkly different from its meek brother in the city, that pitiful draft
that vainly tried to break the heat. This ocean breeze had substance
and was strengthened by an aroma so fresh that Lucy *had* to find its
source. It called to her, luring her to join it out-of-doors.

Since she had the permission, the very encouragement, of her mistress, Lucy put on her hat, secured it with a pin, and set out for the sea.

Lucy slipped out a side entrance of the house and made her way
across the grass, through a formal garden, toward the sea. She purposely
chose a course that kept her slightly hidden from view. She didn't want
anyone in the house to look after her and wonder. Nor did she want to
run into one of the outside workers, who might question who she was
and why she was trespassing on the Langdon property.

She soon found the Cliff Walk on the other side of a low stone wall.
It was barely wide enough for two and meandered in either direction,
tracing the edge of the manicured properties, offering an accessible
divide between land and sea.

She turned south and began to walk. The narrow path, with land
on her right and a sharp drop-off to the rocks on her left, demanded
her attention, and the only time she could enjoy the view was when
she stopped walking. As she did now.

The ocean stretched before her, meeting the sky. She remembered
being on the ship to America, standing next to her father.

"See how the horizon line is always at the level of your eyes?"
Papa had said. And she'd stood and stooped and sat, marveling at this
wonder of wonders.

"But it's so far away, Papa. Is America really out there?"

"So I've heard."

"What will we find there?"

"Whatever we seek," he said. *"Chi cerca trova."* Seek and you shall find.

But had they found what they'd sought? Surely her mother and father hadn't sought poverty, deplorable living conditions, or an early death.

The waves crashed upon the rocks below with such power that Lucy started.

With her sudden movement, her boot slipped upon the small stones on the walk.

And off the edge.

She slid down a short embankment, landing on a narrow ledge. Unloosed pebbles continued from the ledge to their death in the water below.

Her heart pulsed wildly in her throat. Just a few inches more and she too would have tumbled to the sea.

Lucy grappled for handholds. She pressed her cheek and her body against the earthen wall. Surely the frantic beating of her heart would push her away from safety, sending her hurling backward into the greedy sea.

She carefully looked over her shoulder at the guilty waves. They'd come dangerously close to distracting her right into a catastrophe.

Help me. Please help me.

Her prayer was an embarrassment. Why should God help her? She'd ignored Him more oft than not. If she wanted to get out of this predicament, *she* needed to find a way back to the path that mocked her. But how? It rose above her, a few inches higher than her head.

I wish I'd told someone where I was going.

She carefully resituated her feet upon their tenuous ledge, and felt shivers course up her spine as if the sea were a boogeyman intent on catching her. The sound of the waves, crashing upon the shore—too close—intensified her need to get back up to the path in all its dubious safety.

Calm down, Lucy. You can do this. One step, one handhold at a time.

Her eyes grazed across the rocks, dirt, and plants that covered the wall before her. If she put her left foot there, and held on up there with her right hand . . . If only she could let go enough to rid herself of her stupid hat so she could fully see, then—

A man appeared in her sightline, on the path to her left, carefully peering over at her. "Hello there. Are you all right?"

It struck her as a silly question. "Let's just say I didn't plan to be teetering on this ledge."

"Are you sure?" he said. "For it does offer an exquisite view of the waves."

She was in no mood to banter. "If you please? Help me up."

The young man dropped to his knees and studied her situation, his blue eyes darting from one outcropping to the next. "I think if you walk a bit to the right you can step on that flat rock there, which will lift you up enough for me to get my hands around your arms."

"You can't lift—"

"Do you have a better idea?"

"No."

"Then you have no choice but to trust me."

He spoke the truth and went over the plan again, adding a few more details of where she should put her hands and feet. He looked at her hat warily. "I think it will work best if we both rid ourselves of our hats."

Gladly. Heartened by his presence, Lucy kept hold of the world with one hand while removing her hatpin with the other. She dropped it into the sea. Then she handed her hat to the man. He removed his own, revealing a shock of unruly dark blond hair.

"Are you ready, then?" he asked.

"I am." The waves crashed beneath her, mocking her. They were also ready to receive her as an offering if things went terribly wrong.

The man stooped directly above the place they had talked about, then changed his mind and got to his knees again. "When I have you, I'll need you to swing your leg up to the path."

Any thoughts of the action being unladylike were quickly dismissed as Lucy's survival mode took hold. "Agreed."

"Then let's do it. Right foot on the flat rock . . ."

He led her through the plan, just as he'd laid it out. She felt his hands lock around her forearms and begin to pull her upward.

"Swing your leg up!" he ordered.

She did as she was told, and by his pulling her toward him and leaning back, she was able to scramble the rest of the way, falling into his arms, over his legs as they sprawled across the pathway.

"I'm safe," she whispered. His face was mere inches from hers.

"And so you are," he whispered back.

Propriety ended the moment and they awkwardly found their footing and stood. They brushed off their clothes and the man retrieved their hats. Once they were presentable, they stood face-to-face.

"You saved me," Lucy said. "I am in your debt."

He touched the brim of his hat and nodded. "I'm glad I was here to help. I've heard there's not a season goes by where a few are not lost to the sea in just such a manner."

Really? The enormity of the danger made Lucy's legs waver. "I need to sit, please."

He helped her find seating upon a stone wall. "May I?" he asked.

"Of course."

He sat beside her and took an exaggerated breath. "Well, then. That was rather exciting."

"I don't know what I would have done if you hadn't come along."

"There would have been others. Eventually. The Cliff Walk is well traveled."

"But who knows if they would have assumed the part of hero as you did."

He shuffled his shoulders. "I was rather brave, wasn't I?"

"Terribly."

Lucy felt a pain in her calf and put a hand on it.

"Are you injured?"

"I don't . . ." She turned her body away from him so she could lift her skirt enough to check. Her stocking was torn and her leg bloody. She turned back to catch him looking.

"You're bleeding."

"Just a little."

He retrieved a handkerchief from his pocket. "Here."

"No, no, I wouldn't want to dirty it."

"Don't be ridiculous. In fact . . ." He looked toward the private property behind them, scrambled onto the grass on the other side of the stone wall, and ran to a gazebo a few dozen yards away.

Lucy feared he would get into trouble, trespassing as he was. "Come back here. What are you doing?"

Then she saw him dip his handkerchief in a birdbath. He returned, wringing it out. "I'm afraid it's not the cleanest water, but the wetness should help wipe away the worst of it."

She took it and dabbed at the scrape. "You shouldn't have trespassed like that. What if someone would have seen you."

"You're right," he said. "I could have been arrested for stealing bird water. I wonder what the penalty is for that grievous offense."

She allowed herself a laugh. The atmosphere of this land of wealth had intimidated her past common sense. Why should anyone care if someone stepped a few paces upon their lawn? Yet, even as she made this rationalization, she knew they probably *did* care, and in a worst-case situation, there could be repercussions.

Lucy was used to being the best of her class, an achiever, a woman in control. Yet here she belonged to no class and had very little con—

"I lost you there," he said.

"Sorry. I was thinking."

"Be careful with that. It can get you into trouble, especially in this city of frippery, finery, and falderal. It's all about the show and the spectacle. What the eye can see and the ear can hear."

"But never what the mind can think?"

"It's best not."

She laughed again, then realized she needed to get back. Rowena may have returned from her luncheon. "I must be going."

He helped her to her feet and she tested the pain in her leg by putting her weight upon it.

"Would you like me to help you home?"

That would never do. "No, thank you. I'll be fine. I've felt worse."

"Ah. A veritable trooper. An admirable trait."

Lucy felt a wave of pleasure that she'd impressed him. "Well, then . . ." She extended her hand. "Thank you for your heroics."

"Any time. And since we've faced death together, I do believe we should exchange names."

"I'm Lucy."

He clicked his heels together, then shook her hand. "Bartholomew—"

"Bartholomew? That's not a very heroic-sounding name."

"Then what shall I be called?"

Lucy knew little of heroic men and couldn't answer.

"Perhaps Odysseus or Achilles?"

She'd never heard of them.

"Or, I know," he said. "How about Shadrach, Meshach, or Abednego?"

"You're making fun of me."

"Perhaps a little. But I assure you, these were all heroic men. So choose a name, perhaps a name that means something to you."

The only name that came to mind was Dante, her father's name. "Dante."

"Dante Alighieri? The great Italian poet?"

Lucy had never felt so ignorant. This man seemed to know everything, and she nothing. "Dante, my father. He was the most heroic man I ever knew."

He studied her a moment. "Your father was very lucky to have such a loyal and appreciative daughter. I hope one day my children will look upon me in such a way."

Lucy felt herself redden. The conversation had veered into a place too personal. She really needed to get back to the Langdons', so she turned and tapped him on one shoulder and then the other. "I hereby declare from this day forward that you—being a hero—shall be called Dante."

He bowed low, sweeping his hat far to one side. "I am honored, Lady Lucy."

She attempted her first curtsy, then turned back the way she had come. Once on her way she glanced over her shoulder and saw him standing there, looking after her.

The sensation was quite pleasurable.

⊙⊙⊙

"Where have you been?"

Lucy pulled up short at the foot of the back stairway.

Margaret, Rowena's reluctant lady's maid, stood before her, arms crossed.

Lucy wasn't sure whether to bow to her and be contrite, or stand tall and take a stand. She decided on a bit of each.

"I needed some fresh air, and my eyes needed a rest from the close handwork." She looked up the stairs. "Was I needed?"

Margaret hesitated. "You should be here."

"I am here. Now."

Margaret's nose twitched before she spun on her heel and walked away.

Add another enemy to Lucy's list.

Rowena appeared in the corridor leading to the front of the house, wearing a blue smock over her dress. "I thought I heard your voice. Come with me. I've got a project for the two of us."

Lucy followed Rowena into the wide corridor of the main floor, and back to the rear veranda, where two easels were set up, one boasting a blank canvas and the other a partial landscape.

Rowena handed Lucy a paintbrush and a flat piece of wood with a hole in it. "Have you ever painted before?"

It was a laughable question. When in her life would she have had the opportunity or the inclination to paint a picture? "Never," she said.

"Then it's time you gave it a try. Mother has blatantly stated that all young ladies need to learn to be artistic."

Lucy had other things on her mind. She looked over the stone balustrade to the lawn and the sea beyond—the sea that had nearly taken her prisoner. *If not for Dante.*

"What do you think of my feeble attempt?"

Lucy transferred her gaze from reality to representation. She could see remnants of the scene on the painting in progress, though there was something off about the proportions.

"Wear this," Rowena said, bringing forward a green smock for Lucy's use. She helped button it in the back, then showed Lucy a wooden box full of tubes, each wrapped with a colored band. "And here are your colors. Just squeeze a little paint onto your palette and begin."

Lucy had to laugh at Rowena's swift instructions, as if just like that, by wearing the correct costume and holding the correct tools, she would instantly become an artist.

"What?" Rowena asked. "You won't even try?"

"Of course I'll try. But don't expect much."

"That's what I tell my mother every day. Now . . . consider the view."

Lucy did just that. And yet it was a strange experience to look upon something with the intent of reproducing it.

"Come, now," Rowena said, taking up her own palette and brush. "Just begin. You can't get it wrong—at least not really."

Lucy wasn't certain about that, but she looked at the horizon where blue met blue, and noticed the blue of the ocean was slightly darker. The sea was benign at this distance, a powerless swath of color.

She began at this joining of sea and sky and enjoyed the feel of the stroke as paint met canvas and left behind evidence of her intent. When she needed a lighter blue, she added some white to it and swirled the two colors together to make a third.

And what if she added the tiniest tinge of purple to the mix?

Rowena was perched on the edge of a high stool, busy with her own creation. "Where were you?" Rowena asked.

Lucy tried to gauge if there was any anger in her voice, and found none. "I took a walk on the grounds and on the Cliff Walk. I hope you don't mind."

"Of course not. I suggested it. You are not my slave, Lucy. You may come and go as you please."

The level of trust exhibited by Rowena contrasted sharply with the confining attitude of the household staff.

"Did you enjoy the Cliff Walk?" Rowena asked as she squeezed green paint upon her palette.

"The view is breathtaking."

"I love the ocean. I love sailing on my family's yacht—or used to."

"You don't go anymore?"

"I have trouble finding my footing now."

So Rowena's handicap had not always been with her.

Rowena changed the subject. "You must be careful on the Walk, though. It can get very slippery."

"I know," Lucy said. "I fell."

Rowena's brush stopped in midair. "Were you hurt?"

"A little. But I was saved by a very nice man who pulled me up from a ledge—"

"A ledge! You fell to a ledge?"

Lucy marked a place taller than herself. "I was this far down from the walkway. I don't know how I would ever have gotten out if this man hadn't saved me."

"What's his name?"

Lucy smiled at the memory of their banter. "Dante," she said.

"His last name?"

"We only exchanged first names."

Rowena's brow creased. "I don't know anyone by the name of Dante."

Of course not. "It's just as well. I—"

"Was he charming? Do you wish to see him again?"

Did she?

"You do, don't you? You like him very much."

"I'm not one to be attracted so easily." *If at all.*

"But *like.* Do you like him? Would you like to see him again?"

Lucy was not used to talking about romance. Romance was for other women, women who weren't responsible for a mother and sister. Women who had time to swoon and chatter and primp.

Yet Dante was special. He was a "giver," a trait often lacking in people of either gender. She added more paint to the sky, leaving voids for the white of the clouds. "I suppose I'd like to see him. But not in the way you assume."

Rowena's eyes sparkled as she pointed her brush at Lucy. "You pretend to be above romance, but your stance is not quite believable."

"Believe it or not, I'm not searching for a beau. Or a mate. I am quite content to be on my own."

"Then you are one of a thousand. Once a woman is twenty, she is on the road to being an old maid."

At twenty-four I am the oldest maid there is.

In a way, Lucy liked the idea that she was not a normal woman who wanted marriage and children. She was unique.

"Romance or no," Rowena said, "you should go to the Cliff Walk every day in hopes of seeing him. For conversation's sake. Or out of gratitude."

It seemed silly. Contrived. "You assume he wishes to see *me* again. Remember, I caused him much trouble."

"Saving a damsel in distress is hardly trouble for a gentleman. A true gentleman longs for the chance to do just that as a way to prove his worth."

"Then perhaps I should fall a second time."

Rowena pointed her paintbrush at Lucy, and annoyance was added to her voice. "Stop making fun of the situation. A man graciously saved you from great peril. You like him. It's only logical you at least try to see him again."

Lucy regretted causing her distress. "You assume he's a creature of habit?"

"I assume he'll try to be there at the same time tomorrow in the hopes of seeing you. How else can he expect to find you again?"

The workings of a romantic mind . . . Lucy mixed some gray paint with white and applied it in soft swirls, creating clouds. "Perhaps he doesn't wish to find me."

"Perhaps. But just in case . . . you must go. Newport is known for its romantic matches. People come here for pleasure, to relax. And in such a state they are open to the wiles of love."

"I don't use wiles. I don't trick men to love me." *I don't want them to love me.*

"I'm sure you don't."

Lucy couldn't tell if Rowena considered this an admirable quality or a failing.

"Have you been in love before?" Rowena asked.

Lucy sat on the stool, her thoughts flitting back to Mulberry Street. Perhaps if she told Rowena about her one foray with love, she would be left alone. "His name was Angelo."

"Was he as angelic as his name?"

Lucy shook her head. There was little angelic about Angelo, except . . . "He loved me."

"But that wasn't enough?"

The complications of her relationship with Angelo blurred. Lucy didn't want to go into the details. "I had to put my family first. He didn't understand."

"So he didn't love you enough."

"Or I didn't love him enough."

Rowena sighed. "How does one know when they are in love?"

Lucy didn't have enough experience to offer an opinion. "Are you in love with Edward?"

"I hope to learn to love him."

"Is that possible?"

"My mother learned to love my father."

"Did he learn to love her in return?"

Rowena seemed to have no answer to that. Instead she said, "Father has instructed me to love Edward. He says girls like me must not be fussy or choosy."

Lucy took offense on her behalf. "Girls like you . . . that's not very kind."

Rowena moved awkwardly across the room to retrieve a rag. Even with her slow gait there was evidence of her infirmity. "Girls with my impediment are tainted."

"Tainted?"

"We are imperfect and therefore not worthy of a marriage of high esteem."

"That's ridiculous. You're more worthy than a thousand women with perfect legs. Your kindness and loving heart overshadow any physical irregularity."

Rowena lifted her arms wide, palms up. "You are too kind, Lucy, but look around you. My clothing, this house, the grounds, the area around Bellevue Avenue in its entirety . . . it's all about perfection, about attaining something above and beyond what's ever been created before."

"But it's false. It's a dreamland. Life's not like this for most people."

"Which is the point."

The words of Lucy's father interrupted her thoughts, and she shared the phrase. *"Non è tutto oro quello che luce."*

"That's beautiful. What does it mean?"

"All that glitters is not gold."

Rowena considered this a moment. "Perhaps the reverse is also true? All that's gold does not glitter?"

Lucy loved how their conversations made her think. "You are very wise."

Rowena left her perch to study Lucy's progress. "And you are ridiculously talented. Are you certain you've not painted before?"

Rowena sat on her stool, cleaning their brushes. She'd sent Lucy up to her room to ready a dress for a formal dinner they were having that evening. But in truth, it was an excuse to study Lucy's painting against her own.

Unfortunately, she found her own lacking. Where Lucy had captured the sea, sky, and lawn with deft strokes and splashes of expertly mixed color, Rowena's attempt looked like a five-year-old's dabbling.

Was there nothing Lucy couldn't do well? She designed clothing and constructed it, and now was an artist with paint. Creativity flowed out of her with a fresh clarity like water from a spring. Rowena wouldn't be surprised if Lucy could sing like an angel and play Chopin like a virtuoso.

What flowed out of Rowena? She had no ability on any musical instrument, and sounded like a screaming seagull when she sang. Her needlepoint was lumpy and her tatting always got tangled. As for her painting ability?

Rowena loaded her brush in deep blue and painted a large X on her canvas, then another and another, until her feeble attempt was obliterated. She tossed the painting in the bushes on the other side of the balustrade. Her breathing had grown ragged, and she felt her heart beating in her throat. A heat more stifling than anything summer could summon tightened like a shroud around her, making her claw at the smock, needing it off, needing air.

"Rowena!"

At the sound of her mother's voice, Rowena froze with one shoulder of the smock hanging precariously at her waist and the other side caught upon the volume of her dress sleeve. A hank of hair fell across her face.

"What is going on here?"

"Help me get this off, please."

Mother pulled the smock free. Then she spotted the painting. Her face washed with pleasure. "You did this?"

Rowena wasn't sure what to say. It was the first time her mother had given any indication of pleasure upon seeing her paint—

Only it wasn't *her* painting. But she couldn't reveal the truth just yet. Had she been right in thinking Lucy had talent?

"Do you like it?"

Mother moved right, then left, trying to capture the best light. "I insist you enter it in the art show next month. And if Mamie Fish doesn't award you a first-place ribbon, I'll deny her entrance into this house."

Rowena couldn't withhold the truth any longer.

"Lucy will be thrilled to hear that."

"Lucy?"

"Lucy Scarpelli? It's her painting. I thought it showed true talent, but now to hear your opinion . . . she will be thrilled to hear it merits a place in the art show."

Mother whipped toward Rowena, her cheeks a blotchy red. "Don't be ridiculous."

Rowena felt her own cheeks grow hot. "But you said—"

"I thought it was your work."

"But talent is talent. If the work is good enough to be entered, then it shouldn't matter who—"

Mother went back into the house, the train of her dress sashaying wildly across the floor to keep up.

Rowena was left to mull over the status of her own insipid talent and the inequities of her world.

⁂

"Sofia, get me another box of pins."

Sofia looked toward the storeroom with trepidation. She'd been avoiding going back there all day, and so far had managed to tag her need for supplies onto someone else's errand.

Dorothy repeated herself. "Sofia? Pins?"

Mamma stood. "I'll get them."

Mrs. Flynn looked up from the order she was writing. She eyed Mamma, then Sofia. "We aren't dumb, little girl. We've all noticed how you've avoided going in the back today. I'm sorry about what happened to you, and I've talked to Mr. Standish, who's going to talk to the police. We've done all we can do. But you have to do the work required or I'll dock your pay."

"Baby Sofia," Tessie whispered.

"Scaredy cat, scaredy cat," added Leona.

"You can have your mamma do your work for you," Ruth said.

Sofia flushed with anger and embarrassment. She'd like to see one of these ladies handle Bonwitter as she'd done the night before. See if they wouldn't be scared too.

But even Mamma nodded toward the back, indicating she should go.

"Fine," she said, pushing her chair away from the sewing machine. As she walked toward the door, her arms tingled and she got a creepy feeling up her back. Logically, she knew he wasn't there, but . . .

She walked into the storeroom and let her eyes adjust to the dimmer light. Maybe if she kept her gaze straight ahead and walked very quickly, she could get back before her courage left—

She turned toward a tapping on the alley window. There, with his nose pressed against the pane, was Bonwitter!

Sofia ran back into the workroom. "He's at the window! He's come to get me!"

Dorothy and Mrs. Flynn shook their heads in disgust and entered the storeroom while Sofia ran into Mamma's arms.

"Are you sure you saw him?" Dolly whispered from the next worktable.

Sofia nodded with her head against Mamma's shoulder. She let go when Dorothy and Mrs. Flynn came back into the room. "Did you see him?"

"There's no one there. No one in the alley either," Dorothy said.

"I even walked down to the street and looked both ways. He wasn't there," Mrs. Flynn said. "It's your imagination run wild."

"But I saw him!"

Mrs. Flynn shrugged. "I can't have you screaming at every fly on the wall, girl. Get yourself under control." She nodded to the room. "Everyone, back to work."

They didn't believe her? "But why would I make that up?" she asked anyone who would listen.

"Oh, I don't know," Leona said under her breath. "Perhaps so you can go home early? Or have time to go read one of your silly books."

Sofia looked to Mamma for support, but even she pointed toward the sewing machine. "Best get back to work."

"Surely you believe—?"

Mamma's shrug was a wound to her soul.

※

There was a knock on the dressing room door. Good. Dinner. Lucy was famished.

She went to answer it. "I'm glad you're here, Sadie. I was about to wither—"

"Hello."

At the sight of the man she'd accosted because of his dirty boots, Lucy took a step back.

"Your dinner, mademoiselle?"

She collected herself enough to ask, "Where's Sadie?"

"I intercepted her in the hall and asked where she was going." He pressed past her into the dressing room and set the tray on the ottoman. "I think it's time we were properly introduced. I am Rowena's younger, but oh-so-handsome, brother. Hugh is the name. And you are the Lucy I've heard so much about."

"What have you heard?"

He leaned toward her and made his eyebrows dance. "Don't worry. Your secrets are safe with me."

"What secrets?"

He ignored her. "So this is where you've moved."

"Not here, but next—" She stopped herself from mentioning her actual sleeping quarters, hidden away as it was. "Yes, your sister wanted me close."

"Good for her." He winked. "And me."

His very presence made her nervous—and oddly, a little angry. "Thank you. That will be all."

He looked at her askance. "Is this how you dismiss all your servants?"

"I . . . no, of course, I just . . . I'm just hungry. So if you don't mind?"

He strolled along the rows of dresses, letting his fingers skim every one. Did he know about her room? If not, she didn't want him to discover it. He was coming distressingly close to the break in the dresses. He'd see the door and—

She tried to divert him. "So, Mr. Langdon. Are you in college or are you being groomed to take over your father's business?" *Whatever that is.*

He stopped within inches of the opening in the dresses, took a quick glance, then looked at her. "Both."

She sat beside the tray and took a roll, breaking it in two, desperate to divert him. "Would you like to share?"

He grinned, came forward, and took her offering. "Thank you."

Lucy regretted her gesture, in that it prolonged his presence. "Won't your family be waiting for you at dinner?"

"They're used to me being late."

NANCY MOSER

Lucy could imagine they were used to Hugh exhibiting a myriad of faults.

"So, Lucy," he said, "how are you finding life at *Porte au Ciel?*"

"Very well, thank you. I'm glad to be of service to your sister."

He snickered. "Rowena needs all the help she can get."

Lucy felt her dander rise. "Why do you say that? She's extremely sweet and charming. She's a good—"

"All traits that *sound* enticing, but traits that bore most suitors."

"You don't like women who are sweet, charming, and good?"

His eyes held an intensity that made her stomach tighten. "There are other traits more to my liking."

It was her own fault for asking, and Lucy wanted him gone. "Your sister possesses traits most men would covet—beyond the ones I mentioned. She is courageous, determined, and—"

"And broken."

Lucy moved to the door. "If you don't mind, Mr. Langdon, I prefer to eat my dinner alone."

"Ignoring her handicap will not make it go away."

"I do not ignore it; I look past it." She put her hand on the doorknob.

"Do you want to know how she was injured?"

Actually . . . She let go of the knob. "Certainly. If you'd care to share."

He walked toward her, his hands in the pockets of his evening trousers. "My sister is a klutz. When she was thirteen she slipped while running on the family yacht and landed badly on her hip. She has no grace at all. Never has."

"She exudes grace with every breath," Lucy said.

Hugh's eyebrows rose. "Well, well. She certainly has you under her spell."

"There's no spell involved," Lucy said, reaching for the knob again. Opening it. "I see the truth in her, and total loyalty. They are the essence of her character."

He walked past her, through the door, stopping so his shoulder grazed her own. From there he looked down at her. She could feel his

198

breath upon her cheek. "Speaking of truth . . . don't believe everything you hear about me, Lucy."

The trick would be believing enough.

⁊

Rowena dunked her spoon into the shrimp bisque but took to her mouth little more than a coating.

She wasn't hungry, and worse than that, she didn't want to be there.

At least it wasn't a large dinner party, just a few of her parents' friends, and none of her own age, so she didn't have to pay that much attention to the banter. Which was a good thing considering her mood.

Which was . . . ?

She dunked the spoon a second time in the soup, lifted it out of its drowning, then dunked it again. Memories of the painting fiasco dogged her thoughts.

Fiasco?

It was far too strong a word. She'd had the notion to expose Lucy to art. It wasn't Lucy's fault she possessed a natural talent for painting. It served Rowena right for being condescending about it. *See the rich girl enlightening the poor seamstress as to the finer things in life.*

See the seamstress outshine the rich girl, which serves her right for being so patronizing.

Rowena fidgeted in her chair, gaining a look of warning from Mother. She gave up on the soup, setting her spoon down.

"Not hungry, my dear?" Mother asked.

"Not much." She added, "But it's delicious as usual."

"Where is your Edward?" Mrs. Garmin asked.

My Edward? And actually, she wasn't sure why Edward had sent his last-minute regrets. She hadn't seen him all day and had looked forward to his company at dinner. But late afternoon, he'd sent a note giving his regrets and saying he would stop by the house tomorrow. And they *were* going to the musicale at a neighbor's home the coming weekend . . .

A musicale. Another place where Rowena would be faced with talents she didn't possess.

Mrs. Wetmore set down her own spoon and audibly took a breath, her face beaming with obvious anticipation. "I have it on highest authority that Alice Vanderbilt is altering the format of her upcoming housewarming and coming-out party for her Gertrude, and turning it into a costume ball. Isn't that marvelous?"

The look on Mother's face showed otherwise. "And how are we to come up with costumes in two weeks?"

Mr. Wetmore leaned forward. "I would guess the short notice is so Alice will have the best costume, one that was designed and made months ago."

There was a grumbling ascension among the men, and a mumbling resignation among the women. It was just like Alice to create a way for herself to be the queen of the ball. Two years ago she'd been costumed as "Electric Light" at her sister-in-law's ball in New York.

"The Vanderbilts' new home, the Breakers . . . not a piece of wood used in the construction," Mr. Berwind said. He shook a finger to make a point. "They are not going to lose this house to fire like the last one."

"I hear its very Old World," Mr. Langdon said.

"Well, I think it's ridiculous," Mr. Havemeyer said. "I mean what style is it, anyway? Italianate or French or—?"

"Vanderbiltian," Mr. Langdon said.

Amid the soft laughter, Mrs. Garmin set her spoon down with a clatter. "Well, ladies. What are we going to do about this? Alice has thrown down the gauntlet. We can't let her costume overshadow our own."

Mrs. Wetmore looked to her husband. "Are you certain we won't be in town for this party?"

Her husband pressed a napkin to his mouth and cleared his throat. "I am certain."

With Mrs. Wetmore out of the picture, Mrs. Garmin turned to the other women. "So? It's up to us, ladies."

Mother shook her head back and forth. "There simply isn't time—as Alice well knows."

"Actually . . . I've already got my seamstress on it," Mrs. Berwind said.

"As have I," Mrs. Havemeyer said.

Mr. Garmin turned to his wife. "We have the costumes from last year. Those will just have to do."

Mrs. Garmin shook her head adamantly. "I will not be Cleopatra a second time."

Like a bolt from heaven, Rowena had an answer. *Lucy can make our costumes.*

Yet before she let the idea take flight, her hurt pride grabbed hold of its legs, forbidding its freedom. To let Lucy's talent shine yet again? How could she choose such a thing?

How could she not?

"Why not ask Lucy to design and create our costumes?"

"Lucy?" Mrs. Garmin began to smile. "Ah yes, Miss Scarpelli. I had the pleasure of her company on the trip here. She is quite delightful."

Of course she is.

Rowena's mother looked confused. "But how did you travel *with* Lucy? She was in third class."

Mrs. Garmin huffed a laugh. "I can assure you, *I* was in first class. And so was she."

Rowena wanted to melt into a puddle under the table, and could have from the heated intensity of her mother's look. She might as well admit it now in front of her mother's friends rather than risk a private reprimand latter. "I paid for Lucy's first-class passage out of my allowance."

Her father leaned back to let the footman take his soup away. "Your allowance is for *your* use, daughter, not the use of a . . . a . . ."

"Friend?"

Mrs. Garmin came to her rescue. "I think it's wonderful. And isn't it also propitious? For now Lucy is here, and she is available to help us look smashing at Alice's party. Do you think she'll do it?"

With a glance to her mother, Rowena answered, "If I ask her to. She's very creative."

"Then count me in," Mrs. Garmin said.

Rowena's envious side chided herself for creating yet another way for Lucy to showcase her talents, but the side of her that cherished Lucy as a friend shoved the envy aside and took charge.

Friends helped friends be their best.

❦

Lucy enjoyed this time of day. The night had taken away the sun, leaving her with the lesser light of the gas lamps for her work—which wasn't enough. And so she was free to do nothing—at least until Rowena came up from dinner and needed help with her nighttime toilette.

Lucy extinguished the false light in order to see outside. She turned her work chair toward the window, and drew it close enough that she could lean against the sill to look out upon the night. She was glad the dressing room was on the ocean side of the house so the darkness wasn't spoiled by the gas lamps lining the drive or the grounds. The back yard glowed with the reflection of the light inside, but not to the extent that the moon relinquished its prominence.

She saw its light sparkle on the water, and could even distinguish the horizon line where ocean met sky.

Once again Lucy remembered her father's lesson about the horizon and stood in her chair, watching its line rise with her. She sat again and found herself smiling.

Her father, Dante.

Her hero this afternoon, Dante.

Would she ever see him again? Rowena had told her to return to the Cliff Walk, just in case. . . .

It was not a question of whether she *could* pursue seeing him again, but *should* she? She was a visitor in Newport—for a very short time.

But so were most of the people here, residents for six or eight weeks, then gone again, returned to their other life. Their real life. This place was a fantasy, a regal fairyland of gilded halls and glorious balls. It was a city of pleasure and position, of show and splendor. It was as different from her life in New York as diamonds were to glass.

Her thoughts turned to Mamma and Sofia. The same moon that shone upon Lucy shone upon them. But would they—could they—see it amid the tall buildings of the city? And surely they were already asleep, worn out from the strenuousness of their workday, needing to rest so a similar day could begin tomorrow.

Were they safe from Bonwitter?

The draw of the night was interrupted by her fear, and she lit a lamp in order to write them a letter. She'd been selfish to let her thoughts get distracted from their troubles. How were they managing without her to guide and protect them?

Lucy got out paper and pen and used a book as a surface to write upon. *Dearest Mamma and Sofia . . .*

She was interrupted by the sound of Rowena returning. She set the letter aside and stood to greet her.

Rowena burst into the dressing room, her face alight. "Were your ears burning?"

Lucy had no idea what she was talking about. Ears burning?

Rowena laughed. "One of our dinner guests knows you."

"Knows me?"

"Mrs. Garmin? She met you on the train?"

Lucy smiled. "She and her husband took care of me and helped me tremendously. She was here?"

"They both were." Rowena turned her back toward Lucy so Lucy could start unbuttoning her dress. "And here is the good part. Mrs. Garmin wants you to make her a costume for Mrs. Vanderbilt's costume ball."

Lucy stopped her work and turned Rowena around. "She wants me to sew for her?"

Rowena beamed. "She saw my dress and Mother's, and was so impressed with your work that—"

"But I didn't do all the work. The other ladies at Madame Moreau's did much of it, and—"

Rowena's smile faded. "You can't do it?"

"No, I can do it, but—"

"Because you also need to create a costume for Mother and me."

Lucy's thoughts fluttered with all that would be involved in three dresses. No, not merely dresses . . . "Costumes, you say? What kind of costumes?"

"The more elaborate the better. I would like to wear something from the Regency period, and Mother was thinking of a costume from Elizabethan times. And Mrs. Garmin mentioned wanting to be dressed as a very elaborate Hungarian gypsy."

Lucy's head shook back and forth, accepting and rejecting the immensity of it all. "When is this ball?"

"In two weeks."

"But I—"

Rowena took Lucy by the shoulders. "You'll do it, won't you? It will be such a triumph for you, Lucy. If others see your work and appreciate it, who knows what could happen?"

She couldn't say no.

Sleep would not come easy tonight.

CHAPTER FOURTEEN

$\mathcal{R}$owena was up with the dawn, her mind racing with thoughts of the dinner party the night before. She'd offered Lucy's creative talents toward making three costumes for Mrs. Vanderbilt's costume party. Her own envy at Lucy's gifts had nearly kept her from sharing the idea, but luckily, loyalty had won out over petty jealousy.

For now at least.

She opened the curtains wide and let the sunrise and the sea inspire her. The clouds were low in the sky as if the sea had birthed them, and as they rose higher, they lost their newborn pinkness and grew blue and then gray.

Rowena was reminded of a poem by Elizabeth Barrett Browning and recited a verse. " 'Love me with thine azure eyes, made for earnest granting; taking colour from the skies, can Heaven's truth be wanting?' "

The colors of dawn were her favorite colors in all God's creation, which was why she often chose them for her clothing. Happily, with her light skin and hair, they suited her.

An idea for her costume came to mind. The Regency era of history was rife with the pastels of the sunrise. What if she portrayed a character from one of Jane Austen's novels? Her favorite was Elizabeth Bennet from *Pride and Prejudice*. And Edward could go as the romantic hero, Mr. Darcy.

Rowena retrieved some stationery from her desk and held pen to paper.

You're not a painter, and you're certainly not a sketch artist.

She had an image in her mind but hesitated. What if she couldn't get it down on paper? What if it looked like a silly cartoon?

"So what?" she said aloud. She wasn't creating a piece of art but simply illustrating an idea. Lucy would take it from there.

Her doubts eased at the knowledge that she and Lucy were working together in this. Comrades. Partners.

And so, the ink flowed.

❦

Lucy was up with the dawn, her thoughts racing. Mrs. Garmin wanted her to create a costume? And two more for the Langdons?

During the night she'd made a mental list of the supplies she'd need, and the first thing she did upon waking was to start a new letter to Mamma, explaining the situation. If she could have it finished before Rowena woke up—

There was a rap on her bedroom door. Lucy panicked and realized she wasn't even dressed, but there was nothing to do but answer. "Rowena, I'm so sorry. I didn't realize the time and—"

Rowena shook her head. "The time is far early, but I couldn't sleep for thinking about the costumes."

Lucy indicated her letter. "I'm writing my mother right now, telling her what supplies to send and—"

"Your mother is a part of an idea that just popped into my head. Why don't you ask her to come here to help you?"

Lucy was shocked into silence.

"She's a seamstress at the Emporium too, isn't she?"

"She is," Lucy said, "as is my little sister."

"Then have her come too. They can bring the supplies with them."

Rowena tied the bow on her ruffled wrap. "If you tell them the type of fabrics you need, could they bring those too?"

Lucy was overwhelmed. Her legs felt weak, and she staggered to sit on her bed.

Rowena rushed to her. "Are you all right? I should have been more subtle this early in the morning. I *can* be more subtle, but—"

Lucy touched Rowena's hand. "It's . . . it's just that ever since I got here I've been worried about them and—"

"Worried? Why?"

Lucy didn't want to burden Rowena with their problems with Bonwitter again. There was nothing she could do about it anyway. "Remember that man back home who's been bothering—"

"The rat man. What's his name? I'll have Father take care of him."

A laugh escaped and Lucy quelled it. Did Rowena truly think her father could do what the police could not? "It's a complicated matter. The police—"

"Police are involved? What else did he do to you?"

Oh dear. "It's more what I did to him. If you remember, I arranged things so he was caught stealing from my employer. He lost his job and fled. Needless to say, I'm not his favorite person."

"And with you out of town, you fear for your family."

"Yes."

"Then you *must* bring them here, for their safety *and* to help you with the costumes."

It did seem like a feasible solution.

Rowena took Lucy's hand and pulled her through the dressing room into her bedroom. "Come see the sketches I did of a costume I'd like to wear. I even have an idea for Mother's. And Mrs. Garmin is coming over this afternoon to talk to you about hers."

Was this really happening?

❧

Sometimes Sofia regretted learning how to use a sewing machine. The machine made it audibly obvious when she was working and when she was not. And today she was not in the mood to work.

There was a subtle mood of unease in the workroom today, as if the other ladies didn't like her anymore. Could she help it if Bonwitter kept targeting her? If Lucy were here, he would have harassed her. Sofia was an innocent in all this. She didn't deserve Bonwitter's stalking; nor did she deserve the hostility of her co-workers. Considering all this, she was in no mood to work, much less work hard.

The desire to escape into a book dogged her, demanding attention. Maybe if she slipped into the storeroom . . .

Her fear of seeing Bonwitter made her think twice. But after sewing two more seams, she chose escape over fear.

While the other ladies were busy discussing the neckline of a ball gown, Sofia nabbed her latest novel from a basket at her feet and went to the storeroom. She glanced toward the window and was relieved to *not* see Bonwitter staring back at her. Had she really seen him the other day? Or was it all in her imagination as the other ladies—

Sofia pulled up short. For there, on the floor, was one of her novels, torn to shreds.

Bonwitter!

Yet the scene confused her. She looked at the book in her hands, to the debris on the ground, and to the book again. Maybe this wasn't her book at all . . . She knelt beside the pieces and saw the title: *Lovers Once But Strangers Now*. This *was* her book!

She stood and took a step back. Yes, it was her book, but worse than that, it was a book she'd last seen in her bedroom. Her mind raced through her memories, trying to remember if she'd ever even brought this book into the shop.

She hadn't.

Which meant Bonwitter had been up in their apartment, in the room where she slept.

A wave of chills coursed through her, propelling her to race back into the workroom. "He was in our apartment! He was in my bedroom!"

All conversation stopped and Sofia could see by the ladies' skeptical looks that they had already deemed her outburst another false alarm.

She put her hands on her hips and glared at them. "You don't believe me? I have proof." She pointed to the back room. "Come see."

The workroom cleared out in parade fashion as the women followed Sofia to the storeroom, grumbling all the way. She stood over the remnants of her book and presented them with a wave of her hand. "See?"

Mrs. Flynn picked up a piece. "It's a book all right, but who's to say it was up in your apartment or—"

Sofia's anger rose. "You're calling me a liar?" She snatched up the portion that owned the title and turned to Mamma. "Wasn't I reading this book the other evening?"

"You were." Mamma looked at Mrs. Flynn. "Sofia is not a liar."

Dorothy chose another scrap. "I think the main point is that Sofia would not rip up one of her own books. She loves those books."

Finally, a champion. "Exactly," Sofia said.

Dolly hugged herself and looked toward the alley door and window. "Does that mean everything she said was true? That Bonwitter's been peeking in the window at us? That he's coming and going as he pleases?"

They all looked to Mrs. Flynn to give the verdict. "I guess that's exactly what it means. I'll send word to Mr. Standish that the locks *must* be changed immediately."

"Those on our apartment too," Sofia added.

She nodded. Mrs. Flynn and the other ladies went back to work, but Dolly stayed behind and helped Sofia pick up the pieces of her book.

"I always believed you," she whispered.

It was something.

⁂

Mrs. Garmin took Lucy's hands and kissed both her cheeks. "It's so good to see you again, my dear. Are the Langdons treating you well?"

Lucy glanced at Mrs. Langdon. "Very well. Extremely well."

"I knew as much. For why would they not? Women with a talent such as yours must be cultivated like a fine orchid."

Orchid?

Mrs. Garmin took a seat on a burgundy settee beside Mrs. Langdon.

Rowena sat nearby, leaving Lucy standing awkwardly before them. She wasn't sure what to do, what was expected of her.

"I . . ." She nodded at Rowena. "Miss Langdon created some drawings of possible costumes and—"

Rowena raised a finger. "Crude sketches that Lucy has since embellished."

Mrs. Garmin rubbed her gloved hands together. "A collaborative effort. Bravo. Now let me see!"

Lucy handed the ladies their respective sketches. She spoke to Mrs. Langdon first, "Your daughter said you wished to portray a lady in waiting in Queen Elizabeth's court."

"You've always liked that era, Mother."

Mrs. Langdon nodded.

Lucy resumed the commentary. "For your dress I was thinking of a deep olive velveteen with a pink satin in the underskirt."

"What about the stiff collar they always wore?" Mrs. Garmin asked. "How will you ever make that?"

Lucy had thought it through. "I'll starch lace and mold it into the required shape."

"How ingenious."

Rowena sat beside her mother. "I was thinking you could wear your emerald necklace in your hair, with the main bauble on your forehead. I have a picture of Queen Elizabeth wearing a jewel like that."

"That's entirely possible," Mrs. Langdon said as she studied the drawing.

Mrs. Garmin raised a hand. "My turn!"

Lucy caught Rowena's eye as she moved to Mrs. Garmin. They shared a smile. This was going better than they'd hoped.

"For you I was thinking of a rich paisley for a shawl and as a portion of the overskirt."

"What colors?"

"Mostly red with swirls of blue and gold."

"I love deep colors."

Lucy continued. "And the main skirt would be a red satin and—"

"Gypsies wouldn't have worn satin," Mrs. Langdon said.

Mrs. Garmin objected. "They probably had dirty hands and feet too, but I want to be a luxurious gypsy."

"A gypsy queen," Rowena said.

"Exactly. A queen." She waved a hand at Lucy. "Go on. Red satin . . ."

"Red satin, and probably a layer of blue too. Or perhaps a blue-and-gold-striped skirt showing at the bottom."

"And the blouse?"

The picture in Lucy's mind was vivid. "Something simple in a white gauze, with flowing sleeves. And a laced girdle in black."

"A girdle on the outside." Mrs. Garmin put a hand to her midsection and sighed. "To think I'll be able to go without a corset for a night. Now *that* is true luxury. Sometimes I get tempted to go without and breathe free and—"

"We really shouldn't be talking about these things," Mrs. Langdon said.

"And why not?" Mrs. Garmin said. "These *things* may be unmentionable, but truth be told, they are quite ridiculous and worthy of discussion and disdain. Hourglass figures, my foot. I'd like to see a man wear one of the contraptions we endure every waking hour. Would the world come to an end if we began a revolt and simply refused to wear our corsets?"

None of the ladies answered.

With a dramatic sigh, Mrs. Garmin gave up trying to incite a mutiny. She nodded to Rowena's drawing. "And your costume, my dear?"

Rowena turned her drawing around so both women could see. "My inspiration comes from the books of Jane Austen."

Lucy gave the details. "I thought a butter-colored silk would supply color yet represent the pastels of the Regency period. The piece of fabric I'm thinking of is covered with gold embroidery."

"You have this fabric with you?" Mrs. Langdon asked.

"No, no," Lucy said. "But it's in stock at the shop where I work."

Mrs. Garmin studied the drawing. "I do like the feathers in the headpiece, and is this a width of lace fabric hanging down?"

Lucy nodded. "I was thinking of a lace piece we have that's a brick red. It would hang from the headpiece and skim Rowena's shoulder. I think the color would complement the yellow of the dress quite well."

"I have a citrine necklace that would look beautiful with it," Rowena said.

Each lady examined her sketch and nodded—to Lucy's relief.

"So then," Mrs. Langdon said. "We are definitely impressed with your designs."

"Your daughter came up with the initial ideas," Lucy said.

"Then my kudos go to you too, Rowena," she said. "But the next question involves the implementation of these wonderful ideas. How and when?"

Rowena sat forward in her chair, eager to share the answer. "Lucy needs help, so I thought we should send for her mother and sister—who are also seamstresses. They can come on the train with all the fabrics and supplies she'll need."

"Would they be willing to do that?" her mother asked.

"More than willing," Lucy said. She could hardly wait to send word. If only she could see her mother's face and hear Sofia's squeal of joy.

"Then do it," Mrs. Langdon said. "I'll talk to my husband and he'll see that the arrangements are made. Firstly, he'll send a telegram this very afternoon." She looked to Lucy. "Could they come on the train day after tomorrow?"

"I'm sure they could."

"Very well, then. That will be all, Lucy."

Lucy nodded and left the room.

Two days. In two days she'd see her family!

Then suddenly it hit her. What would Mrs. Flynn's reaction be? Would she let them leave? Would she let them take supplies? Would she help them get the fabrics Lucy needed?

Lucy hadn't talked about the expense with the Langdons or Mrs. Garmin, and she wasn't even sure how much such a costume should cost.

But perhaps money wasn't mentioned because money didn't matter. It would cost what it would cost. Money talked.

Surely Mrs. Flynn would let it talk to *her*.

The bell on the front door of Madame Moreau's chimed. "Hello? Telegram!"

All the ladies turned aflutter at the distraction and received a loud "Shush now!" from Mrs. Flynn—who went to the lobby to retrieve it.

Sofia kept sewing a satin petticoat for a day dress. Since finding her book torn apart, and having the ladies finally believe her about Bonwitter, she'd felt relief overshadow any fear that he was still out there. Yes, Mr. Standish had been called, and had assured them the locks would be changed by tomorrow, but it was more than that. Or actually less. Losing her title of "Baby Sofia" made her feel like one of the group again, which made her want to work harder.

If she thought about it, she had Bonwitter to thank.

Sofia barely looked up when Mrs. Flynn returned to the workroom. She didn't see her hand Mamma the telegram, but only knew of it when Tessie and Dorothy exclaimed.

"Lea? *You* get the telegram?"

"What's it say?"

"Who died?" Dolly asked.

Leona slapped her shoulder. "Stop that. Telegrams can be good news. Remember Lucy's?"

Sofia remembered Lucy's. Her telegram had been like getting a summons to a royal feast. But now, getting another one . . .

Mamma's face sagged with worry and she hesitated to open it. Sofia rushed to her side. "Do you think Lucy's hurt?"

Mamma pressed the envelope into Sofia's hand. "You open it."

Her heart pounded and her throat tightened. As much as she envied Lucy, she loved her and . . . *God, please don't let her be hurt.*

She opened the seal and pulled out the note, scanned it, then burst into laughter.

"You're laughing?" Tessie said. "What does it say?"

Sofia cleared her throat and read aloud. " 'Mamma and Sofia: You are needed in Newport to help make costumes for Vanderbilt ball. Train tickets at Grand Centr—' "

Mrs. Flynn tried to grab the telegram away. "The gall! What's Lucy doing, emptying out my workroom!"

"Wait," Sofia said. "Listen to the rest. 'Tell Mrs. Flynn much money coming. List of supplies attached. Come Friday. Lucy.' " Sofia flung her arms around Mamma. "We're going to Newport!"

"We're going to see Lucia!" Mamma said.

Mrs. Flynn clapped her hands. "Hold on there. Only if I let you go."

Mamma and Sofia parted. Mamma took a step forward. "Please, Madame. Let us go see Lucia and do this work for you."

Dorothy gave her defense of it. "It *will* be a feather in your cap, Madame. Not just gowns for a Newport ball, but costumes."

"And not just any Newport ball," Tessie said. "A Vanderbilt ball."

Dolly nodded. "They're richer than Croesus."

Everyone looked at her. "Do you even know who Croesus was?" Dorothy asked.

Dolly thought a moment. "Isn't he one of the Vanderbilts' cousins?"

The laughter was a balm and led to Mrs. Flynn saying, "Let me see the list."

Sofia was going to Newport!

And getting away from Bonwitter.

❊

So much for meeting Dante.

Lucy sat by the window, furiously mending Rowena's wardrobe. She had two days to finish her work before her family arrived and the costumes would need to be started. Her leisurely strolls were a thing of the past.

Oh well. At least she'd had a chance to walk along the sea. Once. It was probably best she didn't go back to see Dante. She knew nothing about him. She didn't even know if he was an honorable man.

He saved me.

But wouldn't any man do that?

She tried to shove the thoughts of Dante away. *"Quando la pera è matura, casca da sè,"* she said aloud. All things happen in their own good time.

But they wouldn't happen at all if she never showed up. Couldn't happen.

Lucy pricked her finger. Served her right for letting the idea of love enter her head.

She looked up when Rowena entered the dressing room. The look on her face was quizzical. "Why are you here?" she asked.

"Pardon?"

Rowena pointed out the window. "Isn't it time to meet your Dante?"

Lucy was surprised she remembered. "I have work to do, especially with the three costumes to make as soon as my mother and sis—"

Rowena plucked the needle from her fingers. "Nonsense. I will not have you ruin a chance with your hero because of a split seam. Outside with you, and you'd better hurry or you'll miss him."

Lucy was ashamed when her heart began to pound. This whole thing was silly.

But Rowena would not be denied. She pulled a pink dress from the rack. "Here, wear this. You can't have him seeing you in the same outfit."

"I have another blouse."

"Save it for the next time you see him. This dress, I say. Come now. Time is ticking."

Lucy stopped her argument. The thought of wearing a truly beautiful dress was exciting, one with lace sleeves, a wide ruffle at the hem, and rows and rows of lace.

Rowena buttoned the back of it, then helped Lucy wind her hair into a soft bun. All finished, she turned her around and beamed like a proud mother. "There now. Off with you!"

"But—"

"I expect a full accounting upon your return."

Rowena stood at the window and watched Lucy run across the grass toward the Cliff Walk. It felt good to be instrumental in bringing two lovers together.

And yet . . . she felt a wistful tug knowing that she would never run into her lover's arms. At best she'd limp, clod, and stagger.

She closed her eyes and tried to imagine meeting Edward and throwing her arms around his neck. How would it feel to have him pull her close, to actually feel his heart beating next to hers?

There was a knock on the door and Sadie entered, carrying a bouquet of flowers. "For you, Miss Langdon. Just delivered."

Rowena's spirits immediately rose. She brought the white flowers to her nose and was met with a biting, sweet smell, not completely pleasant.

"There's a note, miss."

Yes, of course. *Forgive me for missing dinner with you. Yours truly, Edward.* A smile came without effort.

"Would you like me to put them in some water, miss?"

"Of course."

Reluctantly, Rowena relinquished the bouquet to Sadie. Then she sat on the bench at the foot of her bed and read the note again. Oddly, the words seemed capable of issuing two meanings. The culprit was the "missing dinner" line. Was Edward missing having dinner with her? Or was he simply talking about being absent from their house for dinner? One was certainly more romantic than the other.

And the flowers he'd chosen . . .

She remembered a small book her mother had given her on her sixteenth birthday and retrieved it from a shelf. *The Language of Flowers.* She'd only had cause to use it one other time when she'd received a tussie-mussie of dandelions from a distant cousin. The book had said those flowers indicated coquetry, but Rowena, knowing her cousin, had determined they simply meant he was cheap and had pulled a bouquet from a neighbor's lawn.

Edward's arrangement contained two types of plants: daisies and ferns. She found reference to the fern first. " 'Sincerity,' " she read. She nodded once, accepting that meaning with pleasure. Now to daisies . . .

She saw its meaning. "Innocence?"

It was *nice*, but hardly romantic. She thought of Lucy, off on her secret rendezvous with Dante. . . . That was hardly innocent.

She knew Edward's choice was a compliment, but she also wanted him to think of her in more . . . more assertive ways.

Innocent?

She checked the book again and scanned some of the floral meanings. Red roses were still the most meaningful with their message of passionate love. But even asters would have spoken of love. Or red chrysanthemums.

She paged through and found some flowers with symbolisms she hoped never to receive: houseleeks meant "domestic economy" and red clover indicated "industry." Innocence and sincerity were better than those. And a black rose? That was too far in the other direction, meaning "obsession." Rowena never wanted Edward to be obsessed with her, just deeply, sincerely in love with her.

Sincerely. Sincerity. The ferns . . .

Sadie knocked, brought the bouquet into the room, and set it on the table by a chair. "They're very pretty, miss."

With a snap, Rowena shut the book on flowers. "Yes, they are."

༺༻

Lucy burst onto the Cliff Walk and turned right, nearly colliding with a couple taking a stroll.

"Pardon me," she said.

They gave her odd looks and went on their way.

Please help him be there. Please help him be—

Lucy mentally pulled up short. Was she praying? About a man? It was ridiculous. God couldn't be bothered by such a silly notion.

She passed the place where she'd lost her footing, hugging the land side of the path. And then . . .

She saw him. Her heart skipped a beat.

He was facing the sea, his hands behind his back. His chin was held high as if meeting the view and the breeze head-on.

She slowed her pace and quickly stroked stray hairs behind her ears.

He heard her coming and turned. And smiled. And with that smile, she felt an unfamiliar tug inside. Had anyone ever smiled in such a way at seeing her? Had *she* ever felt so excited about seeing anyone?

"Good afternoon, Miss Lucy. I was beginning to fear the worst."

"The worst?"

"That you'd found me a bore during our previous meeting and had shunned me, leaving me to a lonely humiliation."

"No, and no," she said. "You're the most interesting man I've ever met, and if I would have missed our meeting, I assure you it would not be a rejection, but because of some extenuating circumstance." She took a deep breath and suddenly feared she'd said too much. "Forgive me if I sound too forward. Since I was running late I'm not giving my mind time to think before I speak."

He laughed. "I'm glad for the condition, because your words ease my mind—and my ego. Now that we're both here, would you care to walk?"

She could think of nothing better.

They strolled to the south, following the path along the ocean. To their right were the homes of the very rich.

"There, that house with all the chimneys? It's called Ochre Point Mansion."

"It's interesting," Lucy said. "It juts out, falls back, and the many different roofs . . ."

"It's built in the 'Shingle' style. See all the different types of shingles on the walls and roofs?"

He took her along the Cliff Walk to the next house. "This one is Ochre Court. The style is French Gothic, with Renaissance elements in limestone."

Lucy nodded, having no idea what that meant.

A few minutes later, they stopped in front of a sprawling red house. "There, that's Vinland. Miss Catherine Wolfe lives there. I heard she was a large contributor toward the building of Grace Church in New York. I love the red brick, and the Romanesque Revival style."

Now she was really lost.

He seemed to sense this, and changed his description to something more interesting. "It's named for the spot where the Norsemen first landed, centuries ago. Miss Wolfe was also inspired by Longfellow's story 'The Skeleton in Armor' about a Viking who built a tower to honor his love. I've heard there are many friezes and murals inside that depict Norse legends."

Friezes? Norse? Lucy didn't want to admit her ignorance. "You seem to know a lot about architecture. Is that your vocation?"

"If only . . ."

By this admission she felt a connection. "I understand the desire for an education beyond one's means. I would have loved to go to school."

"You never—?"

She shook her head. "My parents taught me how to read and write, and my mother added what little bit of arithmetic I needed for sewing. But beyond that I know little of the world, history, or literature."

"But you'd like to know more."

His statement surprised her. "Of course. Who wouldn't?"

"From my experience, too many are content with knowing too little. They find learning a burden."

"I don't understand such thinking. If I had the means and the—" Lucy suddenly realized she'd led the conversation down a path that revealed her poverty. Not that she wanted to pass herself off as a lady of means—oh, that she could—but she'd hoped to keep the details of her family background to herself. She wasn't ashamed, and yet . . .

"If you had the means and the . . . ?" Dante asked.

"I . . . I don't want you to get the wrong impression of me."

"What can be wrong about a woman who longs to learn? I find the trait admirable."

"I'm glad. I simply don't want you to think that just because my family is—" There she went again, telling too much. Maybe one of her father's truisms would save her. "In regard to schooling, my father used to say, *La pratica vale più della grammatica*."

"Which means?"

"Experience is the best teacher."

"I agree." He paused and looked at her. "Was that Italian?"

Lucy hesitated. Did he share the common prejudice against her roots? "Yes."

"So you're Italian?"

"Yes."

"I suspected as much. Your coloring is lovely, and your eyes . . ." He looked away, embarrassed. "What's your family name?"

How she wished it were something Americanized like Smith.

He stopped walking and faced her. "Lucy. Please. I feel you weighing every answer as if trying to decipher what I want to hear. I want to hear the truth about you. And knowing you, even as little as I do, I know the truth will be sufficient. The truth will be more than enough, a pleasure."

Lucy studied his face. His eyes were a gray-blue with yellow flecks, and his brow was pulled into an interesting furrow, evidence of his sincerity. Could she fully tell him the truth? Although he was dressed nicely, his apparel was not flamboyant or showy in any way. She guessed him to be a tradesman of some sort. And she? She too was a tradeswoman. A seamstress. What did her roots matter, anyway? Wasn't becoming an American an act of moving forward rather than back? An act of achieving a dream?

"I . . . my name is Lucia Francesca Scarpelli."

"Lucia."

"Lucy."

He shook his head. "Not Lucy. Lucia is lyrical."

Lyrical?

"Are you from Newport?" he asked.

"Oh no," Lucy said. "I'm a seamstress." She decided not to mention Madame Moreau's. "I'm here temporarily, sewing some garments for a few of the ladies."

"You must be very talented. From what I've seen, the ladies of Newport are quite demanding, and the fashion ornate."

"As ornate as the architecture," she said.

He smiled. "I'm afraid we live in a time of conspicuousness. The Gilded Age, you know."

She shook her head. She didn't know.

"Haven't you heard it called that? Mark Twain coined the phrase a couple of decades ago. He made fun of the rich and how everything was gilded. They seem to have an insane need to outdo each other—or at least to not be outdone."

Lucy nodded toward the houses they'd just passed. "Summer cottages they call them. Who's fooling whom?"

His voice turned thoughtful. "It's sad."

"Sad?"

"For the most part, the people of society weren't born to it, they earned it."

"That's a good thing, no?"

"It's a very good thing. I don't begrudge anyone money if they've worked hard to get it."

She sensed he wasn't finished. "But?"

"But . . . instead of being content with their achievements, they seem to be in a constant state of trying to prove they are as good as the wealthy people in Europe. They strip entire rooms from estates overseas and reconstruct them here. They copy their architecture to match some castle or palace. They create a set of rules to rival any restrictions of old society as if to say, '*See how we thrive with even more boundaries and limitations than you have endured?*' "He shook his head mournfully. "We fought for freedom only to create our own prison of conformity. It doesn't make sense."

Lucy was moved by his passion—and agreed with it. "So what kind of society would you create if it were in your control?"

He smiled, but his eyes were still serious. "I would build houses with rooms meant to be lived in, not walked through to admire. I would set people free to be friends with whomever they chose. I'd help people achieve their dreams without caring if they fit into a formula set for them by others, and—" Dante looked at her and blinked, as if all he'd said had never been shared before. He hooked a finger in the collar of his shirt. "And I'd ban stiff collars for men and corsets for women, and declare it quite appropriate to only dress once for the entire day."

"You wish to put me out of business? For I thrive on women changing six times."

"Freedom demands sacrifices, Miss Scarpelli."

She loved how he shared his thoughts with her, and how those

221

thoughts made her think more deeply than she was used to. In fact, she couldn't remember ever having such a meaningful discussion with a man.

A large wave broke on the rocks below them, sending spray upon the path. Lucy felt the reality of time passing. She needed to get back to the Langdons'. "I'm afraid I must go."

"Back to the sweatshop?"

She knew he meant it as a joke, but . . . what would he think of her if he knew that's the very place she'd worked for most of her life? "As you said, the ladies are very demanding."

"I can't come here tomorrow, but will you meet me the day after?"

Gladly. But facts overshadowed her wishes. "I'm afraid not." Her mother and sister were coming that day, and with their arrival there would be more work and less time to stroll along the Cliff Walk. "I'm not sure when I'll have time to myself again. Once I finish one project, they seem to find something else and—"

"Sunday, then. They'll have to let you go to church on Sunday and give you the afternoon free."

Would they? Lucy wasn't so sure.

Dante knelt beside a stone wall. He began digging around one stone in particular.

"What are you doing?" she asked.

"I'm making a secret place for us to leave each other notes. If we can't coordinate our meetings, at least we can continue our conversations." He pulled the stone free and brushed out a place inside. "There. Whenever you can, leave me a note and I will do the same." He replaced the stone and stood, taking her hands in his. "I don't know what the future holds, but I do know that just as you find me interesting, I find your company enchanting. I enjoy knowing you, Lucia Francesca Scarpelli, and I want to know you better."

She was moved by his words, but recognized that during this meeting she'd done most of the talking. "You learned about me today, but I didn't let you tell me about your life. I know so little about you."

"Which provides more incentive for you to continue our correspondence via the stone in the wall."

Lucy nodded. She could think of nothing that would give her more pleasure.

✦

Lucy signed her name to the note: *Lucia.* There. She'd done it. She'd written a note to Dante.

She scanned the words, letting her eyes fall upon a few phrases: *I am pleased . . . you ignite my thoughts . . . hope that we . . .*

It was ridiculous. Who was she to say such things to a man? Any man, much less one she'd only talked to twice. A man who was far different from any man she'd ever met. Although she didn't know his last name, she could be assured by his sandy hair and blue eyes that it did not end in a vowel. He was not a Romano, Lombardi, or Marino. She had not had much contact with men of different ethnic backgrounds, but would guess that Dante's family had been in America far longer than her own. He had no accent to give his roots away.

In Lucy's world, Italians married Italians. Jews married Jews. Irish married Irish. A poor immigrant girl did not marry a businessman from any—

Marry? Marriage? Lucy lifted the note and began to tear it in two. But with just a rip started, she stopped herself. She needed time to think about this.

She folded the note into fourths and set it on the table. Then she put out the lamp and got into bed.

The moonlight stretched across the room, up the table, and over the edge of the page.

Lucy turned her face to the wall.

Chapter Fifteen

hey're going to work *and* sleep in here?" Lucy asked.

Haverty, the coachman who'd originally picked her up at the dock, shoved a cot into the corner of the outbuilding. He stood and arched his back before giving her a scathing look. "You want your family to get special treatment like you? Who do you think you are? The Astors?"

"No, of course not, but since my room is in the main house, I'd hoped—"

"Hope all you want, Lucy; this is where the Langdons want them to be. And considering all the work me and the others had to do to clean out this space so you three can have a sewing room . . . it wouldn't hurt you to be a little grateful."

She was grateful—to some extent. And yet she still wondered why they couldn't find some larger room in the main house to set up their work space. To be ostracized out here, in this room attached to the groundskeeper's house, was far from handy.

Haverty set a couple straight-back chairs up to the table they'd use for cutting. "I'm waiting."

It wasn't his fault. And he had done his best making it workable. "Thank you, Haverty. I do appreciate the help. I'm just worried what my little sister will say."

"She won't take kindly to you being in the big house and her being out here?"

"Uh . . . no. Sofia is a princess at heart."

He nodded toward the two cots. "She won't feel much like a princess after sleeping on that thing." He moved to leave, then stopped. "How old is she, anyway? And is she pretty?"

Lucy pushed Haverty out the door, but his questions raised a warning flag. Sofia was fifteen but looked older. And she was pretty. Back in New York, Lucy had felt fairly safe because their apartment was right above their workplace. There was little chance for Sofia to wander or be faced with the usual temptations of youth. But here, isolated in this building that was close to the stables and the men who worked there and close to Hugh in the house . . . Mamma would have to keep a close eye on her youngest daughter.

Lucy took inventory of the room. Her mother and sister would have to share a bath with the groundskeeper, Mr. Oswald, and his wife, and would take their meals with the middle-aged couple. The furniture in the room was sparse and merely functional. Two cots, three chairs, and a large table. At the far end sat a treadle sewing machine the Langdons had borrowed from some neighbor. Mamma was bringing sewing supplies and fabrics—hastily ordered from Madame Moreau's supplier. There would be no room for error regarding the cutting, and no time—

Time. Lucy only had a few hours before Haverty would go to the station to pick up her family. She could either rush back to her room and work on one of Mrs. Langdon's dresses or . . .

She patted the note in her skirt pocket. She hadn't been to the Cliff Walk in two days. Dante had told her he couldn't come yesterday, which was just as well, as Lucy had been busy helping Rowena dress for a special afternoon outing to a neighbor's, plus she'd been occupied arranging for the sewing room and lodging for her family.

And she'd told Dante she couldn't be there today, but . . . but she would like to leave him a note, have it waiting for him. *Il tempo viene per chi sa aspettare.* All things come to those who wait.

She'd reread the note written Wednesday night—the one she'd nearly torn up—a multitude of times. Today, almost without conscious thought, she'd put it in her pocket.

So now . . . note or work?

It was a surprisingly easy choice.

❧

The Cliff Walk was especially busy, and Lucy, walking alone, stood out among the couples taking a stroll, arm in arm, the ladies shading themselves with lace-trimmed parasols.

She was rather surprised to see all status of strollers, from lower class in their simple clothing, to the very wealthy in high style and intricate finery. She remembered what Rowena had said about the owners of the mansions being perturbed about having the full range of society pass by. Apparently they lived to show off but wanted to choose whom to show off to.

When she reached the stone wall that held their hiding place, she was forced to feign gazing at the sea as a couple sat on the very wall, the woman's skirt veiling the stones.

Lucy noticed the tone of their conversation change at her intrusion—which was just what she had hoped for. *Leave! Go somewhere else for privacy.*

Eventually, that's exactly what they did, adding snide comments about "rude people" under their breaths.

Lucy quickly sat upon the wall, inches to the left of the secret stone. She reached down as if adjusting some detail of her skirt, and gave it a little tug. To her relief it moved, but she was forced to sit upright when another couple strolled by.

The man tipped his hat.

"Good afternoon," she said.

As soon as they passed, she looked both ways and determined the time would never be fully right. She had to take a chance. And so she reached down, pulled the stone away from the wall, and began to insert—

There was a note inside!

Lucy quickly set the stone at her feet and removed the note, inching herself to the side to conceal the open space. She slipped her own note between thigh and wall, and opened Dante's.

> My dear Miss Scarpelli,
>
> To go two days without seeing you is pain indeed, and so I have done what little I could do and have talked to you on paper. 'Tis not the same (nor nearly as satisfying) but at least one side of our conversation can be shared. I will await your reaction in person, or in a note if that is all God and circumstance allows.
>
> I have never—never I say twice and more if necessary—met anyone quite like you. The dialogue we have shared in our few meetings has far surpassed the lifetime of small talk I have previously endured with a myriad of acquaintances. For even those of the fairer sex I previously deemed interesting now pale in the light of your being.
>
> We have begun to know each other, and that seed now planted demands full growth. I long for Sunday, at 2 o'clock. I will wait for you here, with the sea as my companion.
>
> Yours truly,
> Dante

Lucy pressed the page against her chest, surprised to feel the beat of her heart through the paper. The words he'd shared with her . . . No man had ever said such things to her, not even Angelo.

And yet . . . She folded his page, put it in her pocket, and removed her own note from under her thigh. Rereading what she'd penned two days before, she found their thoughts were as one. For she too mentioned the depth and breadth of the conversation and had braved saying she longed to see him again. She'd questioned being so bold, for until now her boldness had been reserved for practical matters, not issues such as love that seemed to defy all that was logical. But something in their time together, and in the feelings that lingered far after their time had ended, had led her to take the risk.

And now, to find the risk would be well received? The risk was reciprocated?

It was horribly frightening. And yet . . . She put her note to her lips and whispered into it, "For you, dear Dante," and then slipped the note behind her skirt, into its rocky hiding place. She slipped the rock into place, locking her words away, for his eyes alone.

She hurried home, her hand sharing space with Dante's note in her pocket.

※※※

"Mamma, come to the railing and see!"

But Mamma shook her head and sat as far away from the railing of the steamer as possible. She'd shown a surprising dislike for being on water. Hadn't she traveled halfway around the world to get to America?

Sofia shrugged and turned back to face the wind. She for one was thrilled to be off that awful train and into the fresh air of the sea. When they'd first received the telegram inviting them to Newport, she'd assumed they would travel first class, as Lucy had traveled. But no. They'd ridden hours in a crowded train car, sitting on hard benches, shoulder to shoulder with working-class people traveling to Newport for a quick summer holiday before returning to the city to resume their grind.

The car had been hot, and conversation difficult with the windows open, letting in the loud *clackity-clack* of the train along the rails, along with a feeble bit of air. Sofia's anger over the situation added fuel to the heat, and it had taken a strong dose of determination—and Mamma's chiding looks—to make her say a prayer of contrition, and another of supplication that somehow she'd get over it and make the most of this opportunity.

For that's what it was. A huge opportunity to see Newport and get away from the stifling heat of New York City, and the danger of

Bonwitter's lurking presence. She took to heart Papa's saying "*A caval donato non si guarda in bocca.*" Don't look a gift horse in the mouth.

A few hours into the trip, they'd grown hungry, and Sofia had asked the conductor the way to the dining car. Lucy had written home telling about the luscious sweets she'd eaten in that special place. But there was no such car for their class, and they'd had to spend their money buying stale sandwiches from a woman carrying around a basket. A cup of lukewarm water dipped from a barrel had been their only refreshment—and even that not very enticing after Sofia witnessed a little boy spit into the water.

Transferring their things from the train in Wickford Junction to the steamship had cost more money, and Sofia hadn't even cared to see the room where her third-class ticket dictated she sit. Instead, she chose the rail and the wind and the view.

As they neared the harbor, she saw sailboats and was in awe. She'd never seen anything so beautiful and couldn't imagine the peaceful feeling that must accompany the passengers. She waved at a boat nearby and was pleased when its white-clad skipper waved back.

Maybe she'd get a chance to sail in Newport.

The possibility encouraged her.

❦

Once the steamer docked and Sofia and Mamma landed, a stocky blond man wound his way through the crowd toward them, his height a good six inches above the rest.

Sofia leaned toward Mamma. "I think he's for us."

As if he'd heard, his eyes fixed on her. When close enough he said, "Scarpellis?"

Sofia took the lead—and Mamma's arm—and stepped forward. "Yes, that's us."

He looked from Sofia to Mamma, then back again—and smiled. "Well, now," he said. "I see the resemblance to Lucy."

Mamma pulled free of her arm. "I assume you mean that as a compliment, young man."

"Oh, I do. And the name's Haverty, ma'am." He lifted their

carpetbags as if they were filled with air. "How many other bags do you have?"

Haverty made quick work of collecting their luggage and helped Mamma into the seat of the cart next to him. Sofia didn't mind sitting off the back of the cart, her legs dangling. She regretted not hearing any commentary from the driver, but also liked observing this new place on her own.

She was immediately impressed with the streets. Unlike New York, once away from the harbor, they were little congested and lined with trees. There were neighborhoods with small houses close together, many with shop signs hanging near their doors, but as they drove farther to the east, the streets widened, the lawns broadened, and the buildings became massive. Were these the government buildings for the town? The offices and courthouses?

But then she saw two little boys playing with hoops on a lawn near a front door, with a woman accompanying them, warning them not to get grass stains on their knickers.

These weren't government buildings. These were homes.

She remembered their first letter from Lucy, where she'd written about the Langdon home, but Sofia had been too deep in the throes of jealousy to pay it much attention. What Lucy had and Sofia didn't have held little interest.

Until now. Until being here and seeing these mansions fit for kings.

She passed a couple walking on the sidewalk, the woman's hand around the man's arm, the other hand holding a lacy parasol. She waved.

They both looked downward.

Suddenly, Sofia regretted her fine perch on the back of the cart, for certainly no lady had traveled this grand street in this particular way.

Luckily her discomfort was short-lived as she heard Haverty say, "Here we are." He turned up a long drive.

The house was not as grand as some, but magnificent nonetheless. It rose three stories tall—which was short in comparison to the buildings in New York, but somehow, perched on top of a vast lawn, it seemed taller, and certainly more regal, as if it chose its height for its own purposes and was neither too tall nor not tall enough. Somehow Sofia knew that inside this house, everything would be just right.

She was disappointed Haverty didn't drive them to the front door. Although she sensed her entrance there wouldn't be proper—nor anyone's entrance who arrived via a cart—she would've liked to experience it.

The thought that she would never go through the front doors came, and went. But instead of feeling bad about it, Sofia accepted it. She guessed the number of people who went through the grand entrance of this house was limited. That she was not among that number was tolerable, and even a relief. Although she often thought more of herself than she should, she was no dummy. The world had always been inhabited by the rich and the poor—and everything in between. That she was getting to experience a bit of the former was like walking into a scene in one of her novels. It made her happy. For didn't every one of those stories have a happy ending?

The cart veered away from the house to an outbuilding, a smaller one-story structure nearer the stables than the main house. Haverty stopped the cart there and helped Mamma down. Sofia hopped off the cart a bit reluctantly. Surely they hadn't traveled this far not to see the mansion? Not to stay in the mansion?

Haverty knocked on the front door of the little cottage, and an old woman who looked as though she enjoyed eating very, very much opened the door. They exchanged a few words, then Haverty explained. "This is Mrs. Oswald, the groundskeeper's wife. You'll be staying here."

"And working here," Mrs. Oswald said. She offered no more introductions, but exited the house and directed them around its side. "Many an hour has been spent clearing out the back room so you can use it as a sewing room and sleeping quarters."

Sofia had had her fill of back rooms. . . .

"That's very kind of you," Mamma said.

Sofia looked toward the main house and wanted to pull both ladies to a halt and say, *"But I want to be up there!"*

At the back of the cottage was another door, and Mrs. Oswald led them inside, to a room slightly larger than their main room back in New York. "Mrs. Langdon insisted we clear this room for you, and we found some spare tables and chairs for you to work on. And there's a bed for each of you too."

Sofia looked in the direction she'd pointed and was appalled to see two skinny cots shoved against the wall. Less than two feet separated them from the main worktable.

"See here," Mrs. Oswald said, "the Langdons even found you a machine for sewing. That's how special they think of you."

Sofia wanted to laugh. The minimal nature of the space screamed exactly how special the Langdons thought of them.

"Where's Lucy sleep?" she asked.

"Oh, your sister's up in the main house. I hear she has a room right next to Miss Langdon's."

Of course she does.

"I'll send her word you're here."

Summon the queen. Her poor relations have arrived.

Lucy raced across the lawn toward the groundskeeper's house. She couldn't wait to see Mamma and Sofia.

Mamma must have spotted her from the window, for the back door opened and she ran out, her arms wide. "Lucia!"

Lucy fell into her arms. "I'm so glad you're here. So glad."

The feeling of Mamma's arms holding her close made Lucy feel like a child again, dependent and safe. Cared for and protected.

It didn't last long, for Sofia came out of the house and said, "Come down from the big house to visit, have you?"

Mamma swung around and said, "*Silenzio*, Sofia!" To Lucy she offered a smile. "We are very glad to be here. For one thing, Bonwitter's been causing more trouble."

"Causing me more trouble," Sofia said.

The shelter of Mamma's arms faded and Lucy found herself thrust into the position of protector again. "What has he done?"

An assault, a face in the window, a threat, a torn book taken from the apartment . . . Menace enough for Mr. Standish to change the locks. "Why haven't the police arrested him?"

"They've tried, but he's too quick for them. Too determined to hurt us."

"Hurt me," Sofia said. "Since you left, I'm his target."

A wave of guilt washed over Lucy. Bonwitter wanted his revenge on *her*. Had she been remiss in leaving her mother and sister behind?

She decided to change the subject. "How was your trip? Weren't the furnishings in the train cars luxurious?"

"Luxurious?" Sofia laughed. "Hard benches are hardly luxurious." She put a hand to her lower back. "And it was so crowded. . . . I had a fat lady sitting next to me the whole time, taking up half of my place and—"

Lucy was confused. "You didn't travel first class?"

"Not at all," Sofia continued. "And I don't think it's fair you got all the frills and we got some dry bread and a thin piece of cheese, and loud babies crying in our ears, making it impossible for me to read , and—"

"So-fi-a!" Mamma said, making her name a full three syllables. She turned to Lucy. "We are here, and glad to be here, and that's the end of it. Now tell us about the costumes we are to make."

Gladly.

Rowena tried not to hold on to Edward's arm too tightly, but she was glad to be with him again, and wary of the massive steps leading upward to the neighbor's music room. She held her dress with one hand, and Edward with the other, but unfortunately her bad leg was on the outside and—

The toe of her shoe caught in her dress, and she slipped down one step—

Edward's free hand grabbed her closest arm and his inner arm found her waist. But too late. She fell to the step, landing with a hard *oomph* on her knees. Off-balance, she turned on her side to sit.

Even more unfortunate was seeing her skirt raised on the bad leg, exposing its smaller length and twisted angle.

Forgetting the pain from her landing, she reached forward to adjust her dress, only to have Edward do it for her.

Which meant he'd seen; he knew the awful extent of her injury.

Rowena felt her face grow hot and saw in a blur a throng of onlookers stairstepped around her, their eyes drawn to her leg and her awkward position on the steps, their mouths agape or in conversation with each other, certainly discussing the poor crippled Rowena making a fool of herself.

But then . . .

"I'm so, so sorry, Miss Langdon. It was my fault completely," Edward said as he helped her up. "My foot slipped and I brought you down with me. I am a clumsy man of the highest order."

Rowena regained her footing and further smoothed her skirt. "Not the highest order," she said. "At least not yet. We'll save that designation for a future honor."

There were a few titters of appreciative laughter, and Hattie Tremaine said to her husband, "Actually, I think you own that honor, don't you, Conrad?"

Conrad pretended to be appalled and gave his view of the past incident. "I assure you, I did not mean to make the entire centerpiece disintegrate. It was a design defect, I tell you." He raised his right hand as if taking an oath. "I stand by this limitation of my guilt."

It was enough to defray the moment and get people moving again. Once Rowena and Edward were merely one couple among many, he whispered, "Are you all right?"

"Bruised of body but not of spirit," she whispered back. "And thank you for taking the blame. You didn't need—"

He put a finger to his lips, ending the matter.

And adding to her delight in him.

✦

Edward was a marvel. Not only had he taken the blame for her fall, but when it came time for the professional musicians to step aside and open the event to the amateurs among the guests, he'd stepped forward to perform, leaving it unnecessary for her to decline any polite invitation to sing or play. Of course those gathered were well aware of who had talent and who did not, but of the dozen assembled, only Rowena and Oscar Dudley were known for their nonparticipation.

Not that everyone who performed should have performed. Hattie and her husband, Conrad, had ears of tin and voices just as thin.

But Edward . . .

Upon volunteering, he consulted the hired pianist, who nodded at his choice and presented him with an arpeggio to set the key. Edward put a hand in the opening of his vest, stood straight as a statesman, and began to sing.

" 'Beautiful dreamer, wake unto me, starlight and dewdrops are waiting for thee. Sounds of the rude world, heard in the day, lull'd by the moonlight have all pass'd away. . . . ' "

Rowena was astounded by his mellow voice, and blushed when he looked in her direction to continue the song.

" 'Beautiful dreamer, queen of my song, list while I woo thee with soft melody. Gone are the cares of life's busy throng, beautiful dreamer, awake unto me.' "

Rowena's heart caught in her throat.

Was this what it felt like to be in love?

If so, dear Edward, sing on.

❦

Sofia threw a pillow across the workroom. "This isn't fair. Not fair at all!"

"I'm sorry," Lucy said as she stepped in front of the cots, trying unsuccessfully to hide them from further view. "It was not my doing."

Sofia pointed out the window toward the main house. "You can't tell me in that huge mansion there's not space enough for Mamma and me."

Lucy had no answers, no excuses. She looked to her mother for rescue.

Mamma retrieved the pillow and pressed it into Sofia's arms. "We are not here to sleep, we are here to work, and for work, this space will be quite satisfactory."

"Why does Lucy get all the fun?"

That did it. "Fun?" Lucy said. "I spend hours and hours every day repairing Rowena's clothes, and now I have to create these costumes besides?" She handily kept to herself the free time she'd had for taking walks and meeting Dante. The truth remained: she *had* been working hard.

Mamma moved to one of the trunks. "Let me show you the fabrics we've brought. We have work to do."

Yes, they did. So there, little sister.

⊘⊗⊘

"Thank you for the delicious dinner, Mrs. Oswald," Lucy said.

"You're very welcome." She extended a bowl of boiled carrots to Sofia. "Please have more, Sofia. You're eating like a bird."

"No thank you."

Sofia hadn't eaten much—which was unlike her. Lucy suspected it was done to show her displeasure at having to stay down here in the groundskeeper's house. Her silence was supposedly another punishment. So be it. Lucy had no time for her sister's moping moods.

Mamma rose and helped Mrs. Oswald clear the table. "I can't believe you've worked for the Langdons twenty years."

Mr. Oswald handed Mamma his plate. "That's the year they renovated this place. It was the best of the best, the fanciest of the fancy, until these upstarts came along the past few years and started thinking a summer house had to look like a palace from Europe."

Although *Porte au Ciel* was a mansion by anyone's standards, it was homey compared to the museum quality of some of the other homes Dante had pointed out.

"Yes indeed," Mr. Oswald continued. "We've seen the two children grow up from babes to . . . to . . ."

From the sink, Mrs. Oswald looked over her shoulder at him. "Be kind, Otto."

He sighed and ran a finger along his gray mustache. "Miss Rowena is the kindest of the kind, a genuine lady."

Lucy's interest was piqued. "But her brother?"

"What can I say? Hugh doesn't know the concept of responsibility, taking it or assuming it."

"What's the difference?" Mamma asked.

Mr. Oswald shared a glance with his wife, but when she shrugged, he continued. "I'm still waiting for that boy—that young man—to take responsibility for causing his sister's injury. Until he does that, I just don't think he's going to be capable of assuming the responsibility of the family—"

Lucy was confused. "I thought Rowena fell on their yacht." *At least that's what Hugh told me.*

"She fell all right, after saving Hugh from going overboard."

"She saved him?" Mamma asked.

"He was only ten or eleven, and was misbehaving something awful. I've heard it said he was told many times to quit climbing on the railing. He kept doing it, and when a wave made the yacht teeter, he lost his grip and footing. Miss Rowena lunged for him and got his hand. She held on to him until adults came to the rescue."

Mrs. Oswald finished the story. "In the saving, Rowena broke her hip and her leg in three places. They were far from shore and sped to the nearest port. But it was a tiny town, with no real doctor, and . . ." She paused to genuflect. "The bones weren't set correctly and now she limps. Her leg never did grow properly."

"We certainly hope her marriage to Mr. DeWitt goes through. She's not getting any younger."

Lucy objected to the last statement. Rowena was three years younger than herself. "But Rowena is so lovely in every other way," Lucy said. "Any man who can't look past her limp is—"

Sofia shoved her chair back and stood. "I'm tired. I'm going to bed."

Lucy and the others stared at her, dumbstruck by her rudeness. But before Mamma could chastise her and tell her to sit down, Sofia walked out of the Oswald's living area toward the back room.

Mamma's face reddened. "I'm so sorry. I apologize for my youngest daughter. She's headstrong and . . ."

There was no defense for rudeness.

❦

While Mamma helped Mrs. Oswald with the dinner dishes, Lucy excused herself. Before heading back to her quarters, she detoured to the workroom, expecting to find Sofia in bed, and also expecting to wake her to give her a good scolding. "How dare—"

Sofia wasn't there.

Lucy went outside, hoping to find her sitting against the building, pouting.

But Sofia wasn't there either.

Lucy scanned the grounds, having no idea where to look. Her first fear was that Sofia had stomped up to the main house and made a fool of herself demanding some right she didn't deserve. Her mind filled with the apologies she'd have to make to the staff and, heaven forbid, the Langdons. What could Sofia be thinking to be so brazen and—

Lucy heard Sofia's laughter, and whipped around toward the sound. It was coming from the stables nearby.

Although her anger was still afire, Lucy felt some relief. At least Sofia wasn't breaking some protocol of society.

But then she thought of Haverty and all the other men at the stables. Sofia was a pretty girl. They were virile men. . . .

Lucy walked faster.

She followed the sound of Sofia's laughter and rounded a corner, through the open stable doors. There was Sofia, leaning against a stall, one knee raised to enable her shoe to lie flat against it.

A stableboy stood nearby, his left arm extended to the stall, leaning close.

"Sofia!"

Sofia rolled her eyes and offered a dramatic sigh.

Lucy turned her wrath on the young man. "Leave her alone! She's just a child."

Sofia stomped a foot upon the ground. "I am not!"

Lucy recovered quickly. "That action proves you are. Come with me. Now. Mamma is waiting."

"She's always waiting." Yet in spite of her words, Sofia moved away.

The boy made his defense. "I didn't go after *her*. She came in here. We were just talking."

Lucy knew who was at fault. "I know. And I apologize for snapping at you. But if she comes in here again, send her back where she—"

"I am not a wayward dog, needing to be sent home!"

Lucy exchanged a look with the young man, then grabbed her sister by the upper arm and marched her out of the stable.

"Let go of me!"

"Stop making a scene."

"Then . . . let go!" Sofia pulled her arm loose and ran ahead toward the workroom.

Lucy shook her head, exasperated. Although her sister had grown feisty in recent years, Lucy had never, ever expected her to act up like—

Lucy looked to the left toward the main house and saw Hugh Langdon sitting sideways upon a second-story windowsill, one leg bent. He gave her a one-fingered salute.

Great. Just what she needed. An audience. And not just any audience.

Hugh. A spoiled liar.

She suffered a shiver.

CHAPTER SIXTEEN

"Why can't they come to *us* for the fittings?" Sofia asked as she lugged three bolts of fabric to the main house.

"You wanted to see the house; now you're seeing it," Lucy said. "Mamma, tell her to be polite in front of the ladies. I don't want her embarrassing me."

"Sofia will be the essence of polite to the ladies," Mamma said as she readjusted a bolt of satin against some striped fabric. "As will you be, Lucia, to your sister."

Lucy wanted to argue but knew it would do no good. But she also knew if Sofia didn't watch herself and wise up soon, she'd end up in big trouble. Lucy was already regretting her presence. If only Mamma could have come alone.

They entered the house via the servants' entrance.

Mrs. Donnelly was passing by and gave them a what-for look. "And who are you?" she asked.

Lucy made the introductions. "This is my mother and sister,

Mrs. Donnelly. They've come to help sew some costumes for the Vanderbilt ball." She nodded toward Mamma. "Mother, Sofia, I'd like you to meet Mrs. Donnelly, the housekeeper. She's in charge of . . . of . . ."

"Everything," Mrs. Donnelly said.

Well put.

"And where are you going with all that fabric?" she asked.

"To Mrs. Langdon's morning room," Lucy answered. "We're having the fittings there."

Sofia dropped a bolt and picked it up with difficulty.

"Don't leave a mess for the housemaids or I guarantee you'll hear about it."

"We won't, Mrs. Donnelly." Lucy led her family to the stairs.

"Who does that woman think she is?" Sofia asked. "The queen of the house?"

"Next to Mrs. Langdon and Mr. Timbrook, the butler, that's exactly who she is. You need to show her some respect."

Sofia made a disgruntled face but kept any comeback to herself.

The back stairway emptied out in a rear hall. They passed the dining room on their way to the morning room.

"Well, I'll be," Mamma said.

Lucy turned around and saw Mamma and Sofia stopped in the doorway, taking it in. She remembered her first look at the dining room and allowed them their awe. "Isn't it something?"

"How many can they seat in there?" Mamma asked.

Lucy did a quick count of the chairs. "Thirty or so. At least."

"Look at that ceiling," Sofia whispered.

They all peered up at the painting of cherubs, clouds, flowers, and ribbons that covered the ceiling, which was edged with a carved golden cornice.

"Who are these people?" Sofia asked. "They're rich as royalty."

"Come, now," Lucy said. "The ladies will be arriving soon, and I'd like to have the fabrics nicely displayed before they do."

Mrs. Langdon's morning room was on the east side of the house, across from the dining room. It was radiant with sunshine.

"It's a room made for a princess," Sofia said.

Lucy remembered her initial impression of this room when she'd met with Rowena after arriving in Newport. She too had been struck by its airy lavishness. Unlike the darker hues in the rest of the house, it was decorated in soft tan, fern, and mauve. The delicate furniture, with its light-colored wood, curved legs, and ornamental filigree, revealed a woman's touch.

"Set the bolts over there."

Sofia ran a hand along the silk back of a chair. "So Mrs. Langdon just uses this room in the morning? She uses another room in the afternoon?"

"I don't think 'morning room' is to be taken too literally. I think she uses it all day, but it's *her* room." Lucy moved to a desk near a window. "See? This is her desk, where she handles her correspondence."

Sofia picked up a pen and ran it between two fingers. "I would correspond with people too if I had a desk like this—and had someone to write to."

Lucy took the pen out of her hands. "Please quit touching everything. It's not yours."

Sofia drew back and sulked. "Don't rub it in."

Lucy turned to her mother for support. "Please, Mamma. Tell her to behave. We can't have her making such comments when the ladies come."

Mamma gave her youngest a scathing look. "If I have to order you to silence, I will."

Sofia shrugged but shook her head.

Lucy let out a sigh. Mamma and Sofia were there to help her, yet she'd felt more stress in the last twenty-four hours than she had with the concept of handling all the sewing herself.

The clock on the mantel chimed the three-quarter hour. They needed to get the fabric organized.

With her family's help, Lucy grouped the fabrics according to costume and draped them dramatically over various chairs. Hopefully the fabrics would speak for themselves and delight the Langdons and Mrs. Garmin.

"Take that fringe and lay it over the red—"

As the clock began to strike the hour, Mrs. Langdon entered, followed by Rowena and Mrs. Garmin.

Mrs. Garmin clapped her hands together. "It's a fabric extravaganza!"

Leave it to her to make Lucy feel the extra effort was worth it.

"Well, well," Mrs. Langdon said as she strolled past the three displays. "I can see how the fabrics lend themselves to your designs." She stopped in front of the green cloth for her costume and touched it. "The depth of the velvet is exquisite."

Lucy caught Rowena's eye and received an encouraging nod. Then she held the coral silk that would be the underskirt over her arm. "And see how this one drapes?"

Rowena stepped forward. "It will feel heavenly when you walk, Mother."

Mrs. Langdon studied it a few moments, nodded, then looked at Lucy. "Well done."

Lucy was so happy she could have called it a day right then.

Mrs. Garmin pulled the length of paisley challis from her display and wrapped it around her shoulders, sashaying across the room. "As a gypsy queen I'll need some castanets, or perhaps a tambourine."

Mrs. Langdon shook her head. "Alice will have a conniption if you do."

"All the more reason."

Lucy moved to Rowena's display of butter-colored silk with golden thread embroidered throughout. "Do you like your fabric?"

Rowena's smile revealed her answer. "It's just as I envisioned. More."

Lucy leaned close. "*I* will make yours."

"Which one will I make?"

It was the first time Sofia had spoken, and as the three women turned toward her voice, Lucy realized she hadn't introduced them to her family.

She hurried forward. "I'm so sorry. Please let me introduce my mother, Lea Scarpelli, and my sister, Sofia. Mother, Sofia, this is Mrs.

Langdon, the lady of the house, and her daughter, Rowena, and this is Mrs. Garmin, who befriended me on the train."

Mamma bowed her head. "So nice to meet you. Thank you for bringing us here."

"Do you find your accommodations and work space acceptable?" Mrs. Langdon asked.

"Yes, very. Thank you."

Sofia stepped forward. "Actually, I'd like to stay in this house with my sister."

Lucy grabbed her arm. "Sofia, shush!"

Mamma pulled at Sofia from the other side. "Please forgive my daughter, Mrs. Langdon. She speaks when she should be silent."

Mrs. Langdon's face was stoic, but Lucy could see thoughts moving behind her eyes. She finally said, "If Lucy will have you in her room, I have no objection."

Sofia stepped out of her mother's shadow. "Really?"

Lucy wanted to wave a hand and ask, *What about me? What if I don't want her in my room?*" But she didn't have time, for Mrs. Langdon asked, "Is that agreeable, Lucy?"

No! "Of course, Mrs. Langdon."

"Good. Now, let's proceed with the fittings."

It had finally happened. Sofia had gone too far.

❧

"I'm sorry, all right?" Sofia was done with this discussion. You'd have thought she'd asked to stay in *Rowena's* room.

Hoping to diffuse the scolding, she tossed a tape measure into the air, but instead of catching it, she let it slip through her fingers and die upon the floor.

Lucy pointed scissors at her. "You had no right to complain about anything, especially to Mrs. Langdon."

"But she asked how we liked . . ."

"She was being polite!"

Mamma stepped between them. "This argument is getting nowhere. Sofia, your sister is correct. You shouldn't have complained about our accommodations. They may be simple, but they are satisfactory. The Oswalds are nice people and—"

Boring people. "I just wanted to—"

Mamma stopped her word with a hand. "And, Lucia, you must be more forgiving and stop presenting yourself as some bastion of society perfection."

"I'm not; it's just that Sofia needs to keep her mouth shut when she doesn't know—"

Mamma shook her head. "Remember what Papa said: '*Chi non fa, non falla.*'"

Those who do nothing make no mistakes.

"See?" Sofia said. "Papa would've said it was all right."

Mamma turned on her. "No, he would not have said that. His wisdom only means that mistakes happen. That doesn't mean we should run willy-nilly into them."

Lucy had to have the last word. "From what I've heard and seen, Newport society will only forgive so much. It's far better to remain silent than risk offense."

Mamma spread the red satin for Mrs. Garmin's costume on the workroom table. "What's done is done, and what is not done . . ." She nodded toward the bolts of fabric. "We have much to do, girls."

Sofia picked up the measuring tape. Lucia walked past and took it from her—none too gently. The warning was blatant: Sofia had better work doubly hard today or—

Or what?

She hated when Lucy acted more like her father than her sister. And yet . . . Sofia remembered seeing Lucy and Papa in deep discussion—as equals. Such times had aggravated her, and more often than not, she'd made a point of intruding, of interrupting their conversation by going to sit on Papa's lap.

"*Più tardi, cara,*" he'd tell Lucy. *Later, my dear.* And then, rather reluctantly, he'd give his attention to Sofia—for a brief moment before making an excuse that he had things to do.

With a mental slap, Sofia acknowledged that Lucy had been their father's sounding board, his confidante. And she, Sofia, had been but a child to him, dear in her own way, but of little import or consequence.

If only she'd had the chance to show him that she too could act grown-up, that she too could contribute to the family.

But the fact remained, it was too late to show Papa anything. If she worked hard, it would be for herself. And Mamma.

Although Sofia wasn't one to surrender to Lucy's wishes, she did vow to behave herself.

At least for a little while.

❧

The three women barely talked as they worked on the costumes, each fully engaged in her work.

And good progress was made. All three dresses were cut out. Lucy had been concerned about what Sofia could do. Last she'd seen in New York, her sister had been doing odd jobs, a little handwork, and was only beginning to sew on a machine. She was therefore surprised when Sofia fully took over the sewing machine. "We haven't just been sitting around while you've been gone," Sofia said. "Mrs. Flynn says I have the potential to be just as good at the machine as Leona."

Good for her.

Lucy knew she'd reached a stopping point when her thoughts strayed from sewing to Dante. Had he gone to their hiding place and found her note? Had he left another?

As these questions demanded attention, Lucy decided to fulfill two needs with one act. She set down her scissors and declared, "It's time for a break. I have a special place I want to show you."

Sofia finished the seam she was sewing. "I vote for anyplace but here."

Mamma swept up the fabric scraps and put them in a pail. She rubbed the back of her arm over her forehead. "I too am ready for a change of scenery. Where are you taking us?"

"To the Cliff Walk."

"It sounds dangerous," Mamma said.

"It can be. But it's also stunning." She pointed to the hat tree. "Gather your hats and let's go."

❧

Sofia ran ahead toward the beckoning sea. "Look! It's gorgeous!" She stepped off the path, from rock to rock, drawing closer to the waves below. She flung her arms wide, wanting to capture the sea in her embrace. "I have never smelled such air!"

The others came up behind and immediately Mamma called to her. "Get back here, Sofia! The rocks aren't safe."

Sofia knew Mamma was right, yet she felt just the opposite, as if the rocks, which had been washed by the waves for eons, were as stable and eternal as the ground a mile inland.

She looked around to see her mother hugging the land side of the narrow pathway as she'd hugged the middle of the steamer when they'd traversed the bay.

"Come, now," Lucy said. "I want to show you my favorite place."

Lucy led the way, with Sofia taking up the rear. Mamma was so uncertain with her footing that when the path was wide enough, Sofia took the outside position and held her arm.

"Here we are." Lucy stopped beside a hip-high stone wall. She pointed out to sea. "Isn't it spectacular?"

Mamma eagerly sat on the wall, but Sofia found a boulder to stand upon. "I like the other place better. The waves aren't as violent here."

Mamma crossed herself, then removed her hat and used it as a fan. "I'm not used to such a hike."

Sofia turned around to say something but saw Lucy, sitting next to Mamma, reaching down and pulling at a rock.

Lucy was absorbed in her task, so Sofia pretended she hadn't noticed. When she looked again, Lucy was pressing the rock back into place.

There was something in her hand. . . .

Secrets? Her sister had secrets? That wasn't like Lucy.

Sofia raised her eyebrows when Lucy looked at her.

Her sister adjusted her skirt over the wall, pretending . . . Then she stood and, with her opposite hand, pointed toward a mansion behind them. "See this mansion? It's called Vinland after some Norsemen—or is it horsemen?"

Her attempt at distraction was almost comical and revealed Lucy's inexperience in deception.

Mamma looked toward the house, apparently at the end of her tolerance for sightseeing. "I'd like to go back now," she said.

"Of course," Lucy said. "Sofia? Would you lead the way?"

Absolutely not. Sofia wanted to watch her sister carefully. "You first, sister," she said with a sweep of her arm.

Lucy couldn't refuse without argument, and when she stood, Sofia saw her slip something into her skirt pocket.

Lucy, Lucy, what are you up to?

"Mr. DeWitt is here, Miss Langdon."

Rowena looked up from her thank-you note to the hostess of the musicale. Edward had come to visit her? Unannounced?

She rose and glanced in the mirror on the wall of the morning room. "Show him in, Timbrook."

Edward entered, dressed in a light-colored suit, so appropriate for the heat of the Newport summer. He kissed her on the cheek and took the seat she offered.

"How nice of you to come, Edward. I didn't expect—"

"I was out taking a jaunt this morning and decided to stop by to check on the state of your bruises."

"Sore but surviving," she said, though she had an enormous welt on her knee.

"Good for you." He rose and began strolling around the room. She'd already taken him for a man who couldn't be sedentary for long.

She would have liked to ask him about his plans for the day, but to do so would be asking for an invitation. She was due to see him tomorrow night for dinner. . . .

Suddenly, he reached low and pulled up a painting she'd set on the floor beside a table. "And what's this?" he said, studying it. "This is absolutely beautiful." He raised his gaze to include her. "How dare you keep your talent hidden behind the furniture. This should be hung above the mantel, at the very least."

Unfortunately, it was Lucy's painting he lauded. For a brief moment she was tempted to take credit, for how would he ever uncover her lie? But then, the truth forced itself into words. "Lucy painted it."

He blinked once, then twice. "Lucy?"

"I think I told you I'd befriended a talented seamstress in New York and brought her here. She's sewing our costumes for the Vanderbilts' ball."

"Lucy," he repeated.

Rowena nodded. "Lucy Scarpelli. Isn't that a marvelous—"

Edward looked again at the painting, then set it down in its original place. "Well, then. No matter who painted it, the artist shows true talent."

Rowena sighed. "Which is further proof that it is not mine, for I possess no talents of any kind, neither of music, of yarn or thread, and certainly not of paintbrush."

The look on Edward's face made her ache to take back the words. "I shouldn't have . . . I mean . . ."

He smiled politely, then made his way toward the door. "I really need to go. I just wanted to stop by . . ."

She rose. "Of course. I appreciate your kind visit."

And then he was gone, and with him went the strength in Rowena's legs.

She sank into a chair, her head shaking against the memory of her words. "Stupid, stupid, stupid!" she said aloud. "What was I thinking, listing my absence of talent? I'm supposed to impress him, not shove him away!"

She pressed her hands against her face. "Dear God, what have I done?"

If Mrs. Oswald says "bless your heart" one more time, I'll throw the green beans in her face.

249

Being forced to eat their meals with the Oswalds was like being wrapped in a grandmother's shawl—and having it tied up tight in a large knot. Sofia liked old people—Mamma was old and was her favorite person in the entire world. But to be around them twenty-four hours a day . . .

At least she wouldn't have to sleep there anymore. Mrs. Langdon had given her permission to stay with Lucy. That one fact had helped her endure the work of the day.

On many occasions she'd wanted to mention it to Lucy and ask how to go about it. After the meeting with the rich ladies, Sofia had expected Lucy to take her upstairs immediately. Even if her sister detested the idea, Mrs. Langdon had ordered it, and so Lucy had to obey.

Didn't she?

Mrs. Oswald was finishing yet another tedious story about her daughter. "And she never said another word, bless her heart."

Sofia leaped into the pause between stories. "If you'll excuse me?"

Mrs. Oswald looked surprised, as if she'd only then remembered Sofia was even at the table. "Of course, dear."

Sofia avoided meeting Mamma's gaze and exited to the workroom. Now what?

It was getting dark and would soon be time to go to sleep. If she stayed here and Mamma came in, she would be stuck here for the night. The only way to get to stay in the main house was to take matters into her own hands.

She wrote a quick note to Mamma—*Gone to stay with Lucy*—and put it on her pillow. Then she quickly packed their smallest satchel and slipped outside.

Walking up to the main house in the half dark of sunset, she chose the least obvious path so she could enter the back way, where Lucy had taken them that morning. She paused at the door, uncertain whether to knock or just go inside. She didn't want to draw attention to herself, so . . .

She opened the door and went in. To her left she heard voices and movement coming from the kitchen, dishes clattering as they were washed. To avoid meeting anyone, she hurried up the stairs to the first floor. But two steps from the top she paused behind the newel-post to verify her course.

The stairs continued to the second floor, leading to new territory. It was odd to think she'd seen the grand dining and morning rooms but not her own sister's room.

Voices coming from the main part of the house propelled her upward. She took each tread on her toes, hugging the rail side, which was more apt to be without squeaks.

On the second floor she was faced with a long hallway and many doors. *This was a bad idea. How am I ever going to find Lucy's room?*

Maybe if she walked slowly and listened for Lucy's voice . . .

She moved forward, listening at a door to her left, then her right.

Suddenly a door opened and a young man in evening dress pulled up short.

"My, my, a stalker in the hall. Friend or foe?"

Sofia stepped away, more than a little taken aback by his . . . his . . . dashing appearance.

She'd never even thought of that term before, and had only seen it within the pages of her novels. Yet there was no other way to describe this man. Light brown hair parted in the middle, hazel eyes . . . but it was the package of the whole that made the impression. Sofia had a quick thought: Wouldn't any man, dressed in a tuxedo, be as dashing?

His eyes narrowed and he pointed a finger for emphasis. "I know who you are. Lucy's sister. Part of the reinforcements from home."

She didn't like the designation. "I've come to make a costume for Mrs. Langdon, her daughter, and—"

He smiled. "My mother and sister."

Sofia took another step back. This was the Langdon son? The heir?

He laughed. "Do I suddenly smell offensive?"

"Of course not." He smelled wonderful. Of musky spice.

"Then why do you back away from me?"

She purposely took a large step forward. As she did so, she noticed a stain on the white of his shirt. "Your shirt is soiled," she said.

He looked down. "Oh my. Cook's gravy has done me in again."

He turned back to his room, then faced her fully once more. He clicked his heels together. "Thank you, Miss . . . ?"

"Sofia."

"Thank you, Miss Sofia, for saving me from excruciating humiliation at the casino tonight. How can I repay you?"

Sofia delighted in his attention and regretted the conversation was coming to an end. "You can point me toward my sister's room. I'm to stay with her."

He reached for her satchel, then held out an arm and said, "Come. I will be your personal escort."

Sofia had never taken the arm of any man but Papa, much less a gentleman, but slipped her hand into the space he'd created.

He began to stroll down the hall. "Actually, your sister's room—the lovely Lucy—is to our right here, directly next to mine, as it were."

Sofia felt the fool and started to pull her hand away. "I'm sorry, I—"

He drew it back. "But as you see, there is no access from this charming hallway and so we must find another way. This next door goes to my sister's dressing room, which is full of delightfully excessive fashion, and this . . ." He stopped before a second door and knocked.

It was Rowena who cracked the door to see who it was, then opened it fully. "Hugh? What—?"

Hugh took Sofia's hand and twirled her under his arm before presenting her. "This lovely lady is looking for her sister's room. Would you be so kind as to take over the tour?"

"Of course," Rowena said. "Come through this way, Sofia."

But before leaving her, Hugh kept hold of her hand, bowed, and kissed it. "*Adieu*, Sofia. Until we meet again. *Vous êtes enchanteresse, belle fille.*"

Sofia had no idea what he said, and only found the word *belle* to sound in the least familiar. *Bella* in Italian meant beautiful.

And so she felt herself blush.

Rowena interrupted by stepping aside to draw her into the room. "Good night, Hugh. You're going out?"

He handed Sofia the satchel and winked. "As soon as I change my shirt." With a nod he was gone.

The hallway wasn't the same without him.

❧

Lucy sat by the window of her room and perused Dante's letter for the ninth time. Or was it the tenth?

Your words brought me full pleasure, dearest Lucia. Come to me at two in the afternoon, but not at the Cliff Walk, which will certainly be teeming with people. I have something else to show you. Meet me at the corner of Narragansett Avenue and Annandale Road. I count the hours.

She'd never seen Dante except on the Cliff Walk, but obviously, he had plans to go elsewhere. Oddly, she found herself quite willing, and though there was a niggling inner voice that told her she had no reason to trust him, trust him she—

There was a knock on her door.

"Yes, Rowena?"

The door opened and Rowena entered in her nightclothes. But not alone. "You have a house guest."

Sofia stepped inside Lucy's room, carrying a satchel. "*Ciao*, sister."

Lucy was aghast. After the scolding she'd given Sofia this afternoon, the girl had the audacity to show up? And knock on Rowena's door?

Rowena glanced about the room. "Hugh brought her up. I know Mother gave consent for your sister to join you, but . . . I see there's no other bed."

"I'll sleep on the floor," Sofia said.

Lucy nearly laughed. Sofia, offer to be uncomfortable?

"I could order in another bed."

Lucy shook her head, but Sofia answered. "That would be nice."

Rowena gave Lucy a questioning look, but Lucy knew there was no agreeable way to refuse her offer. And Rowena looked haggard, as if she wasn't up to dealing with this problem. "That would be nice," Lucy repeated.

"Very well, then. I'll ring. Wait in the hall off the dressing room and someone will come up. Tell them what you need and they'll put it in place. Meanwhile, I must say good night."

As soon as Rowena left, Lucy pointed a stern finger at her sister. "Stay here."

She went out to the hall and paced, needing an outlet for her fuming. *How dare Sofia intrude like this? I'm the one who got invited here. Sofia's only here because of me! She has no right to—*

After mentally repeating the rant a dozen times, Lucy saw Sadie coming to answer Rowena's call. She shared the request and Sadie left—after raising her eyebrows at the gall. The presumption. Lucy could only imagine the tattle that would flow belowstairs.

Sofia stuck her head through the doorway. "Is a bed coming?"

Lucy spun toward her, pointing a finger. Sofia disappeared inside.

Lucy felt the last vestige of patience evaporate. Luckily, Sofia made herself scarce for the rest of the wait.

Soon there was the sound of commotion on the back stairs and two male servants appeared, carrying an iron bed.

"Through here," she said.

With some difficulty, they carried the bed through the dressing room and into Lucy's quarters, where they set it in the corner.

The taller of the two made no bones about looking around. "Seems you're setting up quite a home for yourself 'ere, ain't ya?"

"It's a temporary arrangement," Lucy said.

Sofia offered both men a smile. "Thank you for bringing me a bed."

Lucy became invisible.

"You're welcome, lass. What's yer name?"

"Sofia."

"Mine's Connor."

"And mine's Dav—"

Her sister's power of attraction was unnerving. "That will be all, gentlemen." She moved toward the door. "Thank you for your service."

Sofia took a step forward. "There's no bedding." When the men looked at her, she said, "I need bedding."

There was something unseemly in her request, and Lucy hurried the men away. When they were gone she confronted Sofia—again. "You do not speak of bedding to a man."

Sofia sat on her bed, bouncing on the thin mattress. "They don't sleep?"

It was complicated—which anyone over the age of twelve knew. "*I'll* get you bedding."

Lucy went out to the hall, to the linen room, and gathered a set of sheets, a pillow, and a towel. She knew Mrs. Donnelly kept tabs on its contents, but she'd deal with her later. She noticed under the door of Hugh's room there was still a light on. . . .

For some reason it made her nervous.

She hurried back to the room. "Here. Bed—"

Sofia was seated at the chair, holding—

Lucy snatched the note away from her. "Give me that!"

"Who's Dante, and why does he have Father's name?"

"None of your business."

Sofia leaned back in the chair as if she owned it, a smug smile upon her lips. "You're meeting him tomorrow. Can I come too?"

"No, you may not!"

"Does Mamma know about this other Dante?"

Lucy dropped the linens to the floor. "Here. Make up your own bed."

Sofia shrugged. "Help me?"

The audacity.

Lucy left her to do it herself, and while Sofia's back was turned, she gathered Dante's other notes and slid them under her mattress. For now at least.

There were no words exchanged until the lamp was extinguished and both girls were in bed.

Sofia broke the silence by saying, "Mamma said sharing a room would be good for us."

Lucy faced the wall. What was Mamma thinking? The only good Lucy could imagine was that it would keep Sofia farther away from Haverty and the other stableboys.

But closer to Hugh . . .
She closed her eyes and tried to think happy thoughts.

⁂

Sofia turned over on her mattress with a distinct *plop.* It was not her first act of restlessness, nor would it be her last.

Part of the reason she couldn't sleep was regret. She shouldn't have read Lucy's notes. She'd known it at the time but had been unable to control her curiosity.

Lucy had a suitor?

Sofia knew Lucy had come close to marrying Angelo Romano, and she didn't fully understand why it had been called off. But other than Angelo, she'd never seen Lucy be flirtatious; in fact, the thought of Lucy being in love was absurd. Love was all about lingering looks, desperate embraces, and undying passion. Or at least that's how her novels portrayed it. She could *not* imagine Lucy in any of these situations. Lucy was the sensible one, the—

Sofia's thoughts flipped from Lucy to herself, and then to Hugh.

With little effort she could imagine herself in his arms. She would look up at him and he would smile down at her, and then, with a lift to her chin, he would . . .

Yet again, Sofia turned over as sleep eluded her.

CHAPTER SEVENTEEN

amma held on to Lucy's arm tightly. Lucy could tell she was apprehensive and entered the Langdons' church as if entering a foreign land. Lucy understood her disquiet. Mamma liked what was *known*. After all, she'd lived in the same apartment on Mulberry Street for two decades, and had sat in the same pew at the Old St. Patrick's every Sunday. The fact that Mamma had adapted rather well to their new home above the dress shop was a miracle. Now, to ask her to attend a different church, in a different town, in a different state—with strangers?

Lucy patted her hand and whispered, "It's all right, Mamma. God lives here too."

They followed the other servants into the sanctuary, and sat as a group near the back. What surprised Lucy the most was how the church was shared with the upper classes and the servants. The congregation of their old church was strictly immigrants. It wasn't that they didn't allow the rich to enter; it just *was*. But here in Newport, the wealthy residents sat up front, walking past in all their Sunday finery, while the people who served them sat in the back.

Lucy wasn't certain how to feel about it. Wasn't the God they were here to worship the same for all? To be so segregated was a bit disturbing, and yet . . .

It would have felt far more awkward to sit intermixed. There was comfort in sitting among people of like kind.

The church was full, and Lucy sat shoulder to shoulder with Haverty. She'd purposely placed herself so, shooing Sofia into the pew after Mamma. Of course, that didn't stop Sofia from leaning forward and smiling at the man, or the other boys who worked in the household.

"Stop that," Lucy whispered.

"There's no rule against smiling in church."

But how about flirting?

The organ music began and all stood to sing from a hymnbook. They weren't used to singing songs in their church, but Lucy helped Mamma find the book and turn to the right hymn: "The Church's One Foundation." Mamma shared with Sofia, leaving Lucy to share with Haverty. The man had a nice baritone voice and they sang the first verse and started the second. " 'Elect from every nation, yet one o'er all the earth; her charter of salvation, one Lord, one faith, one birth; one holy name—' "

Lucy glanced up and stopped singing. There, across the church, was Dante! He was sitting with an older couple. His parents? She'd always assumed he lived alone, that as a businessman he lived above his shop, or—

Had he ever said he ran a shop? Had he ever told her anything about how he made his livelihood?

Haverty nudged her arm, and she returned to the hymn, but only mouthed the words as her mind raced. From the older woman's attire it was clear she was wealthy, or at the very least upper middle class.

She knew Dante wasn't poor. She had known that from the beginning.

As if he felt her gaze, Dante glanced back and saw her. Lucy offered a subtle nod, but Dante quickly turned forward again. His mother gave Lucy a glance too before returning to her hymnal.

He didn't smile. He didn't acknowledge me. He's ashamed of me!

A moment after the rest of the people in her pew had sat down, Lucy realized she was still standing. She quickly sat and received a questioning look from Mamma for her tardiness.

Unfortunately, Sofia looked directly at Dante, then at Lucy. Her smile was mischievous.

She knows that's Dante. . . .

As the sermon began, Lucy's thoughts sped to what was going to happen at two o'clock. She was supposed to meet him on a street corner . . . *but not at the Cliff Walk, which will certainly be teeming with people.*

He was ashamed of her! Of being seen with her!

Suddenly, Lucy's opinion of being set apart, servants from masters, changed. Forget the comfort of being among like kind. This segregation had to be the idea of the wealthy. It was they who wanted the separation as a way to showcase their position and standing. To sit in the back as *lesser* people . . .

Papa's voice sounded in her mind: *"Chi la dura la vince."* He that endures overcomes.

But she didn't want to endure such a blatant snub. She was very willing to work for the wealthy. There was honor in work. But on Sunday, the day of rest and *no* work, to have her status shoved in her face . . .

Lucy had the urge to storm out of the church in protest.

But even as her mind warred with the notion, she found her body standing and going through with it. "Pardon me, excuse me," she said, edging out in front of Haverty and two others.

She hurried toward the side aisle and, with a single glance, saw Dante watching her go.

What have I done?

It was too late to worry about that now. Lucy ran out of the church and down the steps to the street. She ran toward home.

No, not home. Toward the Langdons' home.

⚜

Where was Lucy?

When church was over, Rowena had seen Mrs. Scarpelli and Sofia milling about, but Lucy was nowhere to be found.

Hugh sidled up next to her. "If you're looking for Lucy, I saw her run out of the church midway through the service."

"But why?"

Hugh shrugged. "Maybe she didn't like the sermon."

As soon as Rowena got home she knocked on the door to Lucy's room. When Lucy answered she looked pale and her expression was distraught.

"You're not feeling well?" Rowena asked.

"I am well. Physically. I just got upset during church and . . . I ran out. I'm sorry to cause you worry."

They moved into the dressing room. "But what's wrong?"

Lucy shrugged, but Rowena would have none of it. "Lucy, please. Aren't we friends? I want to help."

Lucy was still reluctant, but she answered, "*He* was there. At church. And he's rich."

He must mean Dante. Rowena raised an eyebrow. "Really? Didn't you know he—?"

"No, I didn't!" Lucy said, too loudly. "Sorry. I don't mean to shout, but I feel duped, as if he led me on to believe he was something he wasn't."

"What did he say he was? What does he do for a living?"

Lucy was faced with the reality that Dante knew far more about her than she knew about him. "I know he wants to be an architect. But other than that, he let me talk about myself."

"So he knows you are a . . . a seamstress?"

"Yes." Lucy began to pace. "He knows the conditions I grew up in, he knows my family immigrated from Italy, he knows . . ." She stopped and looked at Rowena. "He knows too much."

Rowena took Lucy's hand and led her to the ottoman. "He knows who you are, your background, your occupation, yet he still wants to see you."

"Well . . . yes."

"I think it would be far more of a problem if you'd kept your roots from him than the fact that he has kept his from you. He is the one to blame, not you."

Lucy's worry lines eased. "Perhaps you're right."

"Of course I am," Rowena said. "But just as he doesn't hold who you are against you, so you mustn't hold his status against him. You must see him today, as planned."

"But—"

Rowena put a finger to Lucy's lips. "No *buts*. You have to go. True love should not be cast off for such a trivial issue."

"It's not true love. I barely know—"

"Which is why you must see him. To know him better." She stood and pulled Lucy to her feet. "How can love grow if you suppress it before it even has a chance?"

"But I'm never supposed to be in love."

Rowena did a double take. "Not supposed—?"

"With my father gone, I'm the head of the family. Mamma and Sofia depend on me."

Rowena placed her hands on her hips. "So you're sacrificing your own happiness for duty?" She didn't let Lucy speak, but continued. "Duty is fine, duty is noble, but you can't ignore your own future, your own purpose, for . . ."

She noticed Lucy had crossed her arms and was shaking her head.

"What?" Rowena asked. "Do I not speak the truth?"

"Oh, it's the truth all right," Lucy said. "But it's your truth as much as mine."

Her words caused Rowena to take a step back. Duty. Sacrifice.

Lucy's voice softened. "We're both dutiful daughters, thinking of our family's needs before our own."

Rowena was very confused. She'd never considered her situation similar to Lucy's. And yet . . .

She sat upon the ottoman, bewildered. "I'm trying to love Edward and trying to get him to love me, and you are trying *not* to love Dante while he clearly loves you. All for the sake of duty."

"We are quite a pair."

Rowena nodded. "But what should we do? To ignore duty seems the epitome of selfishness."

"But what about ignoring love?" Lucy asked.

Rowena took Lucy's hand and pulled her down beside her. "I want to love someone. I want to have that ever-after knowledge that I am meant to be with a certain man for the rest of my life." She looked into Lucy's eyes. "Don't you want that too?"

"I didn't think I did. I didn't think I ever could . . ."

"But now that you've met Dante?"

Lucy shrugged.

The gesture sparked Rowena's anger and propelled her to standing. "You must love him, Lucy. You must allow yourself *to* love." Rowena remembered her latest gaffe with Edward, telling him she had no talents whatsoever. It was akin to saying there was no reason for him to marry her. "I wish I had evidence of love like you do."

"Aren't things going well between you and Edward?"

Rowena moved away and fingered the cuff of a hanging gown. "We attend the same soirees; we talk."

"But . . ."

"As much as I wish for him to love me, I'm afraid he doesn't. Not really."

"Do you love him?"

She hesitated. Did she love Edward? Suddenly the words came spilling out. "I want us to adore each other and be all things to each other, and share secrets and dreams and . . . and know the worst about each other but not care." By saying all this aloud, Rowena realized how far her relationship with Edward needed to go. She'd been ordered to love him, but she didn't. As Shakespeare wrote, "There's the rub."

She turned back to Lucy. "My friend Morrie says that Edward would be an idiot not to fall for me."

"Morrie is right. Give it time and Edward will see what an amazing woman you are."

"But I'm not—" *And time is short.*

"Shhh. You are, and that's that."

Rowena offered a smile of surrender. "Enough of me." She began riffling through the rows of dresses. "What are you going to wear to see your Dante?" With a glance over her shoulder, she added, "For you *are* going to see him."

"I can't wear your clothes again."

"They're not good enough for you?"

"Of course they are, but—"

Rowena pulled a pale olive pinstripe from the pack. "This one, I think."

⚘

"Where did you get that dress?" Mamma asked.

At the question, Lucy immediately regretted her decision to stop by the workroom to tell her mother she felt better and was going to meet a friend.

"Rowena loaned it to me."

Sofia let out a puff of air. "When can I wear her clothes?"

"You can't." *She's not your friend.* "They wouldn't fit you."

Lucy turned toward the door. "I really need to go—"

"But why can't I go too?"

Her regret in coming to the workroom deepened. "Because you weren't invited."

"Now, now, Lucia," Mamma said. "It seems very convenient you are suddenly feeling better—just in time to meet a friend."

"He's not just a friend," Sofia said. "Lucy has a beau."

Lucy felt the heat of Mamma's questioning eyes. Should she deny it?

"A beau, Lucia?"

Lucy flashed Sofia a scathing look—to no avail. Sofia busied herself with a bowl of buttons. "He's a very nice man, Mamma. We met on the Cliff Walk. Actually, he saved me when I slipped down to a ledge."

"You slipped?"

Lucy wasn't sure whether to exaggerate her fall or act as though it were nothing. She decided to focus on the aftermath. "He pulled me to safety."

"Tell me about him. What's his name?"

Before Lucy could answer, Sofia did it for her. "Dante. Like Father."

Lucy felt her cheeks flush. "That's my name for him. He was a hero in saving me, and Father was my hero, so . . ."

"What's his real name?"

Oh dear.

"Lucia?"

"Barth-something? I don't really know."

"You don't know his name, yet you're meeting him on some street corner?"

It did sound questionable. "We've had long talks, Mamma. He's easier to talk with than any man I've ever known. He's a good man. I know it."

"They write each other notes," Sofia added.

That was it. Lucy lunged at Sofia, making the buttons spill. "You little brat! You have no right—"

Mamma got between them and, thankfully, pointed a finger at Sofia. "You hush now. This is Lucia's story to tell."

Sofia couldn't resist one more jab. "He was at church this morning."

Since Sofia had seen the glance that had passed between herself and Dante, Lucy wondered who else had seen.

"Why didn't you introduce me to him?" Mamma asked.

"I . . . I didn't feel well, remember?" She glared at Sofia, trying to warn her to keep any additional comments to herself.

Oddly, her sister remained silent.

"I really have to go, Mamma. You need to trust me, trust my judgment."

Mamma studied her face a moment more, then nodded. "Be wise and be good, Lucia."

She'd try.

⸙

I'll follow her.

If she hurried, Sofia could spy on Lucy with this wealthy man who'd captured her sister's heart.

She headed for the door of the workroom.

"Where are you going?" Mamma asked.

"For a walk."

Mamma gave her the look she deserved. "You leave your sister alone."

Sofia saw an opening. "But I thought you didn't approve—"

"I understandably have questions, *piccolina*. A mother always fears for her daughters' hearts."

"Well, you don't have to worry about mine. I'm not the one in love."

Mamma looked heavenward. *"Grazie, Dio."*

Sofia realized too much time had passed to catch up to Lucy now. She had no idea if she was meeting Dante on the Cliff Walk or somewhere else, and now it was too late.

She put her hand on the doorknob. "I'm not following her, Mamma. I'm just going up to our room to read."

"Promise?"

Sofia crossed her heart. What other choice did she have?

As she walked toward the main house, she glanced toward the stables. She *could* go talk to the stableboys. They seemed eager for her company.

Too eager.

She continued toward the house, where she went in the back entrance and up the stairs. But once on the first floor she noticed how quiet it was and remembered passing a certain room she really wanted to see. . . .

Holding her breath in order to listen for others, she heard nothing, which provided a boost of courage to move forward, down the wide hallway, to the room of her dreams.

The library.

She peeked around the doorjamb and found it empty—of people.

It was full, entirely full, of books. Shelf upon shelf, wall-to-wall books, just waiting to be read.

And she, the willing reader.

She entered and took a sharp left, which allowed her to remain out of sight from anyone walking down the hall. But within moments, her fear of discovery faded into the thrill of discovery. The volumes before her weren't like her cheap dime novels, with flimsy covers and minimal pages. These were thick tomes, bound in leather, with gilt lettering and decorative detail on the spines.

Some titles piqued no interest: *Western Civilization*, *The Mechanics of Pulleys*, and *The Complete Works of Sophocles*. But others . . .

She chose one called *Little Women*, opened to the first page, and read:

> "Christmas won't be Christmas without any presents," grumbled Jo, lying on the rug.
>
> "It's so dreadful to be poor," sighed Meg, looking down at her old dress.
>
> "I don't think it's fair for some girls to have plenty of pretty things, and other girls nothing at all. . . ."

Sofia was hooked and backed into a chair, where she read three pages. Only the sound of voices brought her out of the story and into the fact that she was sitting in the Langdons' library, reading one of *their* books.

She started to put it back on the shelf but desired the story enough that she simply moved the two books on either side of *Little Women*'s space toward the middle and tucked the novel into the folds of her skirt. She *had* to read this book, but she couldn't do it here.

Sofia paused at the doorway, listened, and finding the voices to be from farther up front in the house, slipped into the hallway, where she scurried toward the back stairs.

But then . . .

"Miss Scarpelli!"

It was the butler's voice, coming from the front end of the hall.

She turned around, but the movement caused the heavy book to move out of its hiding place. She quickly put it behind her back.

He strode toward her. "What do you have there?"

She pulled the book around front and clutched it to her chest. "I was just going to my room to read."

He held out his hand. Now she was in trouble. There was no way she could ever claim this fine book as her own. She decided no explanation was better than a feeble one. She gave him the book.

Timbrook read the title and harrumphed. "It sounds decadent." Then he nodded toward the library. "And you stole it."

"I did no such thing. I simply borrowed it, to read."

His eyebrows rose. "You? Read?"

It was beyond insulting. "Yes. I. Read. A very lot, if you must know." *More than you.*

He grabbed her upper arm and pulled her down the hall toward the front of the house. "You will make your excuses to the mistress. Let's see what she wants to do with your pilfering."

"But I didn't—"

"That won't be necessary, Timbrook."

They both turned around to see Rowena's brother standing near the doorway to the library. He motioned toward Sofia. "Come, Miss Scarpelli. Retrieve your book, and then come back to the library. There was another book I wanted to show you that you might enjoy."

Back to the library? Had he been in there the entire time?

In taking the book from the butler, Sofia could feel the nettles flow off Mr. Timbrook into the air between them.

"Pardon me, Mr. Hugh," Timbrook said. "I didn't know she was in the library with your blessing."

Hugh motioned for Sofia to join him—which she was very willing to do. "And in my company. Someone has to read all these books," he said. "And it's certainly not me." Once Sofia was safely in the library, Hugh added, "Thank you for your diligence, Timbrook. That will be all."

Sofia took a position on the far side of the room. Hugh came inside and closed the sliding doors behind him. She sensed Hugh was wild and was used to getting his own way. She would rather deal with Mr. Timbrook and Mrs. Langdon than be in here alone with him.

"Well, now," he said with a grin.

She held the book against her chest. "Thank you for your assistance."

He strolled into the room, tracing a hand over the top of the chairs. "Assistance? I think it was far more than that, Sofia. I saved your hide."

She didn't like his attitude. "I didn't need saving. I wasn't stealing the book; I was merely borrowing—"

"Same thing."

"No it's not. As you stated, *someone* has to read these books."

"*Touché.*"

"What?"

He went to the shelves and pulled out a book. "Here. Read this one."

She read the title. "*The Three Musketeers?*"

He put one arm curved behind his head and thrust his other out toward her. "*En garde! Touché!* All for one, and one for all!"

She still didn't know what he was talking about.

He put his arms down. "Read the book. It's all about honor and valor and love."

It sounded like her kind of story. But beyond that, she'd caught him in a lie.

"You've read the books in here."

He put a finger to his lips. "It's best people don't know."

"Why?"

"Because then they'd expect something of me."

"But don't you want people to expect—?"

He swept his arm toward a couch. "Please. Sit."

Sofia sat and Hugh fell upon a chair nearby, slumping into its cushions, his hands taking the armrests captive.

There was an awkward moment when they simply looked at each other. Ordinarily, Sofia would have been the first to look away. But this time, she felt oddly emboldened and stared back, eye to eye.

And, oh, such handsome eyes . . .

Finally, he waved a hand and said, "You win, you win!" He shook his head. "I thought you were supposed to be the meek little sister."

She felt her ire rise. "Who said that? Did Lucy—?"

Hugh raised his hands in the air. "Don't fire! I surrender."

Sofia felt foolish for overreacting, yet she hated that Lucy had portrayed her as . . . as . . .

What she was.

"What happened?" Hugh asked. "I didn't mean to quench your fire."

"I . . . I . . ."

"I don't like living in my sister's shadow either."

His candidness surprised—and pleased her. "You feel you're in Rowena's shadow?" she asked.

He pulled a footrest close with a toe, then crossed his ankles upon it. "Completely enveloped."

"But you're the heir."

"But she's the martyr."

Sofia remembered hearing the story of Rowena's accident, and how she'd hurt herself saving Hugh. If he didn't say more, she wouldn't bring it up.

"Did you know I caused her injury?"

She was surprised he'd continued with the subject. "How did you do that?"

"I was being reckless on the boat and nearly slipped overboard. Rowena saved me. She's a hero, she's my messiah, and I'm scum on the bottom of a boat." He shook his head, as if removing himself from a bad memory. "Yes indeed, she's the good child, the virtuous child, the loyal and obedient child."

"And you're . . . ?"

"Not."

Sofia empathized with him. "Add capable, trustworthy, and dependable, and you have my sister."

"And you're . . . ?"

She smiled. "Not."

He pushed the footstool away and stood. "Would you like to go for a sail?"

"A what?"

"Would you like to go sailing with me in my sailboat?"

Sofia remembered seeing the boats sailing in the harbor. . . . "I'd love to."

"Take your books upstairs and grab a hat. I'll wait for you outside."

Her mind raced with a hundred reasons why she shouldn't go, but she knew she would be dissuaded by none of them. He opened the library doors, then looked back to her. "Are you coming?"

Oh yes.

❦

Sofia was impressed. Down at the harbor Hugh seemed to know everyone, from the scraggly fishermen to his fellow yachtsmen. Gone was his cockiness. Evident was his love of all things seaworthy and of the sea. He stopped at a cart and bought sandwiches, apples, and a glass flask of beverage. Then he took her hand and led her to a short pier between two sailboats. The boats were much larger in person than they'd seemed from the steamship.

He helped her aboard. "Here now. Watch your step."

The boat rocked precariously and she nearly panicked.

"Sit," he said. "And relax. You're safe with me."

She believed him. The way he untied the ropes that held them to shore, pushed them free, then hoisted the sails . . .

"You're as adept with the boat as I am with a needle," she said.

"That's right. You're a seamstress. Perhaps I'll commandeer you to mend any rips in the sails."

She would like nothing better.

Apparently he was waiting for a response. "As the mate you're supposed to salute and answer, 'Aye aye, Captain.' "

She complied, feeling a bit silly but enjoying the feeling. When was the last time she'd allowed herself to be silly?

Hugh turned the sails to capture the wind and the boat headed out into the bay. The wind whipped against Sofia's face, forcing her to put a hand to her straw hat.

Hugh called out from the back of the boat. "How do you like it?"

When she turned around to answer, the wind caught her hat and pulled it away from her head. She saved it from the water and placed it safely under her seat. Her hair pulled free from its knot and she turned toward the wind again, giving it full rein.

Hugh's laughter gave her permission to lift her face to the current, close her eyes, and raise her arms in the air. "I'm flying!" she yelled.

I'm free.

⁂

The boat was anchored in a quiet cove, the sail down. It rocked gently. Sofia surrendered to its soothing rhythm and took a bite of her apple. "My father worked on the docks," she said.

Hugh unwrapped the paper from his sandwich. "He was a fisherman?"

She shook her head. "He handled the goods coming off the ships. The docks killed him."

"I'm sorry," he said. "I'm guessing the docks didn't kill him, the work did. But, oh, what a way to go."

His comment surprised her. "Surely you don't relish hard work."

He smiled and lifted an arm, making a muscle. "*Au contraire, mademoiselle.* I am a man of muscle, not mind."

She couldn't imagine any wealthy man working up a sweat.

"What? You don't believe me?"

"It's just that . . . what about your father's business? Doesn't that involve office work?"

He put a finger to his nose to indicate the rightness of her state-ment. "Which is why I'm completely supportive of Edward marrying my sister. With Edward at the helm, perhaps I will be allowed to . . ." His voice faded, as did the sparkle in his eyes. "Hold on. A wave . . ."

Sofia braced herself for the rocking caused by the movement of other boats in the main channel. Then she asked, "So what would you like to do for a living? If you had your choice?"

He shrugged, but she could tell there was an answer to her ques-tion available; he simply didn't choose to share it with her. Which made her sad.

"How about you, Sofia? If you could do anything, be anything, what would that be?"

No one had ever asked her that. It had always been assumed she would be what she had always been—a seamstress.

When she didn't answer he asked, "Do you enjoy sewing?"

It was her turn to shrug. "It's something I can do."

"Have . . ." He faltered, then tried again. "Have you ever wondered why you're here?"

"In Newport?"

"Here."

"Why do I exist?" It was such a serious question.

"Exactly."

She thought a moment, then said. "It frightens me. Most of the time I feel very small and useless. Back home there are so many people around, all the time, all hurrying about doing *something*, that I can't imagine God has much use for me. I'm hidden away from His sight. I'm not even important in my own family."

"You're important to me."

"You're too kind."

"I'm not actually. And to answer my own question, I've thought about it a lot. Surely I'm supposed to do more than work in an office. We only have one life, so shouldn't it mean something? Shouldn't the world be better for us living? But how do I affect the world by making elevators? What does that really matter?"

Sofia let the boat tip her gently left, then right, and with the movement an answer came to her. "Perhaps your worth—our worth—isn't measured by what we do to make a living, but in . . . living?" Sofia felt silly saying something so serious. It wasn't like her.

But Hugh applauded. "Bravo, matey. Well said. So to my original question I ask another. How do you want to accomplish that *living*?"

Sofia's thoughts flitted through her wishes and desires. Oddly there weren't that many to choose from. Which made her say, "I'm willing to do whatever comes my way. I'd like some adventure. And a husband who thinks I light up his world. I want children and a—" She realized how personal her answer had become and felt herself blush.

"Your answer is my answer," Hugh said softly.

She stole a look at him and found his eyes fully locked upon her. For the second time that day she held his gaze. *"Simpatico,"* she whispered.

He nodded once. "Soul mate."

She looked away—reluctantly.

È perfetto.

※

Dante was there, standing at the corner. Lucy had second thoughts—until he looked toward her. And smiled.

And life was good again. Very good.

Dante extended his hands to her, and when they met, he pulled Lucy close to kiss her cheek. "Finally, we meet again!"

She stepped back, relinquishing his touch. She would not be so easily appeased. "Actually, I saw you this morning."

He looked away for but a moment, but in that moment, she could see his discomfort. "I was with my parents."

"So I noticed."

He attempted a smile. "You were with your mother and sister?"

"And the rest of the servants."

Dante nodded once, then retrieved a basket at his feet. "I have brought refreshments."

He wasn't going to escape so easily. "Your family is rich."

He set the basket down. "It's not a character flaw."

"It *is* a surprise," she said. "Never, during any of our conversations, did you imply you were one of the . . . the . . ." She didn't know how to say it.

"I never said I wasn't."

Lucy stomped a foot and walked away from him, taking refuge along a hedge.

He nodded to another couple who walked by, then joined her. "What does it matter?" He tried to take her hand, but she kept it by her side. "I have never felt such a tie to a woman as I feel with you—as I felt with you from the first moment we met. I love hearing about your family and your roots."

"But I'm poor."

He stepped back and placed his hands at his sides, palms out, presenting himself. "And I'm here. Of my own free will. Because I want to be."

"That's what Rowena said."

His arms fell to their normal position. "Rowena?"

"Rowena Langdon. The woman I'm sewing costumes for." He had an odd look on his face. "You know them. Of course you know them," she said.

He reached for the basket. "Of course. You mention costumes . . . for the Vanderbilts' ball?"

With a start, Lucy realized he might be going to the ball, that he was probably invited. "You're going, aren't you?"

He shrugged, but she knew his true answer. "Will you be going?" he asked.

A laugh escaped.

"Enough of that," he said. "I told you I had an excursion planned and I will not disappoint." He bent his elbow, offering her his arm. "Shall we?"

Her objections to his social standing fell away. If he didn't care, why should she?

❦

Lucy raised her chin, closed her eyes, and let the wind from the trolley ride caress her face.

"You're an outdoor girl, aren't you?" Dante asked.

She opened her eyes. "I don't think so."

He shook his head. "You are. I saw you on the Cliff Walk, and now, relishing the breeze. Most women would be worried about their hair, but not you."

Was her hair out of place? She checked and tucked a multitude of stray strands behind her ears and into her hat as best she could.

He pushed her hand down. "Don't. Leave it. I like the windswept look."

She left her hair alone. "Do you always say the right things?"

"Maybe you simply make everything I say right."

Lucy laughed. He was amazing. Unlike so many men she knew who were argumentative, Dante had the ability—nay, the talent—to dispel conflict and make things good and easy. In this way he was superior to the other Dante, her father, who'd had a boisterous temper.

The other Dante?

Suddenly, Lucy remembered that Dante wasn't his real name. "Since we seem to be clearing the air today—"

"Amid the clear air."

"Amid the clear air . . . what is your real name? Bartholomew . . . ?"

His face turned serious. "My name is Dante."

"No, it's not. I gave you that name when—"

He shook his head adamantly. "Please, Lucy. I love the name because you gave it to me, because it has meaning for you, because it was your father's name. It has a far deeper meaning than my own name. So please. Continue to call me Dante."

He seemed so sincere, so concerned. What would it hurt?

"Fine," she said. "I proclaimed you Dante before, and Dante you shall remain."

His face brightened once again, and he pointed out the window. "We are almost there."

"Where is there?"

"Easton's Beach."

※

Unlike many of the others at the beach who wore full outfits for swimming, Lucy stood with her skirt raised to her calf, her feet bare. Dante stood next to her, his trousers safe, his feet firmly planted in the sand.

"Are you ready? Because here it comes!"

The ocean rushed to meet them and Lucy squealed at its coolness. As it retreated, the sand around her feet filled in the gaps, making her sink deeper into its captivity.

"You like it?" he asked.

"It's wonderful!"

"See? Just as I said. You are an outdoor girl."

Perhaps she was. How would she know? All her memories were of Mulberry Street, where the tenements were tall, the streets narrow, and every space congested. She'd taken a few walks in Central Park, but even the trek there was a luxury. For when did she have free time? From the moment she was five years old she'd worked in the sweatshops six days a week and had spent Sunday with her family at church and inside the house. Or in good weather out on the stoop with the other families of the neighborhood.

But now, on the edge of the water, with sailboats racing the horizon, with the brush of the breeze, the warmth of the sun, the sticky coolness of the wet sand . . .

She held on to Dante's arm for the next wave, marveled at its pull, and made a pronouncement. "I'm afraid the sea frightens me a bit. So perhaps I'm not the outdoor enthusiast you take me for."

He laughed with her. "Actually, neither am I. My family has a camp in the Adirondacks, but it's a little too woodsy for my tastes."

She didn't know which issue to address first. "Where are the Adirondacks?"

He didn't skip a beat. "They're mountains to the northwest in New York State. Far different than it is here, with rolling hills and miles and miles of wilderness. But in the autumn the trees turn bright orange and red and gold, as if God swept a paintbrush across the entire lot."

He may not have liked the wilderness, but his passion for its visual beauty was evident. "I'd like to . . . never mind."

"Stop it," he said.

"What?"

"Being logical. Logic is banned this afternoon."

She squeezed his arm. "And what shall be in its place?"

"Joy," he said. "Pure joy."

"And gratitude," she added.

His eyes were soft as he repeated her words. "And gratitude."

When he leaned toward her, she didn't pull away, didn't even think of pulling away. The kiss was soft and . . . perfect.

She was glad he didn't apologize.

It was not an afternoon for apologies, but for . . .

Joy.

"He what?"

Lucy hadn't planned on telling Rowena about the kiss, but it slipped out. "He kissed me. Once. Very tenderly."

"With your bare feet in the ocean?"

Lucy couldn't tell whether Rowena felt this was scandalous, but she answered with the truth. "You should try it sometime. It's a wonderful feeling. It's very freeing."

Rowena opened her jewelry box and pulled out a necklace of pink stones that matched her pink and ivory evening dress. She was having dinner with Edward's family.

"Actually, I have put my feet in the ocean, at Bailey's Beach, when I was far younger."

"Not Easton's?"

Rowena held the necklace toward Lucy, needing help with the clasp. "Bailey's is where our set goes."

Oh.

Rowena turned around and smoothed her dress. "How do I look?"

"Lovely as usual." She retrieved some ivory gloves. "Is this a private dinner between the two of you?"

"If only. No, our parents will be present." Rowena put on the gloves. "I don't know how Edward and I are ever supposed to get to know each other when we are never alone for more than a few moments."

"Never?"

She shook her head.

"So . . . he's never kissed you?"

She hesitated. "On the cheek."

Lucy wasn't sure how to feel: ashamed at her own experience— meager as it was? Or sorry for Rowena, for her lack.

Rowena reacted to Lucy's silence. "Actually, I have been kissed once by my friend Morrie. We were very young and he was helping me down off my horse and . . ."

"And?"

"He leaned down and kissed me."

"Did you kiss him back?"

"I believe I popped him on the tip of his nose. As children we spent a lot of time together. And when I had my accident, he watched over me. He's always been there for me."

This was the second time she'd mentioned Morrie. "It sounds as though Morrie considers you more than a friend. Perhaps you have feelings for him?"

"No, no. I love him as a friend, and he me. But beyond that? My parents would never approve. They've set their sights on bigger fish in Edward."

"But it sounds as though Morrie is far more suited—"

"I really must go. I shouldn't be late."

The ways of the rich were hard to fathom.

❦

This is the man I'm supposed to marry.

Rowena looked across the massive dining table at Edward. He must have felt her gaze, for he met her eyes and offered a timid smile.

Or was it a tentative smile? Patronizing smile? Smile at the crippled rich girl; she's going to be your wife.

It sounded so provincial, so antiquated, so—

"I hear you've brought in a professional designer to create your costumes for Cornelius and Alice's ball," Mrs. DeWitt said to Rowena's mother.

Rowena was curious as to whether or not her mother would go along with their hostess's lofty version of the facts.

It was the latter. "We were very lucky to get Miss Scarpelli. And because Mrs. Garmin also ordered a costume, two other seamstresses were brought in to help."

"I don't suppose they have time to—"

"I'm afraid not," Mrs. Langdon said. "Do you have a costume you can wear?"

"I do. I was just—"

Mr. DeWitt shook a scolding finger at her. "One costume per season, Rachel." He included the others. "I'm to be Admiral Halsey."

"Complete with a sword," his wife added.

Mr. Langdon looked to his own wife. "And what are we?"

278

"You are Caesar, and I am a lady of the Elizabethan period."

"'*Et tu*, Brutus?'"

It was the first time Edward had spoken, and Rowena relished the opportunity to look at him. "Beware the Ides of March!" she said.

Mr. DeWitt clapped. "Well done, Miss Langdon. Are you a history lover?"

She felt her face flush. "I read a lot."

Oddly, the others at the table seemed embarrassed for her, and she realized they assumed she was well-read because of her handicap. She suddenly feared Edward would think she was too bookish. "I like outdoor pursuits too."

"Like sailing?" Mrs. DeWitt asked.

Rowena shared glances with her parents, and her father answered for her. "Rowena prefers to stay on land."

Another awkward silence as assumptions were made. How she wished she could blurt out what was *not* being said about her injury. She knew they were curious, and who knew what rumors they'd heard about its cause—or its severity.

"I may prefer to stay on dry land, but I do love taking leisurely strolls." She looked to Edward, hoping he took the hint. It was a lovely evening for a walk. Alone. Or if not tonight, perhaps tomorrow?

He remained silent.

"So what is your costume, Miss Langdon?" he asked.

The discussion that had skimmed the subject of her infirmity was over. They were safely back to the costumes. "My costume was inspired by Jane Austen's novel *Pride and Prejudice*." She looked directly at Edward. "I will be Elizabeth Bennet." *And you, Edward? Would you be my Mr. Darcy?*

"You should see the stiff collar they have planned for me," her mother said.

"I'm sure it's nice, but it won't match the drama of my sword," Mr. DeWitt said.

Rowena took a bite of her cod. It was hopeless. As the discussion changed to the new home the Havemeyers were building, she envied Lucy and her Dante. Lucy had only been in Newport a short while, and already she'd met a man, taken long walks with him alone, enjoyed extended conversation, and even received a kiss. Rowena had been told that Edward was to be her intended three months ago, and they'd only touched as a matter of his being the gentleman, helping her out of a carriage or walking her into dinner. As for a kiss?

Just the once. On the cheek.

She'd often tried to imagine what it would feel like to be kissed on the lips. . . . She'd actually dissected the idea of kissing to a great extent the past year. What an odd custom. Family members and friends kissed each other's cheeks, mothers kissed their babies' foreheads, and the occasional gallant man kissed the back of a lady's hand. But kissing lip to lip . . .

She'd never done it fully. With emotion. Not once. How many twenty-one-year-old women could say that—or would admit that?

But almost more disturbing than her lack of a proper kiss was the fact that Edward had shown no indication that the idea of giving her one had ever crossed his mind. She may not have been an astounding beauty, but she was an attractive woman. Morrie had even told her she was pretty and had scolded her to stop thinking otherwise.

"But it sounds as though Morrie is far more suited . . ."

Before Rowena allowed Lucy's words to settle in, she mentally checked the table banter. They were talking about the first United States Open golf championship just held in Newport.

"Who won?" Edward asked.

"Horace Rawlins—by two strokes."

"Willie Dunn should have won it," his father said.

"Because he's a better golfer?"

"Because he's an American. Rawlins is British."

The subject was changed again. "Who do you think will run for president next year?" Mr. DeWitt asked.

"Aren't you for that McKinley fellow, Father?" Edward asked.

"Indeed I am. McKinley's pro-business. We have a responsibility to back men like him."

Edward nodded.

Rowena felt sorry for him. Obviously Edward was under his

parents' thumbs as much as she was. But as the conversation continued on a political theme, she felt her thoughts drifting. Since she wasn't
allowed to vote, elections were not her concern. Besides, as a woman,
she was not expected to know of such things—and was nearly required
not to—so she let herself ponder Lucy's wisdom about Morrie instead.

Was Morrie more suited to her than Edward?

She'd known Morrie since both were children. Before the accident
she'd been a wonderful runner and the two of them had contests to
see who could run the length of the Cliff Walk the fastest. The winner
was always Morrie, but only by the smallest margin.

When she'd been recovering from her injury, it was Morrie who'd
come to sit with her, entertaining her with games and funny stories.

Following, there'd been a few years when they'd missed their play-
times in Newport, a few years when Rowena's family had forgone the
Newport season and *Porte au Ciel* had remained empty. She could never
forget the first summer they'd returned. She'd been sixteen at the time,
a girl blossoming into womanhood. And Morrie? He'd changed too.
He'd grown tall and muscular, and suddenly playing together was not
allowed. And yet he'd remained her confidant and continued to know
more of her secrets—and her true self—than anyone else in the world.

I really should marry him.

Rowena dropped her fork.

Marry Morrie? That was ridiculous. Even if Rowena thought of
Morrie in *that way*, her parents would never allow it. Although Rowena
was no catch, her parents didn't want her to marry *down*.

Timbrook brought her a clean fork.

"What do you think of that, Miss Langdon?" Mr. DeWitt asked.

Think? Wasn't she raised to be vacant of thoughts and opinions?

She had no idea what they were talking about and hadn't the
energy to catch up. And so she said, "I have no opinion."

The conversation resumed without her.

❧

"Why won't you talk to me?" Sofia asked.

Lucy gave her a scathing look.

Oh. That.

Sofia unbuttoned her blouse, readying herself for bed. She knew she'd gone too far that afternoon, leaking to Mamma about Dante and the notes. She didn't know why she said such things, yet they always seemed to slip out.

Actually, she usually enjoyed the tension such comments created. But tonight, Sofia didn't want to remember her earlier mistakes. She didn't want to harass her sister. It was almost as if *that* Sofia and the Sofia that existed now, this evening, were two different people.

A child and a woman.

What Sofia really wanted to do was talk to Lucy about Hugh. And sailing. And the connection the two of them had shared during their lunch on the water. There was an odd tightening in the pit of Sofia's stomach every time she thought of it.

But Sofia knew Lucy's opinion of Hugh involved his misbehavior, and some rumor about a departed maid. Sofia had no facts about what was true and what wasn't. And she could imagine Hugh being a bit wild, especially since he was unhappy about his position in the family and his future.

But the situation with the maid? That had to be a rumor. During their time together there'd been many an opportunity for Hugh to take advantage of her, and he'd been nothing but a gentleman.

She pulled her nightgown on and rid the collar of her hair. "Hopefully tomorrow we can get a lot done on the costumes. I really like the designs you came up with."

Lucy extinguished the lamp and got into bed. There was no "sweet dreams," *sogni d'oro.* Back home they'd always managed to say goodnight to each other, yet here . . .

Sofia didn't like this silence between them, especially since she was the cause of it. She shouldn't have forced her way into Lucy's room here. She shouldn't have looked at Lucy's love notes. She shouldn't have told Mamma Lucy's secrets.

But it's all Lucy's fault. If only she hadn't gotten invited to the Langdons', traveled first class, and—

Stop it!

Sofia was surprised by the inner admonition. It was her habit to complain about what Lucy was and had, and subsequently whine about feeling like a nobody.

But tonight was different.

She was different.

Tonight she was somebody.

Somebody's soul mate.

CHAPTER EIGHTEEN

*L*ucy fastened the top button of her navy dress, collected her hat and shoes, and with one last glance at Sofia to make sure she was still asleep, slipped out of her bedroom, through the dressing room, and into the hall.

She looked both ways, hoping no early-bird servant was up and about. The house was quiet—as it should be at five in the morning.

Lucy took the back stairs down to the basement. She heard commotion in the kitchen, so skimmed the walls, hugging the shadows. She breezed through the exterior door with only the softest click marking her exit.

Once outside she sat on a step and put on her shoes. It was safe to put them on now, for the grass would soften the sound of her tread.

Fortunately, even with few lights glowing from the interior, Lucy's journey across the dark grounds to the Cliff Walk was not as difficult as she had assumed it would be, as the sky was already beginning to lighten.

She entered the path and took a moment to get her bearings. The sound of the ocean was muted, as if it too were still sleeping. The tide was out and the rocky shore was exposed like a child who'd kicked off the covers during the night. The water made soft *slush, slush* sounds. *Shhh. Shhh. It's too early to get up. . . .*

The sky contained a heavy sprinkling of clouds, and the barrier between sea and heavens was just beginning to announce itself as a stroke of orange red.

"It's so beautiful," Lucy whispered.

"As are you."

She turned to her right and found Dante sitting on a rock wall near the Langdon property line. He stood and came to her, handing her a pink rose.

Lucy put it to her nose, inhaling its perfume.

Then he pulled her into his arms. Lucy marveled in his warmth and the way her head fit against his chest and shoulder. A perfect fit. As if it was meant to be.

"Look." He continued to hold her but allowed her to turn her face toward the sunrise. "God is waking up the world."

She held him tightly and felt his chin upon her hair. The band of orange widened and the first sliver of the sun slipped above the water, sending tentative rays of yellow piercing through the clouds. Lucy felt her chest tighten. "Tell it to stop, to hold, right there."

He didn't ruin the moment by offering logic but nodded. "Can you believe He does this every day?"

That simple fact caused her to pull away from him. "Then why is this the first time I've ever seen it?"

He shook his head. "Every morning and every night He puts on a show just hoping someone will take a moment to notice."

Lucy was appalled to feel tears threaten. She put a hand to her mouth, willing them away. "I'm sorry. This is silly. To cry over a sunrise?"

He drew her close again, fully encompassing her with his embrace. "It's never silly to cry over beauty. Ever."

And so Lucy let her tears come. But with his permission also came a strength to let them go.

"So," he said after she was still again. "What do you want to ask the sunrise?"

"Ask—?"

"Since so few witness the show, I like to think God is waiting for our thoughts. Our sunrise requests."

She laughed softly at his reasoning. "And you know this how?"

He put a finger beneath her chin and raised it so he could look at her. "Because I'm here with you and my heart is overflowing."

His kiss was like a seal, confirming all of his words. For as they kissed, Lucy sensed the sun rise above the sea, as if showing its approval, wanting to see more.

When his lips moved away from hers, he kept an arm around her shoulders, facing her toward the dawn. "God? Are you listening? I pray for a lifetime of sunrises with this woman. And sunsets. Storms and blue sky, snow and rain, fog and clear skies."

Lucy was taken aback. Was he asking her to marry him?

"Your turn," he said.

"I . . . I don't know what to say."

He turned toward her and got down on one knee. "Say yes. Marry me, Lucia."

She let out a puff of air.

"Surely you're not surprised?" he asked.

Was she? Ever since their first meeting she'd known their bond was special, and never had she found her thoughts so consumed by another. The need to see him and be with him completely blanketed her senses, providing warmth, protection, and comfort.

Say yes!

And yet.

And yet.

The old argument against marriage demanded attention. "But my mother and sister . . . they depend on me for everything."

He rose from his knee but never moved his gaze from her eyes. "They can learn to depend on me."

Lucy wasn't sure he understood. "They don't earn enough between them. They need—"

Dante put his fingers to her lips. "Can you stop being your family's savior for just one minute?"

If only she could. "But they—"

He covered her words with his lips and murmured his proposal once more. "Marry me, Lucia."

How could she refuse?

❦

Lucy hurried back to the house. After agreeing to marry, she and Dante had lingered on the Cliff Walk, letting the sun fully rise and the waves gain momentum, applauding their promise to be together, always.

It was still early, not yet half past six, but by this time the house would be buzzing with servants.

Hopefully not Rowena. And not Sofia. Lucy was banking on her little sister's penchant for being the last one awake.

Once in the house, Lucy removed her hat, slipped the pink rose into the sash of her dress, and lifted her skirts to more ably take the stairs. She passed one of the footmen on his way down. "Eee," he said as he nearly collided with her. "What you been doing to get yer cheeks all rosy this morning?"

She ignored him and escaped up the stairs to the second floor. But at the sound of voices in the hall, she pulled up short. Hugh was standing outside his bedroom door, fully dressed, but in clothes casual and unkempt. His father stood in the doorway, wearing a morning suit, barring him from entry. They were the epitome of fashion do's and don'ts.

"You cannot continue to come in at all hours, son. And what *are* you wearing?"

"I was just going to change," Hugh said. "If you'll excuse me, Father . . ."

Mr. Langdon put a hand on his arm, stopping him. "Were you out playing cards with your friends? How much did you lose?"

"Who said I lost anything?"

His father seemed taken aback, then stood his ground again. "Show me your winnings."

"I don't have them on me."

287

"Because you didn't win."

Hugh shrugged and began unrolling his sleeves. "I'll see you at breakfast."

But his father wasn't through with him yet. Mr. Langdon thrust a finger in Hugh's face. "I'll suffer much from you, boy, except lying."

"I'll remember—"

Hugh spotted Lucy standing on an upper step. Too late, Lucy put her hat behind her back.

"Well, well. It looks like I'm not the only one getting home in the wee hours."

Lucy raised her chin and strode past them. "I was merely taking a morning constitutional. I enjoy the brisk air."

"And brisk it is," Hugh said.

As she passed the two, Lucy nodded at Mr. Langdon. "Good morning, sir."

"What about me?" Hugh asked. "Don't I get a good morning?"

"Shush, boy." His father shoved him into his room. "I'll expect you down to breakfast at eight."

Lucy rushed to the door of the dressing room and entered before Mr. Langdon had time to question her. Once inside, she leaned against the door and caught her breath.

"Where have you been?"

Sofia stood in the doorway to their room, buttoning her blouse.

Lucy strode past her.

As soon as their door was closed, Sofia pounced. "Were you out with *him*?"

How she wanted to throw her engagement in Sofia's face. But she couldn't. Not until the time was right.

And that right time would be . . . ?

Lucy busied herself making her bed. "You're too young, Sofia. You wouldn't understand."

Her sister tossed a pillow at Lucy's face. "I am not too young! I'm grown-up too."

Lucy threw the pillow back and laughed at Sofia's petulant words. Which was the wrong thing to do.

Sofia pulled all the sheets off Lucy's bed, then did the same to her own. Lucy stepped back, crossed her arms in front of her chest, and waited for the tantrum to end.

"Do you feel better now?"

Sofia was out of breath, her hair half covering her face. "Much."

Lucy checked her own hair in the mirror before heading to the door. "Now you have two beds to make. I need to help Rowena dress. I'll see you at the workroom later."

Upon leaving, Lucy heard a pillow graze the back side of the door.

Sofia walked amid the fallen covers, kicking them around, but also getting her legs entangled.

She sat at the foot of her bed to be rid of the burden, then fell back, exhausted. Although her first instinct was to lash out at Lucy, the words that came from her mouth were aimed at herself. "Why do you let yourself do such things?"

There was no answer, or at least none she wanted to hear.

She thrust her arms straight out from her sides, letting them bounce upon the thin mattress. "I hate being young!"

Suddenly, she heard a muffled man's voice. "You're not so young," it said.

Sofia sat upright and held her breath. "Hello?"

There was a tap on the wall. "How are you this morning, Sofia?"

The voice was coming from the next room! She scurried to the wall, pressing her cheek against it. "Hugh?"

"I'm here, beautiful lady."

Lady, he called me a lady!

Suddenly, as if a lamp had been lit, she realized she was only a child if she chose to be. To Hugh, she was a grown woman, and better than that, a lady.

She touched her forehead to the wall and pressed her hands flat against it. "I miss you."

"I miss you too. *Je t'adore*, Sofia."

She didn't know exactly what he said, but she understood the meaning. He cared for her, he really, truly cared for her.

"I—"

But before she could finish, he said, "I'll come see you today. I promise. Until then . . ."

"Until then," she said.

Sofia lingered against the wall, wishing it would disappear so she could be with Hugh face-to-face.

Until then.

❧

Rowena slipped her arms into the lavender satin dressing sacque that Lucy held for her. She pulled the lace-edged neck ties to the front and made a knot. "It's a beautiful day today, isn't it?"

"Extremely," Lucy said.

That wasn't enough of an answer. For Rowena had spotted Lucy running back to the house across the lawn at half past six. Where had she been? Who had she been with?

There was only one answer. Dante.

Rowena sat on the bench in front of the dressing table so Lucy could do her hair. Being seated put her in an advantageous position to watch Lucy's face in the mirror.

"What are your plans today?" she asked.

Lucy pulled the brush through Rowena's hair, making her head move up and back with the gentle tugging. "I'll be working on the costumes," she said. "It's been four days since the fitting. We'll need another fitting tomorrow."

Still nothing.

The thought of Lucy out in the early dawn hours with a man . . . She didn't want Lucy to get in trouble that way. Lucy seemed to be a good girl, and yet, who really knew? And what girl was ever wholly immune from temptation?

Rowena. Not that she'd ever been given the chance to test herself.

She noticed Lucy smiling—smiling at nothing at all. Something had happened.

"What are you smiling about?" she asked.

Lucy seemed surprised at the question and checked her reflection in the mirror before relinquishing the smile. "As you said it's a beautiful day."

"There's more to it than that."

Lucy twisted Rowena's hair into a high bun and arranged curls around the crown, fastening them with hairpins. "I did see a comical scene this morning."

"Where was that?"

"Right out in the hall here. It seems your brother was just returning from an all-night card game and got caught by your father."

That's all?

"Does your brother make a habit of coming in so late?"

"My brother makes a habit of doing whatever he pleases without care for the wishes of the family or propriety." She hadn't meant to be so brusque, but her disappointment in having the conversation turn toward her brother took hold. "If it weren't for my brother, I could marry anyone I wanted."

Lucy's eyebrow rose. "Really? How so?"

Rowena hadn't meant to open the door, but the gateway to her frustrations had been unlocked and they demanded release. "As the heir, my brother should be concerned with marrying well. But so far he's only succeeded in causing shame to our family name by his carousing and wild ways. No respectable girl will have him. And so it's up to me to marry Edward to save our family from full ruination. After all, I've already caused shame to my family by my injury, by becoming less-than, so I owe them."

"I'm sure your family doesn't think of you as less-than. And your brother's actions shouldn't affect *your* future happiness. That's not fair."

Rowena shrugged and held out a palm full of hairpins for Lucy's use. "In truth I'm not who people think I am." It was a fact that both calmed and irked her, and as soon as she said it, she wished the words back. She shook her head as if that physical act could negate the moment before.

"Who are you, then?"

Rowena turned the tables. "Who do you think I am?"

291

"I think you are a good woman who is loyal to a fault. I think you would do anything for anybody, and—"

Rowena slammed her free hand upon the table. "No, no, no! That's not me at all!" When Lucy took a step back she added, "I'm sorry. I didn't mean to be so adamant." Rowena pressed her fingers to the space between her eyes. She should never have brought it up. She forced herself to smile. "Never mind me. I simply woke up on the wrong side of the bed. You can go now. I can finish up here."

"Are you sure?"

"Of course."

Lucy deposited the rest of the hairpins into Rowena's hand and left the room.

As soon as silence seeped into every corner, Rowena turned her hand upside down and let the pins fall to the carpet. She held her open hand in the air a moment, marveling at how her act had caused no sound at all. It was as if she'd done nothing.

The fuller implications rushed forward to crush her. Nothing she did mattered or had an effect. She had the odd notion that if she stood and jumped up and down until the crystals in the chandelier bobbled, no one would hear. No one would come running to see what was the matter.

Her hand found its mate in her lap and she began to cry.

Why was she stuck playing this awful, meaningless part? Why didn't her image match the woman she felt herself to be? Should they match? Or was there some advantage to being unfathomable?

Yet . . . might she be considered mysterious?

No. That wasn't it at all. For to be mysterious people had to wonder about her; she needed to possess an aura of something hidden, or better yet, something to be discovered. Everyone felt they knew exactly who she was and what she believed, and could rest assured they could spend their curiosity dissecting someone else's personality.

She gathered a handkerchief from the table and dabbed her tears away. What good were tears, anyway? The world saw her as a good girl: polite, trustworthy, dependable, loyal, and true. Traits most people would die for.

Then why did the listing cause her pain? Why did she want to rush to the banister and scream for all to hear, *"You don't know me!"*

She looked at her reflection and repeated the phrase for her ears alone. "You don't know me."

Being polite, her reflection nodded affirmation.

⁂

Hugh came in to breakfast after the serving began. He kissed their mother on the cheek. " 'Morning, Mother."

"One more minute and I would be forced to consider you tardy." She looked at her husband. "Although I did hear you've earned that designation in other ways this morning."

Rowena's brother took a seat and grabbed a scone from the tray in the same movement. He took a piece of bacon, then added, "The bacon being cold is my full punishment for any and all transgressions of time."

"Oh you," Mother said with a shake of her head.

Rowena looked to her father, waiting for his reaction. "So, wife. What do you have planned for the day?"

Rowena was appalled. That was it? Once again Hugh caused offense but got off with nary a word?

"Perhaps I should be tardy too," she said as she poured cream into her coffee.

"Pardon?" Father said.

"Don't be ridiculous," Mother said.

Hugh winked at her from across the table. "You couldn't do it, sister dear. It's not in your nature."

And that was that. The conversation moved on. The very notion that Rowena would break a rule or offend was discounted as impossible.

She fumed—but of course kept silent.

After all, it was the proper thing to do.

⁂

"Come now, Rowena. Try the bicycle. It's not that difficult."

Rowena looked aghast at her friend. "I can't, Millicent. You know that."

"You won't have a problem. Trust me."

As Rowena looked around she spotted acquaintances riding side-saddle on horseback, another two carrying rackets for tennis, and one other accompanying Millicent on her own bicycle. The latter two were wearing absurd-looking bloomers, cuffed at the calf. The outfits looked ridiculous coupled with a ruffled shirt and a short jacket with voluminous sleeves. It was as though a perfectly presentable outing ensemble had been bastardized into a bizarre costume more fitting for a theatrical escapade than proper society.

The recreational options for young females had expanded dramatically the past few years, with golf, swimming, fencing, and yachting also the rage. Rowena was in the minority who chose to abstain. Although she felt she could do these things in spite of her infirmity, being even the least bit unsure caused her to decline the experience rather than risk possible humiliation. Besides, although bicycling was acceptable, Rowena remembered when women had first started participating in the sport they were called . . . whores. The connotation was too awful to contemplate or risk.

Millicent rolled her eyes at Rowena's rejection, said something to the other woman on the bicycle, and walked alongside her own machine, giving Rowena company as the other girl rode off alone.

"Aren't you bored to death spending your afternoons strolling about?" she asked.

"Not when I have good company."

Millicent did a double take. "I assume that's a compliment."

"Of course." Though actually . . . Millicent was not Rowena's favorite person. She was far too brusque and refused to talk of anything beyond rumor-filled tittle-tattle.

They walked to the corner and waited for some carriages to pass before proceeding. "I heard your brother was down on the docks early this morning, dressed like a ragamuffin."

That didn't make sense. Hadn't Hugh been playing cards somewhere until late? "I'm sure what you heard was exaggerated."

"I don't think so. Audrey's cousin was on their yacht anchored nearby and saw him talking to harbor workers."

Harbor workers? "Perhaps he was up early making some repairs to his sailboat. He loves that boat."

Millicent shrugged. "At dawn? Of course knowing your brother, he'd probably been up all night. Maybe he was paying the workmen to cover up some mischief he'd done."

Rowena hated to admit she'd considered the same thing. And yet, to have Hugh's reputation besmirched by others, in gossip . . .

She came to his defense. "I saw him at breakfast with my parents and he was happy and jovial."

"Of course he was. Your brother seems to thrive on being happy *with* trouble. It's quite a feat that he can keep up a good front to your parents. Though parents *are* always the last to know."

Rowena wondered what else her parents didn't know. "I love him dearly, but I do wish he'd behave himself."

"So does Sarah Billings. Just this morning she intimated she will have nothing more to do with Hugh—that her parents will order her to have nothing more to do with him—unless he changes his wild ways. The whole town has heard about that maid of yours. No girl will want him, Rowena. No respectable girl, at least."

Which left the burden of marrying well on Rowena's shoulders. It was not new news.

As if reading her mind, Millicent asked, "Where is your Edward today? Why isn't he strolling with you?"

"We don't see each other every day," Rowena said.

It was Millicent's turn to stop walking. "Whyever not? If he were my intended, I'd demand his full attention. You're much too compliant, Rowena. You need to insist on your due."

Tears filled Rowena's eyes, which caused Millicent to lean the bicycle against her hip and quickly retrieve a handkerchief from her sleeve. "Now, now. I didn't mean to make you cry."

Rowena turned toward her friend, trying to assemble a modicum of privacy from people walking by. She dabbed at her eyes. "I don't know how to insist on my due. I don't know how to make Edward want to see me or spend time with me. It seems every time we're together we're with a crowd. I've yet to spend time alone with him."

"Not any time?"

"A few minutes at most."

"Oh, dear . . . that's not good, Rowena. When my sister was engaged, my parents had to all but force them apart."

Rowena blew her nose. "I have no such problem."

Millicent leaned close. "Then why are you even considering marriage?"

Not one of her friends had ever asked the question. "I have to marry him," she said.

"But why?"

When pressed, Rowena answered, "Our parents want it so."

"But why?"

Millicent could be very pushy, a trait that vacillated between a flaw and a good attribute. "Business reasons, I guess."

Thankfully, Millicent moved on to a different question. "Surely your father's business doesn't need the DeWitt money to keep it going. Or perhaps it's vice versa?"

Rowena could only offer a shrug. She wasn't privy to details about her family's business, and certainly knew less about the DeWitts'. She only knew what had been implied, that this marriage would benefit both families.

Millicent finally provided her own answer. "I suppose you have to marry well because Hugh won't."

Rowena released a puff of air. "Exactly."

Millicent began to walk again. "Men," she said.

Indeed.

I'm engaged!

Lucy sewed each stitch of the sleeve trim on Rowena's costume as if adding brushstrokes to a piece of art. Each stitch was evidence of her happiness.

Yet it was a happiness she couldn't share with her mother and sister—for different reasons. If she told Sofia, there'd be no end to the questions and the intrusion. Any hope of keeping her time alone with Dante secret or private would disappear. Sofia would demand to know more than Lucy wanted to share.

And if she told Mamma? Mamma would say it was too soon, would want to meet him, and would ask questions about the future for which there were no answers. She would be a . . . mother. Right now Lucy didn't want a mother or a sister. She just wanted a fiancé and for the world to consist of only two.

Sofia sat at the sewing machine, her head on her hand. "Come on, Lucy. Give me the sleeve. You're taking forever. Hurry it up a bit."

Mamma stepped in. "Even though it's just a costume, it's still important to do—"

Suddenly, Sofia stood and pointed out the window. "Mr. Oswald's running! Something must have happened."

Sure enough, they heard a commotion coming from the Oswalds' quarters, and then he burst through the door of the workroom. "Haverty's fallen out of the loft! A doctor's been summoned, but I came to get me wife to help. She knows something about nursing."

Mamma set her sewing aside. "So do I."

"And I," Lucy said. A broken limb could be the kiss of death for a working man.

Lucy and Sofia got up to follow, but Sofia suddenly held back. "I'll stay here and continue working."

Lucy started to complain, figuring it was just one of her sister's ways to avoid work, but then Sofia said, "Lucy, you know I grow faint at such times."

It was true. Sofia cowered at the sight of any scrape or cut.

Lucy pointed a finger at her. "Get a lot done while we're gone."

Then Sofia did something odd. She saluted and said, "Aye, aye, Captain."

❦

Thank you for getting hurt, Haverty. . . .

While she was alone Sofia sewed like a wildfire, needing to get as much accomplished as quickly as possible so she'd be free to talk to Hugh when he stopped by the workroom, as promised. All morning she'd worried and fretted about how it would play out. Would Hugh simply come to the door and ask to speak with her?

The thought of Mamma and Lucy keeping tabs on them, watching through the windows . . .

But now, thanks to Haverty, the coast was clear for them to have some time alone.

If only he would come before everyone gets back.

Sofia sewed and prayed, sewed and prayed.

And then, during the umpteenth time she looked toward the house, she saw him hurrying toward the workroom.

Not wanting to miss a moment with him, she met him at the door and pulled him inside. Her first impulse was to fling her arms around his neck, but she restrained herself. "You came," she said.

He kissed her on the cheek. "I came, but alas, not for long. I hear Haverty fell in the stables. He's a good friend. I have to go to him."

Sofia felt her countenance fall, along with her hopes. "But plenty of people are there to help. Mamma and Lucy went, which left me alone here, and I . . . I was waiting for you to come." She didn't like the desperation in her voice but found she could do nothing to stop it.

He lifted both her hands to his lips and smiled. "I promised we would have time together, and we will. Tonight don't eat dinner with your family but make your excuses. At six o'clock I'll meet you at the front gate. Do you like seafood?"

"I . . . I don't know."

"After tonight, you will." With a glance out the window, he took her face in his hands and kissed her fully on the lips, but softly, as if he treasured her as something delicate and rare.

He pulled away and looked into her eyes. "Words cannot express . . ."

Then he rushed out the door and ran toward the stables.

Sofia stood there, frozen in the moment, wondering if the last few seconds had really happened, knowing they had, yet wishing for more.

And then with a blink she came into the present and repeated " 'Words cannot express'? Cannot express what?"

Yet when she tried to get her own thoughts in line, to mentally express her own feelings toward Hugh, she found herself in the same situation.

Words cannot express . . .

Did she love him? Did he love her? Could love happen so quickly, or was this simply infatuation? And how could it ever continue with him being the heir of a great family and she . . . and she . . .

Words could not express her confusion.

⁂

"See you at the costume ball, if not before," Millicent said as her carriage dropped Rowena off at home.

Rowena waved but found herself in a foul mood—which made her question why she'd spent any time with that girl. Gossip, comparisons, and pettiness. Millicent always left Rowena feeling bad about the world, about her life, and her future.

Timbrook opened the door for her, but before she crossed the threshold, she decided going up to her room—being alone—would only add to her dejected state. She needed a friend. And that friend was Lucy.

"If you'll pardon me, Timbrook, I think I'll go check on the costumes."

"As you wish, miss."

As an afterthought she handed him her parasol, then headed across the grounds to the workroom. Nearing the front door, seeing in the windows, it looked as though no one was there.

But then she spotted Sofia, sitting on a stool, her arms wrapped around herself, her head shaking.

Rowena knocked, then entered. "Sofia. Are you all right?"

It took the girl a moment to pull out of her daze. "I'm fine. I . . ."

"Where's Lucy and your mother?"

"They're down at the stables. Haverty fell out of some loft and—"

"Morrie?"

Rowena didn't wait for an answer, but lifted her skirt and hurried across the lawn. *A fall? Is he in horrible pain? Did something break?*

Her progress was accomplished in an exhausting step-hop, step-hop, so by the time she reached his quarters, she fell against the jamb of the opened door for support. Morrie was on the bed, his left leg raised upon two pillows. Lucy and Mrs. Scarpelli were tying some fabric together, creating a receptacle for ice held in a bowl by Mrs. Oswald. Dr. Kinsey retrieved a bottle from his doctor bag.

"You are to take—" When Morrie looked in Rowena's direction, so did the doctor. "Miss Langdon."

She ignored him and ran to the bedside, falling to her knees beside Morrie. She took his hand and pulled it close. "Oh, Morrie. Are you in much pain? What can I do to help?"

"I'll be fine, Ro. Don't fret about—"

The doctor cleared his throat.

With a glance, Rowena realized she'd shocked him by being so familiar with their coachman. She held out her hand to him, wanting an assist to standing. "Sorry, Dr. Kinsey. I just heard the news. Morrie and I have been friends since childhood and—"

Hugh came in, carrying a glass of water. "I've already explained to the doctor that old Morrie here is responsible for teaching me all sorts of mischief."

Morrie managed a smile. "You came up with your fair share."

The doctor handed Rowena the bottle of medicine. "Since Mr. Haverty is such a good friend to you both, then perhaps you should be the ones to administer his medicine. One teaspoon of laudanum every four hours."

"Is his leg broken?"

"Luckily, no. It's just a very bad ankle sprain and some bruises. He needs to keep his leg elevated and iced. The medicine is for the pain."

Rowena had never been on the giving side of medicines, but remembered being under her own dose of this drug when she'd broken her leg. Though it had helped tame the pain, it had caused her to sleep for days. And as far as the break? Her leg had never healed correctly. For Morrie, who needed a strong body for work . . . "Will he recover fully?"

"I have to recover," Morrie said.

"If you're careful and keep off of it for a few days until the swelling goes down, you should be fine."

"Hugh and I will make sure he behaves," Rowena said. Out of the corner of her eye she caught Lucy staring at her.

The doctor closed his bag and put on his hat. "I'll leave you in these good hands, then." He nodded and left.

"Can we get anything else, Miss Langdon? Master Hugh?" Mrs. Oswald asked.

Hugh dismissed them with a hand. "We've got it. Thank you for your help."

As soon as the three women left, Hugh sat at the foot of the bed. "You can leave now, Wena. I will—"

Morrie shook his head. "Let Ro take care of me."

Hugh's eyebrows rose. "That's the thanks I get? To be dismissed in favor of my sister?"

"She smells better than you."

Rowena turned to her brother. "I'll be fine, Hugh. Let Mother know where I am."

"She won't approve."

She wouldn't. Mother didn't like Rowena spending time at the stables, much less having Morrie as a friend. "Move that chair over here, please."

Hugh moved the chair next to the bed. Rowena sat, then shooed him away. "Go on, now. I've got him."

"I can see that." He winked at Morrie. "Cheerio, old chap. Behave yourself."

"I'll do my best."

With his exit, the room was finally quiet but for the normal sounds from the stable. Rowena wrung out a cloth and placed it on Morrie's forehead. "I'm so sorry you got hurt."

He put a hand on her forearm, stopping her movement. "I'm not."

She met his eyes and saw an intensity that made her look away. "Don't be silly. No one wants to get hurt."

"It's given me time with you, hasn't it?"

Rowena froze. Surely Morrie hadn't injured himself just so he could spend time with her.

"Don't look at me that way," he said. "I'm not that crazy."

She let relief wash over her and immediately felt foolish. No man would go to such extremes to spend time with her. From her experience with Edward it seemed just the opposite, that being in her presence was an imposition or a duty.

She shook her head, needing to dispel such thoughts, then took up the bottle of medicine and a spoon. "I should give you the laudanum now."

Morrie shook his head. "Not yet. Now that I have you here, now that we can sit close without fear, I don't want to sleep."

"But the pain—"

"I will endure more than this to spend time with you, Ro."

She pulled back. "Don't say such things."

"If not now, when? After you've married DeWitt?"

Rowena stood and moved behind the chair. "But I need to marry Edward."

"Why?"

It was such a simple question, without a simple answer. "Because . . . because my parents want—"

"What do *you* want, Ro?"

She hated the way her thoughts became a jumble. She moved to a tall dresser and picked up a brush and then a comb.

What *did* she want? She wanted to be loved and to love. She wanted a husband and marriage and—

"I love you, Rowena."

Her legs felt weak and she gripped the top of the dresser for support. She closed her eyes, keeping her back to him. When they were children she'd dreamed of marrying Morrie. They'd talked about where they would live and—

His voice was soft in tone and volume. "Remember how we used to talk about having a farm in the country with dozens of horses? You were going to train them and I—"

She whipped around to face him. "I can't ride anymore."

"Yes you can."

She took a breath to argue with him, but he repeated himself.

"Yes, you can, Ro. You've let other people tell you what you *can't* do so much you've begun to believe it. I would never hold you back like that. Will never."

Rowena didn't know what to say. Morrie had never talked to her like this. "Why say all this, Morrie? Why now?"

He held out his hand. She took it and sat in the chair. The strength of his grip was both powerful and poignant. It spoke of security and refuge, and a constancy that brought tears to her eyes.

"I've always been here for you, Rowena. And I always will."

Her throat was too tight to answer, but she nodded.

"Unlike everyone else, I only want what's best for you, what will make you happy."

Finally, she found her words. "But I don't know what will make me happy."

"Sure you do."

But she didn't. "I've been brought up a certain way. I'm the only daughter, the loyal, obedient child, and I—"

"You are not a child at all."

She knew he was right, yet she was still beholden to her parents, her family's name and reputation, and the expectations of society. "But I . . . but they . . ."

He pulled her hand to his lips and kissed it. " 'A man's heart deviseth his way: but the Lord directeth his steps.' "

Rowena didn't know what to say. Was she doing what God wanted her to do? Had she even attempted to know His plans for her life?

"Don't make any decision on your own, Ro. I've been praying for you to see what I see, to feel what I feel . . . to *know*."

He'd been praying for her while she'd been trying to handle things on her own? She'd always considered herself a godly person: supplicant, dutiful, reverent. Yet when it came down to the meat of her faith—prayer—she found herself lacking.

"There can be duty without blind obedience, Ro. To obey your parents' wishes when it makes a mockery of marriage is wrong. Promising to 'love, honor, and cherish' is sacred."

"I know."

"Do you? Right now you're on a path that will lead you to marrying someone to avoid making your own choice, to avoid responsibility for your own life. God created free will. Use yours, Ro."

Everything he said made sense. But to take responsibility scared her. What if she made the wrong decision? By letting others make her decisions for her, she could blame them for the missteps of her life.

Morrie said the next in nearly a whisper. " 'For what shall it profit a man, if he shall gain the whole world, and lose his own soul?' "

She pulled her hand away, taking offense. "I'm not losing my—"

He took her hand back and once again she felt his strength. "You risk losing *you*."

Rowena bowed her head, wishing she could pull his strength into herself.

He continued in a whisper. "Where is the girl who was joyful and free, who laughed and danced with me, embracing life and all—?"

She lifted her head. "She broke her leg and became a cripple."

Morrie relinquished her hand. "Excuses."

More than anything, Rowena wanted his touch.

He let his head fall deeper upon the pillow. "I'll take that medicine now."

Rowena nodded and poured the dose. "You need your rest."

He shook his head. "You know what I need. What you need."

She paused at the door and blew him a kiss.

He closed his eyes before it reached him.

<hr>

Rowena didn't want to go inside, where the walls of *Porte au Ciel* would loom over her. The name of the house may have meant "Gate of Heaven," but today she felt as though being inside would prevent her from gaining access to God.

She entered the rear veranda from the grass and took a seat on a wicker rocking chair, away from the entrance to the house. Once settled into the cushion, she let the forward-and-back movement synchronize with the rhythm of her thoughts.

How odd that her time alone with Morrie today had changed the very fabric of her thinking. Why was today different from the other times they'd talked?

Because today he told you he loves you.

And yet she'd known that, hadn't she?

He loves me as a sister.

At the lie, she stopped rocking. As much as she'd deluded herself regarding Morrie's feelings, she knew his love was the kind of a man for a woman, a romantic love.

How long had she known?

She grazed through her memories and within seconds realized she'd always known. Their childhood plans of marrying had evolved from a game to something genuine—albeit unspoken.

Until now.

But genuine or not, the fact remained they could never marry. She was a Langdon, and her parents were set on her marrying Edward as a solidification of her father's business partner—

Suddenly, the absurdity of the match hit her like a slap. Marrying to solidify a business partnership? What about love? What about pride, and family honor, and truth, and doing the right thing?

Was marrying Edward the right thing?

She remembered Morrie's words. By gaining status in the world, would she be risking her soul?

"You risk losing you."

Rowena leaned forward, cupping her face in her hands. *Oh, God, please show me the right thing to do. Please show me what you want me to do.*

She sat in silence a moment, hoping God would send her a sign that would guide her and show her the—

"Rowena? Are you all right?"

Mother walked toward her. Rowena sat up, mourning the interruption and the lack of a clear answer from the Lord. "I'm fine, Mother. Do you need me for something?"

She held out a note. "This just came for you."

Rowena opened it and read: *Dear Rowena, I'm sorry but I can't accompany you to the Dashells' this evening. I will see you tomorrow. Yours, Edward.*

Mother was waiting. "Well?"

"Edward can't go with me tonight."

"Whyever not?"

"He doesn't say."

Mother shook her head. "That boy. Doesn't he realize how imperative it is for you two to be seen together at every convenience? People will begin to talk and think you aren't engaged."

And there it was. "But we're not engaged, Mother."

"You nearly are. It's been arranged."

"By you and Father."

"And the DeWitts."

She pushed herself to standing. "What about what Edward and I want?"

Her mother looked as shocked as if Rowena had uttered a string of curses. In a way, perhaps she had, for she'd certainly expressed an opinion akin to blasphemy.

Mother put a hand to the cameo at her neck. "I thought you liked Edward."

"I do. And I believe he likes me."

"Then what is the problem?"

Rowena sighed heavily and looked out to the ocean that cared not a whit about this conversation. Perhaps she should take note. . . .

She faced her mother and offered a smile. " 'A man's heart deviseth his way: but the Lord directeth his steps.' "

"What—?"

"If you'll excuse me, Mother."

This time when Rowena entered the house, she had no fear of the looming walls, for the gates of heaven *had* been opened. God had heard her prayer.

And answered.

⁂

Lucy relished being on Dante's arm, strolling along the busy streets of the city center. Although the experience lacked the intimacy they gained on the Cliff Walk, it gave Lucy a truer feeling of what life would be like once they were married and forging a life together as a couple amongst the world.

She pointed to a shop window. "Ooh, look at that hat. I love the way the feathers are made to bend around each other in a spiral." She stopped to study it. "I'll have to tell Mamma about it so she can copy—"

"No need to tell her . . ." Dante pulled her inside, where he bought her the hat.

"I've never had anyone buy me anything," she said as the clerk put her old hat in a hatbox.

"Never?" Dante asked. "I find that hard to believe."

Lucy remembered Angelo buying her a flower from a cart once, or on second thought, had he simply retrieved a fallen flower from the street?

They left the shop with Dante carrying the box for her. "Everyone's noticing your new hat," he whispered. "They're jealous."

People jealous of her? It was another new—

Lucy stopped and craned her head to see through the other people, walking on the sidewalk.

"What?" Dante asked.

That looked like Bonwitter.

She continued to peer around people, hoping—yet fearing—to see the same man. What if it was him? But how could it be him? Was his hate for Lucy so strong he'd traveled to Newport to get revenge?

"Lucy? What's wrong?"

She shook her head, dispelling the image. "Nothing," she said. "I'm just seeing things."

Dante put two fingers toward his eyes. "Only see these eyes loving you, all right?"

All right.

⸙

"Where are you taking me?" Sofia asked Hugh as he helped her down from the carriage.

"To the best restaurant in Newport, matey."

"But I'm not dressed fancy enough—"

"Not that kind of 'best'—the best food. Come on."

They zigzagged through the crowd on the sidewalk until they came to a restaurant called The Captain's Bounty. When they entered, the man behind the bar called out, "Hugh's here! Dump a lobster in the water!"

Hugh placed Sofia in front of him, his hands upon her shoulders. "Captain McEnery, I'd like you to meet Sofia. Sofia, meet the captain."

Sofia nodded, and the captain winked at her. "You like lobster, young lady?"

"I don't know."

His eyes grew large. "You don't know? Well, now, we'll take care of that." To Hugh he said, "Take a seat and I'll 'ave Molly get you goin'."

"Crab legs, scallops, and shrimp too, Captain."

He laughed. "A seafood feast, coming right up."

Hugh pulled Sofia to a table by the window, where a plump woman accosted them, setting hands upon her ample hips. "So, Hugh. Ale for the two of yous?"

"Just one, Molly. And a root beer for the lady."

"What's root beer?" Sofia asked.

"You'll see."

Soon after, Molly brought Hugh a mug of beer and Sofia a bottle that said "Hires" on it.

"Taste it," he said.

The taste was tangy yet earthy. "It's good."

"It's just the beginning of new tastes for you, Sofia."

She could believe it. "I've never eaten in a restaurant either," she said.

He gaped at her. "You're joshing me."

Sofia regretted her confession.

He squeezed her hand. "I'm honored to be the one to give you your first dining experience. And The Captain's Bounty is the perfect place for it, you'll see."

"It's already perfect," she said. "Without the food."

While they waited for their meal they looked out the window, to the street and the harbor and the bay beyond. "God lives here," Hugh said.

"Here? In this restaurant?"

He laughed. "I meant here, by the sea. On the water."

"I thought God lived in church."

Hugh shook his head, his eyes still on the water. "I know He's everywhere, but out there, on the waves, under a blue sky, that's where I *feel* Him." He looked at her. "How about you?"

Sofia had never thought much about it. God always *was* for her, yet He also always *was* a ways away, as if He were on a throne in the next room, a room where she never gained access. She extended an arm straight out from her body. "God always seems over there."

"Over where?"

"Anywhere I'm not."

Hugh seemed taken aback.

How could she explain? "Maybe it's because I've always lived in the city, where the buildings are high and there's only a narrow slice of sky, where colors are drab and trees nonexistent."

"What about Central Park?"

She shrugged. "That's as foreign a place to me as Newport."

"Oh, the places I will show you, Sofia."

It was her turn to be taken aback.

He noticed. "Do I shock you by being so forward?"

"I don't know forward from backward, but yes, you're talking far beyond our short acquaintance."

He sat back in his chair and sighed. "I . . . I don't know what to do with you, with the way I feel about you. I've never felt like this about any girl."

Sofia's thoughts raced to what she'd heard about him. "What about that maid? The one . . ."

"Addy?"

"The maid you . . . you . . ." She couldn't say it aloud.

He leaned forward, his voice adamant. "I did nothing to that girl beyond exchanging a few words. If she got in the family way, people need to look elsewhere."

Sofia believed him, and yet . . . . "Then why do people say such things about you?"

He took a sip of his drink, then set it down and turned the mug this way and that. "Because I let them."

"Why do you let them?"

"Because it's easier to be thought of as a fool than live under the expectations of being someone who's worthy and honorable."

"That's a horrible way to think."

He shrugged, then took her hands and held them in the table space between them. "But meeting you, finding a connection with you . . . it's made me want to be a better man. It makes me want to be worthy of you."

She was touched and flattered, but also scared. Where could this go? Certainly no good could come from their relationship. For fool or not, he was still the heir to the Langdon fortune, and poor or not, she was still beneath him in status, education, and breeding.

"Do you want to know a secret, matey?"

"Of course."

"When my parents think I'm out carousing, I'm actually down here, volunteering on a fishing boat. Those men teach me about the world, about life, about living."

Her need to respond was taken away when Hugh pointed out the window. "Look there. Why is Lucy walking arm in arm with Rowena's Edward?"

Sofia saw her sister on the sidewalk. She couldn't see the man's face, as he was looking down at Lucy, but by the way Lucy was leaning her head against his shoulder as they walked, there was an evident connection between them. A romance.

The man shifted.

"That's not Edward," Sofia said. "That's Dante. I saw him in church."

"It's Edward DeWitt, I tell you." He pushed back his chair. "I'll go ask them to join us."

Sofia reached across the table. "No!"

Other diners looked in their direction, and Hugh took his seat. "Why not? You're not ashamed of me, are you?"

"Of course not, but . . ."

The list of *buts* was lengthy and complicated.

Luckily, Molly brought them their dinner, balancing three plates heaped with exotic foods.

"Here now. Let's eat."

Rowena paced in front of her fireplace. It was time for Morrie to have his next dose of medicine, yet she was having trouble finding the courage to go see him.

"But I promised the doctor I'd look after him," she said as she paced toward her bedroom door.

"But he'll want to talk about *us*," she countered as she paced back toward the window.

A solution came to her and spurred her out to the hallway. She went to Hugh's bedroom door and knocked. And knocked. "Hugh? Answer. I need you to do me a favor."

Sadie came down the hall carrying fresh linens. "Pardon me, miss, but Mr. Hugh isn't here."

Of course he wasn't.

There was no way around it. Rowena had to go see Morrie.

As she crossed the lawn she rehearsed different ways in which to curtail his talk of love, or their being together. *"It's not the time or place to talk of this, Morrie. You have to focus on getting well and—"*

As she entered the stables she kept her monologue to herself. But at the entrance to Morrie's room she found a crowd of three stableboys. She heard them talk about repairs to a bridle and saddle.

She took advantage of their presence and paused in the doorway until they turned. Caps were removed and conversation stopped.

"Outta here, boys. My nurse has arrived."

But as the boys started to leave, Rowena slid by them and made a beeline for the medicine. "No need to go. Let me give the patient his dose and I'll leave you to your business."

"But—"

She poured out the medicine and virtually shoved it in Morrie's mouth. "There, now," she said. "I'll be back to check on you in the morning."

"But—"

Rowena nodded to the boys and escaped into the stables. She heard Morrie say, "Thanks a lot, fellas."

She felt bad for being so cowardly, but also felt greatly relieved that she had a respite before she'd see him alone again.

A horse whinnied nearby, drawing Rowena toward the rows of stalls. She found the vocal mare and stroked the horse's nose. "There, there. Has everyone neglected you?"

The horse flicked its head, as if nodding. The smells of the horses and the stables were pungent, yet brought back wonderful memories of hours spent with Morrie, helping him tend the horses and even muck out the straw in the stalls. Looking down at her fancy dress with its elaborate trimmings, it seemed ridiculous to think she'd ever gotten dirty through such hard work.

Yet she'd loved every minute of it and had rushed to the stables each day for more.

She walked down the center aisle with horse stalls on either side. Most of these horses were new and unfamiliar to her, but there, in the last stall on the right, was Bessie, the horse who'd been hers.

"Here, girl," Rowena said, clicking her tongue and holding out her hand.

Bessie came to her, limping a bit.

How ironic.

"You limp too, girl? It appears we're two of a kind."

Bessie nuzzled her nose into Rowena's hand, and Rowena leaned her head against her mane. "I miss riding you. Have you missed me?"

I can't ride anymore.

Yes you can.

Could she? Since the accident she'd given up riding horses. And sailing. And dancing. And doing much of anything that brought her joy.

She heard voices coming toward her. The boys were done talking to Morrie.

She should go talk to him and give him a proper good-night.

Instead, she walked out the other end of the barn, her streak of cowardice intact.

✦

Sofia slipped into the bedroom she shared with Lucy and was glad to find it empty. She didn't want to talk to her sister tonight for fear that questions would be asked about how Sofia had spent her evening—and how Lucy had spent hers.

Sofia knew her talent for hiding her true feelings was limited. If Lucy saw her, she'd know something was wrong and Sofia would have to lie, or even worse, confront Lucy with the truth—that Dante was actually Edward DeWitt.

She couldn't fathom such a confrontation, nor the question that would surely arise as to how Sofia knew such a thing. Sofia couldn't let on she was spending time with Hugh Langdon. Lucy had warned her about him, and though her warnings appeared to be unfounded, Lucy would still not approve.

Though how could Lucy talk? She was being romanced by a rich man herself.

But surely she didn't know Dante's true identity. Sofia couldn't imagine Lucy would ever betray Rowena like that.

It was all too complicated to deal with tonight. And so Sofia quickly got undressed, put out the lamp, and got in bed before Lucy got home.

She closed her eyes and prayed for guidance. For clarity.

And for a miracle.

Chapter Nineteen

e ore del mattino hanno l'oro in bocca.

The morning hours are the most precious of the day.

How many times had her father said those words?

Lucy sat on the stone wall, facing the sea, waiting . . . waiting . . .

There it was! The sun.

It began as a sliver of red, like a ball of fire trying to rise out of the sea. As it rose, the sea diluted its fire from red to orange to a white too bright to hold her gaze.

Quick! Before it's fully risen. Say what you've come to say.

"I . . ." It was odd to hear her voice aloud and she checked left, then right, to make sure she was alone before she continued. "I am in love."

It was a simple statement that surprised her with its power.

She repeated it. "I am in love and am loved. We want to get married, and yet . . ."

And yet . . .

Lucy leaned her elbows on her knees, clasping her hands, looking down at the rocky path.

Rocky path. That's what would come with her marrying Dante, a man of higher birth. What would his parents say? What would society say? What would Mamma say?

Mamma and Sofia would be going home soon. The ball was tonight, meaning their reason for being in Newport would come to an end. They would have to go back to their apartment above the dress shop.

But if I marry Dante . . .

Lucy would be living with him. Then what about Mamma and Sofia? She couldn't expect Dante to take on that responsibility—even though he *had* said, "*They can learn to depend on me.*" Without Lucy's income, Mamma and Sofia wouldn't be able to stay in the apartment. Where would they go?

"I feel so selfish. Oh, God, what should I do?"

God? She'd been talking to the sunrise. How had God come into this?

But as she watched the sun move the clouds out of the way, as she listened to the waves wash over the rocks, teasing them with cool relief only to withdraw to tease again, she acknowledged what she'd already known, that God controlled the sunrise and the waves and the shore. With the flip of His will He could stop them all and move heaven and earth: *Smuovere mare e monti.*

So why would you listen to my prayers? I've always stubbornly insisted I could do things myself.

At that moment the sun sprang free from the clouds, making Lucy laugh aloud.

"Fine," she said. "You're listening. So help me do what's right for all of us. Help me . . ." She remembered yet another piece of wisdom from her father. *Ciò che Dio vuole, io voglio*: What God wills, I will.

I need to let Him choose? It was totally against her character. And yet . . .

Lucy looked out to sea and let the sound of the waves accompany her while she waited for His answer.

Where was Lucy?

Sofia awakened early and found her sister gone. Thinking of Lucy's practical nature, her first thought was that her sister was in the workroom, making sure the costumes were ready for the ball tonight.

But then she remembered seeing Lucy walking with Dante— Edward DeWitt. The look on her sister's face, the way she leaned her head against his arm . . . Lucy was in love.

With Rowena's suitor.

Which said little about Edward's character. What was he doing teasing two women with his attention? Although she'd never seen Edward with Rowena, she assumed they were still courting with the intent to marry.

Perhaps Hugh had been mistaken in saying that the man walking with Lucy was Edward.

The thought of Hugh made Sofia turn toward the wall. Was he awake?

She pressed her fingers to the wall they shared and knocked softly. She heard scuffling on the other side. "Sofia?"

"I'm here. Alone."

"Do you want to go for a walk?"

"Give me five minutes."

Any thoughts about the problems of Lucy, Rowena, and Edward vanished with the chance to see this man she treasured.

Rowena awakened from a dream—reluctantly. She'd been riding across lush fields, laughing. Someone was riding with her, laughing with her. She felt the wind on her face, making her hair dance behind her. She wanted to go faster, so she whipped the reins and pressed her inner thighs to the horse's back and—

At the memory, she sat upright. "I was riding astride?" She'd ridden like that as a child, and had just begun to learn the art of riding sidesaddle, like a lady, when she'd had the accident and riding had been taken from her altogether.

But in the dream I wasn't a child. . . .

And in the dream her riding companion was, as it had always been, Morrie.

Which made her remember her responsibility and his need.

The clock on the mantel revealed it was only half past six. She wanted to go check on him, but didn't want to arouse Lucy for the chore of dressing. So she quietly entered the dressing room and chose her simplest day dress. She would not be able to manage the row of buttons marching from the wrist to her elbows, but so be it. Hopefully she could be to the stables and back before any of her family saw her crime of fashion.

She leaned toward her vanity mirror and drew her hair into a hasty bun, securing it with a few hairpins. The tendrils from sleep fell around her face, needing Lucy's skilled hands to tame them. So be it. Morrie wouldn't mind.

Rowena exited into the quiet hallway and tiptoed toward the stairs. But in passing Hugh's room, she heard his voice. She paused at the door and listened.

"Come on, then. I'll meet you outside."

Who was he talking to?

Before she could consider the question, his door opened, and they nearly collided.

"Rowena? What are you—?"

"I ask the same of you, brother," she whispered. She tried to see past him, into the room. If he had a girl in there, she'd be the first to tell their mother. Wild or not, there were limits. "I heard you talking and—"

She was distracted by the sound of a door opening to her left. Out came Sofia, closing the door of the dressing room gently behind—

Sofia looked up. And gasped.

Rowena looked to her brother. "Hugh? What are you up—?"

Hugh pulled her into his room, then went to the hall and beckoned Sofia to join them. Once the door was closed, Hugh pressed himself against it. "I can explain."

Rowena crossed her arms. "You always can."

2

Sofia moved to Hugh's side, and he put an arm around her. "It's not what you think," she said.

Rowena nearly laughed at the absurdity of the statement coupled with their close proximity: Sofia, with her arm around Hugh's waist, and he, protective of her. When he leaned over and kissed her forehead, that was it. "Hugh, she's a child."

Sofia's face hardened. "I am not a child! I'm sixteen. Nearly."

Hugh put a finger to his lips, reminding them all of the need for discretion. Then he said to her, "You're only fifteen?"

"You're not much more, are you?"

"Nineteen," he said. "Nearly twenty."

They were proving Rowena's point. "You are both children, playing at love."

Hugh reaffirmed his protective arm. "We are not playing. I love her and she loves me."

A laugh escaped. "You've known each other mere days and you love—?"

The two exchanged a glance and a nod. "Call it love at first sight."

This was ridiculous. "Love at first sight only exists in fairy tales and novels. People need to know each other a long time and *spend* time with each other to know whether they are in love."

"And how has that worked for you and Edward?" Hugh asked.

It was a decisive blow, causing Rowena to take a step back. "That's not fair," she whispered.

"Is it fair that you judge the love between Sofia and me with just a glance?"

Sofia nodded once and said, " *'L'amore domina senza regole.'* Love rules without rules. My father used to say that."

It was a lovely saying, but like it or not, there *were* rules. "It sounds like an excuse to me," Rowena said. "Those in love may wish for there to be no rules, but let me assure you, there are plenty of them, rules rooted in common sense."

"Like what?" Hugh asked.

Surely he wasn't so blind. Surely he wouldn't make her state them aloud.

Sofia saved Rowena from having to be cruel. "He's rich, I'm not." She looked up into his eyes. "We know that. And we don't care."

They were completely naïve. "But society cares. Our parents will care."

Hugh let go of Sofia and put a hand on his sister's arm. "Our parents are forcing you into a marriage you don't want, one that has nothing to do with love. How can that be right, or make sense—common or otherwise?"

"And what about—?" Sofia cut herself off. "Never mind."

Hugh touched his sister's chin, making her look at him. "Sofia and I are soul mates. That we come from different backgrounds is a detail, not an obstacle. Beyond the trappings we are the same; we understand each other and complement each other. She has changed me for the better and leaves me wanting to be changed even more. I must marry her, no matter what the cost."

Rowena was surprised. His words held a poignancy she'd never witnessed in him before. "But how can you marry her?"

"How can I not?"

Rowena froze. It was like being presented with a page of truth so profound and so undeniable that she had to pause to get a full view of it so she could grasp its edges and make it manageable. They loved and so they would marry. Action reaction. One plus one equaled—

"Now, if you don't mind, Wena, we're off to the Cliff Walk before the day takes over."

Rowena turned to leave.

On the way out, Hugh said, "Are you missing something?"

"What?"

He pointed at the rows of opened buttons at her wrists, at her wagging cuffs. Then he winked at her and ran off toward the back stairs with Sofia in tow.

Their joy apparent, his last words took on new meaning.

She *was* missing something.

Someone.

꧁꧂

319

As soon as they were safely hidden from view on the Cliff Walk, Sofia released the question. "You want to marry me?"

"Of course."

She pulled him to the side, safe from the edge. "I care for you, Hugh, but we've only just met and—"

"Are you saying you don't wish to marry me, matey?" Hugh moved to the outer edge of the path. "Then I have only one choice! Death upon the rocks below!"

She pulled him back from the edge, relieved he was teasing, but needing him to be serious.

"What's with that face?" he asked.

She shrugged, unable to explain.

"Come now, Sofia. I might have exaggerated our relationship to make a point with my sister, but the essence of what I said is true. I do care for you deeply, and I have thought about what it would be like to be married to you."

"You have?"

"Haven't you?"

She couldn't deny it.

He took her hand. "Then, come on. Let's enjoy our day with the knowledge that the future owns many exciting options."

Together they walked, and with each step, Sofia's heart opened further to each and every possibility.

✿

"Love rules without rules. Love rules without . . ."

Rowena walked to the stables with Sofia's words accompanying each step, adding to her confusion.

For after watching Hugh and Sofia run off joyfully together, Rowena's thoughts, feelings, instincts, and logic collided into a morning mush where nothing was distinct or held a flavor of its own.

Hugh and Sofia? It was ridiculous. Hugh was her family's heir. Sofia was an immature girl who had no idea what love was about or what it entailed or—

Rowena pulled up short. Did *she* know what love was about

or what it entailed? She was six years older than Sofia, yet she'd never had a man look at her like her brother looked at Sofia. She'd never had a man call her his soul mate, nor say she'd changed him, or even tell her he loved—

"*I love you, Rowena.*"

Morrie. He'd said it. He'd meant it.

But did she love—?

" 'Morning, Ro." She looked up and saw Morrie standing in the entrance to the stables. And suddenly she knew that more than anything in the world, she wanted to hear that greeting from him every morning for the rest of her life.

"You're flushed," he said as she reached him.

She ignored his statement and gave attention to his ankle. "How is it?"

"I say I'll be fine even as I fear by saying it, I'll cause you to come less often." He slid a finger down her cheek. "If I would've known falling out of the haymow would gain me more of your company, I would've jumped long ago."

She risked a glance and saw his smile. She nodded toward his room. "Did you take your laudanum this morning?"

"A smaller dose. I am done lying in bed. I need to work. With the ball tonight the carriage needs to be made ready."

She'd forgotten about the ball. The thought of Morrie driving her to a ball where she would be with Edward was disconcerting.

They began to stroll through the stables and stopped before her horse, Bessie. "There, girl," Morrie said. "Do you miss your mistress?"

"I miss *her*. I miss—"

"Edward's going to be at the ball, I assume."

"Of course," Rowena said.

"Then tell him you won't marry him. Tonight. Be done with it."

Rowena was taken aback. "I can't just—"

"Why not?" Morrie touched the tips of her fingers, being wary of the stableboys doing their work close by. "You know you want to be with me. When I was hurt you cared for me; you worried after me."

"Of course I did, but—"

"You love me."

She slid past him, unable and unwilling to discuss it here. When he didn't follow, she looked back and nodded toward the exit. Once outside she took refuge under a huge oak tree. Only then did she face him. "This morning I found out something about Hugh that cements my decision to marry Edward."

"What does Hugh have to do with—?"

"Hugh loves Sofia, Lucy's sister. They're intent on marrying."

Morrie laughed. "Hugh wouldn't know love if it was a rock to trip over."

"I used to think the same thing, but the two of them . . ." She shook her head. "Oh, what do I know? But the point is, with Hugh going against the norm by marrying a poor girl, it will be up to me to keep the family's reputation intact. And up to Edward to take the reins of our fathers' business."

"So it's all on you."

She nodded. "With Hugh going against the status quo . . . If I were to also do so, it would be a catastrophe."

His eyes blazed into hers. "Catastrophe, Ro? The world will spin off its axis? Society will collapse into total anarchy?"

She got his point, but . . . "My family will collapse. My father's business will—"

"So Hugh and Edward are the best of the best when it comes to running an elevator business?"

Actually Hugh hated his job, and from what little she'd heard from Edward about the matter, he was more dutiful than enthused.

"Everyone will just be so . . . so . . . disappointed."

He laughed at her inept choice of words. "My, my, we wouldn't want to disappoint people, would we?"

"I've disappointed them enough." She looked down at her leg.

He moved her chin upward with a strong finger. "Enough of that nonsense. You hurt yourself saving your brother's skin. And now you want to do it again? Hugh is reckless and chooses to do what Hugh wants to do, and you think you have to save him?"

"Someone has to."

"No they don't! Hugh is not a child to be saved, and you are not a child who must follow her parents' wishes at all cost."

"But we're to honor our father and mother."

"Is it honorable to marry a man you don't love? For business? They are not honoring you by even suggesting such a thing." He looked around for witnesses, then took her hands and pulled her close. "Honor me and let me honor you by agreeing to be my wife."

Looking into his eyes she knew that she wanted to say yes and have his arms wrap fully around her and never let her go.

A stableboy called out from the barn, "Haverty! Yer needed."

He pulled away. "I'll fight for you, Ro. Fight for me."

Without his presence she felt alone and weak. She was not a fighter. What was she going to do?

But then she remembered her prayers said upon the veranda. She was not alone. She'd asked God to show her the way. Was she brave enough to accept the answer?

She hurried back to the safety of the house.

※

Mrs. Garmin whirled, causing the red satin skirt of her gypsy costume to billow. She finished with a dramatic pose. "Ta-da!"

The other ladies applauded. "You look very striking," Mrs. Langdon said. "Very . . . bohemian."

Mrs. Garmin nodded as if she liked the term, but Rowena had no idea what it meant, and felt no inclination to reveal her ignorance.

Mrs. Scarpelli was marking her mother's Elizabethan dress with a pin. "Do you like your costume, Mrs. Langdon?"

"Very much," she said, adjusting the stiff lace ruff around her neck. "But how did they ever wear such things? It's frightfully uncomfortable."

Rowena laughed. "I would guess history will look back on us and wonder the same thing about our corsets and bustles." As for her gown, she loved the ease and light weight of her butter-silk empire-waist dress. The fabric was spotted with flowers embroidered in gold metallic thread, and the headdress was a concoction of ivory ostrich feathers rising up, and a piece of gathered red lace fabric falling to her shoulders. She unfurled her fan with a flourish. "I say let's go to the Vanderbilts' right this minute. I don't want to take this off."

"Edward is going to faint at the very sight of you," Mrs. Garmin said.

Rowena shrugged.

"Don't you want him to faint?"

Her mother answered for her. "Of course she does." To her daughter she added, "Isn't Edward coming as a Regency gentleman?"

Rowena faltered. "I never asked him to." She remembered thinking how he would look marvelous as Mr. Darcy, but she'd never pursued it.

Mrs. Garmin put her hands on her hips and asked the question Rowena was asking herself. "Whyever not? It would have been the perfect occasion to come as a matched pair."

Her mother shook her head. "Rowena, really. You need to think of such things."

"I'm sorry, Mother." And she was. Yet what was at the core of her *faux pas*? Could it be she hadn't distinctly made the request because she and Edward weren't a matched pair? They shouldn't be matched at all?

When Rowena felt the heat of all eyes, she handily hid behind her fan.

⚜

Sofia burst into the workroom, on an urgent errand to fetch some extra hooks and eyes. The others were in the house, helping Rowena and Mrs. Langdon dress for the ball. At the moment, it was all about them.

Although the focus was a bit annoying, it was also a relief. On an ordinary day there would have been multiple opportunities when she could have told Lucy the truth about her Dante. But today, they'd not had a minute alone. Added to the issue was Lucy's attitude. Sofia had never seen her sister so happy.

Lucy was forever the serious one. Her demeanor and countenance were more often sober and somber than cheerful and glad. And this afternoon she'd even seen Lucy be joyful. How could she rip that away from her?

How could she not?

For even if Sofia didn't tell her the truth, the truth would come out, and then not only would Lucy be hurt, but Rowena. And the families would surely get involved and there would be scandal and . . .

Nothing good would come of waiting. *Le bugie hanno le gambe corte.* Lies have short legs. This lie, this deception, though unwitting, would indeed be tripped up. But who would fall? Rowena? Edward? Or Lucy? Who would be held accountable?

Knowing the way the rich had of deflecting blame, Sofia feared Lucy would be seen as the guilty one, the seductress who lured Edward away from his intended. And Rowena would be seen as the poor crippled girl who couldn't hold the attention of a man. Edward would come off as less guilty, for men were often allowed to be men with little more consequence than a shrug. "Boys will be boys" was an annoying saying that too often negated the need for accountability.

Girls will be girls.

Sofia will be Sofia.

She gathered the supplies and headed back to the house, trying to avoid thinking about it.

She was unsuccessful.

How many times had she heard her mother or Lucy—or even those outside the family—discount her actions with a shake of the head and a "Sofia will be Sofia." She'd never taken offense before; in fact, she'd found it a means to escape responsibility, allowing her to do whatever she wanted to do.

Images appeared, of reading in a hidden corner when there was work to be done, of pretending she couldn't do something, knowing that someone else would do it. And worst of all, memories of tattling or telling secrets *knowing* it would be hurtful, and not caring.

But I've changed.

This afternoon, the old Sofia would have blurted out, *"Dante's real name is Edward,"* reveling in the shocked looks on Lucy's and Rowena's faces, not really caring that her words would be hurtful, nor that they would cause life-changing repercussions.

But she *hadn't* said such a thing.

325

A wave of satisfaction was a balm to her shameful memories. What had changed her? Why was she now considering the feelings of others?

She looked toward an upper window and saw Hugh standing there, looking out at her. He wore a cascade of ruffles at his neck, and a red coat with gold trim at the opening. He was a ship captain of yore. When he'd told her his choice of costume, she'd approved. If he couldn't be a ship's captain in real life, why not play the part when the chance arose?

He saw her, bowed his head, and made a by-your-leave gesture with his hand. She stopped walking and curtsied to him, right there in the middle of the lawn. Then he blew her a kiss—which she caught with a hand upon her cheek. He disappeared from the window and she continued toward the house with the knowledge that he had been the reason for the change in her character.

She didn't have to be the spoiled girl anymore. She had choices. She could be a kind young woman who thought of others *before* she spoke.

With that knowledge came her decision. She'd tell Lucy after the ball. She'd give her this one evening to revel in the success of her costumes. Tonight was a night of fantasy and dreams.

There'd be plenty of chances for reality tomorrow.

CHAPTER TWENTY

$\mathcal{W}$e get to go to the ball?" Lucy said.

Rowena nodded and took Lucy's hand and turned her under her own arm, as if in a dance. She'd been stewing about the idea for days and had finally conjured up the courage to ask her mother. The permission—though reluctantly given—was permission nonetheless.

"However did you manage it?" Mrs. Scarpelli asked.

"At costume parties most of the ladies bring along a lady's maid to help with the headdresses that don't take kindly to the limited space of the carriage, and for help when it becomes necessary to use the . . ." She looked at the women, hoping they would fill in the blank.

"The necessary," Sofia said.

Leave it to Sofia.

Sofia had more to say. "I'm not wearing a maid's uniform. We're not—"

"No, of course not," Rowena hastened to add. "Lady's maids

don't wear uniforms. You may wear whatever you'd like." Then she had an idea. "In fact, if you'd like to wear something of mine, you would be most welcome. It will be my thank-you gift for all your hard work."

Mrs. Scarpelli shook her head. "I couldn't."

Sofia raised her hand. "I could." She linked her arm with her sister. "And Lucy will too."

Although Sofia's outspokenness was often annoying, today Rowena found it helpful. "Will you, Lucy? It would make me very happy."

Lucy looked uncertain, but she nodded.

"Excellent!" Rowena began to go through her clothes. Sofia was a bit shorter than Lucy, but—

"Can I wear this one?" Sofia pulled out an off-the-shoulder pink ball gown.

Rowena didn't know what to say. She hadn't specified what kind of dresses Lucy and Sofia could borrow, and it *had* been her idea, but it would be the height of impropriety for them to come in something so fancy.

Mrs. Scarpelli came to the rescue. "Don't be silly, Sofia. We are not attending the ball, we are merely going to the Vanderbilts' to help." She moved to a section of neutral-colored skirts. "Perhaps a plain skirt—"

"*I* have a plain skirt," Sofia said. "I want something fancier than that."

Lucy smoothed the ball gown back into place among the others. "Think, Sofia. We must look appropriate."

Thank you, Lucy. "Perhaps a pretty daytime ensemble, like this one?" Rowena pulled out a pale green blouse with small floral flowers. "I've worn this to many a party. You could wear it with your own skirt."

Sofia sighed dramatically. "I suppose."

"Sofia!"

Sofia shrugged, then smiled at Rowena. "It's very pretty. Really."

Rowena was quick to seal the bargain. "Try it on. And for you, Lucy . . ." She chose a caramel dotted Swiss dress, with insets of lace spanning the skirt. "The brown in the trim will complement your brown eyes." She turned to their mother. Rowena's skirts would never fit Mrs. Scarpelli's wider frame, but perhaps a blouse she could tuck into one of her own skirts. She pulled an ivory voile from the rack. "Mrs. Scarpelli. Please allow me to dress you as you have dressed me. At least wear this blouse."

Mamma passed her fingers over the intricate lace of the bodice, and Rowena could see she was tempted.

"Please. For me."

"I suppose. If you insist."

Mission accomplished.

⚜

Lucy sat in the carriage with her family and Rowena. Mrs. Langdon was in another carriage with her husband and Hugh. The sun was just beginning to set, and the light had turned a bluish color as the darkness began to fully overwhelm the day. The streetlights were being lit by a man on a ladder, marking the way to the largest mansion in town: the Breakers.

They were not the first to arrive, and the entrance drive was backed up, carriage upon carriage, down Victoria Avenue to Bellevue. Obviously, the Vanderbilt costume ball was *the* place to be.

"I can hardly wait to see inside," Rowena said.

"Haven't you been here before?" Lucy asked.

"The home was just completed. But I hear it has seventy rooms, and thirty bathrooms with hot and cold water piped in—fresh *and* salt water from the sea." She leaned toward the other ladies to add a bit more. "The other Breakers burned down mysteriously a few years ago and Alice Vanderbilt decided she needed to build something bigger than her sister-in-law's house next door. Marble House is grand, and was a thirty-ninth birthday present to Alva from her husband. Since Alice and Cornelius hate Alva, they were determined to make this house grander."

"Why don't they like each other?" Mamma asked. "If they're family . . ."

"There are two reasons—at least," Rowena said. "For one, Alice doesn't approve of what Alva is trying to do to her daughter, Consuelo."

329

"What's that?" Sofia asked.

"Apparently, she's determined to have her marry into an English title. The Duke of Marlborough is the designated pawn. If Alva gets her way, Consuelo will become a duchess. In return the duke will get funds to fix up some English palace. Alice and Cornelius's daughter Gertrude isn't married, and is rather ordinary looking compared to Consuelo's beauty, so Alva will win this round by getting Consuelo a title."

Lucy didn't want to say anything, but was the situation with Rowena's parents that much different? Weren't they forcing her into marriage with Edward—for funds?

Rowena continued. "Also, Alice considers Alva a vixen who lured their father-in-law into bequeathing Alva's husband an equal amount of his estate, even though Alice's husband was the eldest son. Instead of ten million, like he left his other children, by Alva's coercion and wiles, her Willie got an additional fifty-five million."

"Million?" Sofia asked. "Dollars?"

"I know," Rowena said. "It's an astounding amount. Incomprehensible."

"Where do they make their money?" Lucy asked.

"Railroads."

She thought of her train ride to Newport. "So they owned the train that brought us here?"

"If they don't, they'd like to, and probably will. The Vanderbilts tend to get what they want." Rowena adjusted her gloves above her elbows. "Plus, I'm sure Alice is quite pleased Alva was disgraced by asking for a divorce last spring."

Sofia shook her head, unbelieving. "Why would anyone who was this rich get divorced and risk losing it?"

Mamma answered. "People need to marry for love, not money. 'For the love of money is the root of all evil.' "

"But not money itself," Sofia asked.

Her comment seemed strange. As if Sofia would ever have money.

"Actually," Rowena said, "Alice and her husband are very generous to charities, especially colleges. And they met while teaching Sunday school."

The carriage slowed. It was their turn to enter the estate. There was a huge iron gate at least thirty feet tall, bounded by four stone columns topped with enormous stone balls. Crowning the gate was a filigree C and V.

Lucy set aside the bickerings of the wealthy and took a moment to count her blessings. Her family loved each other, and at this moment Lucy felt like a princess. She—she—was going to a costume ball. But better yet, it was a ball Dante was attending, and he wasn't expecting her. She wasn't sure how she was going to do it, but she was determined to find a way to peek at the festivities and see him. And if she did it right, he would see her, and they would exchange a wonderful glance across the room, and she would smile at him and nod as if to say, *"See? I can be here too."*

But then the inner voice that had recently started niggling at her added its two cents: *But if you're going to be his wife, shouldn't you really be there with him? Dancing? Mingling with his set?*

They were questions that had no answers. Add them to the list of things she didn't know about Dante. His full name, his family's financial status, how his family would react to her, what the future held for them as a couple . . .

She'd heard of wealthy people disowning their children if they displeased them in some way. Yet Dante seemed unconcerned or, at the very least, kept his worries to himself. He'd told her to trust him. Their love would conquer all.

But the words that overshadowed his promises were those of her father: *"Ogni bel gioco dura poco."* Every good game lasts a short while. All good things come to an end.

As did their ride. The carriage stopped at the door. But instead of being eager to enter the mansion, Lucy was struck by an overwhelming premonition. *This good thing will come to an end.*

"Lucy, come on. Get out," Sofia said.

Lucy saw that the other three women had already exited. It was her turn.

Stay in the carriage. Don't go inside.

"Miss?" The footman's hand moved a few inches closer, and she saw impatience on his face.

She retrieved a hatbox containing Rowena's headpiece, took his hand, and got out of the carriage. A strangling vise clenched her midsection, offering further warning that she should not enter this house upon risk of her life.

Rowena was already through the door, and there was a little commotion as the footmen weren't quite sure what to do with Mamma and the rest of them. Rowena, in her kindness, had not thought through the awkwardness of the help alighting from the carriage with her. It was obviously not done, and the liveried menservants who were aiding the guests showed various signs of being both confused and perturbed.

There had to be a servants' entrance. They needed to go back there and—

All this flashed through Lucy's thoughts and added to her premonition that the night would not go well.

Finally, a servant leaned toward her and said, "Go around that way and they'll send you up to the rooms set aside for the ladies' use."

Lucy nodded and pulled Mamma and Sofia away from the grand front entrance.

"We can't go inside?" Sofia asked.

"Not with the guests," Lucy said. She wasn't in a mind to explain. "Just come with me to the back entrance."

"This is embarrassing," Sofia said. "I thought we'd get to see the main house, and now we're treated like regular servants."

"Shush now, *piccolina*. We're lucky to be here at all. Don't do anything to get us sent home."

Lucy stopped walking. Sent home. *Go home. Leave this place before it's too late.*

Sofia stormed past her, then paused and turned around. "Now what's wrong?"

"I just can't . . ." There were no words to explain.

Lucy expected Sofia to tease her, to be impatient with her, and was surprised when her sister nodded to Mamma and said, "Just a minute,

Mamma. Let me talk to her." Then she pulled Lucy to the side. "We don't have to go inside. I'll go home with you, if you want me to."

What? Just a second ago Sofia had complained about not being able to see the main part of the house. Now Sofia was willing to miss the ball? Miss seeing inside this mansion of all mansions?

Yet Lucy could see by the furrow in her brow Sofia was serious. "I'll walk you back. Mamma can handle the final primping. You shouldn't go in there. I'll go back—"

I shouldn't go in there? It was an odd thing to say. It verified Lucy's feeling of foreboding, but . . . "Why shouldn't I go in there?"

Sofia's countenance, which had been so adamant just moments before, lost its fervency. Uncertainty took its place and she looked away, as if unable to hold Lucy's gaze.

Lucy took her arm. "Sofia? What aren't you telling me?"

But before Sofia could answer—if she would have answered at all—they saw Mr. and Mrs. Langdon exit their carriage along with Hugh. He looked over to the girls and offered them a subtle two-fingered salute.

Whatever had been bothering Sofia was forgotten. "Let's get inside," she said.

Lucy had no choice but to follow.

God help me.

⚜

Rowena entered a breathtaking two-story grand hall that could be overlooked from a wraparound railing on the second floor. The ceiling was edged with a heavy gold cornice, and was painted with a scene reminiscent of summertime. Rowena had never been to Europe but couldn't imagine any palace being more opulent.

She looked back to see Lucy's reaction, for surely she would find the grandeur even more of a shock. But Lucy was not behind her. And where were Mrs. Scarpelli and Sofia?

Rowena saw her mother enter and went to her. "I've lost the Scarpellis."

Mother spoke under her breath. "They went to the servants'

entrance. There's such a thing as protocol, Rowena. You didn't expect them to enter with us, did you?"

Actually, that's exactly what she'd . . . wanted. Rowena felt bad for not thinking things through. She'd been so enraptured with the idea of letting her friends experience something sumptuous and new that she'd ignored the cruel realities. How embarrassing—for her, but mostly, for them. To arrive in a grand carriage only to be whisked away to some other entrance because they weren't considered good enough?

"It's my fault. I never should have put them in that position."

"What, dear?"

"Nothing." Rowena made her excuses to her mother and walked with the other women toward the ladies' reception room, where they could put the finishing touches on their costumes.

The reception room was as feminine as the other room was grand. It was paneled in white, with murals lining the walls. The furniture was intricate and looked French. Rowena moved as quickly as possible through the meandering women dressed as princesses, glorified milkmaids, and Greek goddesses, looking for Lucy.

"May I help you, miss?" a maid asked.

"I'm looking for my . . . my . . ." How could she describe them?

"Servants? They should be coming in real soon, miss."

Servants. What must Lucy and her family think of me?

At that moment, Rowena spotted the Scarpellis entering the room with the hatboxes, walking among a half dozen lady's maids.

Rowena rushed toward them, her hands outstretched in supplication. "I'm so sorry. I wanted you to see . . . I never thought it through . . . I feel so bad. . . ."

Mrs. Scarpelli put a hand on hers. "Shush now, Miss Langdon. 'Tis not your fault. We know that. And the truth is, we *are* here to help the three of you get dressed."

Her gracious spirit was humbling. Sofia, however, sat in a chair by the window, pulling at a lace arm cover, sulking. And Lucy . . .

Lucy moved past her and opened the hatboxes. She fluffed an ostrich plume. Rowena went to her. "I'm so sorry, Lucy, I never meant for you to be embarrassed and—"

"Let's get this headdress on."

Rowena took a moment to study her friend. The tone of her voice revealed no injury, but the blush in her cheeks and the tightening between her brows showed harm had been done. Rowena stilled Lucy's hands with her own. "I'm so sorry, Lucy. Truly, I am."

With a bit of reluctance, Lucy met her eyes, but then she held Rowena's gaze. "I know you are. You wouldn't know how to be mean. Things are as things are."

"Which doesn't make them easy, or right," she said.

A shrug was Lucy's only answer—unfortunately, the only answer there was. Rowena felt sick inside and wished she could undo the injury that had been done to her friends, erase the slight. Suddenly, the entire event seemed ridiculously frivolous, decadent, and . . . wrong. And as such . . . she wanted nothing more to do with it.

She handed the headdress back to Lucy. "I'm going home. We're going home. We'll spend the evening up in my room and have a wonderful time talking and laughing and—"

Lucy's head shook in short bursts. "What are you talking about? This is what we've been working toward for weeks, to create costumes for this ball. You can't go home. Besides, Edward will be here."

Rowena's thoughts twisted into a tight cord of confusion. Of course she couldn't go home. Lucy and her family had worked long hours to create these beautiful costumes—which deserved to be seen. Surely Lucy would get other commissions because of this night. It was selfish of Rowena to even think of leaving.

Lucy touched her hand and moved close. "I appreciate your offer, but we're fine, Rowena. I am a seamstress and you are an heiress. Neither one of us asked for our roles, but we're stuck with them—and with everything that goes with them. That we are friends . . . that you and I . . ." She squeezed Rowena's hand. "I thank God for you, and I want what's best for you, which is . . ." She nodded toward the door. "To go find Edward and sweep him off his feet with your beauty and charm so he'll propose to you right there on the dance floor."

Rowena was moved by Lucy's words and her hope for the evening.

She kissed her cheek. "I thank God for you too, Lucy. I have never, ever had a friend like you."

"Then put this on and go live happily ever after."

It was the least she could do.

❦

Entering the grand hall of the Breakers was like stepping into a fairy tale. The enormous room was filled with characters throughout history, from fanciful butterflies, imps, and jesters, to courtiers spanning the Italian Renaissance to Henry VIII's court to the Elizabethan age, to the extravagant bewigged creations of French royalty before its fall to revolution.

"There's Edward," Mother said as she entered beside her. "There, dressed as a Shakespearean actor."

Rowena saw him, and as she did, he saw her. But in the instant before he smiled, there was a flash of something else in his eyes.

Fear.

Fear? What was he afraid of?

But as he crossed the floor to ease her into the cheery mayhem, she saw him struggle to set it aside. By the time he took her hand, he had succeeded. Partially.

"You look lovely, Rowena."

"What's wrong?" she asked as she slipped her hand in his arm and they entered the crowd. She kept her eyes straight ahead, smiling and nodding as they strolled among the other guests.

"Wrong?" he said. "Why, nothing is wrong."

She wanted to believe him, but by the pause in his initial step, by the hesitation and catch in his voice, she knew her instincts were right. And so she stopped their progress and faced him. But as she did so, as her words were poised to be spoken, she felt a wave of panic, an inner warning to ignore her instincts and let the ball continue in all its fantasy. To speak the words, to confront what she only sensed . . .

Everything will change. Don't say it. Let it pass.

But she couldn't let it pass. They were face-to-face now, stopped amid the throbbing movement. "There *is* something wrong," she said.

"There has been something wrong. Please share it with me. If we are to be . . ." She didn't finish the sentence, for to mention their engagement when nothing had been said would be the height of presumption.

Edward avoided her gaze, looked down, then into her eyes. "There *is* something I need to tell you."

And then she knew.

The fairy tale was ending before it began.

The female guests of the party had left the reception room, leaving behind their lady's maids. A few women made themselves comfortable, lounging on the silk-upholstered chairs and settees, while others busied themselves with empty hatboxes and valises. They were clearly settling in for the evening, at their mistresses' beck and call.

Lucy couldn't have sat if she'd wanted to—which she didn't. She wanted to go watch the festivities and spot Dante.

A thirty-something lady's maid sidled up next to her. "If you keep eyeing that door, you're going to burn a hole in it."

"If the hole would let me see . . ."

"You want to *see*? You want to watch?"

Lucy's stomach flipped. "You know a way?"

The woman's eyes sparkled. "There's always a way. Come with me."

Lucy looked around for Mamma. She was over by a window, talking with one of the older ladies. And Sofia was slumped in a chair, running her hands across the damask upholstery.

If she left quickly, for just a short look . . .

"Let's go," she told the woman. "By the way, I'm Lucy."

"And I'm Agatha." With a quick glance across the room she headed for the door. "Quickly, so we don't draw a crowd."

They slipped out to the hallway, where a footman in a powdered wig and eighteenth-century waistcoat stood guard.

"Evening, Agatha," he said with a wink.

"Evening, Benny. We're just going for a look-see, all right?"

"Have a time of it," he said.

"Where's the back stairs?"

He pointed with a nod.

But just as they started walking, the door opened again and Sofia came out.

"Go back inside, girl," Benny said.

Sofia pointed to Lucy. "I'm with her. She's my sister."

Benny—and Agatha—looked at Lucy. "She is," Lucy said. "Can she come along?"

Agatha rolled her eyes but nodded. "Get over here, girl, but do exactly as I say or back you go."

Lucy flashed Sofia a look. She'd better not ruin things.

"Where are we going?" Sofia whispered.

"To watch the rich cavort and be merry," Agatha said.

Lucy whispered for Sofia's ears alone. "I want to find Dante."

Sofia yanked her arm, forcing them to stop. "No, Lucy. That's not a good idea."

"I just want to look. I thought you, of all people, would—"

Agatha stood before them, her hands on her hips. "Are you coming or not?"

"Not—"

"I'm coming." Lucy glared at her sister. "Go back to the room."

"No. I'll come too."

Agatha threw her hands in the air. "Well?"

"We're coming."

Agatha led the way down a hall, to a back stairway that led to the second floor. There, they entered an open mezzanine, one like Lucy had seen at Stewart's department store. There was a series of tall open arches connected by black filigreed railing. The arches and railing ran around the enormous two-story atrium hall where the guests were mingling. Agatha led them behind one of the rectangular fluted columns. "There," she said with a wave of her hand toward the opening. "There's the Great Hall, and there's the most wealthy of the wealthy in Newport—in all of New England."

Lucy peeked around the column and let the voices of the crowd and the music from the orchestra waft upward, drawing her forward to see.

"Stay in the shadows," Agatha warned.

AN UNLIKELY SUITOR

Lucy noted the edge of the shadow and pulled her skirt tight to her legs, leaning back toward the column as she edged her way closer to the railing. Sofia pressed beside her, with Agatha pressing from behind, looking over Sofia's shorter stature.

"See there?" Agatha said. "That rather pudgy woman wearing the ridiculous gold headdress is the hostess, Alice Vanderbilt. She may look small, but she rules with an iron fist. Rules all but her children, that is. See the weak-looking young man there near the orchestra? The one in the soldier's uniform? That's the heir, Neily, and the striking woman he's with is Grace Wilson. She was secretly engaged to his older brother Bill a few years ago, but then Bill died of the typhoid and now . . . the parents aren't pleased one whit she's moved on to the younger brother."

Lucy enjoyed hearing Agatha's stories, but was most concerned with finding Dante. He'd told her he would be wearing a costume from Shakespeare's time. Unfortunately, among the hundreds of people swirling below there was more than one man wearing a short doublet and tights.

"And there's your Miss Langdon," Agatha said. "And DeWitt's with her. Are they engaged yet? I hear that's the plan, but . . ."

Lucy stopped listening. The music faded away, as did the murmur of the party. All her senses focused on sight, on *the* sight of Rowena and . . . and . . .

Sofia whispered in her ear. "I'm so sorry, Lucy. That's why I wanted you to stay away."

You knew?

Yet Lucy couldn't pull her eyes away from the awful sight to question her sister. There had to be some mistake.

Once again Agatha's voice sounded in Lucy's ears. "That DeWitt is a handsome chap, that's for certain, but with Miss Langdon's problem . . . I hope she catches him before his head is turned by someone else."

This can't be real. I'll blink and everything will be different.

Lucy did just that. She closed her eyes, then opened them again. But nothing changed.

Dante was Edward DeWitt. Edward DeWitt was her Dante.

339

Not my *Dante. Not mine at all!*

Suddenly, she didn't care about shadows or being discreet. She stepped toward the railing and gripped it like a lifeline.

"Get back here!" Agatha whispered.

Lucy felt hands tugging on her, trying to pull her back.

Dante was Edward. Dante had proposed. But Rowena was supposed to marry him. How could—?

Suddenly, Dante looked up.

He saw her.

His mouth opened.

Rowena saw the direction of his gaze, looked up, and waved happily.

He shook his head, *no, no, no . . .*

Lucy turned.

And ran.

CHAPTER TWENTY-ONE

o!" Edward said. "No!"

Rowena didn't understand. Just a moment ago he'd pulled her aside, wanting to talk with her, and then he'd looked up and seen Lucy peering down from the second floor railing. She was glad Lucy was getting the chance to see her costumes in the mix of the party.

"What's wrong, Edward?"

She looked toward Lucy again, just in time to see her turn and run away.

"I have to go." His voice was frantic.

Rowena grabbed his arm "But why? Tell me what's—"

He stopped and looked down at her, his face a tragic mask. "I'm Dante. I'm Lucy's Dante."

She must have faltered, because he took her arms and held her up.

"I'm sorry, Rowena. I didn't mean for it to happen. That's what I was going to talk to you about tonight." He looked toward the front entry. "I have to go. I have to find her and explain."

But what about me? What about explaining it to me?

"I'm so sorry," he said. "I'm—"

His apology was as ineffectual as offering to kiss a gaping wound to make it better. He was sorry?

Rowena pulled her arms free. "How could you?" she whispered.

He opened his mouth to speak but offered nothing. Except . . . "I have to find her." He kissed Rowena's cheek, then ran off through the crowd.

"Oh dear."

"Did you ever . . . ?"

Rowena was horrified to realize her humiliation was public. As if in slow motion she looked right, then left, to find multiple groups of onlookers, their heads bent one to the other, absorbed in discussing the drama they had just witnessed. Their faces revealed interest, revulsion, and embarrassment.

But no sympathy. No compassion.

And not a single person—for she would not dignify them by calling them friends—stepped forward to console her, or even to ask after the situation. Rowena was society's pathetic cripple, the subject of pity, gossip, and gratitude that they weren't as wretched as she.

She thought to excuse herself from their presence, then decided they didn't deserve it. And so, she walked through the crowd, letting the venerable bastions of society fill in the space behind her.

Out, out, out, out . . .

Her focus was singular: escape. To be away from this party, this house, this moment.

This truth.

Her hurried departure set the doormen scurrying. "Did you have a wrap, miss?"

She shook her head and let them open the door before her and pull it shut upon her egress. Various coachmen flicked their cigarettes away and stood at attention.

"May we help you, miss?" one asked.

Could they?

"Morrie. Haverty."

A coachman looked down the row of carriages, whistled, then called out, "Haverty! Yer wanted!"

Whatever energy she'd had left her, and Rowena's legs gave out. The men came to her rescue, taking her arms, offering her a seat.

"Is there someone at the party I can call?" one asked.

"Just Haverty. Please."

But before the man could call Morrie's name a second time, he appeared from the line, hurrying toward her, resplendent in his coachman uniform. "Ro—" He caught himself. "Miss Langdon. What's wrong?"

"I need to go. Please."

"Of course. Let me get the carriage. It's just five or six—"

She shook her head, knowing she couldn't walk another step, nor stay here another second. She raised her arms in supplication. "I can't . . . Carry me."

He pulled her into his arms and she linked her hands behind his neck. "I gotcha now. No worries. I'll take care of you."

Rowena closed her eyes and nodded against his chest.

⁂

Lucy ran down the back stairs to the servants' entrance and outside. But instead of turning left, toward the main driveway—which was lined with a parade of carriages—she ran around the side of the house toward the back. There were stone steps and balustrades and gardens, but finally only an open lawn stood between her and the sea.

Her lungs burned and she stopped to catch her breath. Glancing back at the house was like looking at a fully lit lantern, with the movement of the people its flame.

A red hot flame that burned her very soul.

The sound of music and laughter from the house mocked her. *See, you silly girl? You don't belong here. Did you really think one of our kind would truly be interested in someone like you?*

But then the sound of the sea swept over the sounds of the house, and she made her choice. The sea was impartial. The sea wouldn't judge her. The sea, the sky, the stars . . .

She staggered toward the edge of the lawn, which in the darkness looked like a line marking the edge of the earth. With one misstep she would fall into oblivion. But then she found courage by focusing on the sea and the white foam of the waves reflecting the moon. When her feet found the path, she felt she'd moved to a place of safety, as if the world of the Vanderbilts, the Langdons, and the DeWitts couldn't touch her here.

On the Cliff Walk the sea drowned out the very existence of the party, and each wave soothed her panic.

Lucy looked upward to see the stars, but found them washed out. The light of the house was to blame. She felt a sudden need to see them fully, so walked to the south, to find a place free from the intrusion of man.

Her progress was slow and careful, for as she achieved nature's darkness, she lost the ability to see the path. She hugged the land side, letting her feet feel their way along the craggy trail. Lucy stopped a few times to test the sky, to see if the stars were visible, but walked farther and farther until the conditions proved right.

Finally, the stars pulsed in the black sky and the moon played peekaboo through wide strands of clouds. The path here had taken a downhill turn, with the view of its mansion entirely hidden. She leaned against the high bank, letting her head find support there. She closed her eyes and sighed. "How could I have been so blind?"

Had there been signs that her Dante was Rowena's Edward? She raked her memories and found no clue but for his reluctance to tell her his name.

And yet she'd been quite willing to continue the game of "Dante." Had she suspected something was amiss and avoided it?

She opened her eyes, looked out to sea, and remembered her time with Dante on this very path. *Go ask the sunrise . . .*

The feelings they'd shared, the hopes, the plans, had been real. Above all else she'd never seen a bit of artifice in Dante. Their connection was genuine, and their feelings . . .

"I love him." But what did she know of love? And so the words were repeated. "I love him?"

Lucy slid to sitting and wrapped her arms around her legs. *Please, God, I do love him.*

But what about Rowena? *She* was supposed to marry Edward DeWitt. Her feeling of betrayal had to be as great as Lucy's.

"Edward is to blame. He should have told me. He should have told her."

She leaned her forehead against her knees and prayed a wave of wisdom would wash over her.

Or let her drown.

⁂

Rowena felt the carriage stop. The jostling and the sound of the horse's hooves on the street were silent. But she couldn't move.

After Morrie had swept her into his arms and taken her to the carriage, she'd pulled the headdress from her hair and let it fall to the floor. Then she'd turned onto her side with her hands to her cheek and lay upon the seat. She'd wanted to die, or at the very least, acquire the ability to become invisible. The rhythm of the horse's stride ignited a mantra she repeated: *Not true, not true, not true . . .*

Maybe if she repeated it enough, time would reverse itself and Edward would never look up and see Lucy, and there would be no moment of recognition, knowledge, and pain.

But even before he saw Lucy, he was wanting to talk to me, to tell me something.

Very true. It was all true no matter how much she wanted things to be different.

Edward was Dante. Edward loved Lucy.

And Lucy loved Ed—

The door to the carriage opened and Morrie's gentle voice broke through her awful trance. "Come, Ro. I'll take care of you."

His words of comfort were as much a balm as the situation at the ball was a knife to her soul. Could one heal the other?

Morrie held out his hand and helped her step out of the carriage. "Can you walk?" he asked.

She nodded. Her legs felt stronger if for no other reason than

345

he was beside her, ready to catch her if she faltered. It was then she noticed he hadn't taken her to the main house, but back to the stables.

It was a relief. Although her family was at the Breakers—hopefully they were still there, hopefully they hadn't witnessed her humiliation— she couldn't imagine being in that huge house by herself.

"Come into my quarters and you can rest. I'll send one of the boys to Mrs. Oswald's to get you some tea."

"That would be nice."

Once there she sat upon a ragged chair and saw him limp away to get the boy. When they returned she said, "You limp, I limp . . ."

"We are a pair, we two." He pulled a footstool close and sat upon it, looking ridiculous crouched upon its tiny frame.

"Here," she said, standing. "You sit in the chair and let me sit—"

He pressed her back to sitting. "Nonsense, Ro. What kind of man do you think I am to ever take the best for myself?"

She knew exactly what kind of man he was. "Thank you for saving me."

"I will always save you," he said. "But you need to tell me what I was saving you from."

She closed her eyes against the memories. If only she could just sit here with Morrie and not think about the other . . .

"Did DeWitt hurt you?" Morrie asked.

Tears came in a rush and she hid her face in her hands. "He loves Lucy! He's her Dante!"

"Dante?"

Her words came with the same rush as her tears and she explained everything.

"He told you he loved Lucy?"

"He was going to tell me, but then he saw her and—"

"Did she know who he was?"

Rowena looked into the air between them and found it filled with the image of Lucy's face. There'd been no satisfaction there, no complicity. Only shock and horror.

She looked at Morrie. "She didn't know."

"The cretin. To lead the two of you on—at the same time."

His words ignited Rowena's pain, and anger sparked. She rose from her chair, needing movement to fan the flames. "He did lead us on! He was supposed to marry me. He went on outings with me and made me feel as though he loved me, when all the while he was seeing Lucy and . . ." She remembered something Lucy had told her. "He left her love notes on the Cliff Walk. While he was courting me he was wooing her." She stopped pacing. "How dare he do that to me? How dare he get my hopes up for a life together, and then destroy all of it? If only I hadn't brought Lucy to Newport, *I* would be marrying Edward!"

Instead of offering support, Morrie sat motionless on the stool, his hands gripping his thighs.

"Aren't you going to say something?"

He gazed at her a few moments, then said softly. "Are you angry because Edward hurt you or because you love him?"

"I . . ."

He pressed his hands against his legs and stood. "Because if you love him, I will find him and make him pay for breaking your heart. But if you are merely angry because he betrayed you, then I . . ."

Morrie moved close and ran his hand across her cheek, letting it rest there, cupping her face. Without thought she leaned against that hand, closed her eyes, wanting to linger there forev—

What am I doing?

She took a step away from him. His hand fell to his side.

"I see, then," he said. "It's the former."

The stableboy brought in the tea, spilling much of it over the rim. " 'Ere's the tea, Haverty."

"Set it on the table," Morrie said, "so Miss Langdon can drink it at her leisure." He retrieved his hat. "I must be off to defend our lady's honor." With a nod to Rowena, he left.

The boy set the tray on the table. "Sorry I spilled some a' it. I's not used to carrying fancy things."

But Rowena didn't listen, or see when he slipped out of the room. Only after he was gone did she realize she was totally alone.

"Morrie!"

She stumbled out of his room and toward the carriage, only to see it pulling away.

"Want me to run after it, miss?" the boy said from the stable doorway.

Yes. Please. Run after it and bring Morrie back to me so I can have his hand upon my face again, so I can linger there and not pull away and let what would have come next happen. . . .

"Miss?"

He was waiting for her answer. "No, no thank you."

"Can I gets you anything else, then?"

She forced herself to look at him so he would be set free. "No. You may go."

Rowena was left in the shadows of the drive. Behind her was Morrie's empty room. In front of her was the house, which was empty in so many ways. . . .

And so she did something she'd never done before. She turned between them both and walked into the darkness.

❧

Sofia ran down the street, the should-have-saids chasing her, pressing her home. *I should have told Lucy about Dante. Then she would've stopped seeing him or told Rowena or . . .*

As soon as she'd witnessed the exchange between Edward and Lucy at the ball, regret had tightened its grip upon her like a corset laced too tight. And when she'd heard her sister gasp, she'd nearly fallen over from the surge of horror that had swept over Lucy and spilled past her to drown Sofia in its nasty wave. Sofia had always known the truth would come out, but had never let herself imagine the *hows* of it. Or the full devastation.

Lucy had run out, and Sofia had run too, to catch her, to help her, to . . .

To what? What could she do or say to make things better? There was no *better*. There was no happy ending as in the novels she loved. Two girls loved the same man.

This could not end well.

But as Sofia tried to leave, Mamma had come out of the ladies' reception room and stopped her on the back stairs, asking too many questions. Sofia was proud of herself for not saying anything other than, "I have to go. No, nothing's wrong. Lucy wasn't feeling well and—"

But then Agatha had smiled smugly and countered, "It appears Lucy and Edward DeWitt have something going on between them. You shoulda seen the look on his face when he saw her. And him standing there with Miss Langdon—who seemed to know nothing about it whatsoever. If you ask me—"

"No one's asking you!" Sofia hissed.

Agatha put a hand to her neck. "Well, then."

Sofia couldn't worry about her. It was Mamma who needed an explanation. "I'm going after her, Mamma. I'll see she's all right."

"But what happened?"

Sofia hesitated, but only for a second. Better to share the truth than have Mamma hear Agatha's version. She lowered her voice. "Dante is Edward. Rowena's Edward."

Mamma pulled back. "Did Lucy know?"

"No." Sofia didn't mention that *she* knew. "I have to go to her, Mamma." She kissed her mother's cheek and found her way out of the mansion.

To run. To run back to the Langdons'. She expected to find Lucy in her room, packing her things to escape, to travel back to New York.

Not that Sofia would stop her. If they'd never come to Newport Lucy would never have met Edward, and he and Rowena would probably be engaged by now, and—

I would never have met Hugh.

She couldn't think about that now. And as she ran she let all selfish thoughts be ground into the sidewalk with her footfalls. Lucy was hurting. Her sister needed her. That was all that mat—

"Ooomph!"

Sofia was knocked to the ground from behind. She tried to break the fall with her hands, but the force was too strong and the side of her face hit the pavement.

Her attacker turned her over roughly, causing her head to knock against the ground. She tried to free her hands, pushing at him, scratching at him, but he was too strong and got hold of her wrists, pressing them against the sidewalk on either side of her head.

She tried to see his face, but it was too dark.

Then he straddled her. His weight pressed all breath from her lungs and she struggled not only against him, but against her corset and the panicked need to breathe.

"You thought you could hide, girlie? Not from me. Never from me."

His voice! It was Bonwitter!

Anger gave her the power to breathe. "Get off me, you oaf! Help! Somebo—"

"No you don't." He pressed a hand over her mouth, but in the process set one of Sofia's arms free.

She punched him, slapped him, clawed at his face.

He slapped her so hard her ear rang with it.

Then again.

And again.

Sofia felt herself slipping away. She knew she should fight, but there was no fight left. He moved off her, and she was so relieved to be able to breathe that she barely noticed him yanking at her skirts, pulling them up—

No, no, no, no, no . . .

But then he was gone. Pulled away? She heard a scuffle nearby. Fists finding flesh. And bone. Labored bursts of air. Groans.

And then silence.

Was it over? Was she dead?

Sofia tried to open her eyes but couldn't. They were swollen shut and her body seemed separate from her will.

But then someone carefully lifted her into their arms. "I've got you. You'll be all right now."

The angel lifted her from this earth and flew her to a better place.

CHAPTER TWENTY-TWO

*R*owena stood at the entrance to the Cliff Walk. She hadn't been on its path since the accident. She and Morrie used to run its length, leaping over stones, even venturing down to the rocks below to play tag with the waves. They'd take turns standing on a boulder, letting the water lick their shoes. The spray of the sea would splash over them until their hair and clothes surrendered to the wetness.

And now, there were not only years as a barrier to venturing out upon the trail, but darkness. And her leg. And her costume with its embroidered train. And her silk shoes with their slippery soles.

The moon chose this moment to extract itself from the clouds. Its reflection upon the ocean was a twin blessing, a dual assurance that she could—and should—hazard to move away from the house and into the tolerance and peace of nature.

With a final sigh she nodded at her decision. "Forgive us, Lord. Help us." The prayer was all encompassing, for there was so much that needed His assistance. Armed with the assurance she would not be alone, she turned onto the Cliff Walk.

Her first steps were tentative, but as she forced herself to surrender to the sky, the sea, the rocks, and the Divine, she gained confidence and strength.

At a place where the path widened, she paused and sat upon a wall. Without the need to gauge every step, she was free to fully take in the scene before her. On the horizon was the silhouette of a ship. Oh, to be at sea again and feel beholden to the boat and the waves for safety and movement. It was so different here, on land, as an observer rather than a participant.

And that's what you are, Rowena. An observer. When are you going to fully participate?

The thought caused her to put a hand to her breast. She could feel her heart beat and knew its increased rhythm was caused by the inner question and not the physical exertion.

She used to be a participant in life. She'd danced and jumped and laughed and . . .

But with the accident she'd lost more than just physical participation. For years she'd retreated from fully partaking in other aspects of life. It had been too easy to let the concern and attention of her family become a shroud, letting her remain still and contained bodily, emotionally, intellectually, and even spiritually. She'd let them tell her what to do, what to feel, what to think, and what to believe.

Saving her brother's life was the last act of free will she'd accomplished. She'd been a heroine—a heroine crippled by her act of courage. "God bless you, Rowena" had become a cozy couch for her to lie upon as the world—and her own life—continued on without her.

The Lord helps those who help themselves.

She knew the saying was only partially right. God could do anything and everything, but it only seemed right that He also expected some mortal effort and participation. Had God allowed Edward to fall in love with Lucy because Rowena had been complacent, watching others do the work of living for her?

"I have no one to blame but myself."

Rowena heard movement on the path. She looked over to find Lucy there.

"And me. You have me to blame," Lucy said. "But truly, I didn't know. I didn't know."

At the sight of her, Rowena stood and extended her arms to her friend. Lucy ran to her and the two girls embraced, both talking at once.

"I didn't know either."

"He never told me his name."

"I'm so sorry this happened."

"I'm so sorry this happened."

As their sentiments found common ground, they stepped apart. Even in the moonlight Rowena could see that Lucy's eyes were swollen from crying. She pulled her toward the wall to sit. "How are you?" she asked.

"How are you?"

They laughed at their shared concern. Finally Rowena asked, "Have you seen him?"

Lucy shook her head adamantly. "Have you?"

Rowena did the same. "He ran after you."

"He did?"

The hope in Lucy's eyes revealed much about her true feelings.

"So you love him?" Rowena asked.

Lucy was quick to shake her head. "Not really. And I never would have consented to marry him—"

Rowena put a hand to her mouth.

They were engaged? While I've been waiting for Edward to propose to me, he proposed to Lucy?

"It was nothing, Rowena. You're the one who is to marry him."

But then Rowena knew, with a flash as bright as lightning. . . . "We will never marry."

"But that's the plan. You need to marry—"

"My parents' need cannot be my own. I need to marry someone who loves me. And Edward—in spite of his great effort to do so—never had those feelings for me." She sought Lucy's hand and squeezed it. "He loved you. He loves you. He was going to tell me as much at the ball, but then he saw you, and . . ." She paused to gain more courage. What was said next would change the future irrevocably. "His face lit up when he saw you."

Lucy shook her head. "Not at all. He was appalled."

"He was surprised. But then he turned to me to say he was sorry—and he ran after you. He didn't stay to explain things to me. His only thoughts were of you. He loves *you*."

"Then why didn't he tell me who he was? If I would have known, I would have broken it off with him. I would never do anything to hurt you, Rowena."

Rowena nodded, knowing it was true. "You have answered your own question. Edward didn't tell you the truth because the consequences of that truth would be losing you. He loves you. He wants to marry you." She swallowed hard. "Not me."

Lucy's eyes darted as if she were trying to see the truth as well as hear it. "Do you love him?"

Ah. It was time for Rowena to face yet another reality. "I loved the idea of him. I was in love with someone being in love with me. Which he's not. And so . . ."

"You really don't love him?"

Lucy was so hopeful, so eager to be affirmed, that Rowena knew she had to say it again. "No, I don't love him." She added to make it fully said, "He is yours to love."

Lucy wrapped her arms around Rowena's neck. "I'm so relieved." She let go. "I need to find him. Talk to him."

"As do I." She stood. "Let's go back to the house. I'm sure he'll come looking for you there."

Rowena took little consolation in the fact that she was no longer just an observer.

Full participation in life hurt.

Deeply.

Sofia felt herself being placed upon something soft.

"Send for a doctor!" yelled a voice. "And the police. And her mother."

She heard other voices and movement around her, but they seemed to come from another place, another world. She sensed they had a connection to herself but couldn't imagine how.

She moved her torso to get more comfortable but was greeted with a wave of pain. When she grimaced, the muscles on her face rebelled, revealing a new source of hurt. She moved her legs, which added a third. . . .

"Uhhhh."

"She's awake. Sofia? Sofia, can you hear me?"

Sofia opened an eye as much as she could—which wasn't much, for it seemed to be swollen shut. But it was enough to see the speaker. "Dante?"

"Yes, yes, it's Dante, it's Edward. I'm Edward."

This didn't make any sense. Why would Edward DeWitt be sitting next to her? And where . . . ? "Where am I?"

"I brought you to the Langdons'. You're in the drawing room. I've sent for a doctor."

"Here, sir, let me." Mrs. Donnelly took Edward's place. She dipped a cloth in water and began to gently dab at Sofia's face.

"Ouch!"

"I know, dear. You've got some pretty bad scrapes, your eyes are swollen, and that nose of yours . . ."

Sofia could taste the blood. And then she remembered falling forward, her face hitting the pavement. "Bonwitter!"

Edward came into view. "I've sent for the police. I'm hoping they'll still find him where I left him."

And then Sofia understood that Edward had been the one who'd saved her from . . . from . . .

The memory of Bonwitter lifting her skirts made Sofia cover her eyes. "If you hadn't come . . ."

"Shush now, Sofia," the housekeeper said. "You forget all that. You're safe now."

❦

Rowena and Lucy came around the side of the house to the front entry, only to find a carriage in the drive and a policeman exiting the house with some speed.

He tipped his hat to the ladies as he mounted his horse.

"What's wrong?" Rowena asked. "What's happened?"

"There's been an assault. Begging your pardon, miss, I need to catch up with the criminal."

He galloped away, a man on a mission.

An assault? Who was hurt?

The girls ran inside, but both stopped short when they saw Edward talking to the butler.

"Edward?"

Timbrook slipped away, and Edward's eyes skirted from Rowena to Lucy, then back again. "I . . ." He looked to Lucy. "I was out looking for you when I came upon a man assaulting your sister, and—"

"Where is she? Is she all right?"

"The doctor's here, and we've taken her upstairs to a bedroom. She'll be all right, but—"

Lucy ran up the stairs, leaving Rowena and Edward alone. Only then did Rowena see the bruises on his face and the rips in his costume.

"Come, sit down. Tell me everything."

They moved into the drawing room and sat. Blood dripped from a cut on Edward's cheek. "You need a doctor too."

He pressed a handkerchief to it, shaking his head. "I'll be fine." His eyes strayed upstairs.

"But Sofia?"

Edward seemed uncertain with his words. "She'll recover, but I'm very glad I came along when I did."

Rowena suffered a shiver. "Do they know who attacked her?"

"She knew him. 'Bonwitter,' she said."

Rowena had heard that name before. "He caused them trouble in New York. He stole from the dress shop and Lucy was instrumental in getting him fired."

"He's obviously one angry man to come all this way for his revenge."

Rowena felt bad for not taking more notice of Lucy's story of him. Yet Lucy had never let on she felt in danger here.

She rose. "I should go to them."

Edward stopped her with a hand. "In a minute. But first. Please."

She sat back down, dreading his words, his explanation. To know the truth was one thing, to talk about it with the man who had caused the pain was another.

"I can say nothing but . . . I'm so sorry, Rowena."

They were words she was glad to hear, yet words that caused their own damage.

"I'm sorry too," she said. "For how could you fall in love with . . . with . . ."

"Two women?"

This shocked her. "You loved me?"

He started to reach for her hand, then withdrew the gesture. "I love you, Rowena. I care deeply for you."

He looked down and Rowena prodded him to finish his thought. "But . . . ?"

"But I'm *in* love with Lucy."

Rowena had never considered there to be a difference in love, but somehow she understood. Yet the understanding did not negate the pain.

"I never meant to hurt you," he said.

"But you did."

He nodded. "But I did."

She remembered something Sofia had told her. "Earlier today Sofia shared something with me that her father used to say: Love rules without rules. I guess that's true."

Edward offered a bittersweet smile. "And Shakespeare said, 'The course of true love never did run smooth.' "

Which begged the question, "Is Lucy your true love? Are you going to marry her?"

"Yes, and . . . I hope to."

The hedging of his second answer brought to mind the reality of their situation. "What will your parents think about all this?"

"They'll be disappointed you and I are not going to marry, but—"

"No, Edward. What will they think about Lucy?"

He shook his head, his eyes down. "I have no idea."

"Yes you do. You know very well what they'll think."

Edward sighed deeply, his eyes sad.

Rowena realized society could stop this marriage. Edward's parents would never approve of his marrying Lucy. If she pressed him with this reality, she just might be able to—

But in the midst of this thought came another, and she heard herself saying, "You won't let them stop you, will you?"

"You don't want them to stop me?"

And here it was. The culmination, the consequence—and the sacrifice. "I want you and Lucy to be together."

He looked upward, toward the second floor. "If she still loves me . . ."

"She does love you. She told me so."

A beam of light seemed to fall across his face. "She does?"

"She does." But even as Rowena was reassuring him, she wondered if she would ever have someone's face light up for her.

"Come, Ro. I'll take care of you."

She closed her eyes and remembered Morrie sweeping her into his arms, taking her to safety. The feel of his hand upon her cheek, and her resting there, never wanting to . . .

She stood. "I have to go."

"Go where?"

"To see the man *I* love, to tell him . . ."

She hurried to the door, ran down the front steps, and across the grass toward the stables.

Lucy stood beside Sofia's bed holding a cloth full of ice chips in one hand and stroking her sister's forehead with the other. Sofia's face was misshapen from the swelling caused by her beating "I'm so, so sorry, Sofia."

The doctor was putting away the tools of his trade. "She's a very lucky girl. If Mr. DeWitt hadn't come along . . ."

Edward?

He clicked his bag shut and handed Lucy a bottle. "Give her a teaspoon of this every four hours for the pain."

"Thank you, Doctor," Sofia said.

"Now rest, child. And thank God it wasn't worse." He left them alone.

As soon as he was gone, Lucy asked, "Edward saved you?"

Sofia started to nod, but stopped with a grimace. "Bonwitter was on top of me. He would have—"

Lucy stood upright. "Bonwitter did this?"

"I can't believe he followed us here."

Lucy thought back to the other night near the docks. "I thought I saw him when I was out with Dante—with Edward, but I didn't let myself believe it." She returned the ice bag to Sofia's cheek. "But why you? He should hate me. I'm the one who turned him in."

"We're sisters. To hurt one, you hurt the other."

Lucy felt tears threaten. As much as she usually focused on the differences between herself and Sofia, they were bound by God—by blood, loyalty, and a tie that must never be broken.

They were cut from the same cloth.

Lucy wiped the back of her hand across her eyes, forcing the tears away. "Why were you out walking, Sofia?"

"I was looking for you. When you ran out, I tried to follow you, but Mamma delayed me and . . . I'm so sorry about Edward. I should've told you as soon as I found out."

"When did you know?"

Sofia told her about seeing the two of them while she and Hugh were out to dinner.

"You and Hugh?"

"He's a good friend. A good man."

Lucy sat on the edge of the bed, needing its support. It was too much to fathom. Nothing was as it seemed. All had been turned upside down.

Sofia's grimace and groan brought Lucy back to the moment. "No more talk," she said. "You must rest."

Sofia shook her head. "What of Edward?"

"What of him?" She had the image of passing Edward upon entering the Langdon house.

"I believe he loves you, Lucy."

Rowena's words came back to her. "Rowena said the same."

"You've spoken with her?"

"She doesn't love him. She's sacrificing her future by freeing *me* to love him."

"*Chi trova un amico trova un tesoro,*" Sofia said. "He who finds a friend finds a treasure."

Of the most precious kind.

Rowena hadn't run since childhood, but her desire to see Morrie was so great she found a brisk but awkward rhythm as she hurried across the grass toward the stables. She relished the darkness, for to enable speed, she lifted the skirt of her costume, revealing more leg than the world had ever seen of the adult Rowena.

Quite winded, she reached the barn and nearly fell into the arms of a stableboy. "Morrie. Where is Morrie?"

He gave her a quizzical look and she realized her error. "Haverty. Where is Haverty?"

"I don't know, miss. I ain't seen him since he rode off last time you were here."

He was still looking for Edward? Seeking revenge for her sake?

"You want to wait fer 'im?" the boy asked.

Yes! "I'll wait in his quarters. Thank you."

She went into his room only to find the tea the boy had fetched from Mrs. Oswald still there, cold. She downed the cup greedily.

Rowena tried to sit but couldn't contain herself. She paced. As she forced herself to calm down, she began to see Morrie within the objects of this room. A shirt and vest hung from a hook on the back of the door. She pressed her face into the fabric and reveled in the musky scent that was his alone. On the dresser she took up his shaving brush and ran it against her cheek, making her remember the lovely feeling of his touch.

Then she sat upon the bed and took up the book sitting on the table nearby. It was a Bible. She opened it and found many passages underlined. She read one aloud. " 'When I was a child, I spake as a child, I understood as a child, I thought as a child: but when I became a man, I put away childish things.' "

She marked her place with a finger and looked up. The verse mirrored her current feelings. Despite her age in years, she'd been acting as a child. It was time for her to act like a woman.

Rowena read more of the passage. " 'And now abideth faith, hope, love, these three; but the greatest of these is love.' "

Her eyes filled with tears. In spite of everything, Morrie had always held on to his faith, his hope in their future, and his love for her. How blind she'd been.

She heard a commotion outside and stood. The Bible fell to the floor. As she picked it up, a pressed flower slipped from between its pages. Rowena carefully plucked it from the floor. It was a violet.

Her memories flew back to a summer day when she'd been barely thirteen. She and Morrie had spent the day on the Cliff Walk, playing pirates. He'd played the hero, rescuing her from the evil captain. From the rocks she'd plucked a purple violet as a token for her savior.

"He kept it all these years."

And with that knowledge came the rest of the memory of that summer, of her accident, and the abrupt end of her childhood *and* a normal future.

She held the flower to her lips. . . .

"Violets stand for faithfulness, you know." Morrie stood in the doorway.

She could only manage his name, said in a whisper. "Morrie . . ."

He shook his head, stopping her. Then he came inside. "Let me speak first, for I've been driving around and around, ostensibly looking for your Edward to ream him out or kill him or . . . I actually don't know what I was supposed to do with him."

He was so sweet, so sincere.

He began to pace, eyeing the floor as he walked, his hands fueled by his movement. "You know I've always supported you and wanted what's best for you, and if that meant marrying Edward DeWitt or the King of Siam, I was willing to let you do it."

She sat upon the bed, smiling. "The King of Siam?"

He offered her but a glance. "The point is, I've tried to do the right thing by you, wanting only your happiness. But saints alive, Ro, the truth is, the only way you're going to be happy is if you marry me." He stopped in front of her. "I'm the one who loves you. I'm the one God's chosen for you. And you're for me. I know it with every breath in my body."

She stifled a laugh. "Oh, Morrie . . ."

"Don't laugh at me. I love you. And don't go telling me you don't love me, because you do."

She rose and took a step toward him. "I do."

He blinked, then took a step back. "You do? You do what?"

"I do love you."

The space between his eyes wrinkled. "You love me?"

She walked toward him again, but this time he didn't retreat. She reached up and put her hands upon his face, tilting it downward to look into his eyes. "I love you and only you. I always have and always will."

Rowena stood on her tiptoes and kissed him softly on the lips. They lingered there, sealing this moment for all time.

Then Morrie pulled her into his arms and spun her around and around. "Yee-ha! You love me!"

Rowena spotted more than one stableboy in the hall, looking to see what all the commotion was about. So when he spun her just so, she kicked the door shut with her feet.

The boys' laughter joined her own.

✦

"Mamma!"

Sofia opened her eyes and saw her mother rushing toward her. "Oh, my poor dear, my *piccolina*. What happened?"

"Bonwitter attacked me."

Mamma looked to Lucy, who nodded. "The doctor's been here. The bruises will heal—the physical ones. He nearly . . ."

Mamma's eyes grew wide, then filled with tears.

"Edward saved me," Sofia said. "Lucy's Dante saved me."

Mamma slowly turned her head to look at Lucy. "He's in the

drawing room. When I came in he introduced himself and asked after you." Mamma held Lucy's gaze and asked the questions that remained unanswered. "Do you forgive him, Lucia?"

Lucy hesitated, then nodded. "I've talked to Rowena."

"And?" Mamma asked.

"She doesn't love him."

"So it's up to you?"

Lucy just stood there.

"And?" Mamma said.

"What should I do?"

"Do you love him?" Mamma asked.

Lucy nodded.

"Then go to him. Hear him out."

"But he lied—"

Mamma held up a hand. "Love is too precious to throw away."

Sofia had never heard that one before. "Did Papa say that?"

"I say that. As your mother. As a woman who loved one man with all my heart."

Lucy's eyes rimmed with tears and she embraced her mother.

Lucy deserved to love and be loved. Sofia only hoped Edward's love was as genuine as her sister's.

As Lucy left, someone else came in.

"Hugh." Sofia wasn't sure what to do. Mamma didn't know about their friendship.

"Come in, Mr. Langdon," Mamma said. "Again I thank you for getting me back here to see my daughter."

What?

Mamma made room for Hugh at the bedside, then explained. "Mr. Langdon noticed the commotion at the Breakers when a boy brought me a note telling of your assault. He was kind enough to bring me home. He says you are a friend."

Hugh took Sofia's hand. "A friend I hold in the highest esteem." He ran a finger over her bruised fingers. "I'm so sorry this happened to you, matey."

"It's not your fault."

"Which doesn't lessen my regret."

He studied her face, his brows furrowed, and she realized . . . "I must look horrible." She touched her cheeks but couldn't even feel the cheekbones beneath the swelling.

Hugh shook his head. "You're a brave girl to fight so hard. If only I'd been there to fight for you."

If only . . .

Mrs. Donnelly stepped forward. "Beg your pardon, Master Hugh, but the girl needs her rest. Doctor's orders."

He carefully lifted her hand and brushed his lips against it. "Get well, Sofia, so we can go sailing again."

As he left, Mamma took his place by her side. "Explain yourself, *piccolina.*"

Exhaustion demanded her attention, but Sofia couldn't rest until something was set straight. "I am not your little girl anymore, Mamma. I am a woman. And Hugh is my dear, dear friend."

"You are still a child. You know nothing of the—" She must have remembered the beating, for she halted.

"I have been taught too much of the world tonight, Mamma. But even beyond that, since coming here I've grown up. Hugh helped me do that. And I have helped him."

"He mentioned sailing. When have you been sailing?"

She didn't want to defend herself anymore—at least not tonight. Whether Mamma believed she'd changed or not, Sofia knew it to be true. And even Mamma's opinion couldn't take that away from her.

"I'm tired, Mamma."

"You must not set your sights too high. He is the heir. You cannot—"

"Edward is the heir of *his* family."

Mamma looked away.

"What happened to love being too precious to throw away?"

Mamma had no comeback. "You are but a ch—" Thankfully, she stopped herself. "You are both so young."

Sofia pressed her head into the pillow and closed her eyes. Sleep beckoned like the sea pulling the waves away from the shore. "Not now, Mamma."

"Mrs. Scarpelli, please."

Thank God for Mrs. Donnelly.

And Hugh.

And Mamma.

And Edw—

Sleep took her captive.

⚜

Lucy's heart beat in her throat as she descended the grand staircase of the Langdon mansion. Her eyes focused on the drawing room. Was Edward really there, waiting for her? What would he say? What would she say?

She reached the foyer, her hand upon the carved ball that crowned the newel-post. Once she let go, once she took a step from the safety of the stairs, she would be walking across a threshold from one life into another.

And then she saw him, pacing up and back, toward the foyer and away.

He looked up.

He saw her. And whispered, "Lucia."

She could tell by the tensing of his muscles that he longed to rush toward her, yet not knowing her reaction, he held his position.

It was up to her.

Lucy relinquished the newel-post and walked toward him. His eyes were darting this way and that, trying to read the moment.

She longed to run into his arms, and yet . . . She walked to the center of the room. She opened her mouth to say his name, then stopped. "I don't know what to call you."

He came closer but still kept his distance. "When I met you, I had no idea who you were."

"But you were supposed to be readying yourself to propose to Rowena."

He swallowed with difficulty. "That's what our parents wanted, not what was meant to be. Not what God wanted for either of us."

Her father's voice whispered to her. *"L'uomo propone ma Dio dispone."*

"What does that mean?" he asked.

"Man proposes but God disposes."

His face lost its dire intensity. "Your father's wisdom is good for many occasions."

"He taught me a lot about life."

"He was your Dante."

"He was my father. You were my Dante." She walked toward the mantel, keeping her back to him. "Why didn't you tell me your name?"

"When you mentioned Rowena and I discovered you were her new friend, I knew I should pull away from you, to stop these feelings. But I couldn't."

She heard him approach and felt the air change behind her. When next he spoke she felt his breath upon her hair. "I didn't want to be Edward DeWitt—Bartholomew Edward DeWitt. Like Romeo I wanted to rid myself of the name that came between us. Once I met you, I fell in love with you, and from that moment all I wanted to be was Dante—your Dante."

Lucy turned and looked into his eyes. She wanted to pull her gaze away, but his eyes were so sincere, so deep. Within those eyes she saw a reflection of herself, and from the emotions that were welling up within her, she wondered if he saw the same within hers.

He took her hands. "Lucia, I regret the hurt I've caused you and Rowena, but I do not regret one moment we've had together. And I believe, with all my heart, that God brought me to the Cliff Walk that day, and He arranged our meeting because *He* desired it. I am meant for you and you are meant for me."

He got down on one knee. "I ask now what I asked before. Lucia, my love, will you marry me?"

She drew him to his feet, and his face was pained with her supposed indecision. But then she put a finger beneath his chin, stood upon her toes, and gave her answer through a gentle kiss.

Yes, oh yes.

EPILOGUE

$\mathcal{S}$ ofia checked the mailbox and raced up the stairs of their apartment to read the latest letter from Hugh.

Mamma trudged up behind her. "Another one? I'm surprised the man has time to eat with all the letters he sends you."

Sofia took no offense at Mamma's words. Hugh's letters had won Mamma over. Sofia often read passages to her, and loved the way her mother's face softened, and her head nodded with appreciation.

And acceptance.

For Hugh had proven himself to be wise in his actions. After Sofia and her family returned to New York, he'd shared with Sofia an idea to talk to his parents about his passion: the sea and Sofia Scarpelli—in that order.

Sofia didn't mind receiving second billing, for Mamma was right. They were both young. Even she was not impulsive enough to declare her love or seriously talk of marriage. There were things to work through first.

Once in the apartment, Sofia went into the bedroom she now shared with Mamma and closed the door. It was silly to close it, for there was nothing for Mamma to overhear. Yet this was her habit, to lock herself in a room to better hear Hugh's voice within his words upon the page. Somehow, fully alone, she was not alone. For he was with her in spirit.

My dearest Sofia, my lovely matey:

The best of news! Because of you I've gained the courage I needed to talk to my parents about my future. I am not meant to work in an office but rather should work upon the sea. I want to use my arms and my back, not succeed upon the arms and back of my father's efforts.

At first Father disparaged my words, but at your suggestion, I came prepared and told him of my plan to start a fishing business. If he would but loan me the money, I would buy a few boats, hire some crews, and earn a good living. He was impressed with my plan to pay him back, and has agreed on one boat—for now.

I am ecstatic beyond words! I never thought this was possible. And but for you, matey, I would never have found the courage to try.

How is your work? Do you enjoy having the extra responsibility of ordering supplies?

I am proud of you—proud of both of us. And before too long, I hope we can be together as true partners, man and wife.

Do you truly think your sewing skills could be used to mend sails and nets?

Send your mother my love.

Yours always,
Captain Hugh

There was a tap on the door. "Sofia? Is Hugh well? What does he say?"

Sofia gathered the letter and opened the door. "Let me read it to you. . . ."

"But I can't do it, Morrie."

He stroked the horse's mane and looked down at her with disdain.

"You know I hate those words, Ro. You promised once we were married they would never cross your lips again."

She *had* promised, and she'd meant it. For she'd uttered the words *I can't do it* too many times in the days, weeks, and months after the Vanderbilt ball—the night that had changed everything.

Her parents had been understandably upset by the happenings of that night. Although they'd not witnessed the dramatic exit of Edward, Rowena, and Lucy, the titterings of those who *had* seen skittered through the crowd of costumed guests, to their ears.

But Rowena's parents had done their best to pooh-pooh the gravity of it all, and had laughed it off and stayed to enjoy the ball. And then Hugh had seen the Langdon servant bringing a note. . . .

Needless to say, when her parents had finally left the ball and returned home, they were not pleased that a despicable crime had been committed close by, the police had been in their house, and the victim was lodged in one of their guest rooms.

Never mind that Edward DeWitt, the man who was supposed to become engaged to their daughter, was sitting in their drawing room holding hands with the victim's sister, or that their son was holding vigil at the victim's bedside. The worst was finding out their daughter was down at the stables, in a coachman's quarters.

Timbrook had been the one to find Rowena and Morrie together. Not that they were doing anything unseemly. They were sharing some coffee and cake with Mrs. Oswald, who'd been kind enough to bring it over.

After being summoned by her parents, Rowena uttered the awful "I can't do it" for the first time, to which Morrie assured her she *could* for the first time, and for the first time he took a position by her side in full support.

The looks on her parents' faces were in stark contrast to the frivolity of their costumes, and Rowena had experienced the odd sensation of being brought before the emperor and queen. She wouldn't have been surprised to be sent to the Tower or fed to the lions in the Colosseum.

Morrie had been wonderful that night, spurring her with

encouraging words to explain that Edward loved another, and by the way, so did she. And that *other* was not a man of society but a humble coachman she'd known her entire life.

Her parents were not amused.

Rowena couldn't blame them. Their lofty plan of marrying their tainted daughter to the son of a business partner was crushed. The brunt of the blame fell on the DeWitt shoulders, but there was plenty left to pour across the Langdon name. And when Edward informed his parents he was marrying Lucia Scarpelli and there was nothing they could do to stop him, they'd kept their pride intact by disinheriting him in the way of so many scorned parents of society.

That he didn't care offended them greatly.

A month later, when Hugh had sprung a surprise upon *his* parents, that he had feelings for Sofia Scarpelli, a sixteen-year-old Italian seamstress, and then offered them a second surprise soon after, that he didn't want to work in the family business but wanted to be a fisherman, Rowena had thought her parents would die in a communal fit of apoplexy.

That the elder Langdons had been able to pull Hugh off from the edge into some semblance of wait-and-see had been a blessing for Rowena's cause.

Which was?

To be allowed her freedom. In a burst of eloquence, Rowena had talked frankly with her parents. She did not have a long line of suitors waiting in the wings, nor would new ones likely be added because of the scandal. So why not let her marry Morrie Haverty, a good man who'd been a loyal servant for decades.

And it wasn't as if Morrie didn't have ambition. He'd been saving his money to buy a small horse farm in upstate New York. Surely her parents knew how much Rowena loved horses. . . .

And so, with there being no other suitable future for their daughter, her parents had said yes—or at least quietly surrendered.

She and Morrie had been married in a small ceremony with Joe the stableboy and Lucy as witnesses, attended by Hugh, Edward, Sofia and Lea Scarpelli, Mr. and Mrs. Oswald—and the Langdons.

Whether Mrs. Langdon's tears were caused by sadness or joy was left to interpretation.

Rowena surprised herself by not shedding any tears at all. She felt bad for her parents but had no regrets about choosing to marry for love. That she and Morrie would struggle to make ends meet, that their little farmhouse would struggle to give them enough hot water to take a bath, were facts Rowena accepted with little worry and much tolerance. She'd expected to miss her lovely clothes and lush house, but as Morrie fortified her with statements that "God will provide" and "God tells us to be strong and do the work," she embraced the challenges of her new home, and found she awakened each morning with anticipation for the day ahead.

The reason for that was this: for once in her life, she had a purpose, a reason to get up each day that went beyond the social requirements of being a lady. On the farm—which she and Morrie had named Morwena—the two of them delighted in working side by side in the autumn air, and spending their evenings by the fireside, talking of the future, and wallowing in the blessing of their marriage.

"Ro?" Morrie broke through her reverie. "Bessie here is getting antsy, and so am I. If you're going to be able to help with the horses, you need to ride them fully—astride."

He was right, of course.

She yanked at the pair of Morrie's trousers she'd put on that morning, which were cinched in with a rope and folded many times over the top to take up the length. Without the camouflage of petticoats and skirts she knew she looked like a sorry ragamuffin, an urchin on the street begging for pennies. To add to her ensemble, her blouse was her own—sans corset. The corset had been relinquished early on after she'd found it impossible to bend over to carry a bucket or brush the horses under the constraints of its prison.

She thought about balking at how ridiculous she looked today, but knew there was no one to see but Morrie, and he'd already assured her she was always beautiful—even after she'd fallen in the corral after a rain and had emerged a muddy mess. And oddly, she believed him. To him she was beautiful and so . . .

She was.

Rowena took a deep breath and faced the horse that used to be her friend. "All right. Help me up."

Morrie helped get her strong foot in the stirrup, then virtually lifted her onto the saddle. Her bad leg found its place on the other side, and Morrie went around and adjusted the stirrup to a shorter length. He handed her the reins. "Press your thighs against her," he said. "Do you feel her muscles?"

Rowena did and was encouraged by the melding of her muscles to Bessie's.

"Now, then, you and Bessie can be one, just like it was when you were little." He checked to make sure she held the reins securely. "Are you ready, Ro?"

Yes. No. She felt Bessie tense, ready to run.

"Ro, you can do this."

She nodded. "I can do this."

"Then *do* it!" He slapped Bessie's flank and the horse took off.

Rowena nearly faltered, but then she heard Morrie yell, "Lean forward! Use your legs!"

As soon as she followed his directions, she felt Bessie's power course through her and felt more powerful herself. She remembered the reins and pulled back slightly, taking control. Bessie responded and together they found a rhythm to their gallop.

And Rowena found joy.

As the wind whipped the hairpins from her hair she swung her head back and forth, giving it freedom. Memories of her childhood, riding just like this, with Morrie at her—

"Wait for me!"

As though filling out the memory, Morrie raced to catch her, coming alongside. "How is it?" he yelled.

It was perfect. Yet that word still didn't fully express her emotions.

And then she knew the essence of what she was feeling. "I love you, Morrie!"

He offered her a wink, then dug his heels into his horse. "First one to the house wins!"

Rowena entered the race knowing she'd already won.

※

The waiter placed a cloth napkin in Lucy's lap with a flourish, and did the same for Edward. Then he handed them menus, nodded, and left them alone.

"Are you certain we can afford this place?" Lucy whispered.

"Do you doubt my new job?" he said. "I'm on the road to becoming a full-fledged architect."

Lucy was so proud of him for pursuing his passion. And prouder still for engaging a position with the budding architect Frank Lloyd Wright. "Do you like Mr. Wright?"

"He's a bit curt, but his ideas are brilliant. To allow the function of a space to determine its form is revolutionary. That we Americans have been stuck copying European design instead of creating our own . . ."

The enthusiasm in his voice and the sparkle in his eyes told Lucy their move to Chicago was well worth it.

Not that they'd had much choice. After the scandal of choosing Lucy over Rowena, Edward's parents had cut him off financially. He'd assured Lucy the loss of the money was of little concern, but she knew he hoped to one day mend the familial ties. *Amor tutti fa uguali*—love may make all men equal, but pride definitely came before a fall, and Edward was willing to forsake his pride to make amends. Someday. After he'd proven himself.

Their wedding day was bittersweet, with only her family, Morrie, and Rowena in attendance, but he'd done his best to assure her that all he needed was her love.

"Now, then," he said, concentrating on the menu. "Shall it be duck à l'orange, chicken cordon bleu, or lobster thermidor?"

Lucy didn't know what any of these dishes were, and actually, would have been content with a simple soup. She was tempted to tell him the reason for her distaste for anything too rich but was determined to wait.

Until she was sure . . .

The third weekend after moving to Chicago, Lucy and Edward walked the sidewalks of Michigan Avenue, enjoying the cool of the autumn day.

"But where will we live?" she asked him, not for the first time. "We can't stay in the hotel much longer. Surely the expense—"

He patted her hand upon his arm. "I've told you I'll take care of everything. Do you trust me?"

"Of course."

"Explicitly?"

"I do."

He craned his neck to see something ahead of them, then stopped. "I need you to close your eyes."

"Close—?"

"Lucia . . . trust. Remember?"

She chided herself for having her trust be so short-lived. But she wasn't used to letting someone else take care of things. Surrender was a struggle. She closed her eyes. "There. See how I trust you?"

He put his arm behind her waist and held her close. "Now walk."

"Walk? But I can't—"

"Oh, ye of little faith."

Why was this so hard? She forced herself to take a step, and then one more.

"You fight me," he said. "Relax."

With a sigh she tried to ease her muscles.

"There. That's better. One step, now another . . ."

"Where are you taking me?"

"It's obviously a surprise."

"I know, but—"

"Shush."

They walked for what seemed like forever, but what was more

likely less than a block. Then he turned her sideways. "Keep your eyes closed. Just a little longer. A little . . ." When he had her set exactly as he wanted her, he said, "Now! Open your eyes!"

She opened them to see a storefront with a large glass window for display. On the window was painted—

"No, Edward . . . it isn't . . ."

"It is, my darling. Lucia's Dress Shop. Just for you."

She stared at the lovely gold lettering, shaking her head in disbelief. "This is mine?"

"It's what you've always dreamed of, isn't it?"

She faced him and bowed her head upon his shoulder. "*You* are what I've always dreamed of."

He wrapped his arms around her and kissed her hair. "Come inside," he said. "The surprise isn't over." He moved her to the door, letting her do the honors.

"Surprise!"

"Mamma?"

"Your first employee," Edward said.

Lucy ran into her mother's arms.

"But there's still more."

He led Lucy to a door that opened to a stairway. He went up first. "There's a two-bedroom living quarters above the store. Enough for three."

For a moment Lucy wondered how he knew, but then she realized he counted Mamma as the third. Once they reached the apartment and he showed them around, she lingered in an alcove off the kitchen.

"This space could be a guest room for Sofia when she comes to visit."

Lucy shook her head. "Only if she's willing to share it."

Edward walked the length of the alcove. "There's no need for her to share it. Your mother has her own room."

Suddenly, Mamma stared at Lucy. Then she put a hand to her mouth. "Lucia? Really?"

Lucy nodded and began to cry.

Mamma took her in her arms and they rocked back and forth.

"Excuse me," Edward said. "What did I miss?"

Mamma let go and Lucy went to Edward, taking his hands in hers. "We're going to have a baby."

She would never forget the look of surprise upon his face, nor forget the way he swirled her around in utter joy—before gingerly placing her on the ground, afraid for her condition.

"I'm fine," she said. "We're fine."

"Il Dio è buono," Mamma said.

She was so right.

God was very, very good.

DEAR READER

I grew up in a sewing household. My mother made clothes for herself and three daughters. I didn't have a store-bought dress until I was in high school. Prom dresses, wool coats, and even our wedding dresses were sewn by my mother. My sister remembers her prom date having to wait while Mom finished sewing her a matching wrap for her dress. Mom is the one who taught us to do our own designing too. It wasn't unusual to take the sleeves from one pattern, the skirt from another, and the collar from a third. My first two jobs were as a clerk in a fabric store, and my first big purchase was a Pfaff sewing machine—which I am still using forty years later.

That background explains my interest in dressmakers of the Gilded Age. Yet sewing a dress nowadays is nothing compared to creating one of the intricate dresses of that era. It's the difference between making a cake from a boxed mix and adding a canister of ready-made frosting, and creating a four-tier wedding cake from scratch, with fondant frosting, lacework, marzipan flowers, and edible pearls and beads.

Yet the seamstresses of 1895 were not that different from seamstresses today. Both learned from experience and were taught by doing—my preferred way of learning anything. I admire the Scarpelli women for their work ethic, and I reveled in being able to move them from a dingy sweatshop, to a fancy dress Emporium, to the halls of Newport's finest homes, where they were set free to fully use their talents.

I love stories about immigrants to America. Their pluck, courage, and determination inspire me. Where did your ancestors come from? What made them leave their homeland behind, to take a chance, to start over? What are their stories of failure and success? Of dreams abandoned and achieved?

Fortunes were made in America, lost, and made again. Some were huge and boggled the mind. Consider the "cottages" of the rich in Newport. The Breakers, which is the location for the climax of this book, has 65,000 square feet of living space. The average size of an American home today is 2,300 square feet, which means twenty-eight houses could fit into this single-family "cottage."

What an exciting place for two poor seamstresses and a crippled heiress to find love. And friendship. And purpose. And yet, the grand mansions in Newport weren't the real setting for Lucy, Sofia, and Rowena to experience their revelations and growth. The Cliff Walk and the spectacle of God's sea, sky, and sun inspired like no creation of man could ever do. *Go ask the sunrise . . .*

Where can I go from your Spirit?
Where can I flee from your presence?
If I go up to the heavens, you are there;
if I make my bed in the depths, you are there.
If I rise on the wings of the dawn,
if I settle on the far side of the sea,
even there your hand will guide me,
your right hand will hold me fast.

Psalm 139:7–10 NIV

Today I urge you to take a few minutes from your busy life and go outside. Seek a place of *the* Creator's design, where His hand will hold you fast and guide you toward love, friendship, and *your* unique purpose.

Blessings,
Nancy Moser

Fact or Fiction in
An Unlikely Suitor

Chapter 1

- Throughout the book I used Italian proverbs as Lucy lives out her father's wisdom. Some are familiar; some are not. I have to wonder which came first, the English or the Italian version. Here's a wonderful source: *http://italian.about.com/library/proverbio/blproverbiov.htm.*

- The tenements on Mulberry Street were torn down and Columbus Park (which is still a vibrant park) was built in their place. The park opened in the summer of 1897, giving the people of the neighborhood benches, sidewalks, and much-appreciated grass.

- St. Patrick's Old Cathedral was—and is—at 263 Mulberry Street. It was the first Roman Catholic cathedral in New York City, and for seventy years was the only St. Patrick's. It was a hub for incoming Irish and Italian families in the Five Points area (the area that became known as Little Italy, and now Soho).

Its "St. Patrick's Cathedral" designation was usurped in 1879 by the more grand (and now more widely known) St. Patrick's built at Fifth Avenue and 51ˢᵗ Street. At that time the Old St. Patrick's was demoted to a parish church. Two scenes from *The Godfather* movies were filmed there: the baptism scene in the original movie *The Godfather*, and the scene where Michael Corleone gets an honor from the church in the third movie in that series.

Chapter 2

- Dime novels were the rage in the second half of the nineteenth century. Yet their format varied greatly, from "story papers," news-papers that ran stories in serial form, to compilations of many stories, to full novels. To add to the confusion, they didn't always cost a dime. But considering that working-class immigrants often made less than a dollar a day working ten to twelve hours, the price was comparable to the same person today buying a seven-dollar paperback. The content of the stories ran from romance to westerns, to crime/detective, and beyond. Dime novels filled the space now held by television, paperbacks, and comic books, and were often reprinted—and resold—in many forms (sounds like a "rerun" to me).

- Laura Jean Libbey was one of the most prolific dime-novel authors. She wrote eighty-two romances with the common theme being a wayward girl falling in love with a man far above her sta-tion. In the end they always married. Ironically, Libbey's mother forbade her to marry, and she held off until her mother died, marrying when she was thirty-six. She and her husband never had any children, and she kept her private life very private, but many doubt she lived the romantic life she wrote about. She was an astute businesswoman and made sixty thousand dollars a year from her romance writing. In today's money that would be one and a half million dollars. The book Sofia is reading, *Little Rosebud's Lovers,* is one of Libbey's books, and the excerpts are real.

Chapter 3

- Indoor plumbing. Most of the tenements around Mulberry Street did not have indoor toilets or baths. Outhouses were lined up in the alleys—with people living in ground-floor apartments just a few feet away. Sometimes there were communal water spigots in the hallway, but in 1895 a tenement with running water in each apartment was beyond rare. Most rich and many middle-class homes had bathrooms, and hotels would advertise if they had private baths. Public bathhouses were opened with signs encouraging use by saying "Cleanliness is next to godliness," but immigrants had been brought up being wary of baths, so these establishments were mostly used in the summer months when even the most hardened nose noticed the stench. The truth was, people smelled bad and often wore the same clothes for weeks at a time. Would there have been a lavatory in Madame Moreau's Dress Emporium? And a full bathroom in the Scarpellis' new apartment? It's hard to say. So I opted to give the characters this luxury. It was my gift to the ladies.

Chapter 4

- Sewing machines were powered by a foot treadle. The machine was used for sewing the longer seams, but the fine work was still done by hand (as it still is today). A dress could easily take a dozen yards of fabric to create, and many dozens of yards of trims were applied. Petticoats and undergarments added more yardage upon the wearer, and corsets constricted easy movement and any chance of comfort. The complexity of the ensemble often meant a woman was burdened with carrying a dozen pounds upon her back—or more. Considering women were generally smaller than they are now, their garments could add an additional ten percent to their body weight.

Chapter 5

- Although ready-made clothes were available in department stores and through store catalogs, the upper crust continued to use seamstresses to ensure that their clothes were one of a kind. By 1895 the bustles of the 1870s and 1880s had given way to a smoother, more body-conscious silhouette. Instead of the skirt providing the interest, the bodice and voluminous sleeves drew the eye. Because of the volume, the waist looked smaller. There were rules for dresses to wear for day visits, outings, bicycling, golfing, picnics, luncheons, dinners, balls, the theater, concerts, and the opera. The opera dress was the fanciest of all, for you went to the opera to be *seen*.

- Delmonico's was *the* restaurant to frequent for New York society. First opened in 1837, it was a pioneer in the business. Prior to Delmonico's, people didn't eat out often, or if they did, it was at a hotel or an inn. There, they ate whatever was being served, at a set price, at a set time. There were no options. Delmonico's was the first restaurant in the States that allowed people to come at their convenience, choose their food items from an extensive menu, and know the cost. It also offered private dining rooms, and allowed women to dine. This family-run business was known for its first-quality ingredients, impeccable service, and unique dishes. Lobster à la Newburg was premiered there in 1876. Delmonico's eventually had four locations, and it closed in 1923. (Any restaurants that now use the Delmonico's name are not affiliated with the original.)

Chapter 7

- Bonwitter's address at 89 Bowery is a real address. I found a picture of the old four-story redbrick building that was there, but it has been torn down. Its most recent use (in 2007) was as an Asian video store.

- The Central Park Reservoir covers 106 acres. It was created in 1858 to hold the water that came from the Croton Aqueduct, which was then distributed throughout Manhattan. It was used for this purpose until 1993. In 1994 it was renamed the Jacqueline Kennedy Onassis Reservoir. She lived nearby, often jogged in the area, and contributed much to the city. She died in May 1994.

Chapter 9

- The quote "I've heard it said that a working professional woman will be satisfied with six dresses in her wardrobe, but a fashionable lady will feel destitute with less than sixty" was from *Demorest's*, a magazine about style and etiquette. Comments like this helped keep seamstresses very busy.

Chapter 10

- The derogatory name of "Tony" for Italians didn't come about because a lot of Italian men were named Anthony. It started because much of the Italian immigrants' luggage was marked "TO NY"—"To New York." Tony.

- The distance from Grand Central Station, New York City, to Wickford Junction, Rhode Island, is 162 miles. Many wealthy families traveled from New York to Newport via luxurious steamships. But you could also go by rail to Wickford Junction, then take a short trip by steamer to Newport. There were no bridges from the island of Newport to the mainland until the twentieth century.

- Toilet paper on a roll was manufactured in 1877 but probably wasn't in use in the places Lucy frequented. Before rolls, toilet paper was distributed in flat sheets with the company's name printed on each sheet. Also in use were newspapers, pages from the Sears catalog, and corncobs.

Chapter 11

- Consuelo Vanderbilt and the Duke of Marlborough got engaged in late August 1895 and were married in November. They were not in love; in fact Consuelo was secretly engaged to someone else. But her domineering mother paid to gain her daughter a title (duchess), which also allowed the duke to have the funds to refurbish Blenheim Castle. He signed a prenuptial agreement that provided him with life interest in a trust fund based on Mr. Vanderbilt's holdings: 2.5 million dollars in 50,000 shares of Beach Creek Railway—a guarantee of 4 percent per year. Plus, he had access to other Vanderbilt money. Their marriage was not happy, though Consuelo provided her husband with "an heir and a spare," a term used one hundred years later with Princess Diana and her children, William and Harry. Consuelo dove into charity work, eventually divorced her husband due to his infidelity, and remarried. During the Gilded Age many wealthy American girls married for a title and became known as "dollar princesses."

Chapter 12

- The décor and style of the Langdon home is based on the Chateau-sur-Mer in Newport. The stained glass in the skylight corresponds to the beautiful entry of the Chateau, the drawing room is inspired by the French Salon, and Rowena's bedroom looks like the Butternut Room. The Chateau-sur-Mer was recently renovated and can be toured. It was originally built in 1851 and was extensively remodeled in 1876. It was the most luxurious mansion in Newport until the rash of mega-mansions were built in the 1890s.

- The song "The Sidewalks of New York" was written by Blake and Lawlor in 1894. It's often known as "East Side, West Side," which is the first line of the chorus. The names of people in the song were real people from Blake's boyhood.

Chapter 13

- In 1895, Gertrude Vanderbilt said, "Alas, when a girl is twenty she is on the road to being an old maid." Gertrude grew up spending her summers at the Breakers, and married Harry Payne Whitney—at age twenty-one. She became a patron of art and formed the Whitney Museum of American Art in 1931. She was also a sculptor and designed the Titanic monument in Washington, D.C., honoring the men who gave their lives so women and children could be saved.

- All the attendees at the dinner are real people—except the Langdons and the Garmins. George and Edith Wetmore owned Chateau-sur-Mer, the house that was my inspiration for the Langdon house in this book. Mr. Wetmore was a two-term governor of Rhode Island, and then a U.S. senator. Theodore and Emily Havemeyer gained their fortune through sugar refining. He was the Austrian Consul-General in New York City for twenty-five years. You can find pictures of these people in historical photographs of Newport.

- The first Breakers burned to the ground in 1892. Its replacement was finished the year of this story, 1895. But Mr. Vanderbilt suffered a bad stroke the following year, so this was the only year the Breakers was fully enjoyed by Alice and Cornelius. Its 65,000 square feet of living space cost $7 million to build ($150 million in today's dollars). Although the Vanderbilt family sold it to the Newport Preservation Society in 1972, all the furnishings belong to the family, and they still have access to the private third floor. Over 300,000 people visit the Breakers every year.

Chapter 14

- The verse "Love me with thine azure eyes . . ." is from Elizabeth Barrett Browning's poem "A Man's Requirements." To read about Browning's life and her poignant love story, read my bio-novel called *How Do I Love Thee?* All of Elizabeth's *Sonnets From the Portuguese* are included in the back of the book.

- In 1884 a book on the meaning of flowers was published: *The Language of Flowers*, by Jean Marsh, illustrated by Kate Greenaway. It became the bible for Victorian flower giving and receiving, allowing people to send messages without speaking. It was cross-referenced by flowers *and* by emotions. Yet problems arose when new books came out, giving conflicting meanings. For instance, a dahlia could mean "good taste" or "instability." Ivy was especially confusing, for it could mean "fidelity," "friendship," "affection," or "marriage." Quite a range there. And woe the hemlock, for it meant, "You will be my death."

- Costume balls were popular, the more elaborate the better. Masks were seldom worn. What's the good of being all dressed up if no one knows it's you?

Chapter 18

- According to *The Language of Flowers*, pink roses signified grace and beauty.

- By 1893, the Hires family sold bottled versions of root beer. Root beer had been around a long time, and some versions included alcohol or were used medicinally. But the kind Hires bottled was made from twenty-five berries, roots, and herbs. It was introduced at the Philadelphia Centennial Exhibition in 1876. In the 1960s, one of the ingredients, sassafras root, was banned as a carcinogen. But brewers discovered it was safe to use if the sassafras oil was removed first.

Chapter 20

- The Breakers had a ladies' reception room off the main entrance, where women could put their wraps and make finishing touches to their ensemble.

- In spite of his family's vociferous objections, "Neily" Vanderbilt (Cornelius Vanderbilt III) married Grace Wilson the next year (1896) and thereby lost a prominent place in his father's will. Neily's mother did not reconcile with him until 1926.

Epilogue

- Frank Lloyd Wright broke away from his mentor, Louis Sullivan, in 1893 and opened his own architectural offices in the Steinway Hall building in Chicago. He expanded upon Sullivan's "form follows function" philosophy and believed that architecture should evolve organically from its function and location, and not be stifled by precedent, by what's been done before.

The Fashion of
An Unlikely Suitor

Chapter 6: The skirt was a pale beige, settling somewhere between cream and tan. The bodice was a light yellow, accordion-pleated *mousseline de soie,* bisected with pearl buttons. The sleeves were of the current leg-o'-mutton fashion—voluminous from shoulder to elbow, padded with eiderdown, yet tight to the wrist. Just as the bustles of the eighties had grown ridiculous, these sleeves and the overt attention to the upper torso often went too far with layers of lace, festoons, and flounces threatening to choke.

Chapter 8: Rowena stood very still while Lucy arranged a lace flourish on her blouse and attached a blue ribbon choker with flat bows that marked the back of her neck.

"The blue of the ocean sky," Lucy said. . . . The pink satin in the oversized puffed sleeves was tucked into elbow ruffles of scalloped lace. A flat lace collar dipped low in a V, and the bodice was covered with a sheer lace overlay that flounced over a blue satin waistband. The skirt wasn't gathered at the waist but folded in deep pleats, and the fabric was a floral sateen of blue and pink flowers.

389

Chapter 17: Rowena began riffling through the rows of dresses. "What are you going to wear to see your Dante?" With a glance over her shoulder, she added, "For you *are* going to see him." . . . Rowena pulled a pale olive pinstripe from the pack. "This one, I think."

Chapter 18: Rowena slipped her arms into the lavender satin dressing sacque that Lucy held for her. She pulled the lace-edged neck ties to the front and made a knot.

Illustrations from *Victorian Fashions & Costumes from Harper's Bazar 1867–1898* (Dover Publications, 1974), and *Victorian Fashions: A Pictorial Archive* (Dover Publications, 1999).

DISCUSSION QUESTIONS FOR
An Unlikely Suitor

1. The Scarpellis need a new apartment. Lucy goes to find one, leaving Mamma to do the praying for her. There's a fine line between doing our part because we shouldn't remain idle and doing our part because we don't trust God to do it. Proverbs 21:31 says, "The horse is made ready for the day of battle, but victory rests with the Lord" (NIV). What does this verse mean? How did Lucy fare in following the instruction in this verse?

2. In Chapter 2, Lucy comes home and says, "When I left this morning I didn't realize it would be the last time I'd see the place as it's always been." Her mother responds, "Consider it a blessing, Lucia. Sometimes it's best not to have time to wallow in the 'last' of things." Think of a "last" in your life (moving, sending a child off to college, changing jobs). How did you deal with your "last"? How would following Mamma's advice have helped?

3. Lucy takes a big risk in catching Bonwitter in the act. There are repercussions for herself and her family. But what good came from her action? Have you ever risked much to see that justice

was done? What did it cost you—or others? What were the rewards?

4. In Chapter 10, Mrs. Garmin explains about men coming to Newport only on weekends, leaving their wives alone the rest of the time. Lucy considers, "What a life they had. As their husbands worked hard to pay for their lavish habits, all the women had to do was sit back and enjoy the benefits." This was a positive aspect of being a woman during the Gilded Age. Or was it? What are some of the other positives and negatives of being a woman of that time? How would you have fared?

5. In Chapter 13, Rowena struggles with jealousy over Lucy's talents. She nearly takes credit for Lucy's painting and is wary about giving Lucy an outlet to shine. And yet "Friends help friends be their best." Name someone in your life who has many talents. How do they make you feel? How have you provided a way for them to showcase their talents? And/or . . . how has someone given you a chance to showcase your talents?

6. In Chapter 14, the ladies of the dress shop finally take Sofia seriously. "Losing her title of 'Baby Sofia' made her feel like one of the group again, which made her want to work harder." When have you felt separate from a group of peers? How did it make you feel? How did you respond? How did the situation change?

7. In Chapter 17, Mamma is uncertain about going to a different church. Lucy pats her hand and whispers, "It's all right, Mamma. God lives here too." Where have you been where you had to remind yourself of God's presence?

8. In Chapter 18, Dante and Lucy "go ask the sunrise"—offer God their thoughts and requests. The "rising of the sun" can contain all sorts of symbolism. What do you see in the sunrise?

9. Rowena realizes that without Lucy coming into her life *and* taking Edward away, Rowena would not have been open to acknowledge the love Morrie has for her, and realize her love for him. And without the scandal and the boundaries of society broken by Edward and Lucy, Rowena would never have been willing to break the bounds herself. God works through all things for good. When have you seen His hand in your life, where something "bad" turned into something "good"?

10. In the Epilogue, Edward tells Lucy to close her eyes and trust him, but she has trouble surrendering control. In the end he shows her a surprise beyond her imagining. Here are two verses that speak to this: ". . . watch—and be utterly amazed. For I am going to do something in your days that you would not believe, even if you were told" (Habakkuk 1:5 NIV), and "Call to me and I will answer you and tell you great and unsearchable things you do not know" (Jeremiah 33:3 NIV). When have you surrendered to God? As a result, what amazing surprises has He shown you? If you haven't surrendered . . . why not? And finally, why not do so now and see what amazing things He has in store!

More From
Nancy Moser

A Novel of Faith, Friendship, and True Love
An heiress trapped by society's expectations. A maid longing for luxury. And the chance of a lifetime. As they risk it all for adventure and romance, will their risky charade be exposed?

Masquerade